The Magic Hour

The Magic Hour

by

James S. Crowley

BONNEVILLE BOOKS ™
Springville, Utah

Copyright © 2003 James S. Crowley

All Rights Reserved.

No part of this book may be reproduced in any form whatsoever, whether by graphic, visual, electronic, film, microfilm, tape recording, or any other means, without prior written permission of the author, except in the case of brief passages embodied in critical reviews and articles.

ISBN: 1-55517-713-1
e.1

Published by Bonneville Books
Imprint of Cedar Fort Inc.
www.cedarfort.com

Distributed by:

Cover design by Nicole Cunningham
Cover design © 2003 by Lyle Mortimer
Cover painting and inside illustrations by James S. Crowley

Printed in the United States of America
10 9 8 7 6 5 4 3 2 1

Printed on acid-free paper

To all those who believe

CHAPTER ONE

"Come on, Mom. We don't have all night," nine-year-old Brian McCourt said as he looked out through the kitchen screen door into the warm autumn night. Dressed in cheery Halloween-print flannel pajamas, he listened to the haunting but familiar call of the owl that lived in the gnarly old pine just across the garden.

"Hoo-hoot, hoo-hoooo."

Long a fixture in the McCourt home landscape, the owl was dubbed Mr. Bones because of all the little bones found under his tree, obvious leftovers from his nighttime journeys.

"Hoo-hoot, hoo-hoooo." Brian perfectly imitated the night-calling bird of prey.

"Hoo-hoot, hoo-hoooo." The response was immediate.

"Ze spirrrrits ah active toniiiiight," his identical twin brother Eddie said in his best Transylvanian accent. A bed pillow flew across the kitchen and landed on the counter by the sink. Another blond boy, also dressed in Halloween pajamas, ran into the room with another pillow held high and the battle was on. Feathers and giggles filled the air.

These young brothers had anxiously looked forward to this day for two long years. Their father had finally finished the construction of their tree house, and tonight, they were given permission to sleep out in it for the very first time.

"Mom! Come on!" Brian said again.

"Yeah, lady. Get with it, will ya!"

The boys' mother entered the kitchen with a raised eyebrow and looked straight at Eddie. She was an attractive woman with short light brown hair. Though a doctor's wife, she still had a sense of humor.

" Since when does a nine-year-old boy refer to his mother as 'Yeah, lady?'"

"When she is making them wait so long."

"Well, at least I know now."

They all stepped out the screen door and made their way through a dark woodland garden by flashlight beams. The night air was thick

The Magic Hour

with the candy-sweet smell of heliotrope blossoms. They paused at a flower bed, which was bulging over with deep purple blooms. By night they appeared almost velvet black.

"This must be what heaven smells like," their mother said.

"Hoo-hoot, hoo-hoooo."

Brian turned and held his light up the owl's tree. "Mr. Bones agrees." High up in the twisted branches his beam landed right on Mr. Bones. His brilliant golden orb eyes looked down and held them spellbound for just a moment, until he blinked, and again. "Why does this pine tree grow so wierd?"

An evil grin spread across Eddie's face. "Because it's bewitched by goblins. Ha! Ha! Ha! Ha! Ha!"

"No goblins home tonight," their mother said. "Not with Mr. Bones on watch."

They continued their walk to the base of a grand old oak. She kissed the two little towheads and directed her flashlight beam up the great trunk. They climbed creaking board steps and clambered through the open bottom hatch into the tree house. Brian jumped to a window and peeked down at his mother with a big smile.

"Good night, mom."

"Good night, you two. Did you both go to the bathroom?"

"Yeah," Eddie alone said.

"Brian? Did you go to the bathroom?"

"Yeaaaah."

"Are you sure? I don't want you climbing down in the night to come use the bathroom. It's dangerous."

A huge grin spread across Brian's face. "We just do it from up here."

"You don't really?"

"Yes we do!" Eddie's face also appeared in the opening. "Out the window."

"Remind me to use my umbrella next time I walk under this tree."

The boys giggled again.

"Now I know why the grass is always so green under this tree. Anyway, if you hear a car pull up in the middle of the night, it's just your father coming home from the hospital."

"We know. Good night, Mom."

"Do you two need anything else?"

"Just some privacy please, thank you," Brian said.

"I can certainly tell when I'm not wanted."

"Nothing personal. We still love you. So please don't go away mad. Just go away."

"All right you two. Sleep tight."

The boys shut the hatch and closed the curtains. For the first time at night, they were thoroughly alone in this their very own little Halloween haven. Cozy with pillows, blankets and sleeping bags, the tree house was boyishly furnished with all sorts of ghoulish delights. Little monster heads lined the walls like hard-won trophies from boyhood fantasy adventures. Even the blankets and pillows had grimacing images of skulls, skeletons and monsters.

The boys broke into their deepest, gruffest voices and spoke at the same time. "Gimme a beer!"

They flipped open frosty cans of Apple Beer and chugged it down.

"Bleccch!" Eddie let out an awesome burp and they laughed together.

"All right. What was it?" Brian said.

"Sketti and meatballs!"

Brian reached for a marker that hung from a string attached on the wall. He handed it to Eddie who then struck a mark beside "sketti and meatballs" on a BURP FLAVOR CHART posted on the wall. Root beer bore the most marks on the chart followed by tuna fish with pickle. Shoe polish down at the bottom of the list carried the least with just one strike.

"BLEEEECCCH! Match that!" Brian put out his hand for the marker, then struck a mark beside "Root beer float."

"Hey! How come if we ate the same dinner, my burp was sketti and meatballs and yours was root beer float?"

"I have a good imagination."

"Or you're a fibber and your burp wasn't really root beer float."

"BLEEECH!" Brian beamed with pride. "Root beer float!"

"Or you went around mom's back."

"You don't know everything. You're not the Burp King. BLEEEECH! I am. Root beer float!"

"Mom wouldn't let us have floats tonight. But that's where you were when you said you were going to the bathroom and you were gone so long!" You were in the pantry making a float. No one can do burps that well without root beer. Gross! I can even smell the root beer."

Brian made two more marks on the chart.

Eddie saw Brian's look of gloating. "That's the last rootbeer float you're ever gonna have. I'm on to you. What do you have to say for yourself?"

"Bleeeccch! Root beer float!"

Eddie slammed Brian with a pillow and they both had another a good laugh.

These mischievous little boys lived the year round with the Spirit of Halloween in their hearts. Not only was October thirty-first their birthday, but they were residents of Middleway, a town that celebrated Halloween on a scale unimagined anywhere else.

"I can't wait to see Bloody Mary," Brian said.

"At the Rub A Dub Pub. It's gonna be so fun!"

"She always gives us free drinks 'cuz it's our birthday."

"Halloween carnival's only three weeks away. We need to coordinate what we get for our birthday so we don't get the same thing twice."

"We never did get the walkie talkies we asked for at Christmas."

"Yeah. With the treehouse done now, we really need 'em."

The look on Brian's face turned serious. "We can think later. The important thing right now is did you get it?"

"I got it!"

"The one?"

"The exact one," Eddie said. "The one Tad says is the scariest story he's ever heard. And he's seen the 'Exorcist' one and three at least six times."

"I know. He says this is even better than 'Bloody Fingers.'"

Eddie dug under a blanket and pulled out a compact disk. "Let's do it!" He plopped the disk into a small player tucked beside his sleeping bag and they both snuggled down into their bags. They shivered with excitement as eerie music began to play.

Brian held a flashlight under his chin. "I am the bogey man!"

"I'm going to take you away! Ha! Ha!" Eddie grimaced at Brian with his flashlight held to his chin.

The music stopped and a deep raspy voice began to speak.

"This is the story of one deep, dark, horrible night in a sleepy little town called Middleway..."

"Middleway?" they both said. They were shocked to hear this story took place right there in their own town.

"Nine-year-old Ryan O'Leary lived with his parents in a quaint country house..."

The boys could hardly believe they were the same age as the boy in the story.

Brian's flashlight rolled out of his hand. "His name sounds almost like mine."

"One October morning Ryan set out with his father, the local doctor on his daily rounds..."

The boys' disbelief deepened still, with the mention that Ryan's father was a doctor, just like theirs. Brian picked up his flashlight and held it tight in his hand.

"The woods were warm and cheery in the autumn sun as Ryan and his father galloped along on their trusted horse Buster. But their journey took them right through the scariest part of the Great Black Woods, the scariest part at night, that is. There are many stories about these Great Black Woods. Spooky stories of witches and goblins that haunt the woods and dance in the moonlight at an abandoned old castle."

The boys both knew the old castle and mouthed the words "Witches' Point."

"But no story is more frightening than the story of the Erlking. Some say the Erlking is the king of the witches and the goblins, who'll devour any child who dares to be in the woods after dark. Some even say that he is the devil himself, and that he rips children right out of their parents' arms."

The night sounds and screeches which had come from the player now appeared to come from the woods all around them. Even the grimacing skulls and monsters on the wall of the tree house which only moments before seemed so friendly, suddenly had taken on a menacing appearance.

Brian reached over and hit the pause button. The two lay there in silence.

"Hoo-hoot, hoo-hoooo." Only the reassuring sound of Mr. Bones' night call punctuated the stillness.

Eddie gulped. "I think we gotta finish the story. Tad's gonna ask about it. He'll think we're total whimps if we can't tell him how it ends."

"Hoo-hoot, hoo-hoooo."

"G. F. I."

With Brian's approval, Eddie pressed the play button.

"The day passed quickly for Ryan and his father, but as they began their journey home night fell over the forest. Thoughts of all the scary stories of what goes on in these woods after dark began to run through Ryan's mind."

"'Daddy, do you believe the stories about the Erlking?' Ryan questioned his father with a look of concern."

"'No, son. They're just fairy tales. But don't you worry. We should be back home before too long,' his father replied reassuringly."

"Eerie night cries rang out through the blackness as they galloped along. The woods which earlier were so warm and inviting now held visions of terror for Ryan at every turn. Big dark boulders looked like lurking demons and dead trees with out-stretched branches appeared as looming ghouls with reaching arms. A cold wind began to blow and Ryan started to shiver. As they neared Witches' Point, where there was an abandoned old castle, the wind blew harder and harder, and harder still. It whipped through the trees like a screaming banshee."

Just then the curtains in the treehouse started to flap in an intense rush of wind, but Eddie and Brian were too spellbound to even notice.

"All of the sudden the wind stopped. Then a strange and deathly silence settled in on the dark forest. Even the sounds of Buster's beating hooves and Ryan's own pounding heart seemed to disappear. All was quiet. Too quiet. Suddenly without warning, Buster jostled about, violently thrashing to and fro, as though being driven by some terrible unseen force. Ryan gasped with alarm and buried his head as his father struggled frantically to maintain control of the frightened horse. At last Buster calmed down and Ryan's father breathed a sigh of relief."

"'It's all right now, son.'"

"Ryan slowly looked up, but gasped again in utter terror! Thundering along right beside them were four black steeds pulling an old black hearse. At the helm sat a dark human form wearing a gleaming gold crown."

"'Daddy!' Ryan cried. 'The Erlking! He's riding along right there beside us!'"

"'It's only the night mist streaking along, son. Don't be afraid,' his father replied in a comforting tone. But Ryan would not be comforted."

"'Don't you see him, Daddy?' Ryan screamed as he struggled to point his shaking hand at the great dark being now directly across from them. 'He's right there!'"

"Ryan's father held him tighter to reassure him, but Ryan froze with fear when a strange and haunting voice called to him from the dark carriage."

"'Dear little child. Come! Go with me! We'll frolic and play along the shore where the beautiful flowers bloom.'"

"Ryan screamed out again."

"'Daddy!! The Erlking is whispering to me! Don't you hear him?!!'"

"'Shhhh, it's all right. It's only the wind rustling in the dead leaves.' His father held Ryan even tighter, but again the voice called."

"'My handsome boy, you will wear garments of gold. You can sing and dance with my three lovely daughters in the moonlight forevermore.'"

"'Daddy, look! The Erlking's daughters! Their hands are reaching out to me.'"

"Ryan's father turned his head to look but saw only a stand of ancient willow trees with branches swirling in the wind as they passed."

"'Son, it's only the old gray willows. They look ghostly blowing in the night wind.'"

"Ryan's father kicked Buster to make the horse go faster."

"'Daddy help!' Ryan cried out hysterically. 'They're touching my face. Aaaaah!'"

"Ryan thrashed about as he tried to push their hands away from his face."

"'Son! Look there ahead at the lights of town in the distance. We're almost out of the woods.'"

"Off in the distance the glimmer of town lights came into view through the trees."

"Ryan's father squeezed him even tighter, so tightly Ryan could hardly breathe."

"'My sweet charming one,' the voice called again, 'if you are not willing to come, then I shall have to use force!'"

"Just then a great powerful arm reached out from the carriage and grabbed Ryan's wrist with a grip of cold steel."

"'Daddy!!! He's got of hold of my arm!' Ryan cried out pitifully. 'DADDY! He's hurting me!!'"

"'Hang on son. We're almost home,' his father offered, as he tried further to calm Ryan."

"They galloped along and at long last passed out of the woods onto a familiar lane and into the courtyard of home. Anxious and weary, Ryan's father looked down at him with a sigh of relief."

"'Son, we're home.'"

"But there in his arms was little Ryan — dead."

Eddie and Brian lay motionless – too stunned to move. Only the sound of their heavy breathing could be heard until a scratchy evil voice blurted out of the disc player.

"Stick around if you dare to hear another tale from the dark side."

Brian slapped off the player. His little lips began to quiver. "I don't wanna hear another story."

"Me neither."

"Maybe we should go back into the house."

"Hoo-oo-oo, hoo-awwww." The owl's normal friendly nightcry had been replaced by some awful warning screech that they had never before heard. They both slid farther down into their sleeping bags, their beaming flashlights held tight in their white-knuckled hands. The sound of their heavy breathing filled the tree house until sleep gradually overtook them both.

Brian immediately began to dream. He saw the Erlking's carriage thunder down a deserted woodland road. The powerful black steeds galloped on and on, up one hill and down the next. The sound of their pounding hooves echoed so loudly through the night air that even the moon seemed to hide from the deafening roar behind folds of forbidding dark clouds.

Brian dreamed that at long last the horses slowed and came to rest beneath an age-old oak tree. The Erlking, still at the helm, craned his neck and looked high up into the branches above. After a moment, he climbed down and walked around to the back of the hearse and unlatched the door. It opened with a loud C-R-E-A-K.

Brian woke with a start and lay frozen with fear inside his sleeping bag. He tried not to breathe for fear the very sound of his breath would somehow betray him. The batteries in both flashlights had long since gone dim. The tree house was completely dark except for a single ray of strange blue light that streaked up onto the ceiling. The thin beam perfectly fell up across a shrunken head hanging in the corner. It created not only a ghastly image on the head itself, but a terrifying shadow across the ceiling as well. Brian turned his head to look at the beam. Something unearthly, something terrible must be causing that light he thought. He closed his eyes in hope that it would disappear, but instantly the image of the Erlking came vividly right back into his mind's eye.

He saw the Erlking right beneath this very tree. A skull-faced lantern burned blue on one side of the carriage. The Erlking lit a similar lantern on the other side.

Brian opened his eyes just as another beam of light flashed up onto the treehouse ceiling. He tried to call Eddie's name but no sound would come out of his mouth. He struggled to sit up in his sleeping bag, then crawled over to the hatch. The door creaked open but did not disturb Eddie. Brian then leaned over the hole and stared down. The blue light from below flooded him with an enveloping brilliance.

He started to climb down but paused on the top step. He looked back at Eddie in the treehouse momentarily, and then started down again when—

"Aaaaaaaaah!" He slipped and fell.

CHAPTER TWO

BONG! The bell in the tower of an old church at the edge of town square struck Twelve O'clock Midnight. BONG! The ivy-covered belfry shuddered against the night sky as the bell rang out across the sleeping town. BONG! Four eventful days had passed since Brian and Eddie slept out together in the new tree house. BONG! Eddie, just like the rest of town, was sound asleep in his own bedroom and in his own bed. BONG! He dreamed of soaring through the night sky over the dark woods east of town. BONG! He sailed effortlessly along so close to the treetops that he reached down and touched the soft leaves. BONG! Through the trees yet ahead, he saw the town cemetery silently come into view. BONG! In the shadow of night, the tombstones below looked like rows of spectral forms emerging from the very graves over which they stood guard. BONG! He noticed an old cathedral with a bell tower that loomed in the dark before him. BONG! The iron Celtic cross atop the spire stood silhouetted against the night sky like a great gun sight. BONG! Eddie playfully dove and passed right through the open arches of the belfry and barely missed the bell as it struck one last time. BONG!

Up and over more treetops, Eddie swept in upon town square all aglow with Halloween lights and festoonery. A gargantuan spider on a giant web completely enshrouded city hall, while across the street, a great jack-o-lantern glimmered on top of an old clock tower. The clock read twelve midnight. Eddie heard singing. It sounded remotely familiar and yet it was somehow strange and eerie. He floated through dark leafy trees that tickled as he drew closer to the music.

A cute pumpkin patch window display at Middleway Floral caught his attention. Chubby teddy bears of all sizes and colors, and all dressed in pumpkin costumes sat atop tiny bales of straw. The front window of the Crystal Ball Beauty Salon next door was trimmed with black lace and orange roses and displayed a magnificent crystal ball surrounded by an enchanting collection of witch dolls. One animated old-witch doll waved.

The Magic Hour

Eddie moved on to a toy store with a fantastical, animated Halloween window, where loudspeakers spewed Halloween carols into the night. The voices sang a familiar Christmas carol but with an eerie Halloween tonality—"O Little Town of Middleway..."

Little ghouls with flashing demon eyes beckoned Eddie into the magical miniature world of the window display. Ghosts and skeletons danced and whirled, twisted and twirled—the window was alive with light and motion, intimate motion of tiny animated Halloween figures.

Beneath a glittering Halloween tree decorated with hand-blown glass ornaments, Raggedy Ann and Raggedy Andy rested arm-in-arm on a doll sized wicker love seat, attired in their Halloween best. Ann coyly held a jeweled mask over her eyes and looked toward Andy.

In the center of the window, the eyes of two grimacing little pumpkin-head goblins flickered from lights inside their heads. The light inside of one wavered, then went out, just when a little ghost train wound past and disappeared into a tunnel leading through a mountain. Eddie moved away from the window and the image of a little blond boy dressed in Halloween pajamas fleetingly reflected on the glass. The image was at once clear and yet spectrally out of focus.

Eddie then moved on down a dark silent street lined with towering trees and passed the local mortuary, where the lights were on. It too seemed dressed for Halloween with its spider-web-design leaded-glass front windows.

On down the road, just beyond the edge of town, Eddie came upon an old country house buried deep in the forest. He passed around to the back of the house and drew near a lighted window on the upper level.

Inside, a single bedside lamp softly illuminated a boys' room warmly paneled in mahogany and brightly decorated with both football and monster posters. Two matching dressers stood between matching closet doors and matching beds. Everything in the room was paired, except that only one bed was occupied. It was Eddie.

A bright light appeared within the room, illuminating his face.

"Eddie. It's me," a soft young voice said.

He opened his eyes and sat up with a look of shock. "Brian! You're here!" Bathed in a beautiful pink-white light, Brian stood right beside Eddie's bed, still dressed in his Halloween pajamas.

"Yeah."

"Everybody thinks you're dead."

"I know. Everybody does just 'cuz my funeral's tomorrow. But I didn't want you to think I was. That's why I came."

"I knew you weren't dead. I could feel it. And I've tried to tell mom and dad, but they wouldn't believe me."

"I know you told 'em over and over. But be patient with 'em. They're having a really hard time with me gone. Especially Mom. I know you told her you don't do funerals when you know the person's not dead, but you gotta go at least to help Mom get through it. She's barely holding it together."

"I really don't want to go."

"I don't like funerals any more than you do, but Grandma is making me go."

"You've seen Grandma?"

"All the time. She says it's the only funeral I'll ever have, and the whole family is going together. So, if I gotta go, you gotta go."

"All right, I'll go. But explain to me how you can be still alive if you died?"

"It's hard to explain, but it was just my body that died when I fell from the tree house. Not me."

"What do you mean?"

"At first when I saw my body lying there on the ground hurt, I thought it was you. I got scared and started to yell for help."

"I didn't hear you."

"I yelled really loud. Grandpa McCourt and Uncle Louie heard me."

"Grandpa McCourt! He died when we were little."

"Yeah. I know. He and Uncle Louie came and showed me it was me on the ground. But it wasn't really me, because I was still me. I was still the same person even without my body."

"But what happened?"

"I had a nightmare the Erlking was coming to get me. I got scared and wanted to go into the house."

"Why didn't you wake me up?"

"I was going to at first, but for some reason I didn't. Then I just fell when I was climbing down. But Eddie, you gotta stop feeling bad about me falling. It wasn't your fault. Grandpa saw the whole thing and said it's not anybody's fault. He said sometimes things just happen. And they do."

"Mom and Dad have been fighting about who's fault it is," Eddie said.

"I know. I heard 'em. They're both blaming each other Grandpa says, but inside they're both blaming themselves. He says they blame each other 'cuz they can't stand the pain inside. You gotta help 'em understand it wasn't their fault. Dad worked so hard at the hospital with all the other doctors trying to save me, but there was nothing anyone could do."

"How do I tell 'em that?"

"Just tell 'em. And you gotta tell Mom it wasn't her fault either, for letting us sleep out. Tell her not to cry anymore, 'cuz I'm all right. Tell her Grandpa and Uncle Louie and everybody is taking really good care of me now."

"Who's Uncle Louie?"

"He's really great. You'll get to meet him. He and Grandpa are the ones who helped me into the light."

"What light?

"The light of life. It's really awesome. You'd like it, Eddie. While we're talking about light, you shouldn't sleep with the light on. You'll sleep better with it off."

"You sound like Mom."

"I sound like Grandma. She keeps telling me to tell you. She also said there is nothing to be afraid of because everyone is watching over you."

The two boys looked at each other almost in tears.

"I miss you, Brian. It's no fun without you."

"I miss you, Eddie."

"What are we gonna do? How are we gonna be together?"

Brian looked to the side for a moment as if someone was there speaking to him. "I've got a plan, but I can't say anything right now." Brian's eyes opened wide with excitement. "But tell Dad to bet on the Giants next Sunday. He can win back all the money he lost last month."

"The Giants aren't gonna win. They're a crumby team this year."

"But they're gonna win. They're gonna kick a field goal with six seconds left and win. And Eddie, there's somethin' else I gotta tell you. Somethin' really important. You gotta help Miss Pleasant. She's not gonna make it without you."

"What's wrong with Miss Pleasant?"

"I can't talk anymore right now. They're calling me."

"Who's calling you?"

"Give everybody a big hug okay? And take good care of Larry for me. Bye, see ya."

Brian turned and walked up a glowing stairway of light.

A look of desperation swept across Eddie's face. "Brian! Wait! When will I see you again?"

"I'll come back as soon as they let me." Brian grinned. "Neat dream, huh? Flying all over town. Except it wasn't really a dream!" He waved good-bye and his image faded into the light, which then simultaneously swelled and faded, leaving the bedroom dark except for the dim bedside lamp.

All sleep was lost from Eddie's eyes. His mind ran back and forth over all that Brian said – he did not want to forget a single thing. And what could he have meant if it was not a dream?

Eddie thought about his parents each blaming themselves for Brian's death, and how Brian said it was neither of their faults. Then he wondered, even though Brian said it was not his fault, if possibly it really was his fault that Brian died. He was the one who said they should finish listening to the story or Tad would think they were whimps. But then again, maybe it was Tad's fault for pressuring them to listen to the story in the first place.

"Grandpa saw the whole thing and said it's nobody's fault --" Brian's words revisited Eddie's mind.

With his heart at peace for the moment, Eddie reached over and doused the light.

"Eddie?" his mother's voice softly called. "Are you awake?"

"Yeah." He rolled over and saw her in the doorway.

"Are you all right?"

"I'm okay. What's the matter?"

"I saw your light go off. Did the bulb burn out?"

"No. I turned it off."

"I know you haven't been comfortable with the dark ever since Brian died."

"I'm okay with it now."

"That's good. There really is nothing to be afraid of."

"That's what Brian said, too."

"When did he tell you that?"

"Just a few minutes ago. I was asleep and he woke me up."

"He didn't say it to you in a dream?" She stepped to his bed and sat down beside him.

"Nope. He woke me up to tell me a bunch of stuff."

"What kind of stuff?"

"He said he's really worried about you."

"Why would he be worried about me?"

"He's worried about both you and dad."

"Why's he worried about us?"

"He knows you and dad are blaming each other that he fell, but inside you're really both blaming yourselves."

"Brian told you that?"

"Uh huh. He said it wasn't your fault, Mom, for letting us sleep out. Don't blame yourself anymore. It just happened and it's nobody's fault."

Eddie's words struck a deep emotional chord within his mother and pierced a hidden pain center about which she thought no one knew.

"Thank you, Eddie, for sharing that." Though it was dark in the room, her eyes broke away and dropped to the floor.

"It wasn't dad's fault either. Dad did everything he could."

"I know he did." She started to cry.

"Brian said to tell you not to cry anymore because he's all right. Grandpa and everybody are takin' really good care of him."

"Oh, Eddie. How can you know all this?"

"Brian told me! But you don't believe me."

"I want to believe you, Sweetheart."

"But you don't. I can tell."

"Right now, Eddie, I'm just hurting so much I can't think clearly. Thank you for sharing all that. It helps me understand things better."

"You're welcome."

"Did Brian say anything else to you?"

"Oh, yeah. He talked me in to going to the funeral."

"How did he do that?"

"He said he didn't want to go either, but Grandma was making him go."

"Really."

"He said if he's gotta go then I gotta go, too, 'cuz we're twins."

Mrs. McCourt smiled. "I'm very glad you changed your mind. That way we can all be there together tomorrow. We're going to need each other to get through it."

"Brian said that, too. I'll be there with you."

"I'm glad. I still love you Eddie."

"Thanks, Mom. Me, too."

"Let's both try to get some sleep now. We have a long day ahead of us tomorrow."

"Okay. Goodnight."

"Goodnight, Sweetheart."

A gloomy gray cloud bank loomed over the town the following morning. Eddie's father, Doctor Patrick McCourt, was a tall man with a neatly-trimmed beard and thinning dark hair. He arose early and stepped to the bedroom window. "That is exactly how I feel—overcast and ready to drizzle at any moment."

Mrs. McCourt sat up in bed. "I checked in on Eddie in the night. He told me that Brian woke him up to tell him that he was really worried about you and me."

Doctor McCourt turned back toward her and the bed. "Brian is worried about us?"

"He said because we're both blaming each other on the outside, when on the inside we're both blaming ourselves for his death."

Doctor McCourt stood quietly. He needed a moment to contemplate what he had just heard. "He's probably right," he said then turned again to the window. A single tear rolled down his cheek. "It's starting to rain."

"Honey. Eddie said Brian knows you did everything you possibly could to save him. It wasn't anybody's fault. It just happened."

"That's really something for a little boy to say that to his parents regardless of how he learned it or where he heard it."

"Eddie knew I didn't completely believe him. I was in shock at what he was telling me. I felt really bad. But there is more. He said to tell us that Brian's okay because grandpa and grandma are taking really good care of him."

"That's a beautiful thought."

"You knew Eddie was boycotting the funeral because he didn't believe in them when he knows the person is not dead. Eddie said Brian talked him into going to the funeral, because Grandma is making him go, too."

"Sounds like those two. Sounds like his little mind has it all figured out. He can help the rest of us make sense of everything."

"I'm sorry for the hurtful things that I said yesterday.

"I'm sorry, too." He sat back down on the bed. "And I want you to know I understand how much my sister's remark hurt you, because it hurt me, too." Doctor McCourt tenderly took his wife's hand. "It was very cruel."

"I think it was meant to be cruel. But this is not a time to be harboring family resentments, so I won't."

"I knew yesterday, when you said you weren't up to house guests, that was your way of saying please take Lois and the girls to a motel."

"They like it better there anyway," she said. "The girls can play in the pool."

A realization struck Doctor McCourt. "That might be why she said it, knowing we would not want to put them up in the house."

"Right now I'm barely holding it together."

"I know the feeling."

"We need to do everything we can to pull together to help us get through this."

"You're right again, as usual," he said.

"Can you live with it if I just throw a black scarf over my head today?"

Doctor McCourt grinned. "Bad hair day coming on?"

"Bad everything day, but I will greet it with a smile." She smiled at her husband then broke into tears. They embraced.

At the grave-side funeral, the black attire of the McCourt family contrasted starkly with the bright rainbow of flowers that completely encircled the casket and the open grave. Eddie nestled in between his mother and his father. Beside him stood his thirteen-year-old sister Melissa, who had dark hair like her father. She was tall for her age and wore a retainer on her teeth.

Everyone stood silently as the Pastor began the sermon.

"Many times things happen in our lives' course that raise more questions than they answer. Losing a child is one of those things. We simply cannot know the full reason why it happens. We can only trust that God above has great purposes and that they are fulfilled in all things, even in tragedy..."

Eddie's eyes wandered all over while the pastor continued. He noticed an owl sitting on a low pine bough just beyond the edge of the funeral gathering. He completely blocked out the funeral proceedings and focused on the owl. Not only did it look exactly like Mr. Bones, it appeared to be looking straight at him. He stared at the owl and it seemed to stare right back.

Eddie looked away then looked back. The owl looked away then looked back, as if to mimic him. He raised his chin and looked up at the sky. The owl raised its head and looked to the sky as well. For the final test, Eddie shrugged his shoulders way up and the owl raised and ruffled his wings. He wondered why this bird could possibly be here and be focused on him this way. He knew it must mean something.

The pastor finished his sermon and a kindly woman of sixty with golden hair stepped to the microphone. She was Miss Margaret Pleasant, Brian and Eddie's grade school teacher. Beloved by the entire community, her forty years of teaching and devotion to the young showed ever so gently in the soft creases of her face. She stood surrounded by children dressed in a rainbow of soft pastel colors that repeated the rainbow theme of all the funeral sprays.

"The children wrote a poem together recently, as part of a class project to create a song. The words are simple and straight forward, but they actually have great depth and meaning. As we put the words to music just last week, we had no idea we would be singing them at a classmate's funeral service this week." She covered her face with a handkerchief for a moment to regain her composure. "The song is entitled 'LET THE FLOWERS BLOOM.' We'll just let the lyrics speak for themselves."

Miss Pleasant led the school children in a simple but lofty chorus of young voices.

> *"The daffodil, the tulip tall,*
> *The rose so sweet, the violet small,*
> *They grace the earth with colors bright,*
> *They fill our lives with joy and light,*
> *Let the flowers bloom.*
> *Let the flowers bloom while they may,*
> *For tomorrow winter will come*
> *And they will all fade away.*
> *Let the flowers bloom."*

Eddie saw that his mother was so overcome while the children sang, she could barely stand. He hugged her and squeezed her tight.

The pastor pronounced the last rites over the casket and rain began to gently fall. Heaven itself wept with all those in attendance. The casket was lowered into the ground and Eddie turned away. He buried his head in his mother's dress. Melissa grabbed her father's arm for support. When the casket completely disappeared below the flowers that surrounded the grave sight, the owl on the branch above took flight.

"HOO-OO-OO, HOO-AWWWW!"

Eddie recognized the sound and quickly turned his head. The owl screeched and swooped down over the open grave, passing right between the people on either side. Those closest felt the rush of energy as the great bird flew by.

Eddie knew this could not be just a coincidence.

CHAPTER THREE

A week and a half passed and Eddie had not yet returned to school. His mother had yet to sleep through the night since Brian fell. She continually woke from nightmares. This morning Mrs. McCourt simply stayed in bed. With the house quiet, she tried to sleep in but the doorbell rang. She put on her robe and answered the door to find Miss Pleasant. Their eyes met in a form of communion and they embraced.

"I'm sorry I'm still in my robe," Mrs. McCourt said, "but, please, do come in."

"No apologies necessary. Is this a bad time?"

"Oh, no. I was just about to start baking cakes for the carnival cake walk."

"May I help you with them? Or better yet. May I make them for you? That will be one less thing for you to worry about."

"Thank you, but actually I enjoy making the cakes. Busying myself will help me keep my mind off of things."

"I understand that."

They sat on the sofa in the living room. Mrs. McCourt did not notice the large carry-all bag Miss Pleasant had slung over her shoulder.

"Elizabeth, I've been really worried about you," Miss Pleasant said. "I can only imagine what you are going through."

"I'm actually doing better. Each day that passes I seem to get a little stronger."

"I'm so glad to hear that. Don't worry if there are relapses. That's normal."

"I cannot thank you enough for that beautiful song. It was the most touching part of the whole funeral—those sweet children singing to their friend and classmate."

"It meant a lot to the children to be able to participate. For many of them it was their first funeral." Miss Pleasant paused a moment. "How is Eddie?"

"I'm not sure, to be honest. He just won't accept Brian's death.

The Magic Hour

He won't accept that he really is gone. He insists that Brian is still alive. But at least he's eating now. At first, he wouldn't touch anything, for days."

"Death is especially difficult to deal with when you're young. It is hard to comprehend the finality."

"Since the funeral, Eddie's been dreaming about the two of them playing together. Now all he wants to do is sleep so they can be together."

"At least they're pleasant dreams and not nightmares."

"I know about nightmares." Mrs. McCourt adjusted her position on the sofa.

"I can imagine. You know there are some young people who never do quite get over the loss of someone special. Older people, too, for that matter."

"I really don't know which is worse. The pain of losing Brian or the pain of watching Eddie suffer so."

"Please be patient with him. Eddie lost much more than his brother. He lost his entire identity."

"What do you mean?"

"All his life he's been special because he's been one of the twins. Now he's just Eddie."

"Oh. I never thought of it that way."

"This has to be doubly difficult for him."

"It does really concern me though, that he insists that his dreams are real. He insists that Brian still tells him things."

"Right now, Eddie is coping the best way that he can. It's not uncommon when someone dies, for a child to pretend that that person is still alive. It shields them from their grief. It's not really any different than keeping yourself busy. It's just his version of keeping his mind off of things."

"You are probably right."

"I am really concerned about Eddie not coming back to school, however. The longer he's out the more difficult his return will be for him. I'm not thinking just of his school work. Socially it gets harder and harder to face everyone the longer you are out."

"Eddie insists that he is not ready for school yet."

"I once knew a young girl who didn't return to school for two years after someone very close to her passed away. Miss Pleasant removed the carry-all bag from her shoulder and took out a large, over-stuffed manila envelope. "All the children in class wanted to make cards for Eddie to show they care. Some are a little strange, but they are from the heart."

"Let me call him."

"No, please don't disturb him. Just give these to him along with our love." She handed the bulging envelope to Mrs. McCourt and then looked back into her shoulder bag with some uneasiness. "This is really awkward to talk about, but the day before Brian died, we made Halloween masks in class. The children all took paper mache casts of each others' faces. It was great fun putting straws in their noses so they could breathe."

"I can imagine."

"All the other childrens' masks are decorated and painted and hanging about the room now. But I thought that under the circumstances, it was best if I didn't hang Brian's and Eddie's." Miss Pleasant pulled two objects wrapped in red cloth from her bag and handed them to Mrs. McCourt. She unwrapped the cloths and her face went white. The sight of two small masks cast from two identical young faces was too much for her. She started to sob.

"I'm so sorry, Elizabeth. I didn't mean to upset you."

"I'm sorry. Anything at all sets me off."

"That's perfectly understandable. Please tell Eddie that he is welcome back in school whenever he is ready. Tell him how we all miss him. The children are concerned, and you know I'll do all I can to make him comfortable."

"That means a lot to us. Thank you so much."

"I'd best be going now." Miss Pleasant stood up from the couch.

"Thank you for coming by."

They hugged and Mrs. McCourt saw her to the door. She then took a moment to compose herself and carried the envelope of cards into Eddie's room. He was still in bed with his face to the wall.

"Knock. Knock. Guess who was just here?" she said.

Eddie neither answered nor turned.

"Miss Pleasant was just here. And look what she brought you."

Eddie rolled over toward his mother. "Miss Pleasant was here? What's wrong with her?"

"Eddie! Nothing's the matter with Miss Pleasant. She brought these cards that all your friends made for you." Mrs. McCourt sat on the edge of the bed and pulled out a pink card. "Look at these. They'll help cheer you up."

She was charmed by a drawing of a teddy bear holding a bouquet of red and black flowers. She opened the card and read the message aloud to Eddie.

"Roses are red,
Violets are black
I can't bear it without you
So please hurry back."

"How sweet," she said. "I wonder who it's from. There's no name." She handed the card to Eddie but he just rolled back over to the wall. "Look, Eddie, this is cute."

Eddie showed no interest so she set it down and removed another that was made of black construction paper with a crude skull and crossbones painted on it. Inside the card it read:

"DEATH SUCKS."

"This one's from Tad. I should have known."

"Tad?" Eddie rolled back over and grabbed the card.

His mother watched as he looked intently at the card. A loving smile broke across her lips. "It hurts, doesn't it? It hurts for all of us. It's a very sad thing, but we have to accept the fact that Brian is dead."

"He's not dead! I know he's not. I talked to him."

"Sweetheart. You know sometimes when we're asleep our minds play tricks on us. And we dream things that we want to have happen."

"It wasn't a dream 'cuz it was real. He's alive!"

"Even though Brian is not here with us anymore, he'll always be a part of our family. He'll always be alive in our hearts."

Eddie started to cry. His mother hugged him tightly and cried, too.

"It's okay to cry," she said. "It will help you feel better."

Eddie cried himself to sleep in his mother's arms.

He dreamed the whole night that he and Brian played together up in the mountains. They hiked and fished and swam in a lake, and then fished some more. Eddie dreamed that he and Brian lazily floated on an old-fashioned log raft, like one his grandpa made for them one summer when they were very young. They wore matching Hawaiian swim trunks, matching sunglasses, and they dangled matching bamboo poles over the side of their raft. He and Brian seemingly spent days at this favorite vacation spot of theirs called Rainbow Lake, where the McCourt family had been going for generations.

Eddie and Brian caught so many fish that all the fun was gone. They barely threw their lines in the lake and they were overrun with fish. The water teemed with fish fighting to bite the hook.

"Can you believe these fish?" Brian said.

"I've never seen anything like it. It's almost disgusting. You don't even have to use bait."

"I know. The fish wanna be caught so bad, they fight over which one gets to bite the hook."

"I just wish they would stop biting and leave us alone," Eddie said.

Their jiggling poles instantly became still.

"Hello-o-o-o-o." A man's friendly voice echoed from across the lake.

Eddie and Brian sat up to greet a young man of twenty with a warm smile, who glided toward them in a hand-made birch-bark canoe. He was dressed in traditional red and black Great Outdoors plaid like their grandfather used to wear.

Brian smiled from ear to ear. "Hey. Uncle Louie."

Uncle Louie pulled right up beside them, and reached out to shake Brian's hand. "Hi, Brian. And hi to you, too, Eddie. I'm Uncle Louie."

"Hi."

They also shook hands.

"Nice glasses, you two," Uncle Louie said. "They must be the latest style."

"They are, thanks," the boys said.

"I should look into getting some for myself."

Eddie handed his glasses to Uncle Louie. "You'd look good in them."

"Do you really think so?"

"Sure. Try 'em on." He put them on.

"See. What'd I tell you? You keep them."

"That's very nice of you Eddie. Thank you. I heard that you boys were bored of fishing so I came to the rescue."

Eddie looked at Brian with amazement. "How'd he know? I just barely said – "

Uncle Louie smiled. "Word gets around. You have to be really careful what you say. If you do not want anybody to hear it, then you had better not say it."

"You know," Brian said, "Uncle Louie's buried right next to us."

"Really?"

"Yes, I am."

"You should go see him, Eddie."

"My grave marker is rather grown over with grass and bushes."

"You should go clean it up for him. Nobody alive even remembers him he's been dead so long. So nobody takes him flowers ever, either."

"What's it like to be in a coffin?" Eddie said to both of them.

Brian frantically put his hands around his throat as if strangling himself. "It's-really-hard-to-b-r-e-a-t-h-e!"

"Don't believe him, Eddie. Neither of us has ever been in a coffin so we cannot really say."

"Who'd they bury in your graves?"

"Just our bodies. Not us."

"Oh."

"You know, when they were all working on me at the hospital," Brian said, "Uncle Louie was there with me, too. Grandpa was telling me all about what the doctors were trying to do to keep me alive, but Uncle Louie was showing me the ropes on how to float and stuff. It's amazing what you can do without your body."

"Brian, I wonder if maybe we should not be telling Eddie about all this."

"It's okay. He's cool—we're twins."

"Didn't it hurt when they were working on you?" Eddie said.

"Oh, no. I couldn't feel a thing. And I was hovering right there above Dad."

Uncle Louie put a hand on each of the boys' shoulders, but looked straight at Eddie. "It is time to hang up the fishing pole and go back to school now."

"I don't wanna go back to school yet."

"I know that it is much more fun to spend your days together up here at Rainbow Lake, but the vacation is over. You both have obligations. I need to tell you that there is someone there at school who needs your help very much."

"Yeah, Eddie. Ya gotta go help Miss Pleasant. She's not gonna make it without you."

Eddie looked puzzled. "What's wrong with Miss Pleasant?"

"She needs help that only you can give her," Uncle Louie said.

"What am I supposed to do for her?"

"The first thing you need to do is just be in class. That alone will help her a great deal. It will also help your parents who are very worried about you."

Brian nodded his head in agreement. "They are very worried about you."

"We cannot tell you anymore right now, but we will talk again."

Brian took a hold of Eddie's hands. "Look for me, Eddie, when time stands still. Remember, when time stands still."

Eddie awoke in his bed to early morning sunlight streaking across his face. He laid there a moment with his eyes open, then glanced at his night stand. The clock read 7:45 AM. He knew he had just enough time to get dressed, grab a bite for breakfast and run out to catch the bus, so he jumped from bed and scrambled to put on his clothes. He overheard his mother in the kitchen talking to his sister.

"How many cookies do you want in your lunch?"

"ELEVEN!" he said, then ran to the kitchen. His entire family looked with surprise as he entered the room.

His father pushed out a chair at the breakfast table. "Good morning, Sunshine."

"Are you going to school today?" his mother said.

"Yeah." Eddie sat down and plopped his elbows on to the table.

"That's great. You must be feeling better."

"Uncle Louie told me I had to go back to school."

"Uncle Louie told you you had to back to school?" his mother said.

"Uh huh. 'Cuz Miss Pleasant needs my help."

Melissa turned and looked straight at Eddie. "Who's Uncle Louie?"

His parents turned and looked straight at Eddie, too, waiting for his reply.

"Uncle Louie's Uncle Louie. He's buried right next to Brian and me."

His parents looked at each other stupefied. Melissa curled her nose. "So, you're dead and buried now, too?"

"Oh. Yeah." Eddie smiled at himself. "I'm not buried yet. But he is. Right by Brian and my tombstones."

"Help me get this straight," Melissa said. "So, you're talking to various dead people now and not just Brian?"

"Just relatives."

"That puts our minds at ease that you're only talking to dead relatives."

No one moved for a moment. Then his mother placed a breakfast setting in front of him. "Are they visiting you here in the house, Sweetie?"

His mouth full of food, Eddie nodded his head.

"Oh, gosh! Call the realtor!" Melissa said. "We need to move. This house is haunted."

"Just in time for Halloween. So shut up!"

His mother frowned. "Eddie! We don't use that word in this house! You know that."

"She's making fun of me and you and Dad are letting her."

"I. . . I'm sorry. It's just that we were so interested in what your answers would be to her questions, Honey."

His father leaned forward in his chair. "You have to understand, Eddie, we haven't had whatever experiences you've had and so this is all very new and even strange to us."

"There's nothing strange about it. I just talk to these people like I talk to anybody else."

Melissa jeered. "Except they're dead."

"Just like you're gonna be if you don't shut up."

"Eddie! You know the rules. Third strike and you're grounded."

"Mom. She's the one causing it. Ground her. I haven't even left the house for two weeks, not since Brian fell. Except for the funeral."

The conversation stopped. No one knew what to say next. Eddie resumed eating then looked at his father excitedly. "Oh, and Dad. I forgot to tell you. Brian said if you'd bet on the Giants this Sunday, you'll win back all the money you lost last month."

Doctor McCourt choked on a spoonful of cereal. He coughed and coughed. Eddie jumped from his chair and whacked him on the back, but he continued to cough.

"Heimlich!" Eddie said. He then threw his arms around his father's chest, locked his hands together and heaved upward.

"Aaaaah! I'm okay now!" His father rose in his chair. "Thank you Eddie."

"Sure thing, Dad."

"I can breathe now."

"Great. I should do the Heimlich on Melissa, too. Get her to cough up what ever is in her craw."

"Human beings don't have craws, Eddie," she said.

A huge smile swept across his soon-to-be ten-year-old face. "I know they don't!"

"Mom! Are you gonna let him insult me like that? He should be grounded. That's his third strike."

Doctor McCourt could barely hold back the laughter at the unfolding comedy. "It's so nice to have everything back to normal around here."

"Hurry and finish your breakfast, Sweetie," his mother said. "You haven't got much time. And how many cookies do you want in your lunch?"

"Four."

"Now, about this gambling bet."

Doctor McCourt looked up and met with his wife's scowl. He turned beet red.

Melissa put her hand down on the table. "Anyway. The Giants could not possibly win. Even I know they are the worst team this year."

Eddie sat straight up. "The Giants are gonna kick a field goal with six seconds left and win."

"Thank you, Eddie. That's a good tip," his father said.

"Don't thank me. Thank Brian. He's the one who said it."

The others all had puzzled looks on their faces. Mrs. McCourt turned to her husband again. "Now, Dear. If I remember accurately, and do correct me if I'm wrong, you promised me in front of the children that you had quit betting."

A school bus honked outside. Doctor McCourt smiled.

"Don't think you're saved by the horn. We'll discuss this later." She hurriedly finished two lunch boxes, kissed Eddie and Melissa good-bye as they ran out the door, then turned to her husband again. "So, who's Uncle Louie?"

CHAPTER FOUR

Eddie hesitated at the school bus door. The childrens' rowdy voices inside made him nervous.

"It's okay, Eddie," Melissa said. "They're all your friends. And I'll be right behind you."

"We all have missed you very much, Eddie."

Eddie looked up and saw the bus driver, Mrs. Forsweat. Her familiar smiling face further helped set him at ease. He stepped up into the bus and an unsettling wave of quiet swept over everyone. In his face, the children not only saw Eddie, but they also saw the face of Brian who was now gone. Eddie hesitated and wanted to leave. Mrs. Forsweat, a middle-aged fifties fanatic in rhinestone cat-eye glasses, stood right behind him without him seeing and lead the entire bus in a cheer.

"WELCOME BACK EDDIE!"

The bus came alive as the children welcomed back their friend. Eddie stepped forward and returned a high five while Mrs. Forsweat kicked and ground the bus into gear.

Once at school, Eddie entered his classroom and first thing saw a large "WELCOME BACK EDDIE" banner stretched across the wall above the chalkboard. Miss Pleasant and the other children were all smiles as they warmly greeted him. A literal swarm of classmates escorted him to his seat. When the children settled into their own seats, the empty desk just to Eddie's left became obvious. It was Brian's. The decision to leave it for the duration of the year was unanimously made in Eddie's absence.

Eddie noticed the room basically looked the same except for the Halloween masks and a few new art posters.

Miss Pleasant stepped to the front. "Good morning, everyone. This is a very special day for us. We are so happy to have Eddie back in class with us."

Eddie studied her eyes to decipher what could possibly be wrong with her. He watched closely for several minutes, but at the end he was no closer to discovering the problem.

"This is a special week for us, too. Who knows what this Saturday is?"

"HALLOWEEN!"

"And what else?"

A blond boy with wily blue eyes named Tad Durban raised his hand. "It's Eddie's birthday."

"That's right, Tad. And we're going to celebrate it here in class on Friday. How lucky Eddie is to be born on Halloween! But what else is this Saturday? Something that only happens once a year in the middle of the night?"

Red-headed and freckle-faced Cindy Crystal raised her hand. Though sometimes a little frumpy as if she woke up late, she always had salon perfect nails. "The Witches' Sabbath."

"Thank you, Cindy, but that's not exactly what I was thinking. This Saturday night we all get an extra hour of sleep. Why would that be?"

A scrawny boy with slicked back black hair and thick dark-rimmed glasses lifted his hand high.

"Yes, Elliott?"

"Because we'll all be so plastered we can't wake up!"

All the children laughed but Miss Pleasant did not respond to his cut up comment. Elliot Carney was not the typical class clown. He was also the class brain.

"Well class, this Saturday night we all set our clacks bock one hour, I mean—"

The class laughed at her tongue tangling.

"What I meant to say was, this Saturday night we all set our clacks bock—"

The children laughed again.

"For some reason I can't say that. This Saturday night—Halloween night, Daylight Savings Time will be over so we move our c-l-o-c-k-s back one hour."

She breathed a sigh of relief and continued. "The clock strikes one o'clock, and then an hour later when it should be two o'clock, we set our clocks back to one again. It is the only time in the whole year when we gain an extra hour. It is almost as if time stands still those sixty minutes."

Eddie's ears pricked up.

"Now to start off this Halloween week in the right spirit, Cindy

Crystal has prepared a special report for us on the origins of our Halloween tradition."

Today Cindy was the perfect picture of school girl Halloween cute—orange and black saddle shoes with orange bobbie socks, pleated black and white plaid skirt and an oversized sweater quilted with images of Halloween. A sequined bat headband and dangling smiley-face-bat earrings completed her ensemble.

She walked matter-of-factly to the front of the room and removed some well creased papers from her little pumpkin-shaped purse. She began to read with monotonic disinterest.

"Halloween. Halloween is a holiday celebrated on October thirty-first when girls and boys put on costumes and greet their neighbors with 'Trick or Treat.' Most people give candy as a treat rather than face some kind of trick, like soaped windows or dog poop on the stoop. Pranks used to be very common, so many towns like ours decided to put on a Halloween carnival to prevent mischief by keeping the young people occupied with other activities. The word Halloween comes from ALL HALLOW'S EVE, which means holy evening."

Cindy became suddenly animated in her speech. "In ancient times, October thirty-first was the last day of the year. That night was considered the most holy night of all. People believed that on Halloween night the spirits of everyone that died during the last twelve months came back to visit their relatives in search of warmth and good cheer for one last time before they passed on forever into the next world."

Eddie squirmed in his desk. The tiny hairs all down his forearms stood straight up with shivers of goosebumps.

"Great bonfires used to be lighted on the mountainsides to guide the way for the spirits of the dead so they would know where to come. Although good spirits were out and about that night, evil spirits also wandered as they looked for new bodies to possess for the coming year."

Miss Pleasant scowled at Cindy's remarks about evil spirits. All the children were glued to Cindy's words, but Eddie was held hostage by them.

"Our costume tradition began when people wore ugly masks to frighten off any evil spirits who might be attracted by the firelight. You see, evil spirits are stupid. They would see the ugly faces of the masks and think Ooooooh, I don't want that yucky body, and so then they move on—"

"Ooooooh Cindy, we need to move on," Miss Pleasant said and stepped again to the front of the room. "You have covered the subject so thoroughly."

"But I'm not finished." Cindy smiled and resumed reading without missing a beat. "Before people left their houses to go to the bonfires, they would leave offerings for the poor outside their front doors. That's where the custom of going door to door for treats came from. This was the last night of the Celtic year and people wanted to send off the old and ring in the new on a generous note. The bonfires were also believed by some to ward off witches, who celebrated their most holy ceremony on Halloween, called Witches' Sabbath."

Cindy's eyes became electrified on the words Witches' Sabbath, so excited they almost seemed to spiral in their sockets. "Some of this town's earliest settlers were Witches, who came here to the forest to escape the vicious persecution that was going on in other areas. Middleway has a long rich tradition of we witches and warlocks gathering up at Witches' Point to offer up our sacrifices to --"

"THANK YOU, Cindy, for that fine report."

"But I haven't told the best part yet. We witches and warlocks gather up at Witches' Point to offer up our sacrifices to --"

"I'M SORRY CLASS." Miss Pleasant stepped right in front of Cindy, determined to not allow her to finish that sentence. "We need to move on now to other things."

But Cindy poked her head around and went right on.

Miss Pleasant noticed the school principal in the doorway. "LET'S HAVE A BIG ROUND OF APPLAUSE FOR CINDY AND HER VERY FINE REPORT." She spoke so loudly that no one could hear Cindy. Miss Pleasant clapped as hard as she could and the class followed suit. Outwitted and outdone with the applause, Cindy reluctantly took her seat. With a pouty face, she stared at Miss Pleasant.

Eddie stared at Cindy. He had to talk to her. He had to know if what she said about the dead coming back on Halloween night was true.

He did not hear another thing said in class. He did not hear a word when Mr. Warburton, the principal, spoke about some important computer disks that were stolen from his office. He was so deep in thought he did not even hear the recess bell.

"Hey, wake up! It's recess!" Eddie's friend Tad said right into his ear.

"Hey!"

"Come on. Let's go. We gotta talk."

"Oh, Eddie," Miss Pleasant said from across the room while children scurried from their desks. "May I see you a moment, please?"

Eddie turned to Tad. "Wait for me outside."

"I'll go secure the merry-go-round and wait for you there."

Eddie walked to his teacher's desk.

"I want you to know, Eddie, that I think you are a very brave boy. You showed real courage coming back to school today."

"It's no big deal."

"It is a big deal, coming back to school after what you have been through. I'm very proud of you."

"Thank you, Miss Pleasant. What did you mean when you said that time almost stands still?"

"This Saturday night at one o'clock, the clock will strike one. But an hour later, after 1:59 when it should strike two, it will strike one again. Because an hour later it is still the same time, it is almost as if time stands still for that one hour."

"I see."

"Now I want you to know, that if you ever need to step out of class to be alone for a few minutes, I will understand."

"Thank you Miss Pleasant. May I ask you a question?"

"Certainly."

"Are you okay?"

"Why, of course I am."

"Are you sure there's nothing wrong? Isn't there something I can help you with?"

"It's very thoughtful of you to ask, but thank you. I'm fine."

"What happened to mine and Brian's masks?"

"I gave them to your mother. Now don't forget that we are all wearing our costumes to school on Friday."

"I won't"

"What are you going to dress up as this year?"

"Frankenstein."

"Oh, he's always been my most favorite monster."

"Are you sure you're all right?"

Miss Pleasant fondled a heart-shaped locket hanging around her neck. "Eddie, you sweet thing. I assure you I'm perfectly all right. But if I need any kind of help in the future, I will be sure to call you."

"You promise?"

"I promise."

"Okay. When is that hour again that time stands still?"

"One o'clock. It begins at one o'clock and ends one hour later, still at one o'clock."

"After midnight?"

"That's right, Eddie. One o'clock in the morning. Most of us are well asleep by then. I know I will be."

"Okay. Thank you. I'm gonna go to recess now."

"You go have fun."

Eddie ran out the classroom door.

Out on the playground, Tad had bullied all other children off of the merry-go-round. Many of them stood at a distance and sneered at him. Eddie walked up. He and Tad gave it a push around and jumped on.

"I'm really glad you're back," Tad said.

"Me too."

"It was boring without you."

"Thanks."

"You okay?"

"Yeah."

"Took long enough to come back after the funeral. Everybody was wondering about you."

"I had a lot on my mind."

"Yeah. It's a raw deal that Brian died. What happened anyway?"

"That disk you loaned us?"

"Oh, yeah. Did you listen to it?"

"Yeah."

"The whole thing?"

"Yeah. The night Brian fell. We listened to your story and the next thing he was gone."

"Hey, wait a mintue!"

"That's just what happened."

"I had nothin' to do with Brian's death. I'm no accessory to murder."

"I didn't say you were. Just telling you what happened because you asked."

"It is kind of weird, though," Tad said. "The story and everything. It was just like Brian—the kid's name, his age, he lived here in

Middleway and his dad was a doctor."

"It's really weird. Did you notice anything weird about Miss Pleasant while I was gone?"

"What kind of weird?"

"Like something was wrong with her."

"Oh, yeah. When Brian died she totally lost it."

"What do you mean?"

"At first I think she thought you died. She started going through your desk, taking things out of it."

"What kind of things?"

"You know those masks we did?"

"Oh, those. That's no big deal. She just gave 'em to my mom."

"Could you believe all that stuff that Cindy was talkin' about? That girl needs a reality check."

"Do you think any of it could be true?"

"I don't believe in witches and all that stuff, if that's what you mean."

"I mean the part about the dead people coming back on Halloween."

"How could it be true if Cindy said it?"

"Do you think that people are really dead when they die?" Eddie said.

"Are you kidding? That's why they bury you. 'Cuz you rot and stink."

"I mean spirits. Do you think people have ghosts?"

"I don't believe in ghosts. Hey, speaking of ghosts. When I was at the funeral I saw a tombstone next to Brian's with your name on it."

"My grandpa gave us tombstones for Christmas a few years ago."

"Yuck! What a rotten present."

"That's what I thought."

"What a rotten grandpa. If my grandpa ever did anythin' like that, I'd tell him where to get off."

"I don't know why he would give us something like that for Christmas. It's not anything you can use."

"You can use it sometime."

"You know what I mean."

The merry-go-round slowed to a stop. Elliott Carney walked up to the far side and started to push. Tad dragged his feet to stop him.

"Merry-go-round is closed, Carney."

"Says who?"

"Says me! So get lost. Unless you wanna get false teeth before you reach the sixth grade."

Elliot gave Tad a dirty smirk and walked around the merry-go-round toward him.

"He's got his nerve defying me like that," Tad said to Eddie.

Elliott walked right up in front of Tad. "I have my rights. So shut up or get off yourself!"

Tad stood tall. "I'm not going to say this more than once more. It's closed!"

Elliott looked Tad right in the eye. "Master Durban, have you ever contemplated the trajectory arc of dirt when moved upon by an exterior kinetic force?"

Tad glowered at Elliott cluelessly.

"Maybe it's time you did." Elliott kicked the loose soil beside the merry-go-round and did not wait around to watch. Dirt flew up and sprayed Tad right in the face.

"ELLIOTT! YOU DIRTBALL! YOU ARE DEAD!"

"You're the dirtball, Taaaaad!" Elliott was already half way across the playground.

Tad jumped up and the chase was on. Elliott tore around the far corner of the school building with Tad way behind but in hot pursuit. No sooner did Tad disappear around the school, then a girlish scream echoed off the building from that far side of the grounds.

Eddie could only imagine what awful fate must have been Elliott's. The hysterical screaming continued, but Elliott came running up and jumped on the merry-go-round.

"If you're here?" Eddie said, "then who's --?"

Elliott just smiled.

Worried for fear of what might be going on, Eddie raced around the building to investigate and stopped—horrified by what he saw. Tad spun Cindy Crystal wildly around by the end of her long orange overcoat. She screamed and screamed and begged him to stop.

Eddie at last came to his senses. "TAD! LET HER GO!"

Tad released her and she sailed off into a heap on the playground.

"What'd you do that for, Tad? You could've hurt her?"

"She deserved it. She's got fleas."

"But you touched her. Now you got fleas."

"Hut uh." Tad quickly rolled up his shirt sleeve to reveal a huge ball-point pen tattoo on his forearm: "SUPER FLEA SHOT."

"Well, I think you ought to know that Elliott's taken full possession of the merry-go-round."

Anger surged in Tad's eyes. He ran off to reclaim the merry-go-round.

This was Eddie's chance to talk to Cindy. Still on the ground covered in bits of grass and playground bark chips, she searched the ground for a missing earring. Eddie walked up to her. "You okay?"

Cindy did not answer. She did not even look up. She picked up her soiled headband and tried to brush it off.

"Is it true what you said about the spirits of dead people coming back on Halloween night?"

Cindy turned her head away from Eddie. "Who wants to know?"

"I do."

Surprised with Eddie's interest, she extended her arm up with a dropped wrist, as if she awaited his kiss or at the very least his help up. Eddie did neither. He just stood there so she pulled her hand back sharply with a jerk.

"What you said about all the dead people coming back on Halloween. Is it true? I really need to know."

Cindy brushed herself off and stood up. "I don't know."

"How can I find out?"

"You'd have to talk to my mother. She's the expert on talking to dead people."

"When can I talk to her?"

Surprised again with Eddie's further interest, Cindy looked at him askance. "She charges for her services."

"I got money."

Cindy scowled at Eddie. "I'm not talking a few dimes and nickels."

"I just inherited Brian's whole life savings."

Cindy looked dead-faced straight toward Eddie. "Come to the Crystal Ball at four o'clock. She leaned right to his face and whispered, "Come alone."

CHAPTER FIVE

The day passed quickly but not quickly enough for Eddie. Just before the final bell he fibbed to Tad and told him he had to go straight home after school today, so he could slip over to the Crystal Ball to talk to Cindy's mother.

Eddie walked downtown, the opposite direction from his home. He gazed in the store windows along Main Street at all the Halloween displays. He knew that he had not yet stopped to look in the windows downtown this year, but somehow the displays all seemed strangely familiar to him.

Eddie knew that his mother would not approve of his appointment at the Crystal Ball. He also knew that if Cindy's mother could help him better understand how he could communicate with Brian, then no risk of being grounded for getting home late was too great.

He approached the Crystal Ball Salon and looked in the front window at the magnificent crystal ball in the center of the display. This window, all trimmed with black lace and orange roses, also somehow looked familiar. He noticed that all the witch dolls in the window had sweet smiling faces. Not one of them had a mean-spirited frightful witch face. One animated witch doll near the front waved and gestured for Eddie to come in. He looked to the door and saw a small sign pasted on the mail box: "Mr. Postman—No Bills Larger Than $20 Accepted," but did not quite understand it.

In spite of his misgivings and fears, Eddie mustered his courage and stepped right in front of the tall glass door. He took a deep breath and reached for the pull bar just when the near-by clock tower chimed. BONG! It was four o'clock. He smiled to himself – he was exactly on time. BONG! The bell chimed again and Eddie was yanked violently forward as the door opened inward. BONG! He fell helplessly forward down on to the floor just inside the salon. BONG!

"Oh, child. I do like punctuality," a mellow-toned woman's voice said. "It is the sign of a true gentleman."

Eddie looked up from the floor to see a large woman dressed head to toe in deep purple standing over him. He noticed that her eye makeup was beautiful but scary, and there was something witch-like and frightful about her, but at the same time she had a soft motherly presence. He saw her head silhouetted against a field of deep blue with shimmering gold stars sparkling all around her, and was momentarily entranced by swirling little flashes of golden light.

The woman's face became concerned. "Are you all right?"

Eddie neither answered nor moved. He knew he was not hurt but he was so uneasy, he just froze in place for a few moments right there on the floor, with his eyes open, as if he was stunned.

"Oh, child!" The woman knelt beside him. "Tell me what you see."

"Gold stars."

"Oh, thank heaven. I was beginning to worry. That's what you should see. The ceiling is covered with gold stars. Let me help you up." She took hold of his arms and he could not help but notice her three-inch-long purple fingernails with gold stars and crescent moons imbedded in them. He had never known anyone with fingernails like that before. He had not known anyone alive had fingernails like that. "For a minute there I thought maybe you were really hurt," she said. "I didn't dare move you. I was about to call an ambulance."

Eddie just let her speak.

"I'm really sorry. I thought you saw me through the lace curtain. I saw you outside the door just standing there. A lot of people think the door opens out, but it's one of those old-fashioned kind that opens in. So I just opened the door for you."

Eddie dusted himself off and then looked again at the woman. She even had purple frosted hair.

"You sweet little pea," she said in a soft, raspy voice, then eyed Eddie over.

Eddie did not know what to say to someone who only wore purple. "I'm Eddie."

"Yes, I know."

"I'm supposed to meet Cindy here."

"Yes, I know. Have a seat Honey. Cindy'll be ready in just a minute." She gestured for Eddie to sit down on one of the sofas in the waiting area by the window. With that, she walked back into the salon toward a client in her chair. "Dolly! Some peppermint tea for our young gentleman."

Eddie took a seat and looked around uneasily. The interior of this salon was a vision into a world of fantasy. The walls and ceiling were a deep shade of blue with gold stars and moons that hung from the ceiling on invisible threads. The stars cast shimmering little flashes of gold light that darted all about.

Fluffy clouds painted along the bottom of the walls just above the gleaming white marble floor gave the entire room the feeling of floating in the heavens. Even the white leather sofa on which Eddie sat seemed to disappear into the overall feeling of closeness to heaven.

Eddie suddenly gasped—a real-life witch sat on the other end of the sofa just beside him. He could see out of the corner of his eye that she was withered and hag like. At first he pretended not to see her, but finally he could not resist and turned to look. He breathed a sigh of relief. She was a nylon stocking person dressed as a witch.

A brilliant flash of colored light streaked across his face. Sunlight streamed in through the window, passed through the great crystal ball and cast a beautiful prismatic rainbow right across Eddie's face. He stared into the crystal ball, entranced by this colorful display of light.

"Do not be afraid, Eddie," a man's voice softly said.

He quickly turned but saw no one.

Again the voice spoke. "Eddie, do not be afraid."

Eddie turned back to the window and the crystal ball, but the rainbow was gone.

"Cindy will see you now," the voice of the woman in purple said.

Eddie turned back around just in time to see Cindy climb down from the lady's chair. He barely recognized her. She had an outlandish tall bouffant hairdo with heavy facial make up. She paraded straight toward Eddie in a bright blue mini skirt and white gogo boots as if she were a model in a fashion show. As she approached, she twirled all the way around for Eddie to see every side of her. He gulped.

The woman in purple walked up beside Cindy. "Mom. This is Eddie."

"Yes. I know." Cindy's mother extended her hand as if to be kissed but Eddie made no gesture. "Call me Sandy."

Both Cindy and Sandy grabbed adjacent white wicker chairs and pulled them up right in front of Eddie.

"You're a Scorpio, aren't you, Honey?" Sandy said, then turned to her daughter. "They're the most romantic." She looked back to Eddie. "Which hand do you use?"

Eddie was clueless. He just looked at Sandy with a blank face.

"Are you right or left handed?"

"Right."

Sandy gently took Eddie's hands in hers and held them with her eyes closed, but suddenly they blinked wide open. She traced her long fingernail down the middle of Eddie's left palm when a look of grave concern flashed through her face. She frantically looked to Eddie's right palm and traced her finger across there, too. She shuddered with a look of terror. "You're the McCourt boy! You just lost your twin brother. Cindy didn't tell me who you were."

Eddie looked sick with worry. "What's the matter?"

"You've got two life lines running side by side. But one suddenly stops."

"I don't know what you're talking about." He started to tremble.

Sandy pointed out the dual life lines running across his palms. "Eddie, you see these two lines? They're called life lines because they represent your life. Most everyone has just one. You have two running side by side. But then see how one stops?"

"I still don't know what it means. I came here 'cuz Cindy said you know how to talk to dead people."

"Oh, child. From what I'm feeling, you could teach me how to talk to the dead."

Eddie squirmed in his seat. He did not know what to make of this place.

"You've heard from your brother since he died, haven't you Eddie?"

Eddie chewed his lip in uneasiness.

"You've heard from your brother more than once. I know. I can feel it. Your brother is very close to you. He's all around you. He may even be here with us now."

Eddie looked back into the salon. For the first time he noticed frightful and grotesque women with mud masks and with their feet in the air drying pedicures. The woman in the closest chair, with her long neck and beady eyes, looked like a meerkat the way she gawked at him.

"Don't worry about any of them," Sandy said. "They can't hear you. I know you have something to say, Eddie. I can feel it. Do not be afraid."

"Somebody talked to me when I looked at the crystal ball when I first came in."

"Oh dear, me." Sandy was overwhelmed. She was so excited she could hardly breathe. She fanned herself. "I want to know every word." She called out at the top of her lungs just as a young woman arrived with a tea tray. "DOLLY! WHERE'S THAT tea?"

Sandy took the tray and set it down on the coffee table. Eddie stared at the tea pot and three mugs all in the shape of an old witch with a hag face. He turned toward the nylon witch.

"I see you've met Lucretia. Do you take sugar, Honey?"

Eddie made no reply. Sandy plunked two pumpkin-shaped sugar cubes into a mug. A little stir with a tiny witch broom and she handed it to Eddie along with two black-cat-shaped cookies.

Sandy then sat at perfect attention. "Now. Every word."

Eddie did not speak. Neither did he drink his tea. He sat perfectly still.

Sandy wiggled in her seat like a little kid. "What exactly did they say?"

Still, Eddie was hesitant to reply.

"Tell me what they said, please, Eddie."

"Don't be scared."

"Don't be scared?"

Eddie nodded.

"Someone said 'don't be scared?'"

Eddie nodded again.

Disappointment crept across Sandy's brow. "That's all they said?"

"I was afraid when I came in."

"Oh, heavens. You don't need to be afraid of me. But if someone from the other side went to the trouble to tell you that, then it must have been important. They do not waste any words over there. It was your brother wasn't it?"

"But it wasn't Brian. It was a man's voice."

Sandy gasped in astonishment and put her hand to her chest. "You've got open lines! Have you seen Brian?"

Eddie nodded.

Sandy could hardly believe Eddie's reply. She leaned back in her chair and fanned herself frantically with her hand. In a moment, she stood up from her chair and turned her back to Eddie and Cindy. No sooner did she do so than Eddie screamed and desperately covered his ears with his hands.

"Aaaaaaaaaaaaaah!"

Sandy whipped around holding what appeared to be a long slender

The Magic Hour

crystal pendant that hung from a cord around her neck. "I thought so!"

Eddie calmed and Sandy sat back down with both a look of concern and a look of excitement at the same time. "I'm sorry I had to do that to you, Eddie, but it was very important."

"What WAS that?"

"This pendant around my neck, it looks like a crystal. It's actually a dog whistle."

"A dog whistle!"

"I'm sorry it hurt your ears but I needed to know what your range of hearing was. I needed to know if you had the ability to hear the whistle. Have you ever heard a dog whistle before today?"

Eddie shook his head.

"Dog whistles make a sound that only dogs can hear. Except you, Eddie."

"How come I can hear it?"

"Before I answer that, I want to ask you another question. Have you ever known who was on the phone before you picked it up?"

"Sometimes I do."

"In answer to your question about why you are able to hear the high pitch of the dog whistle, everybody is given gifts. Some people have the gift to play football. Some people have the gift to draw. Some have good looks." She patted the back of her hair. "You have what we call a psychic gift."

"What exactly does that mean?"

"That means you not only hear things with your ears, but you can also hear things with your mind. For thousands of years people have believed that identical twins have a strange power and ability to communicate with each other without talking. Sometimes this ability to hear or communicate can extend beyond just with your twin. That's all psychic ability is. A special ability to communicate. Like with the phone, when you know who it is before you pick it up. It is because you are hearing or feeling in your mind the energy of the person who is on the other end of the phone that is being sent your way. You have a truly special gift. And now, with your brother passed on—Oh, my. You're still connected to him and it has made you psychic."

Eddie listened to every word that Sandy said.

"Almost everyone has some psychic ability. Everybody has a little voice inside of them that they should always listen to, because it always tells the truth, even though sometimes what it says is weird or hard to believe. The more we listen to it, the better we become at hearing and understanding it. But you really do have a special ability, Eddie. When Brian was alive did you sometimes know what he was thinking and feeling?"

Eddie nodded. "Lots of times we finished each other's sentences or we didn't even have to talk."

"Brian is now on the other side and you can still feel what he's thinking. That's incredible! Do you dream about Brian?"

"Every night."

"Tell me about your dreams."

"We usually go fishing at Rainbow Lake."

"That's fun," Sandy said with a smile. "Is this an actual place where you two have been before?"

"Lots of times."

"Dreams are one way that we can communicate with loved ones on the other side. When we are asleep, our spirits are briefly released from our bodies and their limitations so we can travel or wander freely to spend time with and talk to our loved ones who have passed on. We don't always remember our dreams. Much of the time we are not allowed to remember them. They have very specific rules they have to follow over there. Does Brian talk to you in your dreams?"

"We talk a lot."

"Are you always asleep when you two talk."

Eddie paused and took a deep breath. Sandy noticed his left knee started to shake. She smiled, which put him at ease.

"Brian talked to me when he came to our room the night before his funeral." Sandy's eyes opened wide with intense focus. "You were not asleep at the time?"

"I was asleep but he woke me up."

"What did he say to you?"

"He said he wasn't really dead."

"It's important for you to understand that, Eddie. Did he say anything else to you?"

"Oh, yeah. We talked for a long time."

"Are you comfortable telling what else he said to you?"

"He said I was supposed to tell my mom it wasn't her fault he fell from the tree house, 'cuz she's blaming herself for letting us sleep out."

Sandy was emotionally touched by Eddie's answer. "It is very important Eddie, that you tell your mother that. You must tell her. Okay?"

"I did tell her."

"That is very good."

"Is there anything else he told you?"

"Yeah. He said a bunch of stuff. He said the Giants are gonna win next Sunday."

"Really?"

"Even though they're a crumby team this year, he said they're gonna kick a field goal with six seconds left and win."

"Why would he tell you that? Why would he be allowed to tell you the Giants are going to win? They are a really crumby team this year. I'm going to have to think about this one."

"Brian said that my dad could win back all the money he lost last month."

"Ooooooh. Your father is a betting man, is he? But why would Brian be allowed to tell you that the Giants are going to win? The other side is not usually allowed to give out financial tips unless there are very special circumstances involved."

"My dad promised my mom a long time ago that he wouldn't bet any more."

"Ooooh! Now it's beginning to make sense. Your father doesn't believe you, does he? He doesn't believe that Brian is still alive?"

"Hut uh. I've told them that Brian is still alive, but both he and my mom tell me I just have to accept that he really is dead. They think I'm just making things up."

Sandy sat up with an air of assurance. "Now it makes perfect sense. When the Giants win, and whether your father places his bet or not, he will suddenly gain a new respect for the things you tell him. He will know that you were telling the truth. He will know that Brian is still alive and communicating with you. I can't believe this!"

"You can't?"

"I'm sorry. I do believe every word. It's just that this is so extraordinary. And exciting! I wonder what the odds are against the Giants?"

"You should bet on 'em. You could make some money."

"Thank you, Eddie. That's very generous of you. I'll think about it."

"Why do people have to die?"

"People don't actually die. They just move on. Our bodies are like machines. Sometimes machines break down and don't work anymore. When they don't work anymore, we leave them and move on to the next world. It's kind of like graduating from high school and going on to college. Some people learn what they need to learn and move on faster than others."

"Cindy said in her report that the spirits of people that died come back on Halloween night. Is that true?"

"Our Halloween tradition came from people believing that they do. I can't really say for certain, but if they do, I'm sure that they would only come to those who believe."

"Brian said to look for him again when time stands still."

Eddie's words sent chills up Sandy's and Cindy's spines. They turned and looked at each other with eyes wide open and squealed with delight like giddy school girls.

"Pinch me and tell me this is real," Sandy said to Cindy. She then took a deep breath to calm herself. "I think that's your answer right there, Eddie. The only hour of the entire year when time stands still is this very Saturday night."

"What should I do?"

"You should come to the Witches' Sabbath!" Cindy said, sitting forward in her chair.

"Now, not too fast, Cindy."

"We have bonfires there to attract the spirits --"

"Cindy. The Witches' Sabbath is not for everyone. Yes we have bonfires there. And yes, anciently, they used to build great bonfires to attract the spirits --"

"Each village would light a great fire on a nearby hillside where the people would gather so the spirits could easily see where to come."

"This isn't exactly our tradition today, Eddie," Sandy said while giving Cindy a raised eyebrow. She zipped her lips closed and sat timidly back into her chair.

"I don't know where to go to look, or what to do."

"Eddie, because of the fact you already know your brother is going to come visit you on Halloween night, and because you already communicate with him so openly, I am certain that when Halloween night comes, you will feel deep down inside of yourself where you should be or where you should go in order to meet up with him."

BONG! The near-by clock tower chimed. It was five o'clock.

The Magic Hour

Eddie had lost complete track of the time. BONG! He could not believe he had been there for an hour.

BONG!

"I gotta go home or I'll be in trouble."

BONG!

"I hope we've helped you, Eddie, by answering some of your questions."BONG!

"Thank you Mrs. Crystal. How much do I owe you?"

"Nothing."

"Cindy said you charge for your services."

"Maybe if I cut your hair. If anything I should be paying you for this extraordinary experience. What a gift! Thank you for coming."

"We can talk some more at school tomorrow, Eddie, if you have more questions." Cindy handed Eddie his two black cat cookies. "Here. Take 'em with you."

"Thanks. Bye, see ya."

"Good bye, Eddie."

Eddie glanced at Lucretia the nylon witch, then scurried out the salon door.

CHAPTER SIX

Eddie knew it would take him at least forty-five minutes to reach home. His mother had a strict rule to be home by five thirty when he was out playing after school. This left a fifteen minute window of potential trouble.

He ran until he wore himself out, and then walked to catch his breath. He ate the cookies Cindy gave him as he passed along a big hedgerow lost in thought. All the things Sandy told him about his special abilities and about dreams went around and around in his head. Suddenly someone jumped out of the bushes right in front of him.

"Aaaaaaaaah!"

"GOTCHA!" It was Tad.

"Jerk! What'd ya scare me like that for?"

"What'd ya go to the Crystal Ball for? I knew you were up to something, the way you dodged around the school bus trying to throw me off track. You can't fool me with those first-grade tricks. I followed you. So what did you go there for? Are you secretly in love with Cindy?"

"Are you crazy?"

"Did you touch her?"

"Are you kidding?"

"What proof have you got that you're not secretly in love with this woman?"

Eddie rolled up his shirt sleeve to reveal a large ball point pen tattoo hidden way up on his upper arm: "U.S.F.S."—Ultra Super Flea Shot.

Tad looked at Eddie's arm, but was not sold on his innocence. "Cindy probably sprayed you with some kind of love potion that you don't even know about. Witches do that kind of thing you know."

"She's not a witch."

"Who are you kiddin'? You heard her today. 'We witches and warlocks --'"

"So? I went there to talk to her mom. Not her."

"She's the biggest witch of all."

The Magic Hour

"She's a nice lady."

"You don't get it. Of course she's nice. That's how they lure you in. Witches are always nice at first. Before you know it they'll have you eating frog guts and cat eyeballs, and then it'll be too late."

"Tad. You're full of it."

"No. Really. Did you eat anything while you there?"

"Just some cookies. They were good, too."

"Of course they were. They were all full of weird witches' stuff to make 'em taste good."

"They were not."

"Eddie, I got news for ya. The whole town knows they're witches."

"Not the whole town. You don't believe in witches and all that stuff. Remember?"

"Shut up. I'm trying to protect you. I know for a fact they even help out at the mental hospital. Both of 'em. My mom told me and she works there. Only a witch or a crazy would do that."

"Tad. I got news for you. It's called public service! Nice people do that kind of thing."

"I didn't want to have to go this far, but I'll prove it to you they are real-live evil witches."

"How?"

"Tomorrow at school. I'll swing Cindy around again and you watch her eyes. Watch how they roll back into her head like an alligator's does in a death roll."

"You're sick!"

"That's proof Cindy's a witch! That's what witches do just before they leave their bodies and transform into something else."

"The only thing that proves is how really sick and mean you are."

"I always let her go right then before she can --"

"You said you didn't believe in all that hocus pocus witch stuff."

"Whether I believe or not, it's proof. Eddie, I'm warning you. You're on the road to ruin. They're evil."

"Just leave Cindy alone. And NO I am not in love with her."

"I'm still going to keep my eye on you. I think you need help."

"I do need help finding something in the graveyard. You wanna come with me tomorrow after school?"

"What are you looking for? Dead and rotten bodies? I'll come."

"Talk to ya tomorrow. I gotta get home or my mom will kill me. See ya."

"I'll interrogate you more tomorrow. In the meantime you watch yourself."

"You watch yourself." He waved Tad off and ran on down the street.

Eddie reached home and quietly sneaked in the side door. He tiptoed to his bedroom with his shoes tucked under his arm.

The greeting cards his classmates made for him all hung from a cord strung across his room in front of the window right above his bed. Eddie finally looked at them.

One particular card, painstakingly and meticulously painted to look like outer space caught his eye. It looked quite like the ceiling of the Crystal Ball Salon—a deep blue background with gold stars. The caption on the front read:

"You're outta this world, Eddie!"

He lifted the card off the string and opened it.

*"But please come back to earth.
WE MISS YOU!"*

— Elliott Carney —

Eddie smiled to himself and looked over the many other clever and colorful cards. Finally he noticed the clock by his bed. "EEEK!" It read 6:04 PM. "WHAT TIME IS DINNER, MOM?"

"Oh, are you home?" she said from somewhere else in the house.
"Oh, yeah."
"We'll eat in about half an hour."
"Okay. I'll just be here in my room."

Eddie laid down on his bed and continued to ponder on all the things Sandy told him. He wanted to make sense of it all.

His bedroom was visually split right down the middle with identical halves on either side—matching beds, matching mirrors and dressers, matching desks. Even the posters and pennants on one wall perfectly matched those on the opposite side of the room. Only a large wire cage in the corner by the window was not paired. Inside the cage a single eighteen-inch-long green iguana slept on a small tree branch.

Eddie ran back through his mind how Brian told him he was with Uncle Louie and Grandpa and that he was supposed to help Miss Pleasant. He realized he forgot to tell Sandy the rest of what Brian told him, about how he was supposed to help Miss Pleasant and how Brian talked about the light. His deep focus was shattered by a blood curdling scream from somewhere there in the house.

"AAAAAAAAAAH!"

Eddie sat straight up on the bed. Again the piercing scream rang out. It was a woman's voice.

"AAAAAAAAAAH! EDDIE! GET OUT HERE THIS INSTANT!" Eddie jumped to his feet and ran into the kitchen to find his mother standing in the middle of the room with her hand raised in the air waving a large butcher knife, her eyes wild with alarm.

"GET THIS CREATURE OUT OF MY KITCHEN!"

On the counter beside the sink, a green eighteen-inch-long iguana chomped lettuce from inside a large wooden salad bowl.

"If Harry Houdini escapes from his cage one more time, it'll be lizard steaks for dinner."

"Mom! That's not Harry. That's Larry—Brian's Lizard."

"Harry, Larry. They look just alike."

"Brian and me look just alike."

"Just get it out of my kitchen, please." She shuddered in disgust.

Eddie gently picked up the iguana and cradled it in his arms like a baby. "Larry! Are you all right?"

"They say iguana tastes just like chicken!"

"Mom! Maybe you could try to be a little more understanding. Larry's been having a really hard time with Brian gone."

Caught completely off guard by Eddie's comment, she struggled to reply. "I . . . I'm sorry. I didn't realize that Larry had such feelings."

"Larry's just a lizard and he's dealing with Brian's death the only way he knows how to, through escape."

She did not know how to respond. Reminded of her son's death, she become teary eyed. Instinctively, she grabbed a mixing bowl as if to start making a cake, her way of escape from her feelings—through cooking.

The phone rang and startled them both, but especially Eddie, who stood right beside it. He fumbled to hold on to Larry, then turned to the phone and curled his nose in disgust. It rang again. "Ooooo yuck!" He jumped back to get farther away from the phone.

"What's the matter?" his mother said.

"It's her."

"Who?"

"Aunt Lois."

"No. We haven't heard from her since the funeral. Why would she be calling?"

"I know it's her. I'll bet you fifty cents."

Mrs. McCourt gave Eddie a how dare you look and reached for the phone. "We don't bet in this house, but I'll give you a dollar if you are right. Hello?"

An offensively nasal, snooty voice blared out of the receiver. "Elizabeth? This is your sister-in-law, Lois Beadlewiffer."

Mrs. McCourt pulled the phone away from her ear the voice was so loud. "Yes, Lois? I know who you are."

Eddie stuck a finger down his throat and made vomit sounds, then carried Larry out of the kitchen.

"I don't mean to disturb you at dinner time, Elizabeth, but I wanted to call and see if it's all right if the girls and I come up on Saturday to participate in all the Halloween festivities."

"You know you are always welcome in your brother's home, Lois."

"You wouldn't mind if I brought a couple of extra girls with me would you? They've heard so much about the parade and the carnival and all. I just couldn't dream of saying no to them."

"How many is a couple, Lois?"

"They can all just throw their sleeping bags on the family room floor. It will be no bother to you at all, you have such a big house. I promise."

"How many Lois?" Mrs. McCourt began to pace the length of the kitchen floor.

Lois paused before answering.

"HOW MANY GIRLS ARE YOU BRINGING LOIS?"

"Eleven."

Mrs. McCourt covered the mouth piece with her hand while she cleared her throat and gritted her teeth.

Lois' voice turned sickeningly sweet. "I know that Patrick won't mind if I bring the extra girls. He's always so good with children."

"Well, we wouldn't want to disappoint the children, now would we?"

"I knew you'd be thrilled, Elizabeth. And I know that this is so last minute but I was only able to clear my schedule and reserve the bus just today."

"THE WHAT?" The veins in Mrs. McCourt's neck popped out.

"Uh, the minibus. We will be there at three o'clock sharp on Saturday afternoon. Not a minute early—not a minute late. And I promise we'll leave promptly at 10:00 AM on Sunday morning. Straightway after breakfast. We won't stay a moment once the girls have finished eating."

"That will be fine." Mrs McCourt gently placed the phone down without a good-bye. "PAAAAAAATRIIIIIIIICK!"

"I'm indisposed," Doctor McCourt said from another part of the house.

"THAT WAS YOUR FAVORITE SISTER!"

"I ONLY HAVE ONE SISTER!"

"She's bringing eleven little Brownie girls up for the weekend. That's in addition to her own four."

"Please! I'd like to be indisposed in peace."

Mrs. McCourt suddenly gasped for breath and nearly fell over. She caught her breath and screamed again. "PATRICK! She's bringing the whole blankety blank scout troop for the weekend. I'm not up to sixteen house guests for breakfast on Sunday morning after the carnival."

"I'll send them to The Diner, Dear."

"That's fine then. Thank you, Dear!"

Doctor McCourt entered the kitchen. "The only thing that gives me comfort is that old addage about God gave us our relatives, so thank heaven we can choose our friends."

"I don't want to hate your sister, or even dislike her for that matter, but she tries my patience so. She is always pushing herself on us with her pseudosweet way. If she would just be real."

"I know."

"And she never really tells the truth about what she is trying to pull. That's what get's me the most. She doesn't deal straight up. Sometimes it is all I can do just to be civil to her. Lois is not a bad person," she said. "I cannot imagine that if she really knew how offensive she is, she wouldn't change."

"Somebody needs to tell her then."

"She's your sister."

"The only one I've got."

After dinner, Eddie retired to his bedroom early to be alone with his thoughts. Again he replayed over and over in his head the things

Sandy told him, especially about how he would know inside of himself on Halloween night where he should look or search for Brian.

The evening wore on and his mother came in to check on him. "I'm sorry about earlier, Eddie. I shouldn't have lost my cool like that. My nerves are really on edge."

"Are you okay?"

"I'm just under a lot of pressure this week, with the carnival and all."

"I understand."

"Eddie. I want to talk to you about making some new house rules." She sat down on the bed beside him. "This evening you tiptoed in at 5:57."

"I know. I'm sorry I was late."

"School was over at three o'clock and you didn't come home until three hours later. I know things are different now that Brian is not here. Our rule about being home by five thirty is for days when I know where you are going to be. I was worried about you, Eddie. I had no idea where you were."

"I'm sorry. I didn't mean to be so late."

"I understand you have to look out of the house for playmates now."

"I was making some new friends."

"That is important, but I need to know where you are going from now on. Okay?"

"Okay. But how'd you know when I got home? I didn't make any noise."

"Mother's have extra sensory perception."

"That's like psychic, huh?"

"It is basically the same thing. How did school go today?"

"Pretty good. I learned a lot."

"That's great."

"Mom. Can I ask a question?"

"Sure."

"Do you believe in ghosts?"

"Well. I'm not sure. I guess it depends what you mean by ghosts."

"Do you think people really die when they die?"

"What do you mean?"

"Does only our body die when we die? Don't our spirits still go on?"

The Magic Hour

"I want to believe they do."

"Do you believe in little voices?"

"What kind of little voices do you mean?"

"The little voices that tell you who's on the phone before you pick it up."

"I never thought of it quite that way, but I guess I do. Is that how you knew it was Aunt Lois on the phone? A little voice told you?"

"Sort of. I just knew it was her. I could feel her energy."

"You were right. I should have believed you."

"You should believe me when I say other things, too. I don't make things up."

"I know you don't."

"So do you believe me when I say you owe me a dollar?"

Mrs. McCourt smiled. "Yes, son. I do believe you. And yes I do owe you a dollar. I'll give it to you in the morning. You can buy a treat with it at school tomorrow."

"Thanks, Mom. And thanks for hanging up all the cards."

"You are welcome. I thought that they would make your room a little more cheery."

"They're really nice."

"Do you have a favorite?"

"Probably the 'Outta this world' card."

"My favorite is still the first one. The one with the teddy bear."

"That's because you're a girl, and girls like cutsey wootsie stuff."

"It's a school night and it's getting late. So, I'll say good night."

"Good night, Mom. Oh. Tomorrow after school, I'll be with Tad, okay? I won't be late."

"That's fine. Just as long as I know where you are. Good night."

Mrs. McCourt slept well, right through the night. She did not even stir when her husband woke up at 4:00 AM to go to work. But the door bell rang early, very early. She could not imagine who could possibly be on their porch at six in the morning.

She rolled from bed and dragged herself to the front door. "Hello?" No one was there. She turned to close the door and something caught her eye, something tucked into the pillows on one of the bent-willow arm chairs—an adorable Dracula teddy bear.

"Well, hello. Where did you come from?" She picked up the bear. Tied to its paw with red curling ribbon, was a small envelope typed with "EDDIE." She looked around, then carefully opened it.

"MY NAME IS COUNT BEARACULA.
I'VE BEEN DYING TO BITE YOUR NECK.
WILL YOU SLEEP WITH ME TONIGHT?"

She chuckled to herself then quickly licked and resealed the envelope. After tucking the bear back into the chair she returned into the house.

Later while she prepared breakfast, she heard Eddie stir in his bedroom. "Eddie, there is someone here for you."

"Who is it?"

"Come and see."

Eddie ran into the front room still in his pajamas.

"Out on the porch."

Eddie shoved open the screen door and looked out. "There's nobody here!"

"Over in the chair."

He saw the Dracula teddy bear. "Who left this?"

"I don't know. A secret admirer, I guess."

Eddie ripped open the card. "I wanna know who left this!" He carried the teddy bear into the house and passed Melissa in the hall. She tried to grab the bear and the note.

"I'll tell you who left this, a secret lover, someone who wants to suck on your --"

"Melissa!" her mother said. "That's enough."

Eddie placed the bear at the breakfast table in his father's chair. Melissa continually looked at it with contempt while she ate.

Mrs. McCourt sat down at the table. "I once had a secret admirer. It was so romantic."

Melissa gave her mother an icy stare. "So, what happened to him?"

"I married him."

"How boring!"

"Why are you so impish this morning?"

Eddie grinned. "She's just jealous 'cuz nobody wants to suck on her neck."

"That's enough! Finish your breakfast. Both of you!"

CHAPTER SEVEN

Eddie avoided Cindy all day so as not to confirm any of Tad's suspicions about them, even though he dearly wanted to talk to her again. He also wanted no part of Tad's bully crusade today so he hung out at the swings.

Miss Pleasant walked the school grounds on recess patrol, scanning for any evil in progress. She heard screams around the corner of the building and ran to investigate.

"EDDIE! COME QUICK—LOOK AT HER EYES!"

Eddie heard Tad calling but sat put.

Miss Pleasant rounded the building and spied Tad, again wildly swinging Cindy around this time by the end of a long lavendar sweater vest. "TAD DURBAN! YOU STOP THAT THIS INSTANT!"

Tad looked up in horror and let Cindy go. He ran away as she rolled across the grass and landed in a heap.

Miss Pleasant ran to her side. "Cindy? Are you all right, Dear?" She knelt beside her and tried to help her up, but she was too dizzy-headed to stand. "Just sit a minute until you regain your balance. That Tad! I am going to have a word with his mother. Are you sure you are not hurt, Cindy?"

"I don't know." Her frazzled hair was covered in grass. "I may have suffered some internal damage."

"Shall we go see the nurse? I'll take you there if you think we should."

"Maybe I'll be okay." Cindy looked at a broken nail and sighed.

Miss Pleasant helped her stand and brushed her off. "Let me shake out your coat." She helped Cindy out of her long lavender sweater vest and shook out all the grass. "My that's a pretty sweater!"

Cindy cracked a little smile.

"I wish I had one that beautiful. Did your mother make it?"

Cindy smiled again and nodded.

"She's very talented."

"I know. She designs all my clothes."

"Cindy. You walk along with me so I can keep an eye on you. I want to make certain that you are all right."

"Okay. I don't understand why boys are always so mean."

"Maybe it's because they are not as smart as girls. I probably shouldn't say this but I think it's because they are jealous of girls."

"You think so?"

"Maybe. They also might think they need to be mean to make them feel important."

"Whatever it is, I wish they would get over it."

"Cindy, I've been wanting to thank you again for giving such a thorough presentation on Halloween, yesterday, but I haven't had the right moment to speak with you. In all my years of teaching, I have never heard such an in-depth report. I learned all kinds of things that I didn't know."

Cindy beamed and completely forgot about the incident only a few moments before. "You're welcome."

"You must have spent days researching."

"I did."

"I felt really bad that we didn't have enough time to hear the whole presentation."

"There was so much more! I didn't even get to tell the best parts."

"But don't you think all that about the spirits makes Halloween rather frightening?"

"Oh, no! It makes it exciting! It's the one night of the year when the veil between life and death is so thin that you can almost see right through it."

Miss Pleasant was helplessly interested in Cindy's words.

"The spirits are closer to us on Halloween than at any other time of the whole year."

"They are?"

"Oh, yes. The spirits are so close on Halloween that people used to go lie down on top of the graves of loved ones so they could hear them whisper."

"Oh, how morbid!"

"It's all how you look at it."

"They must have been awfully desperate to contact someone."

"You shouldn't look at it that way. Just look at it as a chance to talk to your dearly departed. Is there someone you'd like to contact on the other side?"

"I should say not! Why would you even ask such a question?"

"Because most old people have someone they love that's died. I just thought maybe you had somebody, too."

"That's a very nice thought for you to have on my behalf. But there is no one. I assure you."

"I'm sorry."

"There's no need to be sorry. I must say, though, how amazed I am at your knowledge and understanding of all these sorts of things. Where did you learn all of this?"

"My mom. She knows all about the dead."

Whatever interest Miss Pleasant may have had abruptly ended. "Well, that explains things. Your mother is quite the authority then, isn't she?"

"You should talk to her sometime."

"Perhaps. You run along and play now. And be sure to tell me if Tad gives you any more trouble. I'll report him right away."

"I will. Did you find out what Eddie's gonna be for Halloween?"

"Frankenstein."

Cindy skipped away smiling.

Miss Pleasant walked back around the school and saw Eddie, still at the swing sets just sitting in a swing. She walked over to him.

"The swings aren't fun any more?"

"Just thinking about things."

"Is it anything that we can talk about together?"

"Not really. I'm just trying to figure some stuff out. But what about you?" Eddie looked right at Miss Pleasant. "What can I help you with?"

"There is something. I've got lots of Thanksgiving pictures that I need colored. Does that sound like something you could do?"

"Sure."

"See me after school and I'll give you the pictures. I'll even give you extra credit."

"Thanks."

Cindy skipped around the building and ran into Tad again. He sneered at her.

"You just better watch out, Tad. Miss Pleasant said if you're mean to me again, she'd report you to the principal."

"Whoop tee doo. Go right ahead. I'll tell him how you provoked me 'cuz you're a witch."

"Toad."
"Witch."
"Toad!"
"You worship the devil."
"Do not! You are the devil! You hurt people and think it's funny."
"This town burned witches once, you know. We can do it again."
"You are mistaken. That was some other towns. I know. I also know that you are the one who stole the CD's from the principals office."
"You don't know anything!"
"I know they're in your desk, and that you'll be expelled if they find out it was you."
"Sweet! Then I won't have to come here everyday and see your ugly mug."
"And the air will be clean and fresh because the stink from your rotten soul will be gone."
Tad sneered viciously, even more angry that he could not verbally one up Cindy.
"As a good citizen, it is my duty to report any criminal activity that I know about."
"You wouldn't dare!" Tad said.
"Might as well start packing your things."
"You tell and I'll --"
"You'll what? I'm not afraid of you."
"You really are evil."
"Evil is as evil does. And I'm not the one who stole. Have a nice life, Tad Durban." Cindy smugly skipped away but then turned back. "And by the way. The little water drops on your forehead, they're called guilt sweats."

Back in class, Eddie still studied Miss Pleasant, always watching her eyes for some clue to the mystery of what was really wrong with her. He knew that helping her with the coloring project was not the big issue.

The main occupier of Eddie's thoughts today, however, was the cemetery, where he and Tad would venture the moment school was out. Eddie had never been there without his family. He had also never been there with an agenda to search for someone's grave—Uncle Louie's, just as Brian suggested.

Before the final bell stopped ringing, Eddie and Tad were already out the school door and down the road. They raced toward the south end of town and did not even stop until they reached the cemetery gates.

They both bent over to catch their breaths before they passed through the wrought-iron gates. The old stone columns that supported the gates looked ominous as they loomed over the boys. Tad made the sign of the cross over his chest.

"You're not Catholic!" Eddie said.

"Catholics just invented it. Anyone can use it. You should always cross yourself before you go anywhere there's dead people."

"I thought you didn't believe in ghosts."

"I don't. But just in case there are any, you'd better do it."

Eddie followed Tad's lead and made the sign of the cross over his chest.

They walked through rows of decaying tombstones overshadowed by towering dark pines. Even in broad daylight, with the cloudy sky and the dense canopy of trees, the cemetery was dark and gloomy.

At last they arrived at the McCourt family plot where Brian was buried. The funeral flowers were withered and brown. Emotion swelled in Eddie's eyes while he and Tad silently looked on. Beside Brian's grave marker sat another with the name Edward A. McCourt engraved in the stone. It had the same birth date as Brian's, but there was no date of death.

Tad drew a long breath. "I don't think God is a very good person. He lets little kids die." A sudden gust of wind whipped a cluster of dried leaves right into his face. "I think we'd better go now."

CRACK! A tree branch right over head creaked and swayed as the wind blew harder. A small dust devil full of whirling leaves swirled right between them. They both stepped back with alarm, but Eddie kicked leaves aside and continued to search for names on the flat gravemarkers.

"Come on, Eddie. We need to go."

"We can't leave. I haven't found Uncle Louie's tombstone yet."

"I don't care whose tombstone you're looking for. They're all dead."

"Brian said he was buried right by us."

"Are you stupid or what?" Tad grabbed Eddie's shirt. "Now, come on. We're leaving." The wind continued to blow harder, whipping through the great black pines over head. They looked all around them almost expecting something or someone. Just when they were ready to break into a run toward the entrance, a tall figure of a man in black leaped straight down out of the trees overhead and landed right in front of them.

"AAAAAAAAAAAAH!"

The boys turned and ran the other way but the dark figure darted out from behind a tree ahead of them, again cutting them off. Again they ran the other way, but the same figure jumped out in front of them there and grabbed them both by the scruf of the neck, stopping them dead in their tracks.

"AAAAAAAAAAAAH!"

The man spoke out with sinsister theatricality. "SCREAM ALL YOU WANT BOYS, BUT YOU'LL NEVER ESCAPE THE GRAAAAAVE DIGGER!" He burst into a hideous evil laugh that echoed through the whole cemetery. At last he let the boys go, but both stood frozen. They stared at him. Dressed all in black, his wiry arms and legs made his big feet appear even bigger than they were. He had black rings under his eyes and his mop of dark hair looked as if he used garden shears to cut it. His deep-set piercingly beady eyes wiggled in their sockets. Eddie and Tad both looked away.

"I'm Grover. The G-r-a-v-e-digger."

The boys did not respond.

"You got a problem with that?"

They shook their heads.

"Scared ya pretty good, huh?"

Tad and Eddie stared at him once again.

He leaned right into their faces with an evil ear to ear grin. "How about some Cracker Jacks?"

The boys stood mum.

Grover snatched a box of Cracker Jacks from off a tombstone right beside them. "Don't mind dinin' with the dead, do you?" He ripped open the box with a single movement of his hand and held the box out to the boys. "I get the toy!"

Eddie and Tad looked at each other with shock and disbelief. They did not know whether this freak was a friend or fiend.

Grover crunched a mouthful and again held out the box. "Don't worry. Andy won't mind if we eat his stuff. He can't eat it. He's D-E-A-D!"

The boys looked at the grave again. The name on the marker was "ANDREW VALENTINE."

"You're weird!" Tad said.

"But weird is relative. And I got lots of 'em. Weird relatives. Ha! Ha! Ha! Ha!" He burst into another fit of hideous, evil laughter. Right in the middle of his fit of laughter, his brow suddenly dropped in a look of concern. He made cute, pouty faces at the boys. "Okay. I'm sorry I scared you so bad. Not sorry I scared you, just so bad."

Tad stepped forward a little. "You're a rotten person!"

"Give - me - a - break. It's part of my job description. Whatcha expect a g-r-a-v-e-d-i-g-g-e-r to do in his spare time?"

Eddie scolded him with his eyes. "You scared us to death!"

"Perfect place for it, don't ya think? I mean if you're gonna be dead and all."

The boys were not amused. They just wanted to get away.

"Okay. If I show ya somethin' really neat will ya forgive me? I don't want any guilt over this. I need my sleep at night. Buryin' bodies is hard work, ya know. Wait here. I'll be right back." Grover walked briskly off. Eddie and Tad both ran the other way toward the entrance as fast as they could. They approached the gates, but Grover appeared from outside the entrance driving a front end loader. He blocked the entire way so there was no escape.

"You two were trying to walk out on me. Didn't I say you would never escape the g-r-a-v-e-d-i-g-g-e-r? Get on."

The boys did not move.

"Whatcha waiting for? Halloween?"

Still Eddie and Tad did not move.

"Do I have to come down and throw you on? GET ON! I haven't got all night. I've got bodies to bury."

With hesitation on their faces, Eddie and Tad stepped up into the lowered bucket of the loader. It lunged forward, nearly throwing the boys out. They held on for dear life as they sped across the cemetery.

"You guys wouldn't believe some of the things that people leave here in the cemetery," Grover said, yelling to be heard above the noise of the engine. "People leave everythin' from hamburgers and tater chips, to toys and tennis rackets. Hikin' boots, garden shears, new suits of clothes—you name it and they leave it. Once I even got a whole set of new steel belted radials for my truck. Workin' here is the greatest."

They arrived at the grounds keeper's house and workshop on the far side of the cemetery and Grover drove them around the back of the old garage where they came to a stop beside a dilapidated old hearse from the days of horse drawn buggies and wagons. Eddie shuddered at the sight of the old death wagon. Grover jumped down and the boys stepped out of the bucket.

"You boys have to promise never to tell anybody about what I'm gonna show ya. Okay?"

They did not answer.

"I SAID – you guys have to promise never to tell. Do you promise or not?"

Eddie and Tad half nodded their heads, just enough to pass Grover's approval. He held open the garage door. Inside was complete blackness.

"Go on inside."

The boys looked in and then looked at each other. Grover saw the trepidation in their faces. He stepped into the dark garage and flipped on a light. Eddie and Tad were immediately enticed in by what they saw.

Inside the garage, a single light bulb dangled from the ceiling and dimly illuminated a room completely filled to capacity with all the things that people had left at the cemetery. Shelves from floor to ceiling of this shadowy dreamworld were filled and tables were covered with toys and dolls, sporting goods and photos, tools and books, all weathered with time. Anything and everything that could ever have held a special place in someone's life was here. Eddie and Tad looked around this bizarre and yet dreamy place with awe. They could hardly believe their eyes.

Tad picked up a Mickey Mantle baseball bat. "Wow! Look at all this stuff!"

"Pretty neat, huh?"

Eddie walked off through the rows in almost somber reverence. "People brought all these things to the cemetery?"

"Yup. Gifts of love and gifts of guilt. 'Member the truck tires I told you about? Some sleazy person left 'em on a grave with an apology note. Said he stole some tires from the dead guy when he was alive and he was sorry. Apology's no good if you wait too long."

Eddie continued to walk along, somehow sensing that each item here was the symbolic center of a life once lived. Somehow he understood the importance that each of these mementos once held for someone when they were alive.

Tad picked up a colorful man's Hawaiian shirt.

"I get all my clothes here," Grover said. "Hardly even have to go to the grocery store, neither." Grover moved and stood watch over a collection of Cracker Jacks toys that went back forty years, to make sure neither of the boys made off with any of his favorite goods.

Eddie made his way back up one particular aisle full of photographs and stopped to look at an obviously old black and white photo of two young boys taken beside a lake. In the picture, both of the boys, who looked like brothers, held up strings of fish as they stood in front of an old-fashioned log raft. Eddie studied the picture. It reminded him of himself and Brian. He even recognized Rainbow Lake, where he and his brother had idled away many hours on a raft built by their grandfather.

Grover walked up beside him. "That's a really old photo! Long before my time."

"How can you tell?"

"I might be old, but I'm not that old! Let me see it." Grover grabbed the photo and turned it over. On the back were coded numbers written in ink. "Judging by the number, I'd say this is a good seventy years old or more."

"How can you tell?"

"Ol' Luther, the g-r-a-v-edigger before me, was an absolute freak. Neat freak. He had this place organized like it was a library or somethin'. It was so boring. Didn't have to dig for nothin'. Personally, I like the supermarket approach to organization. A little notions here. Lotions there. A little dancing in the aisles." Grover broke into a dance routine and twirled right in front of Eddie. He quickly caught on that Eddie was not amused so he stopped. "I'm a wee bit of a slob, if I do say so myself. But that's the trouble with puttin' stuff away. Can't never find it again. So if you just leave it out, you always know where it is. Anyway, Ol' Luther gave ever' grave here in the cemetery a number and coded numbers for everythin' that was ever left. I could look it up sometime. It'll take a while to find the log, but I could tell you exactly what grave this here photo was left on, and the date it was pulled."

"What does pulled mean?"

"Taken off the grave."

"That makes sense."

"Most likely, one of these little brothers died, or somethin'."

"My brother just died two weeks ago."

Stunned by Eddie's remark, Grover bit his lower lip. Eddie laughed right out loud Grover looked so stupid with his top teeth extended like a gopher.

"Is your name McCourt?"

Eddie nodded.

"You okay?"

Eddie nodded again.

"I'm really sorry, kid. If I'd a known who you were, I wouldn't a been so rough on ya. I just thought you two were a couple of mischief makers like all the other kids who come through here."

"It's okay."

"You're doin' great, kid. Back on your feet only two weeks after your brother turned into worm food."

"Worm food?"

"I'm not makin' fun of your brother or nothin', it's just that sooner or later, we all turn into dirt – worm food. It's a fact of life."

"All the dead flowers are still on his grave."

"I'm runnin' about a week behind."

Tad showed up wearing an old Daniel Boon coon-skin-cap, with his arms full of treasures. "You ever gonna have a garage sale? You could make a fortune selling all this stuff."

"I can't sell this stuff!"

"How come? 'Cuz grave robbin's against the law?"

Grover's eyes instantly went wild. They started to wiggle in their sockets just like they did before. "I DON'T STEAL THINGS FROM DEAD PEOPLE!" He let out a big puff of air and then resumed talking calmly. "What kind of a weirdo d'ya think I am? Cemetery policy is to leave things on the grave for two weeks and then I have to clean up. Otherwise the graveyard starts looking like a junkyard."

"So after two weeks you can have anythin' you want?"

"Great job, huh?"

"Yeah! D'ya have any openings?"

"You're a bit young still for grave diggin."

"How old d'ya have to be? I dig fox holes in my back yard all the time."

"It'll be a few years yet."

"Do you ever get scared working here?" Eddie said.
"HECK NO! What's there to be afraid of?"
"Have you ever seen a ghost?"
"Been working here near thirty years and ain't seen one yet. Don't believe in 'em."
"You don't believe in 'em at all?"
"What's there to believe in? Dead is dead. That's why we bury you. 'Cuz you rot and stink. Scariest thing I ever see is the crazy lady. She's the one who leaves the Cracker Jacks."
"Is she really crazy?"
"Heck, yeah. She oughtta be put away. Can't imagine what could drive a woman to her state of mind. Must a been somethin' purty terrible."
"Do you know all the graves in here?"
Grover leaned right into Eddie's face. "Do you know all you're A, B, C's?"
"I'm looking for Uncle Louie."
"Louie? Louie McCourt? He's over hidin' under the bushes 'tween Lucy and Hortense. He died real young. Like four years old."
"Hum. Thanks."
"Any time, kid. Hey! Are you Eddie?"
"Yup."
"You've already got a tombstone!"
"His grandpa gave 'em it for Christmas," Tad said from across the aisle.
Grover's nose curled up in disgust. "Yuck! What a rotten present."
"That's what I said."
"What a rotten grandpa! Now. I'll let you each have one thing, only if you promise to never tell anyone about this. So go ahead and pick ya somethin'."
Tad chose a pair of like-new high-top red sneakers in just his size. He already had them on his feet.
"I don't want to take anything," Eddie said to Tad's and Grover's disbelief.
"Are you sure?"
"Things are better left here."
"Can't say I didn't offer."
Tad stepped forward. "I'll take somethin' for him!"
"Offer's only good once and its nontransferable. Can't come back,

kid, when you change your mind."

"I think things are best left here with you, Grover."

"I can respect that. But if I find out that either one of you has done told somebody about our little visit here in the garage, or if I find out that you done told somebody where you got those shoes, well. I can't even say what might happen or I'll be arrested. So don't go forgettin' your promise. You two git along home now. I've got work to do—bodies to bury."

"Thanks for everythin'." Tad extended his hand to shake.

"I don't do handshakes." Grover threw his arms around Tad and kissed him on both cheeks. Tad jerked himself away and wiped his cheeks in disgust.

"I'm never coming back here ever again!"

"Promise?"

"I promise!"

"Just click your heels together three times and say there's no place like home. There's no place like home. There's no place like home."

The boys just stared.

"It's a joke. All right then. Bye see yah." POOF! Grover disappeared in a cloud of green smoke. "Don't touch anything on your way out." Grover's voice resounded through the building. "'Cuz I'LL BE WATCHING YOU!"

The boys were as stunned by the way he left as by the way he came. Still, they did not quite know whether to think of Grover as a friend or a fiend.

"How come all the weirdos get all the best jobs." Tad said. "It's not fair."

"I gotta get home. My mom let me be late yesterday, so I don't want to push it today. See ya tomorrow."

"See ya."

The boys ran off in their separate directions.

On his way out of the cemetery, Eddie remembered that he still needed to find Uncle Louie's tombstone. He also thought about the photo of the two little boys all the way home. Something about it haunted him. He could not get over how much the boys looked like him and Brian, even though they were of different ages.

When he did arrive home, on time with no issue, he headed for the family photo cupboard. He dragged out all the old family photo albums and took them to his bedroom.

He scoured over them and found a photo very similar to the one that was at the cemetery, two boys and all their fish. He was certain they were the same two boys at the same lake. Now he wished he had taken the photograph when Grover offered. He knew he needed to go back and compare the two photos, to see for sure if those boys were from his family.

Eddie spent the rest of the evening coloring the Thanksgiving pictures for Miss Pleasant. While he colored, he thought about all the things he had learned this week and about all the things for which he was thankful. He realized he had lots of stuff. Too much stuff really, now with all of Brian's stuff, too.

His mother entered the room. "What are you coloring, Punkin?"

"Just some pictures for Miss Pleasant."

"That's nice."

"Mom. Do you know who's in this picture?" He showed her the photo of the two little boys.

"I'm not certain, but I think one of them is your grandfather. Maybe the other one is his cousin."

Now Eddie was more determined than ever to go back and compare with the photograph at Grover's garage.

"Time for bed, Punkin."

"Okay."

Mrs. McCourt tucked Eddie and his Count Bearacula teddy bear in for the night. "Good night you two little monsters."

"Mom?"

"Yes, Sweetie."

"Why do you think Grandpa gave us tombstones for Christmas that one year?"

"I don't know. Grandpa liked to be crusty on the outside but inside he really cared about you two boys."

"Do you think it was because he knew Brian was going to need it?"

"I don't know that either. Everybody needs one sometime."

"Maybe it was because he lost his brother when he was young, just like me?"

"I didn't know he lost his brother when he was young."

"Uncle Louie was only four years old when he died."

"I didn't know that."

"He and Grandpa are the ones who met Brian when he fell and was really scared."

"They were?"

"Yeah. When Brian first fell, he saw the body lying on the ground and thought it was me. He started screaming and yelling for help. That's when Grandpa and Uncle Louie showed up."

"Eddie. I can hardly believe what you're telling me."

"It's all true. Brian told me himself."

"I do believe you. I just mean it is so incredible for you to know this. When did he tell you?"

"The night before the funeral."

Mrs. McCourt had to think a moment on what Eddie had just shared. "Eddie. We want to make your birthday really special. Is there something in particular that you would like?"

"Not really. I just wanna be with Brian. That's all I want."

"I know. We all do. But isn't there something you've been wanting that we can get for you?"

"Maybe some walkie talkies."

"Is there anything else?"

"Don't worry about buying me lots of stuff."

"We're planning on having a party."

"Don't make a big deal out of it. It won't be the same when I open the presents all by myself."

"We want to make it as special as we can for you, though."

"I don't want a party, please. We can cut a cake, but don't get me lots of stuff. I already have lots."

"Well, you have sweet dreams tonight, Sweetheart."

They hugged and Mrs. McCourt walked out of the room.

CHAPTER EIGHT

Cake batter, cake pans and more cake batter filled the kitchen. Mrs. McCourt was literally up to her elbows in liquid cake. By her own choice, she alone was in charge of making all of the cakes for the upcoming Middleway Halloween carnival cake walk. This morning she rose early to begin the assembly line production.

She was the only one awake in the house when the door bell rang bright and early yet again this morning. She wiped kitchen goo off her hands on the way to the door but found no one there. Over in the bent willow chair, though, a little monster teddy bear with a snaggletooth and a humped back looked up at her with one eye. The other little eye drooped halfway down his face. An envelope tied to its paw with blue curling ribbon clearly had Eddie's name printed on it.

"You poor little thing." She walked toward the chair and pulled a paring knife from her apron pocket. Ever so carefully she opened the envelope.

"I'm the Hunchbear of Notre Dame.
I'm all bent out of shape over you.
May I sleep with you tonight?"

She chuckled and slipped the card back into the envelope. She then pulled a glue stick from her pocket and sealed it again for Eddie to find later when he woke up.

He was thrilled to wake up to another surprise gift. His sister became even more green with envy. She sabotaged Eddie's shower with the old honey-shampoo switcheroo and found herself grounded as a result. That only served to further fuel her fire of jealousy.

Before Eddie left for school, he tucked the one photo of the two boys from his family's album into his school pack. Then he also stopped at the tool shed in the car port where he stuffed a small pair of garden clippers into his pack.

Elliott Carney arrived at school early that day because his mother drove him. Near the merry-go-round, he passed Cindy, who was a study in red this morning. He did not pay particular attention to her, but moments later, he saw Tad walk onto the school ground in his high-top red sneakers. Elliott swung around and looked back at Cindy. She also wore high-top red sneakers with her red outfit. Elliott's eyes opened wide with the energy of anticipation.

He darted across the playground toward a large group of girls sitting around the swings chatting. Within seconds, the girls all skipped straight toward Tad. They neared him and broke into a loud happy chant.

"LOVE BIRDS. LOVE BIRDS. TWEET. TWEET. TWEET. TAD AND CINDY—MATCHING FEET!"

Tad instantly became enraged at their teasing. He was proud of his new shoes. But the girls continued to chant, with slight variations.

"TAD AND CINDY—LOVE BIRDS SWEET. MATCHING HEARTS AND MATCHING FEET."

The very thought of being hooked up with Cindy was so repulsive to Tad, he lashed out at the girls. "SHUT UUUUP!"

But the girls chanted louder. More children gathered around and joined in the tease fest toward this bully who had hurt them all at one point or another.

Cindy heard the commotion and rushed over. She listened to the chants and saw Tad's shoes. She thought it was hilarious.

Tad saw her laughing histerically. "HOW DARE YOU WEAR THE SAME SHOES AS ME, WITCH!"

"What's the matter Tadpole? Can't take a little of your own medicine?"

Tad swung his fist at Cindy's face. She screamed and ducked, but his hand grazed the tip of her nose. She put her hand to her face in shock. This was war!

"EVEN YOUR MOTHER KNEW YOU WERE GONNA GROW UP TO BE A TOAD. THAT'S WHY SHE NAMED YOU TAAAAD-POLE!"

All the children laughed and laughed. They chanted his new nickname.

"TAAADPOLE. TAAADPOLE. TAAADPOLE…"

"SURE CAN GIVE IT OUT, WHIMP!" another student yelled at him.

The taunting continued louder and louder as almost the entire playground closed ranks around Tad and completely encircled him. He became even more aggressive, snarling and thrashing like a caged beast.

"LET ME THROUGH!" a deep male voice shouted. "LET ME THROUGH, PLEASE." Mr. Warburton, the principal, pushed his way through the children. "Tad Durban. Come with me please."

The crowd broke up so the principal and Tad could pass back through.

Eddie's school bus arrived late, just as Tad walked off with Mr. Warburton.

He rushed over to Cindy. "What happened?"

"Tad was like out of control. Like an animal! Growling and snarling and—" Cindy was still shaken from her brush with the beast.

The morning bell rang and everyone went to class except Tad. Now there were two conspicuously empty desks in Miss Pleasant's room, Brian's and Tad's.

An hour later in the middle of morning mathematics studies, Mr. Warburton, Tad and Tad's mother appeared at the classroom door. The class went silent. The principal had a quiet word with Miss Pleasant while Tad slowly walked to his desk. He was red-eyed, swollen-faced and moved with a labored painfullness. Everyone watched while he collected things from his desk, then walked out.

The very children who just sixty minutes before were taunting him, were now all hurting with him. Miss Pleasant's face, too, showed great concern for him.

"Tad has had some family problems and may not be with us for a while," she said. "He may or may not show up tomorrow. If he does I want you all to show him that you missed him. I know that he is not always nice to everybody, but I want you all to be nice to him and treat him like a friend if he does come back."

Miss Pleasant knew she would not be able to bring the children's focus back to math. "All right class. In continuing our studies of great artists from around the world, today we are going to learn about an artist born in the Netherlands in the year 1853. Who can tell me another name for the country of the Netherlands?"

Elliott Carney raised his hand.

"Yes, Elliott."

"Holland. Vincent van Gogh was born in 1853."

"That is correct. Very good. And he is the person who painted these great masterpieces I'm about to show you."

Miss Pleasant invited Elliott to come forward and help her hang some posters. Before the children left for recess, the room was filled with over-sized posters of van Gogh's masterpieces such as

"Sunflowers" and "Starry Night."

The school ground buzzed with gossip. Kids everywhere swapped ideas and stories about what happened this morning. Eddie and Cindy sat together on a concrete planter near the front of the school.

"One good thing about Tad being gone is that we can actually talk," Cindy said. "He's always in our faces."

"I know. Another good thing is I don't have to ditch him to go back to the cemetery today?"

"You're going there?"

"After school."

"Would you like some company? I love cemeteries."

"Today, I just really need to go alone."

"I can understand that."

"Thanks anyway."

"Sure. You know Tad is really mean and all, but I am worried about him. He must have been the one who stole the CD's."

"Did you tell on him?" Eddie said.

"No. I was just accusing him to get back at him for being so mean. I just thought he is so creepy he probably is the one who did it. But I didn't know if he was."

"He looked like they beat him. I didn't think they could do that anymore."

"Not unless your parents sign a special release." Cindy opened a little satchel and pulled out some cookies shaped like playing cards. She handed an Ace of Hearts cookie to Eddie. "Here. I made some good luck cookies for us to eat."

"Thanks. The black cat cookies were really good."

"These are even better."

"The family problem thing might just be a cover up."

"I did notice he didn't take everything out of his desk," Cindy said.

"That's right. I saw that, too. So, maybe he will come back."

While they continued to talk, a large perfectly formed maple leaf fluttered down from one of the adjacent school ground trees and dangled momentarily in the air right in front of Eddie's face. Both he and Cindy watched as it gently landed right on top of Eddie's cookie."

"Eddie! To catch a leaf before it hits the ground brings good luck. But for a big leaf like that to land perfectly right on you—it trumps it all. You're swimming in luck."

"I hope so. Because I still don't know what I'm doing this

weekend. I don't know how or where I'm gonna find Brian."

"I really want you to think about The Bonfires. That's what they are for—reaching your dead loved ones."

"I don't know how I could ever pull it off. My parents would never let me go there."

"Just keep an open mind. Like my mom said, that night you should feel it out."

"Okay."

The moment school was out Eddie raced to the cemetery. This time as well he crossed himself at the entrance. He looked back and forth and all around expecting Grover to jump out at any moment, but he did not appear.

Eddie went straight back to the McCourt family plot, and quickly found his grandparents and then Hortense, his great grandmother, who Grover mentioned yesterday. A big bush grew just beside her grave with long grass sticking up through it. Eddie remembered that Grover said Louie was between Lucy and Hortense.

Eddie looked around the bush and found Lucy. The only space between the graves was occupied by the bush.

He leaned right into its woody branches, grateful it was not a sticker bush, and pulled up tufts of grass. The more he pulled, the more there seemed to be. At last, he yanked a large clump, roots and all, and he saw something stone. Frantically he pulled and dug with his bare hands. A small flat marker became visible at the base of the bush. It grew out of the ground right next to and then out and over Louie's tombstone, completely covering it.

Eddie whispered to himself. "Uncle Louie was only four years old when he died. Grover was right."

"GROVER IS ALWAYS RIGHT."

Eddie knew Grover was standing right over him. He turned but no one was there. Not Grover. Not anyone. Except an owl sat on a low tree limb, looking right at Eddie. It looked just like Mr. Bones.

Eddie cleaned up Louie's marker as best he could, then made his way to the caretaker's cottage, right next to the garage. Eddie knocked. There was no answer so he knocked harder, but still no answer. He walked toward the garage, and paused to look at the old hearse. The sunlight glared off its dirty rain-spattered windows. Just the sight of the old death coach gave him the heebie-jeebies. He dragged his hand along the side of it when a black figure sat up inside. Eddie screamed.

"Aaaah!"

Grover screamed. They both screamed. Grover kicked open the door and hopped out.

"You sleep in the hearse?" Eddie said.

"That's where I take my afternoon naps."

"How do you breathe in there?"

"Can't. Wasn't designed for livin' folk."

"Well, then how --?"

"Just climb in, shut the door and sleep till I wake up 'coffin' when the oxygen's gone. Get it 'coffin' from no oxygen. Ha! Ha! Ha! Ha! Ha!"

"Isn't that kind of dangerous?"

"Oh, sure. I could suffer brain damage—go totally wacko."

"Why do you do it then?"

"I knew the job was dangerous when I took it."

"You were right about Louie's tombstone."

"Of course Grover was right. Grover is always right!"

Eddie stared long and hard at Grover. "How did you do that when I was at Louie's grave?"

"If I told you, it would spoil all the m-y-s-t-e-r-y." Grover suddenly sort of withered and slumped over. "I just ran out of steam. I don't usually like to show this here deflated side of me to the public, but right now I can't help it."

"What's wrong?"

"The black bags under my eyes --"

"They do look darker today."

"Ever'one thinks they're makeup. But they're real. I earned 'em."

"How? Protecting the graveyard?"

"So to speak. They're from I can't never sleep."

"How come?"

"It's embarrassing to talk about."

"Are you sick?"

"You might be too young to understand."

"Get over it. I'll be ten years the old day after tomorrow."

"It's called the heart break of psoriasis."

"What's that?"

"A nasty skin disease. That's the real reason why I always wear black, to cover up all the red scaly patches."

"Maybe you should see a doctor?"

"I have. That's not the problem. I can't sleep at night 'cuz the itching keeps me awake."

"Take some medicine so you can sleep."

"That's the problem. I can't afford it."

"Is it really expensive?"

"Average I guess for prescriptions. You'd think they'd pay a g-r-a-v-edigger enough to at least buy a few cans of beer and one prescription a week. I provide a real service for this here community, but I'm goin' broke workin' here."

"I've got some money." Eddie reached into his pockets.

"Thanks, kid, but I can't take your money. T'wouldn't be right."

"My dad's a doctor. What if I brought you the medicine?"

"Can you really get it?"

"I think so. Tell me what it's called again. The heartbeat of what?'"

"Heart-break of Pso-ri-a-sis."

"So-ria-sis. Okay. I'll ask my dad tonight and I'll come back tomorrow around the same time."

"You sure?"

"Yeah. I'll be back tomorrow with your prescription."

"Anythin' you want kid. You bring me that medicine—it's yers."

"Can I just look around in the garage again?"

"Yawh—The light bulb burned out today and I can't afford a new one until my next pay check. Were you wantin' to look for somethin' special?"

"I just wanted to look at a couple of those photographs again. But it's okay."

"Tell you what. I'll round up a bulb from somewhere and you can look in there tomorrow. Deal?"

"Deal!"

Eddie ran home and arrived on time. "Mom! I'm home."

"Hi. Sweetie. I'm in the kitchen."

Eddie sat down and watched his mother prepare dinner.

"Did you have fun with Tad?"

"I didn't go to Tad's after all. Something's wrong with him. He left school today with his mother."

"I hope they're all right. So, where'd you go?"

"I just went to the cemetery."

"You walked all the way there and then home?"

the magic hour

"It's not that far. I just wanted to be there alone."

"I can understand that feeling."

"Grandpa was only seven years old when Uncle Louie died."

"Oh was he?"

"Yeah. They were only three years apart. Almost like me and Melissa. What time does Dad get home?"

"Early tonight."

"Good. I gotta talk to him about something."

"Eddie. You remember our talk last night?"

"Sure, Mom."

"I thought you were going to Tad's today. You really should have called me to tell me about your change of plans. What if something had happened to you? We wouldn't even know where to look."

"Okay, Mom. I just didn't think."

"I know this is all new. I didn't worry so much when there were two of you."

"I know how to take care of myself."

"I know you do."

Doctor McCourt arrived home and Eddie wasted no time at all hitting him up. "Hey, Dad."

"Hi, Eddie."

"Did you have a good day?"

"I did, actually. How about you?"

"I did, too. Listen. Can you do me a little favor?"

"I'll certainly try."

"Can you get some medicine for me?"

"Are you sick?"

"No. It's for a friend."

"Can't your friend have his parents pick up the medicine?"

"They don't have enough money to afford it."

"I'm sorry to hear that. What kind of medicine does your friend need?"

"He has Heartbreak of Soraisis."

"The heartbreak of Psoriasis?"

"That's it."

"That's a skin disease."

"That's what he's got."

"He must have a lot of itching."

"He does. It's really bad. So bad he can't ever sleep at night. Can you drop a prescription by the school to me tomorrow so I can give it to him. It's really important."

"You know I really can't give out prescriptions without seeing the people as patients first. Can you tell me who it is for?"

"It would be too embarrassing for him. Can't you just give me some itching creme or something?"

"All right. If you think it's important, I will do it for you."

"Thanks, dad. I really appreciate it. He will too."

Eddie ran off to his bedroom.

Doctor McCourt turned to his wife who also heard Eddie's unusual request. "I can't imagine who he wants the prescription for. He said his friend had heartbreak of Psoriasis. Only an adult would call it that."

"Isn't that from a television commercial?"

"From at least twenty years ago."

"Maybe it's for someone like Tad's mother."

"I really doubt that she would have extra money for prescriptions."

"Eddie said something was wrong with Tad. He left school today with his mother. But, regardless, Eddie is obviously trying to help someone, and we should be proud of that and support him in it."

"I intend to. I really wonder how Mrs. Durban is doing. She is a good woman. We should go say hello to her one of these days. I have a feeling that she has her hands full."

Mrs. McCourt drained pasta into a collander over the sink. "Did you notice how perky Eddie was?"

"Those little surprises in the morning, those monster bears, they have been a Godsend."

"Eddie's back to his old self. I am so pleased."

"We all are."

They kissed.

The following morning the doorbell rang yet again. Mrs. McCourt started for the door with her glue stick and her pairing knife. She walked straight out the door and over to the big bent willow chairs. A hairy, little werewolf teddy bear with fangs looked viciously up at her. She picked up the bear and began to open the envelope tied to its paw with gray curling ribbon.

"HEY!" Eddie said. "WHAT ARE YOU DOING?"

She froze.

The Magic Hour

Eddie bolted from the doorway in his pajamas and grabbed the bear out of his mother's hands. "THAT'S MINE!"

"I, I was just going to…"

"Save it." Eddie opened the card.

"My name is Bearwolf.
I howl every night I spend without you.
Let's spend the night together."

Eddie beamed with joy over this additional attention. He darted back into the house howling like a wolf. "AaaOooooooo!"

His mother followed him into the house. Melissa did not even want to know about this bear. She was about at the end of her rope with jealousy.

"Come on, Eddie," his mother said. "It's time to do your makeup or you'll be late for the bus. Go put on your black shirt and then come into the kitchen."

Mrs. McCourt applied green makeup and Frankenstein stitches to Eddie's face.

"AaaOoooooo! I should've been a werewolf."

"You know Frankenstein has always been your favorite monster. You shouldn't ever get too excited about having a secret admirer. You never know who or what they might turn out to be."

"AaaOooooo."

"Eddie. I'm really sorry that it looked like I was invading your privacy earlier. Really I am."

"It's okay, Mom. AaaOooooo. It's no big deal. It's not the first time."

"What do you mean it's no big deal—it's not the first time?"

"It's one of the perils of childhood."

"What is?"

"Privacy invasion by your mom. It's okay though."

"It is not okay. Where did you hear that?"

"No where."

"Eddie, you tell me where you heard that. I want to know who put that idea into your head."

"I reserve the fifth."

"Hah! It was your sister. That's her line! I reserve the fifth. I won't answer on the grounds that it might incriminate myself."

"For the record, I didn't tell you it was her."

"You didn't have to. For the record, that's your sister's line, too. It's bad enough when she acts that way, but now she's corrupting her little brother."

"I stand innocent."

"You look pretty guilty to me." She painted the final row of stitches across Eddie's brow. "Go look at yourself in the mirror and tell me what you think."

Eddie hurried off to the bathroom still howling like a wolf. "AaaOoooooo!" His voice echoed through the entire house. "Looks great, mom. Thanks." Dressed head to toe in black, Eddie looked the part of Frankenstein with with his hair sprayed black and spikey, and his green face held together with stitches and bolts.

Eddie's bus approached the front of the school, and he saw Tad sitting alone on the concrete planter where he and Cindy sat and chatted yesterday. Tad was barely recognizable, all decked out as his favorite historical figure, the pirate Captain Blood.

"Great costume, mate," Eddie said.

Tad looked up. "Same to ya."

Eddie could see that Tad was low key and nonaggressive today. "You okay?"

Tad shrugged his shoulders.

"What happened yesterday?"

"Can't talk about it."

"Why not?"

"Can't say."

"Yeah, right. Only the biggest thing that happens in the whole school and you won't even tell your best friend."

"I told you I can't talk about it! At least not now."

"Is it really bad?"

"Worse."

"Are you gonna be all right?"

"We'll see."

"Since you won't tell me what it is, the best thing I can do for you is to make sure you don't ruin your Halloween with a long face. Whatever it is, you gotta shake it out, at least for the weekend."

"You just don't know."

"No I don', but Halloween only comes once a year. You gotta

lighten up! The class party is today and the carnival and the parade are tomorrow. There is plenty of time to be sour next week after Halloween's over."

Tad cracked a smile.

"You see. You're loosening up already. You can have a good time if you want to."

"You're right," Tad said.

"And we get out early today."

"Wanna do somethin' later? I was thinkin' of goin' back to the cemetery. I've got some ideas I wanna run past Grover."

"I wouldn't push it with him. He's weird. And besides, you promised you'd never go back."

"But I can't stop thinkin' about all that free stuff. We could sneak into the garage when he's out diggin' graves."

"No, Tad. That's dishonest. Just give it a little time. Then maybe he'll forget about your promise."

"We can do somethin' else then."

"I gotta bunch of stuff I gotta do, so I'm gonna take the bus right home. And besides. Won't your mom need you to look after your little sisters?"

Tad did not answer.

"We've got all day tomorrow. You are coming over aren't you?"

"You kiddin'? Your mom's cakes are the best in town. Why don't you sleep over tomorrow night after the carnival."

"I'll have to ask my mom, but I don't know why not. There won't be any room for me at my house."

The morning bell rang and with the front door of the school right beside them, Eddie and Tad were two of the first children into the classroom.

Miss Pleasant smiled when she saw them. She was dressed as Raggedy Ann, complete with red yarn wig and MaryAnn shoes with lace bobbies. "My, what great costumes you, two."

"Thank you, Miss Pleasant," Eddie alone said.

"We're glad to have you back in class today, Tad."

Tad cracked a smile and Eddie nudged him with his elbow. "You're supposed to say thank you."

"Thank you, Miss Pleasant."

Excited costumed children milled around out in the hall and gradually trickled into the room. A group of girls dolled up in cute animal costumes entered the classroom door giggling. They looked right at Eddie and giggled more intensely.

Every child who entered the room looked straight at Eddie and laughed. Elliott entered dressed as Dracula. He also looked at Eddie and burst into gales of laughter. Eddie became extremely self conscious not knowing what was wrong with him or his costume. He jumped from his desk and walked toward the door.

"Frankenstein! Don't go. Your destiny awaits!" Elliot broke into a fit of laughter as wedding music began to play somewhere very close. The music quickly became louder and louder with the familiar blare of Mendelssohn's Wedding March. The music announced the arrival of the bride and Cindy appeared in the doorway. She and Eddie stood face to face. Dangling a portable compact disk player from one hand, she was dressed in a shredded pink satin and lace dress with a three-foot-high kinky black hairdo with white lightning streaks running up through it. She was the Bride of Frankenstein! The entire classroom erupted into hysteria at Frankenstein and his Bride. Tad laughed so hard he fell out of his desk sideways. When he hit the floor, everyone laughed all the harder.

Eddie was the only person in the room who did not laugh. Even Cindy thought it was great fun. She turned to her adoring fans and paraded into the room. No expense or effort had been spared with her costume. She had little green Frankenstein head earrings that looked just like Eddie, dangling from her pierced ears, black finger nail extensions, and black stitches up the length of her neck. Even a pink diamond wedding ring sparkled on her left hand. Her costume was so good the other students clapped. At last, everyone looked to see Eddie's response. No one had even noticed that he passed out cold on the floor.

When he came to, he was on the cot in the school nurse's office. He moved his eyes around the room to gather his bearings.

"You just lie there as long as you need, Eddie," the nurse said. "When you're ready, I'll give you this prescription that was just delivered for you."

"From the hospital pharmacy?"

"Yes, marked urgent."

"I'll just take my prescription and I'll be fine." Eddie jumped to his feet.

"But it's just for itching."

Eddie took the bag and stepped toward the door. He became dizzy-headed and wobbled. The nurse noticed and caught him before he fell.

"I think you'd better lie back down another minute. And next time don't get up quite so fast." She helped him back to the cot.

He laid down and closed his eyes. Instantly in his mind's eye he traveled at the speed of light through the vast expanse of outer space. He passed comets and planets. Colorful solar systems and complete galaxies whizzed and whirred past so close he felt he could touch them. Just as quickly as these spectacular images appeared in his mind, they vanished, leaving his mental screen blank. He laid still with his eyes closed, breathing heavily from the exhileration of the space flight. He wondered what had just occurred and why. The only experience he had ever had even remotely like it, was flying over town in his dreams the night before Brian's funeral. But Brian said it was not a dream.

Cakes, cookies, and candy galore covered almost every desktop of the classroom when Eddie returned. The kids all rocked and grooved to the sounds of "Monster Mash."

Miss Pleasant drew the blinds and they all settled in to watch the talking mule movie "Francis and the Haunted House."

When school let out, Eddie boarded the bus as if he was simply going home. He figured out that he could never ditch Tad without actually getting on the bus. He also realized that the first bus stop was actually closer to the cemetery.

Eddie scanned for a vacant seat near the front. The only one was right beside Dracula, Elliott Carney.

"Hey, Elliott. Is it okay if I sit here?"

"I don't know. There's always an empty seat next to me. I wouldn't want you to break any unspoken rules."

"It's okay, right?"

"Sure. If you want to."

"Thanks."

"How come you're sitting up front? You always sit way in the back."

"I have to get off early. At the first stop."

"That's where I get off."

"Really?"

"Yeah. I live right by there. You going somewhere special?"

"I have to deliver a prescription to somebody over by the cemetery."

"That's a nice thing to do. You're a pretty nice kid."

"Thanks."

"Why do you hang around with a loser like Tad? He's nothing but a thug."

Eddie was surprised at Elliott's question. "I guess 'cuz we've been friends since we were little. We used to live next door to each other, before my family moved."

"Up onto the hill?"

"Yeah. Tad didn't use to be so mean. He was nice when he was younger."

"From my perspective he's always been a bully."

"He really does pick on you, doesn't he?"

"He picks on everybody except you. I do my best to just brush it off. It helps knowing that he's just going to end up in prison like his dad."

"His dad's in prison?"

"Like the federal penitentary in Indiana."

"Really? How do you know?"

"It was in the paper in the news of record. I follow all that."

"Tad said his dad was working in Indiana but—"

"It's called prison detail."

"Oh, my gosh. I had no idea. What did he do?"

"I think it's best if I don't say."

"That bad?"

Elliott nodded his head.

The bus slowed and kids crowded toward the door. Eddie looked for his sister, so she could tell his mom he was getting off with Elliott, but she was not there. He remembered she stayed at school for a dance.

"This is where we get off," Elliott said.

They exited the bus and walked along together. Elliott looked at Eddie with hopeful eyes. "So, you're going over by the cemetery for your delivery?"

"Yeah. Right by it."

"Do you want me to come with you?"

"It's somebody I know and he's old, so I'll probably be there awhile. It would be really boring for you. But thanks for asking."

"Sure."

"This is the end of the road then."

"You live right here?"

"Yup."

"Nice talking to you, Eliott."

"Thanks. Hey Eddie! Stop by on your way back from your delivery if you have time. I'll show you my space simulator."

"That would be fun."

"See ya later."

Eddie walked on the few blocks to the cemetery. Today he did not cross himself when he entered the gates. Still dressed like Frankenstein, he walked straight on to the caretaker cottage and knocked on the door.

The front door opened a crack and a scratchy high voice called out. "Trick or treat's not 'til tomorrow! Go away!"

"Grover! It's me, Eddie."

"Go away. Go away!"

"I got your prescription."

The door swung wide open. "Well, why didn't you say so? What's with the Frrrrrrahnkensteen getup."

"It's Frankenstein."

Grover jumped down onto his haunches and put his face right into Eddie's. "Did you like that movie?"

"It's my favorite!"

"Mine, too! Mine, too, Mine, too!" He spun around on his heel like a top. Dropping his other foot down, he stopped right in front of Eddie's face again. "D'ya wanna come over and watch it sometime?"

"We can talk about it. Anyway, here's your prescription." Eddie handed a pharmacy bag to Grover.

"Golly-be-jeepers, kid, I owe you big time. I'd give you a hug, but I don't do hugs."

"I thought you didn't do handshakes."

"I didn't back then. It's part of the ever evolving me. Now I just do nods and circular waves, like Queen Lizzy. Saves energy and it's very dignified." Grover tilted his head ever so slightly, and with a hint of a smile, slowly rotated his hand with his fingers up. "Been thinkin' about yer little friend wantin' to work here 'n all. Could use a little help. I'm not quite as limber or long-winded as I used to be. What's his name?"

"Tad."
"Tad?"
"Yeah, Tad"
"Taaad. Taaaaad. Nope. It's flat. He'd never work out here."
"How come?"
"Bad name for a gravedigger. Names are all important. Everythin' is in a name. What's yer name again?"
"Eddie."
"Edward yer real name?"
"Yup."
"In this business, we don't hide behind nick names. We're proud of who we are. But, see—Edward the gravedigger just don't work neither. It's bad. Not a bad name—just a bad match. But names like Luther and Grover, they roll off yer tongue the way g-r-a-v-e-digger does. Anyway, kiddo. Couldn't sleep last night a'tall, so I done took a light bulb from inside the house out to the garage. Spent all night diggin', 'n this is what I come up with."

Grover handed Eddie a large box with the top flaps folded shut. Eddie could barely lift it.

"What's in it?"

"Don't open it! Wait 'til ya git home. I really searched last night, mind you. Confirmed and verified all the coded numbers and dates. Everythin' in this here box was left at yer family plot over the last seventy or eighty years."

Eddie was speechless with surprise and delight.

"It's all yers, kid."

"Are you sure?"

"You went out of your way fer me. I 'preciate it. There's pro'bly more, but this was all I could find last night. Seems your family was busy cemetery goers. Now hurry up and go home before I embarass myself." Grover's eyes welled as he looked down at the prescription in his hands."

"I'll check on you," Eddie said, "so when you run out --"

"Thanks, kiddo. One other thing. Yesterday, when I told ya I sleep in the hearse 'til I wake up 'coffin.' I was done prevaricatin' ya know—stretchin' the truth. I done drilled some air holes in the bottom. Otherwise I would die in there. Just wanted to clear it up with ya now that we're good friends 'n all."

"Thanks for telling me."

"Now scram."

Eddie could barely make it across the cemetery with the box. He knew it was too far to walk home with such a heavy parcel, then he remembered Elliott lived nearby and that he invited him to stop on his way back. He could call his mom to have his dad pick him up on his way home from work since this evening he was coming home early.

Eddie struggled a half block and then rested, a half block then rested. Eventually he saw Elliott's house and knew that was all the farther he could go before his arms broke off.

Elliott's house was small but charming with picture perfect shrubs and gardens abloom with orange marigolds and all colors of chrysanthemums. Halloween cobwebs enshrouded the bushes on either side of the front door and green witch's hands reached up from the side of the porch. Eddie managed to lift the box up onto the side of the porch and then pressed the door bell.

"AAAAAAAAH!" A deafening hideous scream cried out, severely startling him.

Elliott answered the door still in his Dracula costume. He grinned when he saw Eddie. "Do you like my doorbell?"

"The scream?"

"Yeah. I rigged it myself."

"It's awesome."

"I got the idea from 'Young Frankenstein.'"

"Oh, I love that movie! That's my most favorite."

"Well, come on in, Frankenstein. Mom!" Elliot then hollered with glee. "Come meet Eddie."

A pretty woman with curly dark brown hair entered the front room.

"Mom, this is Eddie McCourt, from my class."

"It is very nice to meet you, Eddie. That's a very convincing Frankenstein costume."

"Thank you."

"We were so sorry to hear about your brother. I hope everyone in your family is doing all right."

"We are, thanks."

"Please know that you are welcome in our home anytime, Eddie. Now, if you'll excuse me, I'll leave you two to your business."

"Walk this way, and I'll show you the simulator."

Elliott opened the door to a small room at the back of the house to reveal the vast expanse of outer space. They entered the room and instantly traveled at the speed of light past comets and planets. Colorful solar systems and complete galaxies whizzed and whirred past so close it appeared the boys could touch them.

Eddie's mouth fell open in awe. "Elliott. This is like the real thing. Like a real space simulator."

"It is a real simulator just scaled down."

"How much did this thing cost?"

"It's worth way more than our house. My parents feel that education for their children is the most important thing. You should see my sister's aquaculture habitat—real lion fish and sharks. She wants to be an ichthyologist."

"This is like really freaky."

"What's the matter? Don't you like it?"

"No. It's awesome. I love it. But today when I blacked out at school, I had this dream about traveling through space. This is exactly what I saw."

"I won't try to explain that one," Elliott said.

"Anyway. This is the most incredible thing I've ever seen. How did you --?"

"My dad builds simulators for a living—aircraft, submarine, space flight. He and I assembled it from an old one being dismantled."

"I knew you were really smart, Elliott, but this is genius level."

"Thanks."

"I'm in shock. I had no idea."

"No one does."

"Has anyone else from class seen this?"

"You're the first."

"We should have a field trip and bring everybody. At least you should invite all your friends over."

Elliot hesitated. "I really don't have any friends."

"All the kids in class."

"They all pick on me."

Eddie had to think what to say next, to not say the wrong thing. "When you asked me on the bus if I was sure I wanted to sit next to you, you weren't joking?"

"Nope. Nobody ever wants to sit next to me. I have cooties or fleas." Elliott raised his hands like a monster in pursuit. "I'm an untouchable—the bottom of the caste system."

Eddie had to think again, very carefully, to find the right words. Elliott saw Eddie struggle.

"It's okay, Eddie. I've gotten used to it. I appreciate that you are even here. You're cool. You don't pick on me directly."

"Permission to enter, Captain." Mrs. Carney stepped into deep space with a tray of brownies.

"Those are the Graveyard Brownies from school," Eddie said. "They were the best thing at the whole party. They're all full gummie worms."

Elliott glowed with pride. "My mom made 'em."

She handed the tray to Elliott.

"Thanks, Mom."

"Yes. Thank you Mrs. Carney"

"You are both welcome." She stepped away.

Eddie was afraid to even ask to use the telephone, for fear he would hurt Elliott's feelings. He did not want Elliott to find out the real reason why he stopped by.

"Do you wanna come over some other time and like watch 'Young Frankenstein' or we could give you a space workout in the simulator?" Elliott said.

"I'd love to."

"Great. You know my mom and me have to go out right now. Would you like a ride home? I saw you had a big box and all."

"Are you sure it's no trouble?"

"Positive."

"That'd be great."

Mrs. Carney and Elliott drove Eddie home.

"You should come over sometime, too," Eddie said. "I don't have a space simulator, but I've got a great treehouse."

"I'd really like to come over."

"We can talk more at school. Thank you Mrs. Carney. Thanks for everything."

"We'll look forward to seeing you again, Eddie. Bye."

"Oh, Elliott. I never thanked you for making me such a nice card. I really appreciate it."

"Sure."

"See ya later."

"Yeah. See ya."

Eddie lugged the big box up the driveway but could not decide whether to take it into his bedroom or to the treehouse. He thought about the weight and having to hoist it up and ruled out the treehouse. But then he thought of his sister grabbing things and he ruled the treehouse back in.

He set the box down just outside the kitchen door and stepped into the house to let his mother know he was home. He told her he would be out in the treehouse, because he wanted to be alone for awhile.

"I can understand that feeling," she said. "You haven't been back up in the treehouse since—"

"Since Brian fell."

"Will you please be very careful?"

"I will."

"Okay, Sweetheart. What's that box out there?"

"Just some old stuff I'm bringing home from school."

"Oh."

"See ya in a while."

Eddie carefully tied the box onto the hoist, then climbed up. Everything was exactly as it was on that fateful night, but he was only interested in the box. He struggled to pull it up then yanked open the top flaps. There it was—the photo Eddie looked at the other day in Grover's garage was right on top.

Eddie stared at the picture. Deep inside he knew he knew these boys. They were his grandpa and his brother Louie.

Old-fashioned toys nearly filled the box. Eddie reached through them and pulled out a little burgundy-plaid beret-like hat with a pompom on top. Then he found a matching muffler with mittens all stitched together. He next picked up a stuffed-sock monkey toy, with a faded "Merry Christmas" ribbon tied around its neck.

Almost everything in the box was left at Uncle Louie's grave. Eddie could tell by the coded numbers. They were almost all the same as on the photograph.

Eddie dug to the bottom and found cards of all shapes and sizes. One particular brown envelope caught his attention, however. It had "Louie" written across it. He carefully lifted it from the pile and saw it had never been opened. The paper was water-spotted and the ink was smeared all down the envelope from either the rain or snow that must have fallen when it sat on the monument.

He opened the envelope. The date on the letter inside told Eddie that this was written to Uncle Louie two years after he died.

Dear Louie,

My new Sunday School teacher, Mrs. Richie, you know her, she made us all promise to write an apology letter to someone this week. She said it didn't matter if the apology was long past due because it is never too late to apologize. I don't know where else to write you but at your grave. It has been two and a half years since you died. Every day I think about not jumping in to help you. I have nightmares about the scared look on your face as the water took you away. I am very sorry little brother I didn't help you. I hope if you ever can read this letter, you can forgive me.

Love,

Georgie

Overwhelmed by what he just read, he laid down on the sleeping bag to take it all in. Emotions swelled inside of him. He thought about his grandpa as a young boy going through the same thing as he was going through. He thought about how Brian did not want to finish the story but he said they should.

"EDDIE? Are you up there?" His father's calling voice woke him up.

"Yeah, Dad."

"Come on in for dinner."

"Okay."

It was almost dark so his father held a strong flashlight beam up the trunk into the open hatch. The light filled the center of the treehouse. Eddie realized the apology letter was still in his hand. He tucked it and the photo into his school pack and slung it over his shoulder.

"Come on down, Eddie."

"I'm coming."

Eddie and his father walked into the kitchen door together to find dinner set and waiting on the dining room table, complete with candles.

The dining room opened right onto the kitchen, which was a disaster zone of countless unfrosted plastic-wrapped cakes, stacked in every corner and on every counter and cabinet. Melissa walked into the kitchen. She saw Eddie and broke into a hyena laugh.

"Shut up! It's not funny!"

"Eddie!" his mother said. "We don't use that word in this house. Remember?"

Melissa continued to laugh. "It is, too, funny! Frankenstein and his bride. That's all anybody in school talked about today! Ha, ha, ha, ha. ha!"

Doctor McCourt sat at the dining table. "I haven't heard what happened yet."

"Oh, Dad. It was the funniest thing ever!" Melissa recounted for him the events in Eddie's class in the minutest detail, just as if she had been there in person.

Eddie looked at her angrily. "How do you know everything? You weren't there."

"The video was circulating everywhere."

"Who taped it?"

"Some kid named Elliott."

"I was over at his house. He didn't tell me. I'm gonna have a talk with him."

"OH! Get a copy p-l-e-a-s-e! I'll be nice to you for a whole week. I promise."

Mrs. McCourt turned to her daughter. "Melissa. You'll be nice to your brother anyway."

"But, Dad. No kidding. When he fainted, I thought I was gonna wet my pants."

"Melissa," her mother said. "You are a young lady now. Let's try to act like one."

Doctor McCourt looked right at Eddie. "You fainted?"

"Out cold."

"Eddie. That's dangerous. You didn't hit your head on that concrete floor?"

"I don't think so. But I woke up in the nurses office."

Melissa jumped into the air with excitement. "I GOT IT! Send it to 'Funniest Videos.' And I get all the money 'cuz it's my idea."

Mrs. McCourt walked to the table with a platter of food. "I have a better idea. Let's eat. Because tomorrow we'll all be running separate directions at the carnival and the parade, tonight is Eddie's birthday dinner." She had prepared his favorite meal, curried coconut prawns over brown rice. "This is the only quiet time we will have in the next thirty-six hours, so let's enjoy it."

The Magic Hour

After dinner, Mrs. McCourt and Melissa disappeared into the kitchen then walked back into the dining room with a beautiful Frankenstein cake aglow with ten candles.

Eddie, still sitting at the table, could only see the side view of the cake as they approached. Everyone broke into song and wished Eddie a happy birthday. Mrs. McCourt placed the cake down on the table. It was a spectacular creation, with painstaking detail in the frosting, but Eddie's face went pale.

"Frankenstein?"

"I made it special just for you, Sweetie, because Frankie is your favorite monster."

"Don't you have a ghost or a pumpkin or something? I don't think Frankenstein will taste very good to me right now."

"Oh, dear! I didn't even think about that. I don't have any other cakes frosted yet."

"I'm sorry, Mom. I can see you went to a lot of trouble."

"Do you want a ghost, a jack-o'-lantern, a witch or a bat?"

"Definitely a ghost."

"I'll frost one right now! Give us ten minutes and we'll have an instant replay. Melissa, come help me, please." Mrs. McCourt and Melissa disappeared back into the kitchen.

"Did you get the prescription I sent to the school today, Eddie?" his father said.

"Oh, yeah. Thanks, Dad."

"How'd it work out?"

"Great, I think. I gave it to him. I know he'll take it right away so the itching will stop. I really appreciate it."

"Happy to do it. Your mother and I appreciate you wanting to be generous and help other people."

"Then they help you, huh?"

"Exactly. And the world becomes a better place."

"Is that why you became a doctor—to help people?"

"It is one of the reasons."

"I think that's why grandpa was a doctor, too. So he could help save people."

"Very likely."

"Did mom tell you I found Uncle Louie's tombstone?"

"She did."

"I gotta picture to show you."

Eddie jumped over to the kitchen door, where his backpack rested on the floor. He pulled out the photo and the card and then placed only the photo on the table by his father. "This is grandpa when he was seven." Eddie pointed to the older boy. "And that's Uncle Louie. He was four."

'Honey. Come look at this," Doctor McCourt called to his wife. "We're almost ready."

Eddie handed his father the card. He read.

Mrs. McCourt walked back with another cake. "Let's try it one more time, Happy birthday to you..." Melissa joined in and the two of them sang together.

Eddie closed his eyes, made his wish and blew out all the candles.

Mrs. McCourt saw the old card in her husband's hand. She also saw that he was emotionally choked up. "What is that?"

Doctor McCourt could barely speak he was so emotional. "My father wrote this when he was a little boy." He handed her the card.

She read and was filled with emotion as well.

"Let me see," Melissa said, then took and read the card. "This was grandpa?"

Her father nodded. "When he was nine and a half. Eddie. Where did you get these?"

"There's lots more. I haven't even seen it all. It's in a box up in the treehouse."

"Let's go get it! Honey, will you serve the cake? Eddie and I will be right back."

Eddie and his dad rushed out the door with flashlight in hand and returned with the box. Eddie explained how everything was left as an offering on a grave, and how most of these things were left for Uncle Louie. The family looked through everything, thoroughly amazed.

"What a treasure trove," Mrs. McCourt said. "Oh. Look at this adorable tam-o'-shanter."

Melissa turned her head. "What's that?"

"This flat little hat with a pompom on top. And there's a matching muffler and mittens."

"And look," Eddie added. "There's something in one of the mittens. A note."

To keep you warm my love—Mother

"I'm going to cry."

Doctor McCourt shook his head in disbelief. "That is from your great-grandmother to her little son who died, your grandpa's brother."

"Uncle Louie," Eddie said.

Melissa looked right at her little brother. "And you've met him?"

"Uh huh."

"So are you what they call a medium or something?"

"I don't know. I just know he's really nice and he's really tall."

"He was only four when he died?"

"But now he's grown up."

"Dead people grow up?"

"Live people do, Melissa," her father said. "If Uncle Louie is still alive somehow, it doesn't seem so preposterous."

Mrs. McCourt looked up from the box. "Maybe there are things we don't know, Melissa. Eddie is teaching us all here."

Doctor McCourt put his hand on his son's shoulder. "Eddie, is this what you have been telling us all along that Brian is still alive?"

"He is alive. I talk to him. He talks to me."

"We're sorry we didn't believe you right from the start," his mother said.

Melissa shook her head. "This is heavy! My brother the psychic. I should probably write a book."

"Melissa! First you need to learn how to write. I saw your score on that last English composition."

"I'm not being rude, Mom. It would probably be a best seller. A story about two twins—one dead, one alive. It's a good premise."

"Anyway, this is Eddie's story right now. He's in the middle of it. And speaking of which, someone has gone to great pains to care for all these things. They obviously saw value in keeping them. They have coded dates in the same code we used at the pharmacy where I worked as a girl. I can read them all. And then there's some other number."

"It's the grave number," Eddie said.

"I'm astounded."

"We're astounded," his father also said.

Melissa nodded. "Make it three."

Mrs. McCourt shuffled through more letters. "Just the fact that these things are still around is remarkable, let alone the fact that they have come back into our hands. You have to tell us how you got these, Eddie."

"I made a promise not to tell, but they were given to me by someone."

"We believe in keeping promises in this house." She looked to her husband and smiled. He smiled back. "So, we'll just be grateful."

"This has turned out to quite the family party," Doctor McCourt said.

Eddie scooped his finger through the frosting on the side of the cake. "Can we eat some cake?"

"Of course, Sweetheart. You can eat as much as you like."

Melissa's eyes gleamed mischievously. "Maybe your secret admirer will bring you something tomorrow for your birthday, Eddie."

"That's what I'm worried about."

"The darling girl who's been sending you the bears?" his mother said.

"What if it was Cindy Crystal? Yuck! Her mother is a witch!"

"Melissa! That is not a nice thing to say."

"She is a witch. The whole town knows she's a witch."

"It was the way you said it. For all you know Mrs. Crystal could be a very nice lady. Which reminds me, your Aunt Lois called last night. She and the girls are coming up for the carnival."

Eddie stuck his finger down his throat and made vomit sounds. "Blaaaaah."

Melissa was delighted with Eddie's discomfort. "You're just jealous 'cuz there aren't any boy cousins."

"Lois is bringing eleven of her Brownie Scouts with her, too."

Melissa sneered at Eddie.

"There is no possible way I'm sleeping in this house with all those girls. Tad invited me to sleep over after the carnival and that's what I'm gonna do."

"We can talk about it later, Honey."

"I'm not coming home until they're gone. Every last one of 'em." Eddie vomited his way out of the room past all the cakes in the kitchen.

Doctor McCourt glanced at the kitchen. "Between the cakes and the Brownies, I'm not sure there's room here for me either. Maybe I'll sleep over at Tad's, too."

CHAPTER NINE

Halloween morning found the front room of the house literally filled with people dressed in stylish period costumes, all come to help celebrate. A "HAPPY BIRTHDAY EDDIE" banner hung above the mantel, and all across the hearth sat presents large and small beautifully wrapped in colorful Halloween papers and ribbons.

Everyone excitedly chatted and ate cake. It was quite a lively party.

Seemingly dozens of historical eras were represented in the clothes of all the party guests. Some women wore Victorian era dresses while others donned early twentieth-century clothing. One young couple stood right in front of the hearth in 1940's country club attire. The man even held an old nine iron golf club in his hand. They chatted away with another young man dapperly dressed in 1940's argyle, and the man with the club whopped the woman on the derriere. She shrieked.

The doorbell rang and everyone looked to the front entry, almost with a look of worry.

Eddie called out from his bedroom. "Let me get it!"

The people in the front room, who all looked somehow familiar, began to fade away as Eddie's footsteps approached. Their now watery image dispersed like ripples on a pond.

Eddie walked toward the door, but sensed something. His attention was drawn into the living room. He looked but no one was there. There was no "HAPPY BIRTHDAY EDDIE" banner. There were no presents on the hearth.

"Who's here? Brian? Mom?"

"I'm in the kitchen, dear."

Satisfied, but not really, Eddie threw open the front door. He found no one. He looked to the big bent willow chair where not one monster teddy bear, but two monster teddy bears sat facing each other with their arms outstretched as if locked in an embrace. They were Frankenstein and Bride of Frankenstein teddy bears, dressed exactly as Eddie and Cindy were dressed the day before at school. The Bride had exactly the same shredded pink satin and lace dress with the same black kinky hairdo with white lightning streaks. An envelope dangled from a black curling ribbon stretched over both their paws.

"Frankenbear and his Bearide."

The blood flushed from his face. He gasped for breath. "MOM! MOM!! MOM!!!"

Mrs. McCourt rushed from the kitchen to see what could possibly be wrong. She stopped right beside Eddie and started to giggle.

"IT'S NOT FUNNY!"

Mrs. McCourt held a frosting-covered hand over her mouth to muffle her laughter. "You're absolutely right. It's not funny. It's awful." She could not help herself and burst into laughter again. "I'm sorry, Sweetie. I can't help it. They're just so cute."

"Then you have 'em. I don't want 'em."

Eddie ran back in the house while she stood there, still charmed by the bears.

Eddie called from his bedroom. "You can open this one, Mom. I don't even wanna know what it says!"

"I don't have time just now, but thank you. Maybe later."

"I WANT A NEW COSTUME!"

WHAM! Eddie's bedroom door slammed shut.

With Eddie out of sight, Mrs. McCourt did her best to wipe off all the frosting from her hands onto her apron then stepped back into the house. She opened the door to the front hall coat closet where a "HAPPY BIRTHDAY EDDIE" banner lay atop a stack of presents wrapped in Halloween paper. She then carried the presents and the banner to the fireplace and set them up just exactly as they seemed to have been set up only moments before.

Eddie laid on his bed and colored while listening to a Halloween sound effects CD that was one of his birthday presents. Both iguanas, Harry and Larry, lay beside him. Eddie stuffed birthday cake into his own mouth with one hand and into the mouths of the iguanas with his other hand. The iguanas appeared to enjoy this arrangement.

Out in the Halloween-cake-filled kitchen, a haggard-looking Mrs. McCourt, put the final decorative retouches on the Frankenstein cake that she originally made for Eddie's birthday. "I hate to send Frankie to the cake walk after I spent so much time on him for Eddie."

Melissa poured powdered sugar into mixing bowls spattered with all colors of frosting. "I don't know why you go to so much trouble for that cake walk anyway. For all you know, some slob could wind up with all of 'em."

"Please Melissa, I don't want to hear that. We do it because it needs to be done. And because it goes to a worthy cause."

Melissa shook an empty sugar bag. "We are now officially out of powdered sugar."

"I don't want to hear that either. I'll have to go to the store. Go take your shower and I'll go."

The doorbell rang.

"Maybe it's the girls!" Melissa said with a gleam in her eye.

"It better not be! It's not three!"

Eddie hollered from his bedroom. "I'll get it."

"I'LL GET IT!" Melissa yelled back.

Eddie raced Melissa to the front door.

"Ladies first," she said.

"You're no lady. And next comes children, so get out of the way."

Melissa held the door shut but Eddie shoved her away.

"And besides, it's my birthday. I get preference." Eddie opened the door and heard a familiar voice.

"Roses are red, violets are yella..." Tad sat out on the porch with the Frankenbears in his arms. He rocked back and forth and recited Cindy's poem. "You're forever my Prince, Forever my Fella. I'll forever be yours. Love, Cindy-rella." He rubbed the two teddy bears' faces together and made kissing sounds.

Melissa looked on from the doorway. "Oh, Eddie. Your dreams have come true." She ducked into the house laughing.

Eddie glared at Tad.

"P.S. I LOVE YOU. P.P.S. I REALLY LOVE YOU."

"SHUT UP, TAD!"

"I REALLY REALLY REALLY LOVE YOU."

Eddie grabbed the note from Tad's lap.

"P.S.S.S. Halloween is the best day of the whole year to talk to dead people. Tonight might be your last chance to see Brian before he passes on forever into the next world. Come with me to the Witches' Sabbath tonight."

Eddie threw down the note and returned into the house. Tad followed him. They passed Melissa in the hallway as she went into the bathroom. Tad and Melissa sneered viciously at each other.

"Hi, Taaaaaaaaad."

"Hi, Melissssssssa."

The boys disappeared into Eddie's bedroom. Tad saw the iguanas and sat on the bed beside them. "Hey Larry. Hey Harry." He then saw the meager pile of presents on the foot of the bed. "Walkie-talkies, crayons and a couple of CD's? Is this all they got you?"

"It was really cool. They wrapped each crayon in a different box so it looked like lots. Some of the boxes were huge."

"You guys having money problems?"

"No."

"Then your parents are the biggest little cheapskates I've ever seen. I couldn't believe it when your mom called and cancelled the party."

"I told her I didn't want a party."

"I didn't believe her for a second it was at your request. I know a cop-out when I see one. You need to get on their case. They owe you a lot more."

"Tad? Are you okay today?"

"Heck, yeah. It's Halloween."

"When are you gonna learn not everybody is like you? I did tell my mom I didn't want a party! And I told her I didn't want a lot of stuff."

"What's wrong with you? You gotta take it when you can get it."

"Some people don't actually care so much about stuff."

"If my parents cheated me out of my birthday like this, I'd divorce 'em." Tad yanked the curtains shut and whipped around. "Shut the door!"

"What's going on?"

"Sit down and I'll tell you." Tad pushed Eddie down by his shoulders all the way to the floor, then dropped down, also. "I have the best birthday present ever."

"What is it?"

"Worth way more than all those pitiful gifts."

"What is it?"

"We're going to talk to your brother."

"Oh, no. We're not doing that again."

"It's the prefect thing to do on Halloween. And besides, now I know all the words by heart."

"I don't care. I don't need to burn a bunch of candles to talk to Brian."

"I even figured out how we could hold hands." Tad reached into his back pocket and pulled out two life-sized floppy rubber hands.

Eddie laughed. "Very clever."

"We need Brian's help to exorcize flea bag Cindy from our lives."

Eddie gave Tad a half sneer. "You don't even believe in ghosts."

"Maybe I'm wrong. Anyway, we gotta do somethin'. If we don't stop this right here and now, you two are gonna end up married with a zillion ugly kids."

"I'll tell you what. If you promise to just shut up for two minutes, then I'll show YOU how to talk to the other side."

Just then a cool breeze blew through the room and fluttered all the curtains. Tad looked at Eddie questioningly. Seeing the seriousness of his face, he dared not say a word. The room was silent except for the soothing sound of shower water running in the adjacent bathroom.

Eddie drew a deep breath. "Brian, this is our birthday. Are you here in the house? Have you come home to celebrate?"

The two sat perfectly still until Tad shivered in excitement.

Eddie took another deep breath. "Brian, if you are here in the house, then give us a sign."

"AAAAAAAAAAH!" Melissa screamed hysterically in the bathroom.

Tad and Eddie nearly jumped out of their skin.

"AAAAAAAAAAH!" She continued to scream and stomp her feet.

Terrified, Tad dove under the bed. Eddie froze. The screaming grew louder and louder and LOUDER. Eddie jumped to his feet and ripped open the door just as Melissa screamed across the hall in a towel and into her bedroom. SLAM! And shut the door.

Eddie turned back into his room with a puzzled look. It was only then that he noticed just one iguana was sleeping on the bed. He turned white as a ghost. He knew what had happened.

He timidly stepped into the bathroom. After confirming his worst fears and turning off the water, he walked solemnly back to his room. Tad was still under the bed.

"Come on, Tad. We've got work to do."

An hour later, Eddie and Tad stood over Brian's grave at the Middleway cemetery with little garden trowels in their hands. A shoe box all wrapped up in Halloween gift paper lay next to a freshly-dug shoe-box-sized hole. Eddie and Tad bowed their heads and Eddie pronounced the eulogy and the last rights.

"Dearly beloved. We are gathered here today, to join in holy ceremony, this dead lizard, Larry Iguana, to his dearly departed owner Brian McCourt. Larry wasn't supposed to die but since he did, we offer him as a birthday present to keep you company along the road ahead. Larry was a good lizard. He liked to climb walls. He liked to scare girls. He hated macaroni and cheese, just like Brian and me. Larry will be missed by his brother Harry and all his friends. Larry never ever asked for much. He met his end with dignity and courage, but he will be happier now that he is with Brian. Amen."

"Amen."

Both made the sign of the cross over their hearts and Eddie put the box down in the hole. They filled in the soil and stomped the sod back into place. Tad then stuck some wiry fake flowers into the ground.

"Where'd you get those? Did you steal 'em?"

"Who cares? They're Larry's now."

Eddie crossed himself again.

The boys climbed onto their bicycles and rode off.

"I can't believe that Larry's gone," Eddie said. "He was eating cake one minute, and the next —"

"Life's like that. That's why you gotta take what you can get when you can get it."

"You know, I think maybe we shouldn't have killed the bears."

"You don't love her do you?"

"NO! But I just have a feeling that maybe —"

"That maybe what? You had no choice but to kill the bears. It's the only way to get rid of Cindy. I know what I'm talking about."

"I don't know. I feel kind of bad about it. I think we should go home and take 'em down."

Tad looked at Eddie with disgust. "When you two get married and have lots of ugly kids, just remember I warned you."

They neared the grave site where before there was a box of Cracker Jacks.

"Hey! Maybe the crazy lady left us a treat."

"Tad. You can't."

"Can't what?" Tad rode right up to the tombstone. "Trick or

treat." He swiped a new box of Cracker Jacks.

"Tad, don't!"

"The guy's dead. Besides, it's Halloween."

The boys rode back across town to Eddie's house. A green school bus filled nearly the entire driveway.

Tad read out loud the name painted on the bus. "CAMP BOUNTIFUL. What's that doing here?"

"That's the reason I'm sleeping over at your house tonight."

Eddie and Tad rode around the bus and something colorful on the porch steps caught their eyes. They stashed their bikes on the front lawn then hurried over to investigate. Pink frosting and cake were smashed all over the front steps, down the top of the driveway and out onto the edge of the grass.

"Talk about mega-gross!" Tad said. "How big was the cake?"

Eddie focused on the mess and did not move. Doctor McCourt walked around the side of the house with a half-carved jack-o-lantern under his arm.

Tad looked up. "What happened?"

"I was just carving out this pumpkin and heard a blood-curdling scream. I thought maybe one of Lois' girls had fallen off the roof or something, so I came running and there was the cake smashed all over the porch. And this chubby little Cinderella girl was running down the driveway."

Eddie looked faint. "I knew we shouldn't have done it."

A huge grin spread across Tad's face. He bent down to pick something up off the edge of the grass. "Hey! Lookey what I found." Tad plugged his nose with one hand and with the other he held up a pink ballet shoe. "Looks like Cindy-rella dropped her slipper!"

"I wish I were dead."

The front door of the house swung open and a tall, painfully skinny girl in a ballerina costume skipped across the porch. Using her hook nose as a forward rutter, she steared gracefully over the smashed cake descending the stairs and moved right up to Tad. Without so much as a word, she snatched the slipper from him and skipped back up and into the house.

Just then car brakes screeched and horns blared.

"AAAAAAAAAAAAH!" A woman screamed!

Driving up in front of the house, Mrs. McCourt turned into her own driveway right in front of an on-coming car. The driver slammed on

The Magic Hour

his brakes to avoid a wreck.

"LEARN HOW TO DRIVE, LADY!"

She narrowly escaped disaster, then barely squeezed past the bus to park in the driveway. A shaken Mrs. McCourt emerged from the car.

"Did you hear that rude driver?"

"I did," Doctor McCourt said.

"He needs to learn how to drive so other people can see him. All I could see was that great big, green school bus that probably seats thirty."

"A bus this size holds forty-four passengers to be exact, plus driver. I know because I stepped up into it and counted the seats. And to answer your next question, yes. They descended on the house like a plague of locusts. There was nothing anyone could do."

Mrs. McCourt was so upset she did not even see the smashed cake as she stormed toward the house. Everyone else was so amazed, they just watched her walk right through it. She splattered huge globs on to her own pant legs as she clomped up the porch stairs. She reached the top and stopped. Sensing something above her, she craned her neck back and saw Eddie's five monster teddy bears hanging right above her head. They all dangled from individual rope nooses tied around their necks. The Bearide of Frankenbear teddy had a paring knife stuck into its chest.

She stared. She said nothing. Her attention was somehow drawn down to her feet. She looked down as if in slow motion and saw the cake smashed all around and on herself.

"AAAAAAH! MY CAKES!"

She frantically ran up and into the house.

CHAPTER TEN

"Reporting live from the Crystal Ball Salon as we continue our Halloween coverage," a young male reporter announced. The camera panned to show the salon alive with witches, monsters and goblins, all volunteer workers, scrambling to apply last minute makeup and don costumes in preparation for the evening's events. Werewolves practiced their howls and zombies rehearsed their screams as they, too, made ready for a night of ghoulish work.

The reporter began again. "We are here with the Grand High Witch herself, Ms. Sandra Crystal. Thank you for allowing us to intrude on your preparation for tonight's festivities."

Sandy, who now had pale green skin with huge hairy warts on her face, raised up in a client chair so she could greet the interviewer. "It's our pleasure." She presented the reporter with a blinking jack-o'-lantern necktie. "Here is just a little token for you to remember us all by, here in Middleway."

"Well, thank you. I didn't expect this."

"You are most welcome."

"Will you be reigning in tonight's parade again, as in years past?"

"I will, thank you."

"That must be quite an honor for you."

"Oh, it is."

The reporter again looked around the room at all the incredibly detailed costumes. "I am amazed at the level of commitment everyone here obviously has to their costuming and preparations for tonight in general. Is it because of the large purse offered in the costume contest?"

"Actually, many of the best costumes are not even entered. It is simply a reflection of not only a desire to have fun tonight, but of a personal commitment to excellence in everything."

"You have to forgive me." The reporter reached his hand toward Sandy's face. "It looks so real!" Before Sandy could tell him not to touch the big hairy wart on the end of her nose, he did, and it slid right off and plopped in her lap.

Dolly shrieked just off camera.

"I am so sorry!" He bent over to pick it up.

Dolly shrieked again. "DON'T TOUCH IT!" She ran right in front of the camera. She, too, was made up as a witch. "I don't want your finger oils on it!" Dolly picked it up with her long black fingernails.

"Please accept my apologies, both of you. And my thanks for allowing us a behind the scenes look at Middleway's Halloween festivities. Now, back to you at the station."

The camera lights went off and Dolly shooed the reporter and the cameraman away and shoved Sandy back down in the chair. She plopped a protective eye cover over Sandy's upper face and went about gluing the big wart back on her nose. "Now don't you move a muscle for the next five minutes until this bond is set."

While she worked, the front door of the salon flew open. Cindy, still dressed in her dissheveled Princess costume, streaked in through the crowd of ghouls in black cloaks near the entrance. She cried hysterically as she fought her way around mummies half in and half out of bandage. In her red-stained dress, she blended right in.

She frantically fumbled over boxes and buckets and ran right past her mother before she disappeared through the back door into their house. Between the noise and the commotion, no one even noticed her.

A sudden burst of wind slammed a particular succession of doors closed, beginning with the salon front door and ending with the house door way in the back. BAM! BAM! BAM! BAM! BAM! Somehow through the blaring rock music and all the noise and commotion, Sandy heard the doors. BAM! BAM! BAM! BAM! BAM! She knew that that succession of slams could only happen if the doors in the back in her house were open. She pulled the protective eye cover from her face and sat up.

"You sit right back down," Dolly said. "You're not getting out of this chair until that glue dries. There is no possible way I'm going to do that wart one more time."

Sandy raised her left eyebrow at Dolly. "Who pays whom around here?"

Dolly's mouth crinkled.

"Did Cindy come home?"

"She might have. Something blew through here a few minutes ago."

"Let me out. Let me out."

Dolly stood back to let Sandy out of the chair. She walked through the salon to their house in the back, where she heard crying through Cindy's bedroom door. She knocked softly.

"Sweetie, can I come in?"

Cindy did not answer so Sandy pushed the door open. Inside, her bedroom was Teddy Bear Kingdom. Teddy bear wall paper covered the walls with teddy bear print curtains at the windows. Shelves every where were stuffed with every imaginable kind and color of teddy bear. At a small tea table near one of the windows, life-sized bears dressed in lace, enjoyed a mock tea party.

Sandy saw teddy bears scattered all over the floor. She also saw two pink ballet slippers sticking out from the bottom of a mountain of teddy bears on the bed. She picked up some bears off the bed to make room to sit down.

"Tell me what's wrong, Sweetie," she said.

Cindy cried and the pile of teddy bears on top of her all wiggled with her every sob.

"Tell me what happened, Honey."

Sandy gently removed one bear after another from off of Cindy until she could see her.

"Please tell me what's wrong so I can help you."

"No!"

"Sometimes it helps to talk about hurtful things to others. It helps the pain to go away."

"I don't wanna talk about it!"

"Was Eddie home?"

Cindy clammed up again.

"Did you give Eddie the cake?"

Still Cindy would not reply.

"You remember our agreement that we don't keep any secrets from each other? You know I don't keep any secrets from you." Sandy stroked Cindy's hair. "It makes me feel like you don't trust me when you won't tell me what's wrong."

"You'll just tell me to forgive and move on with my life."

"Is that what you should do? Forgive and move on?"

"NO!" Cindy rolled over.

Sandy gasped. Cindy looked pathetic—her hair wet, her makeup smudged and smeared across her face, her dress splotched and stained with frosting. "I'm so sorry."

Sandy could hardly bear the sight of her sweet daughter in such a state. She saw Cindy's lips struggle to speak. "You can say it."

"I, I don't wanna live anymore."

Sandy hugged Cindy. "Whatever it is, it's not so bad as that. It's not the end of your life."

Cindy looked up at her mother. "Eddie hates me!" She burst into uncontrollable sobbing. "And I even made the love potion cookies. We ate them together."

"You know, Sweetie, that we don't believe in forcing people to do anything against their will. Love potions can help if someone is already drawn that direction. I wondered what you were making the other day after you got home from school."

"I even delivered everything exactly at the Venus hour. Everytime!"

"I am so sorry you had to go through this. First loves are always the hardest to get over."

"He really, really hates me!"

"First loves are also the ones we grow from the most."

"I don't wanna grow from it. I just want him to like me."

"Sweetie, you know we can't force people to like us. We can only be the best that we can be and the rest is up to others. I have to go check on clients for just a minute, but when I come back I'm going to bring you a nice cup of your favorite, Dragon's Pearl Tea. And then we'll finish our talk. Okay?"

Cindy just looked at her mother.

"You don't need to answer. I'll be right back."

Sandy lovingly stroked the back of Cindy's head and stood up.

Cindy heard her bedroom door shut and she abruptly sat up with a vicious look in her eyes. She looked around the room and spied a Cinderella teddy bear on the bed right beside her, dressed just like her. She picked up the bear and threw it at her bedroom door as hard as she could. WHAM! It hit the door with a smack. It felt so good, she grabbed another bear. WHAM!—and threw it, too! She grabbed another bear, and another, and another – WHAM! WHAM! WHAM! She continued to hurl bears at the door one right after another until only one remained down on the floor right beside the bed. She leaned down and snatched it up—a little witch teddy bear. She looked at it, then hugged it tight.

"Cindy? Why are you blocking the door?" her mother said.

Cindy looked to the door. A mountain of teddy bears barricaded it closed. "It's not me."

"If it's not you, then who is blocking the door?"

"The bears."

"Be sure and remind all the bears that this is Halloween, and tell them the Grand High Witch has a very tight schedule and a very short fuse today. They basically have ten seconds to move their furry little heinies before this Dragon's Pearl Tea goes warm. You don't even want to think about what will happen if that occurs."

Cindy jumped from the bed and scrambled to move the huge pile of teddys.

"Do I hear the pitter patter of little paws?"

Cindy grasped the door knob and struggled to kick the last bears to the side.

Sandy greeted Cindy with a grin almost as big as the tea tray she held. "I have your favorite." She set an unusual dragon shaped tea tray down on Cindy's night stand and then sat down herself on the bed. "I think under the circumstances, the usual four pearls isn't enough. You could probably use a double."

Cindy just watched her mother.

"I thought so," Sandy said. She plucked eight small round white cookies from a dish on the tray and plopped them into a dragon-handled cup full of crimson-colored tea. She then handed it to Cindy on a black doily. "Drink this and you'll feel better."

"Mmm. How come these are so good?" Cindy said.

"I put a little truth serum in the batter today because today is special. It's Halloween."

"Truth serum? Is that the secret ingredient?"

"That's why they taste so good, but you can't use it all the time, or you build up a tolerance."

"What happens?"

"Then it won't work for you when you need it. But you know what that means? You have no choice now, but to tell me everything that happened."

Cindy half smiled and fished another dumpling from her cup.

"Whatever it is, Cindy, I know it hurts to talk about it, but believe me it helps to share it with someone who cares about you."

"Eddie..."

"Take your time."

"Eddie—he hates me." She again broke into a fit of tears.

"Oh Sweetie." Sandy put her arms around Cindy and squeezed her tight.

"He hates me! He hates me! He hates me!"

"How do you know he hates you?"

"He killed all the bears."

"What do you mean he killed the bears?"

"I can't talk about it. It hurts too much."

"As human beings we have to respect others' feelings and opinions."

"He doesn't respect my feelings. Why should I respect his?"

"Because it's the right thing to do. You know full well that two wrongs don't make a right. Try to put him out of your mind."

"I can't."

"I know it's difficult."

"It just hurts so much."

"At some point in time Eddie will know how he hurt you and how he made you feel. And he will feel sorry for it."

"I don't care about some point in time. I want him to feel bad now!"

"Karma is very real and it is fair. The universe truly is balanced. It may not be until the next world, but no one ever escapes the consequences of their actions. No one can hide from any mean thing that they do. Just know that."

"But I love him so much."

"Eddie is not the only fish in the sea. What about that little blond Durban boy – Tad I think is his name. He'd make a cute boy friend."

"He's mean to me." Cindy sniffled. "He's the one who always ruins my clothes."

"Sounds like your father."

"I don't want him."

"What do you want?"

A Cheshire cat grin spread across Cindy's face and her eyes sparkled with a devilish gleam. "REVENGE."

Sandy stared at Cindy. Cindy stared back and her big grin slowly faded.

"You know how I feel about revenge," Sandy said.

Cindy ever so slowly nodded her head up and down. "If you're gonna do it . . ."

"Do it right! There is nothing more satisfying than the feeling that comes from revenge when it's done right."

"I can't wait to see Eddie squirm."

"The feeling of peace that comes when you've taken a distasteful situation and turned it around to a pleasant one." Sandy noticed the look in Cindy's eyes and realized what her daughter was thinking. "Cindy. The ONLY way to do revenge is to 'Do It Right.' And you know what I mean."

"But Mom!"

"But nothing."

"It isn't fair!"

"This isn't about fair. This is about doing the right thing. We've certainly had this talk before. You know full well that two wrongs do not make a right. The ONLY way to set a wrong aright, is to do them better."

"But he deserves it!"

"But nothing! The only way to handle a situation like this where someone has hurt you is to kill 'em with kindess even when, or especially when they don't deserve it. Then their own guilt will eat them from the inside out, and they have to deal with their bad behavior themselves."

Cindy looked at her mother coldly.

"Cindy. You have to trust me. A nasty act aimed back at a nasty act only brings you down to their level. Now, I have an idea that will help perk you up. But we need to hurry." Sandy pulled Cindy up off the bed and out the bedroom door.

CHAPTER ELEVEN

A wailing siren at the far end of Main Street signaled the beginning of the parade and all the Halloween festivities in Middleway.

Eddie and Tad stood curbside amidst crowds of anxious costumed children lining the avenue. Eddie was now dressed as a frog in a full-length green sweat suit, with ping pong balls sewn on top of the hood for eyeballs. This was his mother's best attempt for a new last minute costume change. Tad was again decked out as a pirate.

A police car with flashing lights passed followed by the flag bearers.

Two rows of men in hooded black robes with ghoulish skeleton faces marched solemnly by. Just behind them, a burly executioner with his axe in one hand, lead an ox drawn tumbrel cart with the other. Riding in the cart in the premier position of the entire parade, the Grand High Witch threw whole candy bars to screaming and scowering children.

"OVER HERE!" Tad yelled as loud as he could. He wanted to draw her attention away from the other side of the street.

She turned around and looked right at Tad.

"AAAAH! IT'S HER!"

It was Cindy dressed as a witch. With a fist full of candy ready to throw in one hand, she quickly raised her other hand to her mouth and with a sweet smile blew a kiss instead.

"DUCK!" He dropped to his knees to avoid the in-coming kiss. Cindy threw the candy off in the other direction.

"What a witch! She could have thrown it to us."

"Tad. There's more candy," Eddie said.

"But nobody else throws whole candy bars. I'll get her for that. Come on, we've got work to do."

"I'm not going up in the tree."

"Fine! I'll do it myself. Somebody's got to."

Tad bullied his way through the crowd and shimmied up one of the large maple trees that lined the street and disappeared into the leaves.

The elegant Miss Middleway and her beautiful Glory of Autumn float approached. The blond beauty shimmered in a sequined orange dress and held a bouquet of orange roses in her white-gloved hands. She gracefully led with the wrist as she waved to adoring crowds.

The parade goers began to clap when Miss Middleway suddenly winced, and then winced again. She threw her arm across her face as if shielding herself from some sort of attack. Something splatted right above her eyebrow and her black mascara ran all down her cheek. She dropped her roses, then swatted and thrashed both arms in front of her face.

Eddie's face, already green with frog makeup, turned even more green while he watched. Little kids and adults alike, pointed and laughed as if it was all part of the show.

"SHE'S UNDER ATTACK!" a woman's voice shouted out of the crowd.

Everyone looked all around to find the source or the perpetrator. The offensive instantly ceased. The float moved on with a crying Miss Middleway trying her best to compose herself.

Eddie did not dare look up into the maple tree above for fear that he might implicate himself in the dastardly plot. No one else looked up into the tree either.

The mayor's slimey green sea monster float entitled "Reach Out And Touch Someone" passed without incident so no one thought further on the events of a few minutes before.

Ghoulies, monsters and madmen next filled the street just ahead of a fantastical haunted castle float. The monsters all threw candy everywhere and children scattered in search of every last piece. The Middleway High School Drill Team and Marching Band followed, dressed appropriately in orange and black uniforms.

The drill team girls marched by in a complex routine of interweaving. One girl flinched violently, breaking their otherwise perfect rhythm. Another girl jerked her leg to the side and broke right out of formation to reach down and scratch. Yet another and another flinched and jerked in quirky, spastic maneuvers that belied their many weeks of practice.

The crowd loved the show. Everyone laughed and clapped at the unexpected routines, unaware of what the circumstances really were.

Eddie, too, could not help but laugh at how ridiculous the girls looked. He finally, though, could not bear to watch any more. He turned from the scene and slowly walked away toward town hall where he sat on the side steps and waited for Tad to show up when the parade was over.

"Hey! You deserted me back there," Tad said. "What kind of a friend are you?"

"The only friend you've got. What's gonna happen if they find out who attacked Miss Middleway and the marching girls? We already can't go into the Haunted House because of what you did last year."

"Just how are they going to find out?"

"They've got ways."

"Did you see the look in Miss Middleway's face when all that grape slime hit her? It was so awesome."

"You're lucky they couldn't see you."

"I know what I'm doing."

"You could've been arrested as a domestic terrorist."

Tad laughed right out loud.

"It's not funny, Tad!"

"Arrested for peeling some grapes? Yeah, right. And those stupid marching girls, they didn't even know what hit 'em."

"Shooting all those wheat kernels at 'em was dangerous."

"And the best part of all was them spazzing out right in front of the T.V. camera. The dumb cameraman set up right under the tree."

"What if one of the girls fell and got hurt?"

"Then it would be her fault. They should give 'em training under fire practice."

"You need to lighten up and stop hurting people."

"You need to lighten up so we can have some fun. Come on. LET'S PARTY!"

The entire town and more celebrated at an old-fashioned Halloween carnival complete with a midway of rides. Town Hall had long since been converted into a carnival hall. It had even been officially renamed Halloween Hall.

Eddie and Tad headed straight for their favorite part of the carnival, the Rub A Dub Pub—a delightfully ghoulish place where children and adults alike celebrated the happy side of Halloween.

"Who had the Death Warmed Over?" A buxom zombie waitress approached Eddie's and Tad's table with a large serving tray full of weird-looking food balanced high up on her shoulder. "Oh! Wrong table. But don't go away, gentlemen. I'll be right back to take your orders." She turned around to the table right behind them.

The boys observed as she served the people at the next table.

"And the two orders of Gall Bladder Parmigiana with Petite Kidney Stones? That leaves the Fist Kabobs Flambe for you."

"That's what I want" Tad said.

The waitress struck a match and lit a pan with two hands skewered between large pearl onions. Eddie and Tad excitedly watched the flaming hands curl up around the onions.

A zombie-faced waiter walked past with a large tray of mugs.

"Excuse me!" Eddie said.

"Yes?" He stopped.

"Could we move to the smoking section, please?"

"Didn't they tell you? We had a power surge and it blew out all our smoke machines. I'm really sorry. I know how much the smoke adds to the dining experience."

"What's that over there?" Eddie pointed to a plume of smoke floating across the far side of the restaurant.

"That's just coming from the grills in the back. They're blowing it into the restaurant to make up for the machines being broken."

"Bummer."

"Either of you boys care for a beer on the house? Has a really nice head on it?"

Tad sat tall in his chair. "I'll have a beer."

The waiter plopped a mug of apple beer right in front of Tad. He fidgeted and wiggled with glee at the sight of a shrunken head afloat on top.

"Could I have a Bloody Mary instead?" Eddie said.

"MARY! OVER HERE!"

Another zombie waitress with big poofy black hair wheeled over to Eddie dragging a metal hospital cart that supported a huge I.V. drip bag. She handed Eddie a martini glass from the bottom of the cart, then held a catheter tube up to the glass. Red fruit punch gushed down and out the catheter.

"Olive?"

"No thanks. I like it straight."

Eddie and Tad took in the sights of their favorite place in the whole world. On a small decorative stage life-size marionette skeletons, the Skeletonettes, dressed in big plumed hats and full skirts, kicked their boney legs high in the air while they danced a lively can

can. They swished their skirts for all the excited patrons and flashed lots of pelvic bone.

A skeleton piano player in Gay Nineties attire accompanied them, while a squirrel skeleton did a cane-and-hat routine on top of the piano. A ghoulish array of monsters sat at the old fashioned cherry wood bar.

The first waitress returned to take their orders. "Sorry for the wait, gentlemen. Tonight's special is Fist Kabobs."

"I'll have those," Tad said.

"It comes with your choice of either cream of cockroach soup or a haunted house salad with assorted cemetery greens."

"Soup."

She turned to Eddie. "And you, sir?"

"Do you still have Dead Man's Spaghetti?"

"Always! It's one of the house specialties. It comes with either a blood red sauce or a creamy white sauce made with fresh pus."

"Does it have meat in it?"

"Meat and the noodles are the same thing—worms."

"That's what I'll have, with red sauce."

"Soup or salad?"

"Salad."

"Dressing?"

"Bile and vinegar."

"Thank you very much. Enjoy your drinks. Dinner won't be long."

No sooner did she walk off than yet another zombie faced waitress rolled a dessert cart up to their table.

"I'm not trying to rush your dinner. Just so you'll know whether or not you want to leave room for one of our Halloween desserts."

The boys gazed with delight at all the fiendish confections on the cart.

"Tonight we have Mississippi Mud Pie—mud flown in fresh this morning, Baked Road Apples, Lady Fingers, Gentleman Toes, Blood Pudding, and last but not least Mouse au chocolat. Take your time. I'll be back and you can name your poison then."

Eddie could not help but think about how much Brian loved the Rub A Dub Pub. He especially loved Bloody Mary. She was his favorite. It was almost like the whole town was celebrating their birthday with the carnival and the parade.

When they were younger, Brian and Eddie rode in the parade

almost every year dressed as pumpkins or ghosts or some other cute thing. Because they were born on Halloween, the town showered them with gifts as babies. The woman who designed the mayor's float always asked them to ride with him, but then the mayor changed and they were never asked again.

Eddie and Brian used to talk about how great it would be when they became old enough to ride in the Coffin Patrol. The local Shriners all dressed as monsters and mummies and buzzed up and down the parade route in little motorized coffin cars.

Eddie recalled how out of everything in the parade last year, Brian's most favorite part was when the marching girl stepped right into the horse doo.

Even though everything was still fun, it was all different this year, without Brian to share it with him. Eddie wondered if he could really reach Brian later tonight. He wondered whether Brian would really know about the bonfires or any of the the ancient traditions. Would somebody on the other side tell him to go to the bonfires?

The Rub A Dub Pub opened right onto the rest of the hall, set up with a full compliment of carnival booths. Eddie glanced over and saw his mother dressed as the Queen of Egypt in all her regal beauty reigning over the carnival Cake Walk. With her beautiful painted eyes and glimmering jeweled costume, she drew more attention than all the cakes displayed across two banquet tables.

She had one official helper, who removed a chair each time she stopped the music. Thematically, Mrs. McCourt was very disappointed. Melissa was scheduled to help her dressed as an Egyptian maiden, but then her cousins came and Melissa went off to play. She was left to settle for a scarecrow as a helper.

An odd assortment of children in an even odder assortment of costumes circled around a cluster of chairs while the bouncy song "DON'T GO OUT OF THE HOUSE AT NIGHT" played over and over. Two familiar faces among the children vied for the coveted cakes, Elliot Carnegie in his Dracula costume and Cindy Crystal dressed as a cute witch. The children fought like demons to each get a chair every time the music stopped.

In the dunking booth next door, Doctor McCourt looked funny sitting high up in a steel dunking contraption dressed only in a Pharaoh skirt, to hide his swimsuit, and an Egyptian head piece. He dodged stray bean bags and prayed for people to miss the target.

A young couple dressed as Raggedy Ann and Raggedy Andy stopped at the booth. Andy threw the bean bag. WHAM! It hit the back of the booth, barely missing the dunk target. Doctor McCourt knew he was in trouble. WHAM! The young man threw again.

"I know you," Doctor McCourt said. "You're pitcher on the —"

WHAMMM! SPLASH! The Pharaoh fell into the River Nile.

He raised his head out of the water. "Baseball team."

"Raggedy Andy and Ann enjoyed a good laugh."

A painfully skinny woman in a ridiculous carrot costume strutted toward the dunking booth. Doctor McCourt started to climb up out of the tank and saw her. Her hooked nose extended forward like the beak of a toucan. Dressed head to her pointy carrot shoe toes in orange, even her Leaning Tower of Pisa hairdo swirled high above her head, was henna colored, topped with green ostrich plume feathers. Doctor McCourt was even shocked by how stupid his sister looked in her costume.

He sank back down into the water and held perfectly still. She passed straight on to the Cake Walk.

"Elizabeth," she said. "It was so gracious of you to invite us up again this year."

Mrs. McCourt just allowed Lois to talk.

"And I knew you wouldn't mind if I brought a few extra girls along. You have such a big house."

She smiled at Lois, her special smile that she reserved for Lois alone—a gritted-teeth, "I will smile at you because you are my relative" smile. Lois saw her warmth and smiled back.

"It's so unfortunate," Lois said, "that every town does not provide their young people with such wholesome entertainment as this on Halloween."

Mrs. McCourt studied how absurd Lois looked with her earrings and necklaces made of real withered carrots and her carrot-shaped hair style with feather plumes stuck in the top. "That's an interesting costume, Lois. Did you make it yourself?"

"Yes, I did. I call it Carrot Souffle. The carrot is such a practical vegetable, don't you think?"

"I do. Practical...ly a vegetable. Lois, have you ever heard of anyone in the family named Uncle Louie?"

"No."

"Maybe someone who died a long time ago."

"My father had a younger brother, Louis. But I don't know of any Uncle Louie."

"What happened to him?"

"He drowned in a canal or something when he was only four."

A look of both satisfaction and intrigue struck Mrs. McCourt. "Technically, he would be Uncle Louie if he were still alive."

"I suppose. Why do you ask? Why would you ask about him? No one has asked about him for years."

"No reason."

"Come to think of it, no one has ever asked about him. I want to know why. You tell me right now! I insist."

They both stared at each other without a word.

"You know you're always welcome in your brother's house," Mrs McCourt said with her special Lois smile.

Lois squinted her eyes and coquettishly tilted her head to the side. The already leaning tower of hair and feathers atop her head toppled over.

"Oh! Ooooh!!" Lois reached up to catch her hair. "I'd best go fix my fallen souffle." She walked spastically away with her hands held high up on her hairdo.

Miss Pleasant, dressed as Raggedy Ann, approached and passed the scuttling sour-faced carrot. She stared at Lois and her ridiculous costume and her even more ridiculous posture. She finally turned to Mrs. McCourt. "What was that?"

"A practical vegetable."

They looked at each other and giggled.

"Don't you look queenly," Miss Pleasant said.

"You're kind of cute yourself, Annie. Where is Andy?"

"Oh, he's around here somewhere, I suppose. I've been secretly drooling over your cakes all night long. I can't imagine all the time and trouble you went to. Everyone of them is a work of art."

Mrs. McCourt's demeanor suddenly darkened. "I slaved like a dog for days to make these cakes, and that little witch there has won every single one of them."

Miss Pleasant looked again to the table with disbelief. All but one of the cakes had a little flag stuck in it with the initials "C.C." written on it. "She won all those?"

"The little witch won't leave. What kind of a mother lets her little girl bring home twenty cakes? Who is she?"

"That little girl is Cindy Crystal."

Mrs. McCourt looked seethingly at Cindy just as the line of the song "ON HALLOWEEN YOUR WORSTEST DREAM BECOMES REALITY" played. She heard the words and moaned. This was her worst nightmare. She sent fire darts from her eyes straight at Cindy, who fought with two other remaining children for the one last cake. No way would she allow Cindy to win this one. She stopped the music abruptly. Cindy threw herself right at one of the two chairs. Her sheer weight knocked the skinny little girl dressed as a bright blue alien off the chair and onto the floor with a thud. Cindy glowered gluttonously and the little girl in blue bawled her eyes out. One more chair was pulled away.

Mrs. McCourt started the music again. Dracula and the witch, Elliot and Cindy, were the only two children left. They circled the last chair like two vultures waiting for their prey to die. The music stopped. Again Cindy threw herself at the chair with all her might, knocking Elliot right to the floor. It showed in her face that she thought she had won, but the music started again. Elliot squeeled with delight and jumped back up.

Again the vultures circled, both dragging their hands across and along the edges of the chair as they moved around it. Elliot passed over the chair and the music stopped. He plopped straight down right onto the seat.

Once again, Cindy hurled herself like a battering ram right at Elliot, pushing him off. He landed in a heap on the floor. Cindy grabbed both sides of the chair seat and held on as tight as she could. But Elliot hopped back onto his feet. He held his head high in the air and bared his Dracula fangs. With a loud hiss, he dropped down and bit Cindy in the leg. She screamed and jumped off the chair. Elliot leaped up onto the chair seat and with his arms in the air, did a victory dance. Cindy jumped up and down on one leg cringing in pain. Mrs. McCourt rushed over to Elliott with a congratulatory ghost cake and kissed him over and over.

Miss Pleasant chuckled to herself and walked away. Just then the young man dressed as Raggedy Andy stepped up behind her and grabbed her by the wrist. "Ann, come on. I've been looking all over for you."

Miss Pleasant turned around to see who had taken hold of her hand. She took one look at Raggedy Andy and fainted flat to the floor.

The Magic Hour

The young man scrambled to catch her and managed to save her head from slamming against the concrete.

"Help! GET A DOCTOR!"

"SPLASH!" Doctor McCourt fell into the tank yet another time.

"HELP! WE NEED A DOCTOR!"

Doctor McCourt heard and scrambled to climb out of the water. He grabbed his black bag sitting behind the booth and ran over dripping all the way. He pushed through the gathered crowd and saw Miss Pleasant face up on the floor.

"What happened?"

" I just took a hold of her hand by mistake and she passed out."

"Did she hit her head?"

"No. I was able to catch her."

"Margaret?"

She was out cold. Doctor McCourt dug smelling salts out of his black bag and waved them under her nose. She started to come to.

"Margaret?"

"Oh. Dear me!" She saw Doctor McCourt and struggled to sit up.

"Just lie still a minute until you get your bearings."

Her eye makeup began to smear down her face from the water dripped on her by Doctor McCourt. She wiped her face and smeared her makeup even more.

She looked at the young man dressed as Raggedy Andy and his Raggedy Ann standing beside him. Their costumes looked just like hers.

"Gee, lady. I'm really sorry," the young man said. "I didn't mean to scare you like that. I just saw the red hair and thought you were somebody else."

"That's quite all right, son. I can certainly see how you could make the mistake. It could happen to anyone."

Doctor McCourt helped her to her feet, but she was obviously still dizzy and shaken from her fall.

"Let me take you home, Margaret."

"I'll be fine."

"I think maybe you've had enough merry-making for one night."

"If you'll just help me over to that table there, I'll rest a bit and then make my way home. I just live a block away. A walk in the night air will help me clear my head. I'm very sorry for all the bother."

"Margaret, it's no bother."

Doctor McCourt helped her over to the closest table at the edge of the Pub.

"Rest a bit, and call me over if you need anything. I'll just be right over there."

"Thank you."

No sooner did Doctor McCourt walk off than Bloody Mary wheeled up with her metal cart and her I.V. blood bag.

"Oh, Honey. I can see right through your makeup that you don't feel well. You're all pale—like you just saw a ghost or something."

Miss Pleasant looked up at Mary's frightful face. She gasped. Normally good-natured, right now she was not amused by all the fiendish fun.

"Ma'am. Are you all right?" Mary's hand suddenly went up to her face. Kerchew! She sneezed. KERPLOP! A big blob of slime from one side of Mary's face SPLATTED right onto Miss Pleasant's shoulder and oozed down. She almost passed out again.

"Oh, Ma'am. I am so sorry!"

Kids all around laughed and pointed at her.

"I know just the thing." Mary wiped up Miss Pleasant. "You just sit here and I'll be right back." She stepped over and whispered to the bar tender, a smiling ghoulish faced man with frizzy hair. He poured clear bubbly fluid into a tall glass, then reached into a large candy bottle and pulled out a green gummy frog. He plopped the frog into the glass and FWOOM, lit the drink on fire with a lighter.

"One Hot Toady, Ma'am. Ma'am?"

Bloody Mary turned to find Miss Pleasant, who was nowhere to be seen.

Outside Halloween Hall eerie organ music wafted out over Main Street and filled the town square with spooky sounds. The entire town put on their Halloween alter egos for this one night. Even the church organist, Mrs. Waverly, dressed as the Phantom and played like she never did in church. This was the only time of the whole year when the pastor allowed her to play that kind of music on the church organ.

Eddie stopped to admire the prize-winning jack-o-lanterns. "Wow! Look at these!"

Tad walked up from behind. "There's nobody looking right now. Should I smash all three top winners or just number one?"

"NONE! Just knock it off! You need to let go of this mean streak that's gotten into you."

"You're starting to sound like my mother."

"Maybe you should listen to her."

They next stopped at the CREAMATORIUM ice cream stand where Halloween carolers right out of Dicken's England, serenaded with "God Rest Ye Scary Gentlemen."

"Two waffle cones with toe jam topping please," Eddie said.

"How many toes?"

"Three each, please."

The boys watched with big eyes while two waffle cones were filled with soft ice cream and then were jammed with cookies that looked like big toes. They walked past the Halloweenery hot dog stand with their treats and neared the entrance to the Haunted House where a large banner asked: "Do You Dare Cross The Deadline?"

One of the Torture Masters from The Dungeon in the Haunted House stood by the door and taunted potential patrons. With a studded black leather hood over his head and a large stature, he appeared quite intimidating. He noticed Tad and Eddie.

"Hey kids. What's the matter? You too afraid to cross The Deadline and come into the Haunted House?"

"You guys are all a bunch of whimps!" Tad said. "Last time I came through there, you all screamed like a bunch of babies."

The Torture Master stared at Tad a moment. "Oh! I know who you are. You're the little monster who came through here last year with the mace gun."

"Now you all have a security check to frisk everybody because you're so afraid."

"Don't think for a minute, kid. They banned you to protect the people in the haunted house. They banned you for your own protection, because you're such a whimp."

"You guys can't even take a joke. It was hilarious. The monsters did the best screams I've ever heard."

"I'll tell you something funny. You come anywhere near the inside and I guarantee you the blood will be real—yours. Laugh at that one punk, until your stupid little skull hurts."

"I'm not afraid of you."

"You'd better be!"

"Tad! Come on!" Eddie grabbed Tad's jacket and tugged.

"He's not kidding!"

"Listen to your friend and get lost!"

Eddie pulled Tad away, fuming. They walked over and sat down on the steps of carnival hall to finish their melting ice cream cones.

"Sometime Tad, you're gonna get into real trouble if you don't start being nice to people."

"You're really starting to sound like my mother."

"Why are you so mean anyway?"

Tad slurped his ice cream and completely ignored Eddie's question. "What do you wanna do next?"

"Go to the Witches' Sabbath."

"You kidding?" Tad turned to Eddie with a scowl. "You didn't fall for Cindy's crystal ball stuff did you?"

"But what if it's true?"

"There's a sucker born every minute."

"Why do you hate Cindy so much, anyway? It's possible she knows some things you don't."

"Oh. I get it. You're still worried about the teddy bears? Guilt never did anybody any good. You had to kill 'em. If you hadn't, Cindy'd be buggin' ya all night and the rest of your whole life. Trust me on this."

Some kind of commotion was stirring inside the building behind them and both turned to look. They were surprised to see a determined Cindy stomping toward the door of the building with a large cake in her hands. She barked at some little kids to get the blankety blank out of her way.

An idea struck Tad. "Hey, watch this." He jumped over and hid beside the doorway, then stuck out his foot just before Cindy exited the building. She tripped on his extended leg and flew forward out over the steps, landing face first right in the cake. She slid along the pavement on the frosting and came to a halt as she rammed into a large landscape rock. WHONK! Her glasses went flying. She laid there perfectly still. Eddie stood stiff and motionless. Tad laughed and broke the tension. Eddie ran to Cindy and knelt down beside her.

"Cindy! Are you all right?" She did not respond. He shook her harder and harder. "Cindy! CINDY WAKE UP!"

She finally moved a little and started to cry. Eddie helped her to slowly sit up and a single trickle of blood dripped down from her forehead through thick globs of cake stuck beside her nose. Tad laughed

The Magic Hour

all the more at the hideous sight of her face.

"Ha, ha, ha, ha, ha. Look at her! That's the best she has ever looked in her whole life! Ha, ha, ha, ha, ha." He laughed so hard he nearly fell over.

The harder he laughed the worse he made Cindy feel. She started to sob.

Eddie picked up Cindy's glasses and looked furiously at Tad. "You are a creep!"

"What are you worrying about flea bag Cindy for? You must really be in love with her."

"You're the flea bag. You can go sleep out by yourself. You're not my friend. You're not anybody's friend, because you don't have any friends. You're just mean."

"I knew you loved her all along."

Tad walked away laughing but suddenly turned back and threw something through the air at Eddie. "You can have your cheap walkie-talkie back so you and lover girl can talk in the night. Ha! Ha! Ha!"

Eddie jumped to catch it but missed. Luckily, it hit on the grass before it rolled over onto the pavement. He turned to Cindy with a worried look. "Are you all right?"

"I think so. That was really really weird."

"What was?"

"When I hit my head. All of the sudden I was looking down from all the way up there." Cindy pointed up to the bell tower high above them. "It was almost like I was sitting up there, but I really was just floating in the air."

"That is weird."

"I saw you down here trying to wake somebody. Then I realized it was me. But you couldn't wake me because I wasn't there, because I was up at the tower. But then, when you shook me really hard, it was like I was sucked up by a vacuum back down here into my body."

"That is really weird."

"It was a icky feeling. Kind of like after your leg goes to sleep but when it's waking up." Cindy stared into Eddie's eyes. "I think you saved my life, Eddie."

He took a deep breath.

A big blob of green frosting fell from her brow right above her right eye and plopped down. Eddie wiped another black blob from above her other eye.

"Was that a Frankenstein cake?"
"Uh huh."
"My mom made it."
"I know."
"It was really for my birthday cake."
"I was gonna shove it in your face. I was so angry with you, but I feel different now after that experience. I don't want revenge anymore. And I'm really sorry that I didn't throw you any candy at the parade. I was just being mean."
"It's okay."
"You should come with me to the Witches' Sabbath."
"Do you really think I'll get to see Brian?"
"There's a really good chance because of The Bonfires. It's worth a try."
"My mom will kill me if she ever finds out I went."
"She'll just think you slept out over at Tad's. It's the perfect cover."
"What do you do at a Witches' Sabbath?"
"Sing and dance and stuff, but mostly we just party all night."
"I've never partied all night before."
"It's really fun. You'll love it!"

Cindy looked at the frosting smashed across the front of her costume. "I'm sure glad your mom doesn't use grease frosting like everybody else, otherwise my costume would be ruined. You wait here a minute while I go inside and clean up. Then we'll go."

CHAPTER TWELVE

The bright lights and the exuberant sounds of the carnival dimmed and waned as the two of them walked off down a dark street lined with tall trees. They both held flashlights toward the uneven sidewalk and took particular care not to trip or stub a toe.

A black cat suddenly darted right in front of their legs, then stopped and stared at them. Entranced with its glowing ember eyes, Eddie and Cindy both stared back for an uncomfortably long moment. Just as suddenly, the cat disappeared into the shadows leaving Eddie uneasy.

"Black cats are bad luck!" he said.

"Black cats are good luck tonight! Did you see those eyes? He was trying to say something."

"How can you tell?"

"Animals know things and can see things. They can see right through the veil between this world and the next, because there is no need for their eyes and understanding to be blocked. The fact that he looked right at us so long, means good things are gonna happen."

"You think so?"

"I know so. That was a really good sign. You know, I was gonna tell about black cats in class, but Miss Pleasant wouldn't let me finish. I was gonna tell about a lot of things."

Eddie paused briefly. "Have you ever heard the story about the Erlking?"

"Shhhhhhh! Don't even say his name!" Cindy paused to take a breath, then turned and looked straight at Eddie. "I don't know how to tell you this except to say it."

Worry swept across Eddie's brow.

"The shortest route to Witches' Sabbath is right through the graveyard."

Eddie hesitated. He also wondered why she did not answer his question. "Do you think it's safe to go into the cemetery at night?"

"My mom says you should never be afraid of spirits, because they're just people like us who've already passed on."

"What do spirits look like?"

Cindy shuddered. "They're really ugly with boney faces and hands."

"Brian didn't look like that!"

"Maybe he hadn't been dead long enough yet."

"I don't think Brian'll ever look like that."

"But there's another reason we need to go through the cemetery, anyway."

"What for?"

"Tonight of all nights, we have to do everything we can to let Brian know we're trying to reach him. We need to go stop at his grave before we go on to The Bonfires."

Eddie began to wonder about their safety. He remembered that his walkie-talkies were tucked in his pockets and pulled them out. "Here. Take this." He handed one to Cindy. "Just in case we need 'em." He showed her which button to push in order to speak.

"Come in Eddie, this is Cindy."

"This is Eddie. We're almost at the cemetery."

"Oh, good. What's this for?" She pushed a bright red button on her walkie talkie.

"Aaaaaaaah." A high pitched squeal rang right in Eddie's ear. He yanked his walkie-talkie down. "It's the search button! In case you lose one of 'em."

"Oh. I know what search buttons are for."

Right in front of them loomed the dark stone columns that marked the entrance to the old town cemetery. Without a word, they both stopped and silently looked into the dark through the open gates.

"Eddie, do you know anything about the phases of the moon?" Cindy said.

"I know what they are."

"Tonight's Halloween moon is New, which is very good. The New Moon means that the coming year will be full of new beginnings and new experiences, but the New Moon can be very dangerous. DO NOT look at your moon shadow for any reason. It'll bring very bad luck, not just for tonight, but for the next twelve months."

"How come?"

"Tonight is the last night of the ancient Celtic calendar. So whatever happens tonight, sets the tone for the whole next year."

"Eeeek."

"Basically, don't look back. Another reason to not look back is if we hear footsteps behind us tonight at any time. DO NOT look back to see who is there. Not on All Hallow's Eve. I say these things to warn you and to keep you safe."

The bouncy music of "Monster Mash" from the carnival in the distance became audible in the quiet. Those happy sounds lightened their spirits and after a few moments they walked on.

They passed through the gates and Eddie secretly crossed himself.

"You're not Catholic!" Cindy said.

"I know. Catholics just invented it, but anyone can use it. You should always cross yourself before you go anywhere there's dead people."

Cindy was intrigued. "I've never heard that before."

"You'd better do it just in case we need any extra protection."

With a shrug, Cindy made the sign of the cross over her chest as well.

The cemetery was quiet. Deathly quiet. The carnival music which they heard only seconds ago, was now completely gone. Their every footstep echoed and yet at the same time the sound somehow became swallowed by the night. They cautiously placed one foot in front of the other and proceeded by the light of their flashlights.

They made their way around a curve in the main cemetery road when a dim flickering light ahead of them came into view. A single tombstone faintly glowed against the blackness. They both breathed shallowly but continued on when Cindy gasped with excitement.

"Awesome!" She broke into a run toward the glowing grave marker. "Come on, Eddie. It's okay!"

Eddie hustled to catch up.

Cindy stopped beside a burning jack-o-lantern set just in front of an old grave marker. "I've heard about this!"

The name on the tombstone read:

"B. A. WARE."

"She was a really famous witch," Cindy said. "I think she was best friends with my great great grandma. I'll have to ask my mom, but I think she was Middleway's first lady mayor."

"Was that her real name?"

"Beatrice Alexandra Ware. This is very good—someone is keeping a vigil over her grave. This gives me even more confidence."

"What's a vigil?"

"Kind of what we're doing—sending out energy to reach someone on the other side. We'd better keep going."

Eddie quietly took it all in.

He and Cindy pressed deeper into the cemetery. The towering black pines overhead obscured even the starlight above.

WHOOSH! Something ghostly whizzed past right in front of them.

"Aaaaaaaaah!" Something brushed against Cindy's face.

WHOOSH! WHOOSH!! More ghostly figures flew past them so fast they could not even see what they were.

"Aaaaaaaaah!" Eddie screamed as well.

A deafening evil laugh echoed out through the dark. They both stood frozen in their tracks.

"HA, HA, HA, HA, HA, HA, HA, HA, HA!" The laugh continued on and Eddie suddenly recognized the voice!

"G-R-O-V-E-R!"

KATHUNK! A slim black figure dropped from the trees and landed right in front of Cindy. She screamed and fell backward.

"You dirtball!" Eddie helped Cindy up.

"I'm just protecting the cemetery from kids like you who get bored with the carnival. Most kids are long gone by now. What's you guys' problem?"

"I see the medicine must be working?" Eddie said.

"Last night I slept like a baby—thank you very much. Back in full form tonight."

"What were those?"

"Ghosts."

"You don't believe in ghosts."

"I made 'em."

Ghostly shapes made of sheets dropped from the trees all around them and dangled in the air. Again Eddie and Cindy were startled.

"Pretty cool, huh?" Grover oogled over Cindy while shining a heavy duty flashlight beam up and down her. He held it right in her face. She turned to Eddie in dismay.

"Who is he?"

"Grover —"

"The G-R-A-V-E-D-I-G-G-E-R."

Cindy glowered at him. "You could have scared us to death!"
"Perfect place for it, don't you think?"
Cindy sneered at him.
"This your ghoul friend?"
Eddie did not answer.
"Get it? Ghoul friend." Grover laughed and laughed at his own joke. "So, is she? Your girl friend?"
Cindy looked at Eddie and anxiously waited for his reply. He took a deep breath. He knew no matter what he said there would be trouble.
"A friend," he said.
Cindy took his arm and pulled him along. "Come on, Eddie. We were just passing through." They walked away, but suddenly, Grover was right beside Cindy, walking in step with her.
"You gotta protect me!" she whispered into Eddie's ear, then gripped his arm even tighter.
"No one can protect you from the crazy lady!" Grover said.
Cindy pretended not to hear him. But after a few paces, Eddie could stand it no longer.
"Is she here tonight?"
"The crazy lady a-l-w-a-y-s comes at night."
Grover pelted the night yet again with his evil laugh. Eddie and Cindy stopped dead in their tracks.
"Who is the crazy lady?" Cindy said.
Grover's eyes appeared right in front of them, opened wide like a mad man. "The living d-e-a-d!"
Before Cindy could even scream, Grover was gone. She took Eddie's arm tighter still and the two of them walked on in silence.
Somehow the night seemed a little darker than it was just a few minutes before.
"Before you said not to be afraid of dead people," Eddie said.
"That's real dead people. Not the living dead!"
Neither uttered another word until at last their flashlight beams illuminated the McCourt family plot. They stepped past the old tombstones in the front to Brian's new monument in the back. Cindy's flashlight beam strayed off to the side and lit up another gravemarker that was identical to Brian's.
"Is this you?"
"My grandpa gave it to me for Christmas."
"What a neat present. What a neat grandpa!"

Eddie was too surprised at her response to reply.

"We'd better hurry. It's getting late. You lie down there on Brian's grave and I'll read the rune I wrote. That way the spirits will know we're trying to reach 'em."

"What's a rune?"

"A magical poem. Now turn off your flashlight and put your head right up next to the tombstone so you can feel any vibrations."

Eddie laid down on the grass while Cindy fumbled to pull something from her satchel. "I wrote this special just for us to use here tonight."

"You knew we were coming here?"

"I hoped so. Now, be real quiet."

Cindy held her light on a small heavily creased piece of paper, raised her head to the sky and began.

"New moon, true moon
On this hallowed night,
Shine down and help us commune
And with Brian reunite."

They waited in silence—silence—silence. Finally Cindy broke the stillness.

"Did you hear anything?"

"No."

"Did you feel anything?"

"Hut uh."

"It doesn't always work because you can't always get through. Spirits have just as much trouble reaching us as we do them. I'm gonna read the second verse, but really concentrate hard so they can feel our energy."

"Okay."

Cindy stood tall and this time threw her voice to the night as though she owned it.

"NEW MOON, TRUE MOON
SEND TO OUR WORLD BELOW
IN LANGUAGE WE CAN UNDERSTAND,
A WORD FROM SOMEONE WE BOTH KNOW."

A feeble voice racked with pain called out from the grave.

"Cin-nnn-n-nn-dyyy."

Every muscle in Cindy's body turned to stone. Eddie nearly jumped out of his skin as he flew up from the grave to his feet. Again the shakey voice called.

"Cinnnnnndy. Oooooooh Cinnnndy. Heeeeelp me."

"Talk to Eddie! Not me!" Cindy shook so violently she almost fell over.

The voice moaned as though in great agony. "Oooooooh Eddie. Pleeeeeease come. I need your help."

Eddie and Cindy stamped up and down and clamored to hug each other.

"Come where?" Cindy said.

"Over here. Oooooooh!"

The two of them locked arms and inched their way toward the voice. With every step the voice moaned again and again. "Ooooh, please come. Please hurry."

They bravely ventured on until their flashlights revealed a gruesome human figure arising from a grave with outstretched arms.

"AAAAAAAAAAAAH!" Cindy threw her flashlight right at the hideous form.

"AAAAAAAAAAAAH!" it squalled.

She raced to catch up with Eddie, who was already half-way across the cemetery.

The voice called out pleadingly. "E-D-D-I-E. C-I-N-D-Y. DON'T GO! IT'S MISS PLEASANT."

They stopped cold. "Miss Pleasant?"

The two of them walked cautiously back to the grave where Eddie directed his flashlight right on the ghastly face. They were stunned to see that it really was Miss Pleasant. Her heavy costume makeup had smeared and streaked all down her face. She really did look like the living dead. She was still dressed in her Raggedy Ann costume, but with a heavy black shawl draped up and over her head and shoulders.

Miss Pleasant moaned a great sigh of relief. "You two can't know how glad I am to see you."

"Miss Pleasant! What are you doing here?" they both said.

"I was just out for a night walk to clear my head when I caught a dreadful chill and my knee cramped. Please help me up." She sneezed. They struggled to raise her to her feet, but she cringed in pain with her

the magic hour

right leg doubled up beneath her. She awkwardly bent over to pick up something. "You might be needing this." She handed Cindy her flashlight. "You're a pretty mean shot with your right arm there young lady."

"Did I hit you in the face?"

"I know you didn't mean to."

Cindy cupped her hands to her mouth in embarrassment. "I'm sorry."

"It's all right, Cindy. I'm sorry to be a bother, but I need you two to help me get home. There is no possible way I can make it there by myself."

Miss Pleasant cringed again and again as they hobbled together across the cemetery.

"I couldn't believe my fortune, Cindy, when I heard your voice. I thought I would have to spend the whole night right there on the cold ground. I can just see the headlines: SCHOOL TEACHER FOUND DEAD IN CEMETERY. Everyone in town would think I was crazy."

"Are you the crazy lady who brings Cracker Jacks for dead people?" Eddie said.

"I should say not!"

"Well, how come you were here in the cemetery then?"

"She was lying on the grave trying to reach someone on the other side," Cindy said. "All old people have someone they want to contact."

Miss Pleasant was less than pleased with Cindy's comment. "I assure you, Cindy, I was only taking the shortest route home from the carnival when I caught a dreadful chill. And then my leg collapsed."

Cindy leaned over and whispered into Eddie's ear. "She lives between here and the carnival. This is not the shortest route."

Miss Pleasant overheard her whispers. "I know the two of you are just on your way home from the carnival as well."

Cindy and Eddie exchanged a look.

"Please just help me home. I don't live far."

The three of them hobbled out of the cemetery, down the street and up to Miss Pleasant's house.

"It's a good thing I don't live too far from the cemetery. I know that I can't go another inch."

"Do you want my dad to come and check on you?" Eddie said.

"I'll be fine after a hot bath and a good night's rest. Thank you though. I think you two probably saved my life. Will you stay for some hot cocoa?"

"We can't," Cindy said. We'll be late for—" She stopped mid sentence.

Eddie took a quick breath. "Our parents will worry if we're any later getting home."

"Certainly they will," Miss Pleasant said. "I'll have you over for cocoa another time. You two run along home now. Thank you again."

Miss Pleasant leaned against the doorway under her porch light and watched Eddie and Cindy run on down the street—the little witch and the little frog. They made a charming image. Just before they disappeared around the corner, they turned and waved. She waved back.

CHAPTER THIRTEEN

Eddie and Cindy continued their walk toward the Witches' Sabbath along a heavily wooded stream-side path. With the lack of moonlight, the forest around them appeared blacker than Eddie ever before remembered seeing.

"How much farther is it?" he said.

"Not too much to the entrance, but then we still have to walk a long ways from there. And it's all up hill. So let's rest a minute."

They spied an old wooden bench beside the path and plopped down to catch their breaths.

Cindy scooted way back onto the bench. "Could you believe that was Miss Pleasant there in the cemetery?"

"I'm just glad we were able to help her. Both Brian and Uncle Louie told me I had to help her. They said she wasn't gonna make it without my help."

"Really? They told you that?"

"Yeah. They must have known she was going to get stuck there, and that she'd have frozen to death right there on the grave."

"She'd have been cold and stiff by morning."

"That's spooky."

"And we'd have needed a new teacher. Spirits do know all kinds of things. That's why it's so important to listen to 'em when they speak."

"Well, it's good we've completed that."

"But you still haven't seen Brian. And one thing that good spirits know is to go to the light of The Bonfires. That's the main reason we're going to the Witches' Sabbath."

"How do the spirits know to go to The Bonfires?" Eddie said.

"It's instinct. But they all tell each other about them anyway, 'cuz good spirits all hang out together."

"What do you do at The Bonfires?"

"It's very simple. We have a prayer inviting the spirits to come and to set a reverent mood and then everyone sits around the fires in absolute silence so you can hear any whisperings. The entrance to

Witches' Sabbath is just ahead over a little hill. I need to go over a few rules with you so you'll understand the code of conduct." She scooted closer to Eddie. "When we get there, there is absolutely no talking, not for any reason. Even if you trip on a tree root and fall down, if you whisper a single word, the men in the black robes —"

"With the skull faces?"

"Those."

"I saw them in the parade."

"They will grab you and throw you out. They're really strict, but they need to be. They're dealing with all kinds of monsters. Later on we'll be able to talk, but not at first. No one under twenty-one is allowed into the Witches' Sabbath except you and me. I have special permission for both of us from by the Grand High Witch. So we're fine, but you still need a numbered ticket. Put this in your pocket and don't lose it." She handed him a little ticket.

"I won't."

"And they won't let you in without the Seal of Samhain."

"What's that?"

"A special tattoo that lets them know you're one of us."

"I'm not old enough to get a tattoo? And my mom, if she ever —"

"Don't worry. It's not really a tattoo. It's more like a stamp. And besides, it's invisible. See." Cindy extended her left hand toward Eddie with her palm up. "You can't see anything even though it's right there on my wrist. You can only see it under a black light." She pulled a small foil packet from her satchel. "Give me your left hand." She opened the little packet and peeled away what looked like a clear decal, and then applied it to the under side of Eddie's wrist. "Count to seventeen then rip it off fast. Otherwise it'll hurt."

"What is it?"

"Usually they're jack-o-lanterns or skulls, but yours is a surprise. You'll see when we get there."

Cindy held up her wrist and looked at it admiringly. "Yours will wash off in a few days, but mine is permanent. I'm the first person under twenty-one ever to be given special accommodation." She turned to Eddie. "I wanted to do a chart on you today, but I didn't have all the information I needed so it's not complete. But what I did looked really good. As far as I can tell, the planets are perfectly aligned for someone with your sign."

"That's good I guess."

"It's really good. 'Cuz if the planets aren't with you, you can forget it, Baby!"

"I didn't know that."

"Take my word on it." Cindy's voice became stern. "I need to warn you, Eddie. You are going to see some pretty scary stuff tonight. Just remember that all the monsters are fake. Not one of them is real. Just remember that they're all good people in really good costumes having fun. Okay?"

"Okay."

"Are you ready for Witches' Sabbath?"

"I guess so."

"Then let's go."

They stood up from the bench.

"HOO-OO-OO, HOO-AWWWW!" A large owl swooped down almost into their faces and they both dropped right back down onto the seat.

Cindy struggled for air she was so startled. "Did you see that? Out of nowhere, that owl almost knocked us over."

"I couldn't see it real well, but I think it's Mr. Bones."

"Who's he?"

"An owl that lives in our yard."

"Really?"

"He lives in a really old pine tree just out our kitchen door. The sound the owl just made, that was the same sound he made just before Brian died. It's not his normal call. The only other time I've heard it was at the funeral, when Brian's casket was going down in the hole."

"That's right! I remember! I saw it, too. Eddie, I don't know enough about it but I think we're really onto something. You know I was telling you about how animals see things?"

"Yeah."

"Native American medicine men consider owls to be messengers from the dead."

"They do?"

"Oh, yes. They're sacred."

"It's almost like he's been following me around."

"My gosh, Eddie. With all these good signs, the moon, the owl, the planets—it looks good for tonight."

"Great."

"You don't have anything metal on you besides your flashlight do you?"

"No."

"Good. They have metal detectors at the entrance. You have to take the batteries out of your flashlight and show 'em. So, are you ready for Witches' Sabbath?"

"I'm ready."

The petite witch and the little green frog walked over a knoll and emerged from the dark woods into a huge dusty parking lot packed with cars. Headlights glared everywhere as more cars jammed the road to enter. Cindy and Eddie scrambled through the moving vehicles with their blinding lights, like little lost puppies in a crowd. At last they reached the far side and a reverential quiet spread all around them.

Eddie blinked his eyes several times to see if they still worked. He could not believe what he saw—ghastly ghouls and goblins, witches and warlocks, vampires, ghosts, zombies and demons of every imaginable and unimaginable sort. These were not Happy Halloween costumes. These were all terrifying and life like. This unbelievable sight was straight out of Eddie's worst nightmare. His simple frog costume and Cindy's cute witch outfit seemed grossly out of place.

Each creature that passed them appeared more frightful than the last. A gruesome man with a hatchet stuck in his head brushed past Eddie's arm. Eddie's eyes followed him and the pulsing blood that dripped down his neck.

Cindy saw that Eddie was rattled by the sight. "Don't mind him," she whispered into his ear. "Frank wears that same stupid old costume every single year. He's the only person in the whole Witches' Sabbath into gore. He hasn't gotten it yet that gore is out."

Cindy's whispers were met with grave looks of disapproval as demon faces leered at them from every direction.

Great flaming skulls high in the air on tall stakes announced the entrance to the Witches' Sabbath. A WELCOME banner with letters that appeared to be written in dripping blood stretched over a woodland path that disappeared up the mountain. Throngs of costumed people quietly filed onto the well-worn trail.

Men in black robes with skeleton faces, the ones from the parade, stood as sentinel guards along the torch-lit path. Eddie recognized them. They and many of the other monsters were in the Halloween parade, but here in the forest they looked different—they looked real. They looked and felt as if they were unleashed from some dark and horrible place.

"If you have anything to say, say it now," Cindy whispered again. "Once we enter the path, mum's the word."

They looked at each other. She smiled. Eddie half smiled, trying to hide his feelings of dread. Cindy put her arm over his shoulder and they walked ahead.

They fell in line right behind a lady vampire with horrific eyes and salt and pepper hair down to her ankles. Eddie's eyes were glued to her while they waited to check their tickets and pass through security. She looked like she had sucked the life out of more than one person, Eddie thought to himself.

They both handed their tickets and their flashlights to the cloaked sentinels and filed in among the Sabbateurs. No one spoke on the way up the mountain through the forest. Eddie realized that he and Cindy were the only children present.

He glanced back over his shoulder and drew a short breath. A ferocious-looking nearly-seven-foot-tall werewolf with green cat eyes and drooling fangs walked along right behind them. Eddie began to have second thoughts about being there. He had never seen anything so life like before. If not truly a werewolf, this must have been a close relative of one, he thought. He looked back again for another glance. The rippling muscles on this hairy creature, not to mention the two inch claws, he knew could tear him to shreds with no effort at all.

Eddie took a deep breath and focused forward. Remember they're all fake he told himself. Cindy said they're just good people in really really really good costumes.

The flickering light of the torches cast eerie shadows that darted and danced through the trees. A tall dark shadow fell forward over Eddie. A large man dressed all in black walked determinedly up the path past all the other pilgrims. He passed by Eddie and his black cape partially swooshed up over the top of Eddie's head. The hem on the bottom of the cape caught on one of the ping-pong-ball eyeballs sewn onto the hood of Eddie's sweatshirt. It hooked so well that Eddie was pulled forward face down right into the trail. The man himself was jerked backward to a stop by the cape ties that were knotted around his throat. He angrily turned and saw Eddie's legs sticking out from under his cape. He grabbed his cape and aggressively yanked it free. Eddie pushed himself up and their eyes met—and locked.

What ever feelings of fear Eddie may have ever felt before, were instantly vanquished. Inhuman red eyes held him paralyzed. They burned like the very flames of hell. Every part of this demon was as black as pitch—his skin, his hair, his fingernails. Even his teeth that showed through his dark grimace, were the color of coal. Only the gold crown atop his head reflected any light at all.

Cindy reached down to help Eddie up. The man turned and she, too, received the evil eye, but she quickly looked away so as not to be taken in. The man drew a dramatic deep breath, then abruptly walked on.

Eddie looked at Cindy as though the wind had just been knocked out of him. He struggled for air. Cindy's concern showed clearly in her face. They both knew they could not speak. They both knew that for even a whisper they could be thrown out.

The big werewolf behind them lifted Eddie to his feet. He turned to look. The werewolf brushed the dirt and pine needles off of him, then nodded to Eddie before he resumed his trek up the path. Eddie returned the nod.

Cindy dug around in her little satchel and pulled out a small pad of paper and a tiny pencil. She quickly scribbled out a message and handed it to Eddie. The trail-side torch cast just enough light to read:

"You okay?"

Eddie nodded. Cindy wrote again.

"Hurt?"

Eddie shook his head. She scribbled a long message. He started to tremble as he relived the encounter in his mind. He felt as if he had just faced the devil himself. And when he drew that long breath, Eddie had felt his own air being sucked right out of him.

Cindy shoved her note pad at Eddie:

"Don't worry about that jerk in black.
He thinks he owns the whole Witches'
Sabbath just because his name happens
to be Earl King."

Eddie's eyes bugged out and he mouthed the word Erlking.

Cindy held her index finger over her mouth and tried to be reassuring with her eyes. He nodded. The two of them just stared at each other until Cindy noticed that many pilgrims were backed up behind them, politely waiting to pass. She scooted Eddie and herself off to the side and motioned for them all to go on around.

In a parade of frightful creatures that passed by, two giant munchkin witches suddenly stopped and waved their hands back and forth in silent shrieks of joy. They recognized Cindy. These roly-poly, perfectly round twin sisters gave her a book end hug—a one arm hug with one on each side. Lucinda and Ludwiga were mirror image twins. Where one had a wart on the left side of her nose, the other had the exact same wart on the right side of her nose. They were perfect mirror images of each other right down to the hairs in their moles. They were also the ladies who had made Lucretia, the nylon witch at the Crystal Ball.

Dressed as classic witches with green and black striped stockings, and floppy hats rather than the tall stiff ones that were so popular with younger witches, these jolly souls without even a word, just by their presence, released the air of tension and brought back a much appreciated feeling of fun to this Halloween night.

Lucinda and Ludwiga looked at Eddie in his cute green frog costume. As he stood beside Cindy, who was almost a whole head taller without her pointy witch hat, he looked like her very little brother.

Lucinda motioned for Cindy to give her the pad. She obliged and Lucinda wrote.

"Too young."

Cindy shook her head and grabbed back the pad to scribble a reply.

"Bonfires."

The sisters smiled. One sister's mouth crooked left, the other sister's mouth crooked right. Together they made the perfect smile. They immediately knew what Bonfires meant. They, too, would try to reach the dead later tonight.

Lucinda and Ludwiga literally took Cindy and Eddie in tow.

Lucinda the left witch took Cindy's right hand and Ludwiga the right witch took Eddie's left hand, and together they walked four abreast up the mountain. Though these two looked like real witches with their countless grotesque warts and nasty green skin, there was a sort of grandmotherly softness about them that helped settle Eddie.

He felt big warts on Ludwiga's hand and looked down. She had more hair on her hand than his dad had on his head. But at least for the moment he felt safe.

They continued their solemn walk up the mountain with only the muffled sound of countless footsteps on the soft forest soil. On and on they walked, forever climbing. Some places on the trail were so steep that it would almost have been easier to crawl.

Just when Eddie began to wonder if they would ever arrive, at last they crested a hill where the trees parted to reveal the granddaddy of all haunted castles, Witches' Point.

Lucinda and Ludwiga stopped totake in the view of the decrepit stone structure. The sheer Halloween glory of the sight enraptured their souls. The old stone walls gently glowed in the light of fires placed strategically throughout the castle and its grounds. The velvet black silhouette of the mountain behind and above the dark towers completed the haunting visage. Eddie shuddered at the sight.

They continued on and approached the castle itself, where they passed under the arch of an old stone guardhouse on the edge of the castle moat. They found themselves flanked by two particularly ghastly cloaked men. Their skull faces glowed with a flame blue light that seemed to jump right out of their hooded black robes. These sentinels firmly took hold of each person's wrist as they entered and turned it over to verify their mark. Ludwiga entered just ahead of Eddie. He saw that her tattoo was a steaming cauldron. He wondered if his tattoo would really show up or if it would even pass inspection. If he was rejected, would he have to walk back all alone?

A big dark hand grabbed his wrist and turned it over. Eddie only saw a fleeting glimpse, but there on his wrist the unmistakable shape of a teddy bear wearing a witch hat flashed just for a second.

He breathed a small sigh of relief and they all continued on without even a break in stride. What was Cindy's tattoo, he wondered. He did not see it because she was over on the other side of the guardhouse with Lucinda. Was her tattoo the same as his? Were they joined at the wrist?

They crossed the moat and climbed twisting old stone stairways past dark towers and arrived at an old stone arena. The pilgrims all quietly filed in and took seats in the shadowy unlit amphitheater. Ludwiga and Lucinda also took seats, but gestured for Eddie and Cindy to continue on.

With Cindy in the lead, the two of them climbed on up through the gathering silent crowd to the top of the arena. They passed a small fire along a well-rutted dirt road and arrived at the tower door. Cindy pushed it open without hesitation.

The forbidding-looking tower disguised a state of the art sound control room with a large window down onto the scene below. A stocky man in a shiny red leather devil costume greeted them.

"Hey, kids."

"This is Mike, my mom's boyfriend," Cindy said.

"Isn't your friend kind of young for Witches' Sabbath?"

"He's with me and my mom."

"Whatever you say, girl. You're the boss."

Eddie watched Mike resume his work on a large control panel of switches and levers. He was a little embarrassed that Mike's costume barely covered his hairy body. But he was intrigued by Mike's realistic horns and his life-like big tail. It looked like real red skin. He reached to touch it when the tail suddenly moved. He jumped back.

"Ha! Pretty neat, huh?" Mike turned around. "Remote controlled."

Cindy looked up at a big clock on the wall. It read 11:57. "Wow! We barely made it before midnight. It took us longer than I thought to take Miss Pleasant home. Eddie, I couldn't help but notice your socks back there on the trail when you fell. They are green with black polka dots." Cindy lifted her dress to show Eddie her black socks with green polka dots. "We go together really well. And these are both accepted patterns for apprentice witches." She smiled at him then scurried across the room and pulled two orange pillar candles from a large box. "Help me set these candles. We have to light them on the stroke of midnight."

"What for?"

"It's for good luck. We have to let them burn 'til sunrise."

They set the candles on the ledge of the big window.

"Take a match and when Mike counts down to one," Cindy said, "strike it and light your candle."

The Magic Hour

They watched closely while Mike further prepared the control panel to begin the show. They looked out the window to the dark arena below and saw pilgrims scurry to find the few remaining seats.

"Ten seconds and counting," Mike said. "You two be real quiet now. The show's starting. Five—four—three—two—one."

Cindy and Eddie quickly struck their matches. Bong! The church bell in the far distance signalled twelve o'clock midnight. Bong! The Witching Hour. Eddie's match ignited and he lit his candle. Bong! Cindy struggled and struggled to light her match. Bong! The silent crowd below sat motionless while the bell continued to ring. Bong! Again Cindy struck her match but to no avail. Bong! She reached over to Eddie's candle with what was left of her match. Bong! Holding it into the flame, at last it took. Bong! She then moved too quickly toward her candle. Bong! The flame died out. In desperation she grabbed another match. Bong! And held it right into Eddie's candle's flame. Bong! It burst alight and she shoved it at her candle's wick. Bong! And at long last her candle lit. Bong! She breathed a huge sigh of relief.

With the last stroke of the distant bell, the Witches' Sabbath had officially begun.

Down on stage, an eerie upward-shining light illuminated a witch's face. It was Sandy, Cindy's mother, disguised as the Grand High Witch. Dressed head to toe in purple velvet, she stood over an enormous steaming cauldron. Her green skin was covered with huge warts on both her face and hands. Her long hair shimmered a dark green as she ritually stirred the great cauldron with a gnarly-handled broom that only a witch could love. She stirred and stirred with measured focus and intensity to work her potion, when the flames below the cauldron suddenly grew. Sandy slowly looked up and raised her palms to the dark sky.

"That's your mom!" Eddie said.

"Shhhhhhh."

"Purple must be her favorite color."

"It's a sign of her position. Shhhhhhh."

Sandy cried out to the night. "OH, ANCIENT SPIRITS, ON THIS NIGHT OF HALLOWEEN WE GIVE THEE CALL. RECEIVE THIS FIRE'S WARMTH AND LIGHT. FROM SILENT REALMS—COME ONE, COME ALL.

COME FORTH AND JOIN THE DANCING FLAME, AND CELE-

BRATE A BLESSED RITE. THIS SABBAT NOW WE DO PROCLAIM AS OUR TWO WORLDS DO REUNITE.

OH, BLESSED ONES—COME JOIN US HERE, COME JOIN US NOW.

COME P-A-R-T-Y!"

FWOOM! A bolt of lightning flashed down from the heavens and ignited a great bonfire right beside Sandy. Demons in red burst up and out of the giant cauldron and wildly danced around the mighty blaze.

The up to now unseen silent crowds screamed and thrashed about ecstatically. Dramatic night lighting flooded on, beams flashing everywhere. The howl of wind and wolves sound effects reverberated off the old stone walls.

Mike picked up the microphone in the booth, adjusted the volume knob, and flipped the loudspeaker switch. His deep voice boomed out over the dark amphitheater with a Transylvanian accent.

"Good evening and welcome, all my lovelies, to the most spooktacular celebration of them all – THE WITCHES' SABBATH." He switched off the microphone and glanced backward. He noticed that Eddie looked pale and uneasy. "You okay, kid?"

Eddie did not answer, so Mike turned back to the show.

Cindy was glued to the window and the witches' dance down on stage.

"I'm gonna go home," Eddie said, but Cindy did not hear him. He tugged at her sleeve and she turned. "Cindy. I'm gonna go home."

"But the show just started."

"I don't feel good here. I don't think Brian would want to come here either."

"But you can't go. The Bonfires. The spirits only know to come to The Bonfires here on the mountain. It's been this way for centuries."

"I need to go, Cindy. I need to go now." Eddie started for the door.

Cindy jumped ahead of him and put her arm across the doorway. "And besides, they close the trail, if they haven't already. And you can't just go off into the woods alone!"

"Your mom told me I would know where I am suppose to be on Halloween night. Right now I just know I'm not suppose to be here." Eddie spoke with such conviction that Cindy not only stepped aside, but she actually opened the door and walked out with him.

"Okay. I can respect that, if that's how you feel. But before you go there is one thing you must do. It is important because it follows in the ancient tradition. Also, it will help you know for sure if what you're doing is the right thing."

Along the road at the top of the amphitheater, where earlier a single fire burned, now a row of fires burned brightly. Cindy reached into her satchel and pulled something out. "Here. Take this." She placed a single walnut into Eddie's palm.

"What's this for?"

"You make a wish and then throw it in the fire. If it catches on fire and burns up, then you know your wish will come true."

The fire beside them seemed to crack and pop right in time with the wild music and sound effects of the witches' dance down below. Cindy and Eddie both gazed a moment into the dancing flames.

"Go ahead," Cindy said. "Make your wish."

Eddie closed his eyes, then tossed his walnut into the blaze. POOF! A brilliant flash of blue and purple light streaked through the fire as his walnut exploded into flames.

"WOW!" she said. "What did you wish for? I've never seen a walnut burn so good."

"I wished I could see Brian."

"Well, you know you're gonna see him after that. I don't know where you're gonna see him but at least you know you're doing the right thing then, to leave."

Cindy kissed a walnut she held tight in her palm. She cupped her hands together and shook it around and around as if it were a pair of dice. Finally, she released it into the flames. They both leaned forward and watched closely to see the nut's fate.

It lodged right between two red hot logs. Cindy bit her lower lip and double crossed her fingers on both hands, but the walnut quickly turned black and shriveled. Her lips puckered with disappointment.

"What does that mean?" Eddie said.

"My wish won't come true. If your walnut just turns black and doesn't burn."

"I'm sorry."

"It's not your fault. Sometimes we just have to accept our fate."

"I better go."

"Stay on the path."

Eddie walked on down the road. Still dressed in his frog costume, his form disappeared against the night, except as he passed the fires.

Cindy watched nervously for his silhouette to pass the last fire before he entered the woods.

"EDDIE!"

Somehow he heard her call over the blasting music so he turned back. She ran to him as fast as she could. Gasping for breath, she forced out the words just as she reached him. "I LOVE YOU." She threw herself at Eddie, grasping him round about and lifted him right up off the ground, then laid a juicy kiss right on his mouth. Too stunned to even react, Eddie fell limp in her clinching arms. When Cindy at last released her passionate embrace he dropped to his feet and faltered as he walked off into the woods alone.

CHAPTER FOURTEEN

Doctor and Mrs. McCourt arrived home from the carnival so exhausted they could hardly move. They both struggled just to remove their costumes and put on their pajamas.

"I think I'm going to reconsider the idea of doing the cake walk all by myself again next year," Mrs. McCourt said. She then dropped onto the bed. "I know it goes to a good cause and all but —"

"All those cakes all by yourself is a bit much. Except nobody else would go to the trouble that you do to make them so beautiful."

"Thanks. I would think maybe you'd want to volunteer for something other than dunking duty."

"At first it's kind of fun, but after about the fifth dunk—drudgery is the word that comes to mind, climbing back up on that contraption again and again, hour after hour."

"But you do put on a good show for the kids," Mrs. McCourt said. "They love you."

"At least I only got hit twice this year, and not in the face."

"Just be grateful it's over for another twelve months."

"I think the thing that gets to me the most is the noise and the clamor."

"At last we can enjoy some peace and quiet around here."

"Sweet silence."

"Sublime silence."

They both lay silently just to enjoy the silence.

"NO BEARS ARE OUT TONIGHT." A mob of girls' voices yelled just outside their bedroom window. "DADDY KILLED THEM ALL LAST NIGHT..." All forty-four of Lois' Brownies, still in their Halloween costumes, played an outdoor night game of hide and seek. They skipped around and around the house through the garden, all the while they chanted the same thing over and over again. "No bears are out tonight. Daddy killed them all last night. No bears are out tonight. Daddy killed them all last night..."

Melissa jumped from behind a big evergreen bush and growled like a bear. The girls all screamed wildly and ran off with their arms flailing in the air.

The Magic Hour

Then the chanting started again.

Doctor and Mrs. McCourt tossed and turned in bed with pillows over their heads. The screaming-chanting cycle continued on outside unrelentingly.

"I never imagined myself saying this," Doctor McCourt said, "but for the first time in my life, I can actually see why someone would become a mass murderer."

The screaming outside doubled in volume. The chanting began again and Doctor McCourt chanted along.

"No Brownies are out tonight..."

"Daddy killed them all last night," Mrs. McCourt chimed in to finish the thought. They had a good laugh.

"We should all be sleeping out over at Tad's," he said with a sigh. "Eddie's the only one in the family who'll be getting any sleep tonight."

"This is going to be a long night."

"Longest night of the year with that extra hour."

"Oh, that's right. We set the clocks back. I completely forgot."

"Isn't that great. We actually get an extra hour of —"

"AAAAAAAAAH." The girls screamed right outside their window.

"That's kind of a strange thing when you really think about it," she said."

"What's that?"

"At two o'clock we move the clocks back to one, so that actually the clock strikes one o'clock twice. It's almost as if time stands still for sixty minutes."

"That's the kind of thing college professors love to debate with their students. If time stands still, you could live a lifetime in a moment."

"That's kind of a magical thought. You know, I asked Lois about Uncle Louie. She knew your father had a brother, who drowned when he was only four years old."

"I think I actually did know that a long time ago," Doctor McCourt said. "The apology note that Eddie found certainly confirms it."

"I'm still amazed that Eddie not only knows of him, but says he knows him."

"Didn't he say that he met him in one of his dreams?"

Mrs. McCourt nodded her head. "There must be more to his dreams than we really know?"

"There must be more to dreams that we simply don't know or understand. Eddie is a smart boy. I do believe him now, that Brian really is telling him things."

"I do, too," she said. If Brian's essence does still exist, why wouldn't he want to still tell Eddie things? Those two boys were inseperable."

"We hear more and more all the time, about near death experiences where people are brought back to life. I've worked on some of those people."

"You never told me about them."

"This one patient I revived from a motorcycle accident had some incredible story about leaving his body and passing through a tunnel of light. He said his deceased grandmother met him and told him he needed to come back and find a new set of friends. Funny thing is, his mother says he's never acted the same since. This kid is in high school and he actually spends all of his weekends now teaching people how to read."

They lay silently and contemplated all that they may have discovered.

"Hey, listen," Mrs. McCourt said.

"I don't hear anything."

"I know. That's the point."

All was quiet outside. The Brownie girls had stopped their noise making. They began to hum a strange and haunting campfire melody.

"It's beautiful. Listen," Doctor McCourt said.

"Maybe we will get some sleep after all."

"Don't forget, I'm on call at the hospital tonight."

"Oh, joy!"

They tenderly snuggled together. Mrs. McCourt became teary eyed and started to sniffle.

"What's wrong?"

"I'm just concerned about Eddie. I feel like he needs me, somehow. The only thing he wanted for his birthday was to be with Brian. I miss Brian. This is their birthday. Eddie and Brian should be spending it together."

"Maybe they are together. Maybe sleeping out there under the stars, Eddie is having one of his special dreams."

She smiled. "That's a pleasant thought."

They kissed good night and curled up to sleep. They both lulled off in slumber, but Mrs. McCourt suddenly awoke with a start as if from a nightmare. She sat straight up in bed and stared at the telephone on the far night stand as though waiting for it to ring. It did ring and sent Doctor McCourt straight up in bed as well.

"The hospital."

"No. I don't think so," she said. "For some strange reason I think that it's Margaret Pleasant."

"At this hour? Maybe she's had some more problems." He fumbled to answer the phone. "Hello?"

"Doctor McCourt?"

"Yes."

"This is Margaret Pleasant. Eddie's teacher."

Doctor McCourt turned to his wife with a perplexed look. "Are you all right, Margaret?"

"I'm fine, thank you. Really I am." Miss Pleasant took a deep breath. "I'm dreadfully sorry to ring you up at this hour, but I'm calling to enquire whether Eddie is at home or not."

"No. He's sleeping over at Tad Durban's tonight."

"Actually, that's the reason I am calling. I am not one to meddle in other people's affairs, but I happened to see Eddie walking with Cindy Crystal through the cemetery a short while ago."

"The cemetery? What would they be doing there at this time of night? What were you doing there at this time of night?"

"It's a long story, but I am really worried about Eddie. He and Cindy said that they were on their way home. But if I didn't know better, I'd say that the two of them were on their way to Witches' Point."

"Oh, boy! Thank you, Margaret. I really appreciate your call. We'll go find him."

"I'd be happy to come and help."

"That's fine, thank you. We'll take care of it. You get some rest. You had quite a spill earlier."

"Thank you. Good night."

"Good night."

Mrs. McCourt was frantic. "WHAT?"

"Get dressed. We're going to the Witches' Sabbath!"

They both scrambled to put their clothes on.

Outside the front door, a sea of Brownies was seated across the verandah, down the steps and out onto the front lawn. The glow from barely burning jack-o-lanterns perched on the porch railing flickered in the girls' faces as they continued to hum their eerie melody.

Their calm was shattered by the bang of the front door. Doctor McCourt fell head over heals onto five Brownie girls seated right in front of the door. They screamed and scattered. He grabbed the railing, where he accidentily knocked a burning jack-o-lantern down onto the steps on top of more girls. They screamed and jumped aside just before the pumpkin hit the porch and splattered all down the steps. He stumbled his way down the stairs and jumped in the car.

"ELIZABETH! BRING THE KEYS!"

Mrs. McCourt stumbled out the front door just the way he did, plowed her way through the bodies, and jumped into the car. The engine revved and the car backed out. KATHUMP— KATHUMP— KATHUMP—KATHUMP.

Doctor McCourt slammed on the brakes. "Something is really wrong with this car."

They both jumped out. He looked at the front left tire. "We have a flat!"

"Two of them!"

"Three of them!"

"FOUR OF THEM!" she said.

"I thought the carnival was supposed to keep kids out of mischief!"

"No one from this town would do this."

They both realized the humming had stopped. All was quiet. They looked toward the house. All the Brownies had magically disappeared. Not one of them was to be seen anywhere. They both looked to the bus.

"CAMP BOUNTIFUL HAS FULL TIRES!" he said.

"I'd bet fifty dollars this is the work of some little Brownie Scouts."

"You could bet the house on that one. Go get Lois. We're taking the bus."

"Lois is your sister! You go get her!"

Inside the house, Doctor McCourt knocked softly on the guest bedroom door. "Lois? Are you awake?" There was no response, so he knocked again, more loudly. "LOIS?"

"Patrick? Is that you?"

"Yes. There's an emergency. I need to talk to you."

Lois frantically opened the door. She was a sight with big orange curlers in her hair and a high-neck, long sleeve carrot print flannel night gown. Night-pack creme on her face completed the awful visage.

"Did one of my girls fall off the roof?"

"Eddie is up on the mountain somewhere and we need to go find him. The wagon mysteriously has four flat tires and the Mercedes is in the shop. Can I use the bus?"

"Do you have a chauffeur's license?"

"Lois! I'm just driving me and Liz."

"We can form a search party. We'll cover the mountain in no time at all."

"Lois! The last thing we need is forty-four girls lost up on a dark mountainside."

"My girls are specifically trained in outdoor survival! ARE YOU?"

Doctor McCourt could not respond.

"I will round up the girls and then we will depart."

Lois blew a police whistle out in the driveway and stood before the bus. Brownies instantly appeared from every direction and filed into a perfect line of ascending height. From the shortest to the tallest, Lois strutted up the line like a military general. The only difference between her and a military warlord, was the flannel nighty, the curlers and the night pack creme. She had the attitude and the boots.

"What kind of parents would allow their young child to go up on a dark mountainside all alone at night," she said, "on Halloween none the less, is beyond me."

Doctor and Mrs. McCourt were beside themselves at what they heard. Mrs. McCourt stared seethingly at Lois as she continued her oration.

"Nevertheless, we have been called upon to use our skills. When a need for service arises, a Brownie does not shrink. When we arrive at the mountainside, we will orderly break into our predetermined groups of eight. We will spoke out radially from the bus and comb the area until the child is found. I will remain with the bus with my whistle, which I will blow at precisely thirty second intervals to serve as aural reference. Any questions?"

The Brownies all knew better than to ask questions. Melissa, who was new to this military order and unacquainted with the practices of the regime, stood sort of in line. She raised her hand. "What are YOU going to do, Aunt Lois?"

Lois looked at her incredulously. "I will remain with the bus with my whistle, which I will blow at precisely —"

"I heard that. But what are YOU going to do to help find EDDIE, your nephew?"

Lois' face flushed red. She had never dealt with such impudence. She and Melissa stared each other down.

In desperation to control the situation before it became further out of hand, Lois blew her whistle again and again in rapid succession and the girls methodically filed into the bus in descending height order.

Much to Melissa's behest, her parents insisted that she stay home in case Eddie showed up. They instructed her to call them immediately on the cell phone if he did.

Lois looked at Doctor and Mrs. McCourt with her eyes squinted. "When I blow the whistle, that means you board the bus. NOW BOARD!"

Melissa watched her humiliated parents step up into the bus. "Aunt Lois?" she said. She had had a realization when she and Lois were staring at each other. She stepped over and whispered in Lois' ear. "I am so glad to finally realize that my father's sister doesn't genetically have a hooked witch nose. It just looks like she does because her upper lip is permanently curled up in a look of disgust. I can't tell you how relieved I am. I was really beginning to worry about our family gene pool." Melissa turned away and smiled to her parents up inside the bus. "Good luck finding Eddie!"

"Thanks, Sweetie. We'll talk to you."

Lois was still frozen in position just outside the bus door. Only her eyes moved while Melissa walked up the drive toward the house, they followed her all the way.

"Lois. Come on," Doctor McCourt said.

At last Lois turned and boarded, her eyes open wide like a crazed maniac. She stepped around the McCourts who stood because all the seats were full. "Regulations require that all persons be seated."

"It's a full batch of Brownies," Mrs. McCourt said. "There are no seats."

"THERE IS A FLOOR!"

The McCourts sat down on the steps just inside the bus door.

Lois looked utterly ridiculous as she drove the bus in her army boots and flannel nightie. "Girls? How does that lively tune from the carnival go about not going into the woods alone? Would you sing it for us please?"

The Magic Hour

Mrs. McCourt knew Lois asked the girls to sing that song just to insult her further.

Lois raised her right hand into the air and started the song.

"DON'T GO OUT OF THE HOUSE AT NIGHT AND INTO THE WOODS ALONE. DON'T GO OUT OF THE HOUSE AT ALL, IT'S BETTER TO STAY AT HOME..."

Mrs. McCourt knew the song. She had listened to it all night long at the cake walk. She knew every word of the blessed song and every word made her feel worse.

"FOR MONSTERS, SPOOKS AND GOBLINS, TOO, ARE LURKING THERE IN WAIT FOR YOU..."

The girls went wild mimmicing the evil laugh that came next in the song. Mrs. McCourt plugged her ears. She finally unplugged them just as the girls sang "THE GRAVES ARE GIVING BACK THEIR DEAD, SO DON'T YOU WISH YOU WERE HOME IN BED?" She wished they were all home in bed. "Can't you drive this thing any faster?"

"There are speed limits," Lois said.

The bus passed through town and off onto a lonely woodland road while the girls continued to sing. The line "ON HALLOWEEN YOUR WORSTEST DREAM BECOMES REALITY!" was almost more than Mrs. McCourt could take.

"I'm the one who's going to become a mass murderer," she said almost in hysterics. "I can't take this. They're singing that song just to taunt me, to tell me what a bad mother I am."

Doctor McCourt put his arm around his wife. "Don't worry. We'll find Eddie."

"They'll probably find all our bodies in the morning."

The bus approached a woodland crossroads.

"Turn right and just keep going until the road ends," Doctor McCourt said.

The bus turned onto a narrow bumpy road that ran right into the thickest part of the woods. They followed along and soon approached the entry to Witches' Sabbath. Everyone saw the parking lot packed with cars and the flaming skull torches—all the signs of a major Halloween event.

"Is this some kind of Halloween party?" Lois said in a pleasant tone.

"Some kind," Doctor McCourt said. Two skull-faced men in black robes approached the front of the bus and motioned for it to stop. Doctor McCourt stepped to the opening bus door but turned to his wife. "What's the Crystal woman's name?"

"Sandy."

Lois pulled the lever to open the door and one of the men stepped into the bus.

"I'm Doctor McCourt. It's an emergency. We're here at Sandy Crystal's insistence."

"No one gets in without a pass number."

"Take it up with her." Doctor McCourt stood firmly and held his ground.

The man radioed to speak with Sandy but was told she was unavailable—she was on stage. The two men looked at each other. After a tense moment, the man in black waved the bus on through. "Let 'em pass!"

The door closed and they drove on.

"Aren't you the clever one?" Mrs. McCourt said.

"You do what you have to."

Lois cleared her throat loudly. "Patrick, why didn't you tell us that there were more Halloween activities to participate in? My girls and I, we came to do it all!"

"Believe me. Here, you may be able to do just that."

The road narrowed even more as they climbed the mountain. Pulsating rock music became audible. The bus pulled around a curve, and there before them through the trees was Witches' Point and the Witches' Sabbath!

The girls became wild hearing the blasting rock music and seeing the dancing throngs. The McCourts jumped out of the way just before the girls rushed the door in one giant frenzied wave before the bus even stopped.

"GIRLS! GIRLS PLEASE!"

The screaming girls pounded the door with their fists and stomped on the floor. The whole bus rocked. Two girls grabbed the release lever right out of Lois' guarding hands. SMACK! The door flew open and the wave of screaming girls rolled out of the bus and disappeared into the riotous crowds.

Lois jumped down out of the bus and frantically blew her whistle. "GIRLS! GIRLS!!!" She jumped up and down but the girls were long gone. She slowly turned around and stared back into the bus at the

McCourts, who still cowered behind the driver's seat where they had hidden to avoid the stampede. "PATRICK! HOW COULD YOU? A DRUNKEN OOOOOOOOOOOH! I can't even say it!" Lois suddenly gasped for breath. She gasped and gasped and nearly fell over.

"Lois, have you ever read "Mutiny on the Bountiful?" Doctor McCourt said. She did not even hear his question. She caught her breath then screamed some more.

"I am never coming back to your house. EVER! FOR AS LONG AS I LIVE!!!" Lois ran off into the crowd. "GIRLS! GIRLS!"

Mrs. McCourt looked at her husband disapprovingly. "You are cruel."

"And now we have one more thing to celebrate on Halloween. A disinheritance!"

She hit him and they both giggled.

Doctor McCourt grabbed his wife by the hand. "Come on, Sweetie. LET'S PARTY!" They ran out the door and into the crowds.

"We need to find that Crystal woman," she said.

"What does she look like?"

"A big witch."

"Over there," he said, pointing to a tall witch hat that stuck above the crowd. They fought their way through the dancing crowds toward the hat. They reached the large witch and touched her on the shoulder. She turned and both their hearts skipped a beat. She was a hideous witch with a nasty green face. They looked away and noticed another witch hat.

This witch was a tall slim red head with smooth pale green skin and exotic amber-colored eyes. Doctor McCourt was briefly spellbound by her strange beauty. He looked at her. She looked at him. Mrs. McCourt looked at them. WHACK! Something hit him in the back of the head.

"What was that?"

"A stray broom. Come on!"

They looked around and spied another witch hat and another and another. Witch hats poked up everywhere above the crowd.

"This place is crawling with witches!" Doctor McCourt said.

"That's probably why they call it the Witches' Sabbath."

Doctor McCourt spied a stairway that lead to an observation point high above the crowds. "Come on. Let's go up there. We can see better."

They pushed their way through dancing bodies up old stone, open-air stairways to reach the upper level of the castle and looked down upon the mass hysteria below. They saw Lois screaming, caught up in a bouncing throng of snake dancers. A burly man in an executioner's costume grabbed her hand and yanked her along. They could read his lips.

"Great costume, wench!"

"Aaaaaaaah!" Lois screamed.

Doctor McCourt laughed the harder of the two. "I knew this thing was well attended, but I had no idea it was anything like this. There must be half the town here!"

"The OTHER half!"

"No wonder they close the carnival early. So everyone can come here."

"There she is!" Mrs. McCourt saw Sandy. "The big witch!" Down below amidst the crowd, still dressed in her gorgeous purple as the Grand High Witch, Sandy lead a long train of people in a wild conga line. Mike in his devil costume danced along right behind her.

The McCourts fought their way back down through the crowds to Sandy. Doctor McCourt shouted to be heard over the music. "I'M DOCTOR McCOURT. EDDIE'S DAD."

"IT'S NICE OF YOU TO COME!" Sandy shouted with a smile.

"IS EDDIE HERE?"

"HE'S UP IN THE TOWER." Sandy pointed up to the highest part of the castle.

"Thank you."

He dragged Mrs. McCourt up more narrow stone steps, through more passage ways. At last they broke from the throbbing mass of humanity and arrived at the uppermost reaches of the castle.

"Can you believe people actually enjoy this?" she said.

"Yeah. Maybe we should come next year," he said.

She hit him on the arm.

They reached the tower door and did not wait to knock. Inside, Cindy slept on a small sofa, still in her witch costume.

"That's the little witch that got all my cakes!" Mrs. McCourt said.

"Just take a deep breath."

"I'm sorry. I didn't mean it quite the way it sounded."

Doctor McCourt gently shook Cindy. She woke but was groggy.

"I'm Eddie's dad. Is he here?"

The Magic Hour

Cindy yawned. "He left."

Mrs. McCourt became frantic.

"When did he leave?"

Cindy yawned again. "A long time ago."

"Did he leave with somebody?"

Cindy rubbed her sleepy eyes. "He walked home alone."

Mrs. McCourt became hysterical. "I knew something was really wrong. I felt it. Now I've lost two sons."

"I told him not to go," Cindy said, "but he wouldn't listen."

"He wouldn't have come here if it weren't for you!" Mrs. McCourt said in desperation.

"Liz! We'll find him! Everything will be all right."

Cindy finally came to her faculties. "Didn't Eddie get home?"

"No, he didn't."

"OH, NO!" Cindy jumped up and grabbed the loud speaker microphone. She flipped the switch and cranked the volume on to HIGH. She cringed from a deafening electronic squeal, then her voice blasted out over the pulsating music. "MOMMMMM!"

The dancing crowds below were shaken to a standstill. Everyone covered their ears to protect themselves from the head-splitting volume of Cindy's cry.

Looks of horror flashed over Sandy's and Mike's faces as they looked up to the tower.

Now that she had everyone's attention, Cindy screamed again. "EDDIE'S LOST IN THE WOODS."

Sandy looked at Mike with worry on her face. "If anything has happened to that boy I'll hold myself personally responsible."

"I'm afraid a lot of other people might hold you responsible as well." After his remark, Sandy looked even more sick.

The two of them pushed their way through the crowds and rushed up the steps to the tower. Sandy reached the booth first, huffing and puffing, and threw open the door.

"CINDY! How could you let Eddie go off alone? Tonight of all nights!" Sandy looked down at the control panel. "How do you work this thing?"

"You flip this —"

Mike ran in the door and grabbed Cindy's wrist. "First you adjust the volume, and then you flip the lever and speak."

Sandy took the mic. "My fellow Sabbateurs, this is your Grand

High Witch speaking. I am going to cast a spell over each and everyone of you to make you comply with my wishes." The theatricality in her voice changed to soft motherly concern. "A little ten-year-old boy is lost in the woods. He is dressed as a frog and his name is Eddie. We need all of your help to find him."

The entire crowd below uproariously cheered approval.

CHAPTER FIFTEEN

The torch-lit trail, which earlier was so frightening because of all the Halloween ghouls, now deserted was even more frightening. Eerie shadows darted about through the trees from the flickering torches. They caused Eddie to constantly look around with unease while night sounds played further havoc with his mind.

He heard deep men's voices and heavy footsteps. Getting closer. Getting louder. Four sentinels appeared down the path below him. Their black robes and painted skull faces created a foreboding image. Eddie breathed heavily. Their hideous faces became more frightful with each on-coming step. He broke from the path and ran into the woods. At first he gave a sigh of relief, but then the sound of his own feet crunching in the dry leaves unnerved him even more. He stopped every few feet to look all around himself.

The wind started to blow and the trees overhead heaved and cracked. But Eddie continued deeper and deeper into the woods.

Suddenly he stopped in pain, then limped to a large nearby rock. He sat down and nervously removed his shoe to pull stickers from his stocking. A twig snapped somewhere behind him!

"Who's there?" He looked around but saw only darkness.

Another twig snapped!

Eddie rose to his feet. "Who's there? Cindy? Brian?"

Again came the sound of crunching leaves. Footsteps. Getting louder. GETTING CLOSER!

With his left shoe still on the ground beside the rock, he broke into a dead run. Twigs and branches lashed at his face as he scrambled through thick underbrush in the darkness. Rocks and sticks poked his unshod foot. His own heart beat so loudly its pounding nearly drowned out the sound of his own footsteps.

"Owwwww!" He cried out in pain but continued to run.

FOOTSTEPS! GETTING LOUDER! GETTING CLOSER. HOT BREATH BREATHING DOWN HIS NECK! Eddie crossed himself and frantically looked back over his shoulder.

"Aaaaaaaaaaah!"

He tripped and fell head-long into a ravine and hit his head on a fallen tree. THUD! He lay motionless, face down on the ground. All was quiet. Even the wind had stopped. In the distance the faint sound of the church bell in the old cathedral chimed one o'clock. Bong! Eddie groaned and slowly sat up with his hand held to his forehead. He sat motionless, still too stunned to move.

Before Eddie could even take a deep breath, a man's hand reached out of the darkness and grabbed his shoulder. He tried to scream but no sound could escape his breathless body. The black silhouette of a tall man with a long cape towered over him. A gleaming gold crown topped his head. The night was dark, but this human form before him was even darker than the night, all but his burning red eyes. Without question, Eddie knew who this was and why he had come – the Erlking had come to drag him off to some dark and dreadful place.

The Erlking gestured for Eddie to stand up, but he was frozen in place. Seeing no response, the Erlking took hold of Eddie's shoulders and pulled him up to his feet. He then motioned for him to move on ahead. Eddie knew he was helpless. He knew that he could not refuse. He was simply compelled to obey the Erlking's request.

Eddie slowly walked ahead of the Erlking down a narrow path into a clearing along a woodland road where he stared in disbelief at his own worst nightmare. Bathed in moonlight just ahead stood four shimmering black steeds before an old glass-enclosed hearse. A mysterious ground fog swirled and twisted like a snake around the horses' feet. One of them whinnied—a deep throaty sound that was more like a groan from hell than anything Eddie had ever before heard.

The Erlking's black cape whirled in a sudden burst of wind when he opened the door to the death coach. He entreated Eddie to climb aboard. Eddie knew he was totally under the Erlking's power. Again he knew he could not refuse. He stepped to the door and felt a terrifying bone chill surge all the way down to his toes from an icy wind that blew out from the inside of the hearse. One last time the Erkling gestured, more strongly, for Eddie to climb aboard.

His face filled with trepidation, Eddie climbed in. SLAM! The door shut with a vacuum grip and instantly the hearse thundered off with Eddie's two little hands and face pasted to the back window.

Faster and faster the charging steeds pulled the hearse through the dark woods. Up one hill and down the next they traveled, all the while the Erlking's black cloak flapped maniacally at the helm.

Eddie's heart and thoughts raced along as fast as the horses feet. He wanted to close his eyes and never open them again for fear of what might lie ahead, but he did not dare close his eyes for fear of what did lie ahead.

Thoughts of the night Brian died spun around and around through his mind. Was this how Brian met his end? Was this the same demon come to take him to the same terrible place?

On and on and on the clamorous frenzy continued at dizzying speeds, passing harrowingly close to rocky crags along the narrow roadside. The hearse whipped around a tight curve and Eddie suddenly felt his throat constrict as the temperature inside the hearse increased drastically. He gasped for air but could not breathe at all. He banged on the window desperately trying to be heard when the coach reeled to the side and drove head-on toward a peculiar fold of solid granite at break-neck speed.

Just at the point of impact, in a brilliant explosion, the mountainside burst open into a great blinding tunnel of light and allowed the hearse to enter.

As the brightness gradually dimmed, the hearse seemed to float gently along through a lush, green valley beneath towering snow-capped peaks. Wonder and awe filled Eddie's face, still glued to the window of what had now become a beautiful white carriage with gold trim. Even the ghoulish skull lamps on the sides of the hearse had magically been replaced by faces of beautiful women. He could scarcely believe his eyes as four white horses effortlessly glided the coach to rest before a flower-filled terrace.

Eddie looked around the wonderland in awe and amazement at beauty beyond anything he had ever even dreamed existed. The driver of the carriage, who was now also dressed in white, smiled warmly and opened the door for him to climb out. Eddie glanced at him briefly, but cautiously avoided looking at his eyes. He did notice that the driver looked vaguely familiar, but once outside the carriage, his interest lay in the new extraordinary surroundings.

Flowers and more flowers covered almost every inch of the landscape. Even the trees were blanketed in glorious pink, coral and lavendar blooms.

The sweet scent of something very familiar blew past Eddie on a gentle breeze. The familiarity of the lovely smell of home helped set him at ease and even gave him a distinct feeling of deja vu. Just ahead,

Eddie saw an exquisite bed of flowers aglow like purple neon along a small stream embankment.

"That's purple heliotrope!" He ran over to the flowers and buried his head to take in the heavenly fragrance.

"You are right. That is heliotrope," a distinctive man's voice said.

Eddie looked up to see a handsome young man with light brown hair and a neatly trimmed beard walking toward him down a golden path. He sported a loose-fitting linen shirt, light blue jeans and sandals. "Put your nose right down in them. It is almost more than you can stand the fragrance is so rich and sweet."

"It's my mom's favorite – flower."

"You are right again. That is your mother's favorite flower. She has a beautiful bed of heliotrope right outside her kitchen door so the fragrance will waft into the house with even the slightest breeze."

Eddie looked at the man, not quite knowing how to think or feel.

"Eddie. Do not be afraid."

Eddie knew this voice. He had heard it before. He recognized the distinctive tone and the words he just spoke. "You're the man who talked to me when I was at the Crystal Ball?"

"That was me." He smiled again. "Oh, Eddie. I cannot believe that you are actually here!"

"Where is here? Where am I?"

"I think you know where you are."

"Why am I here?"

"I should be asking you why you have come, but I already know. We have all been expecting you."

"You have?"

"Oh, yes. We all know that you came because you wanted to see your brother, and because you wanted to prove something to your mother."

"She doesn't believe me that he's not dead."

"Your mother is afraid to believe that your brother Brian is still alive. She does not fully understand death so she fears it."

"How come you know all about my family?"

"Because I am your brother. I am Brian."

Brian moved toward Eddie with his arms open, but Eddie's expression of total disbelief stopped him cold. Eddie was completely confounded. He not only could not believe what he had just heard, he did not want to believe what he had just heard. He stared at the man.

He studied his nose, his beard, his eyes. They looked into each other's eyes and Eddie started to soften. He realized this was in fact his brother Brian.

"You have the two little brown moles right below your left eye. That's the only difference between us."

Brian smiled again and then Eddie's bewilderment and disbelief was completely replaced by warmth and tenderness. Their eyes communed momentarily and they grabbed each other and hugged. But Eddie quickly pulled back to look at Brian again.

"Except now you've got a beard?"

"Do you like it?" Brian chuckled to himself.

"How'd you grow a beard?"

"You can grow a beard here whenever you want, because there is no time. I know that you have many questions but there are some people who just cannot wait to see you."

Before Brian finished his sentence, he and Eddie were instantly removed to an elegant reception room with carved, gilded walls and ceilings and custom-loomed oriental carpets. While Eddie tried to catch his breath, a handsome young couple of twenty-five, finely dressed in 1940's country club attire approached the two of them. The man actually wore golf shoes and carrried an old nine iron in his hand. The woman outstretched her arms toward Eddie and his eyes bugged out in disbelief.

"Grandma? Grandpa?"

Eddie's grandmother dropped to her knees and gave Eddie a big bear hug. "Oh, Eddie. I've waited all your life to give you this hug. You know, I was right there when you were born —"

"We were all there when you were born," Grandpa said.

"But I could not hold you because I was already passed on." Grandma simply doted over Eddie. She pulled back the hood of his costume and straightened his hair. "You know I was there when you got your first tooth. I was there when you lost your first tooth, and on your first day of school, too. In fact, I haven't missed a single family party since you were born." She noticed Eddie's feet, his left clad only in a green stocking with black polka dots. "Oh, and your missing shoe makes you even more adorable. I cannot stand it." She hugged and kissed him again.

"I cannot stand it." Grandpa whopped Grandma in the derriere with his golf club. "Lucille. Let the boy breathe."

Grandma released Eddie. "Do not worry about your shoe back there in the forest, Sweetie. You will get it back." She then turned to Grandpa with a sneer. "Oh! You old coot."

"The last thing Eddie wants is to be smothered by some blubbering old lady."

"Just hush! You seem to forget that I am not old and wrinkled anymore."

"But you are old in spirit. That is what counts!"

"You will never change, will you?"

"I hope not."

"You are incorrigible!"

Grandpa gave Eddie a little hug around the shoulder. "Good to see you, my boy."

Eddie hugged him back. "My friend Tad thinks you're a really rotten grandpa for giving us tombstones for Christmas."

"I know. I heard him say it."

"You did?"

"Oh, sure. We get all the news from home."

"You do?"

"Sure we do. We do not miss a thing."

"But how come you gave us tombstones for Christmas anyway?"

"Just remember that a tombstone is the one gift that everybody needs and will never get. Oh, how I used to love to give them to newlyweds." Grandpa laughed right out loud at his own joke.

Grandma scoffed. "At least you think it is funny."

"You would not know a good joke if it crawled across your face, like that little spider there." Grandpa pointed his finger right at the side of her nose.

Grandma shrieked and swatted at her face.

"Ha, ha, ha, ha, ha! Got ya."

"There is no spider! You are terrible! And that is a terrible thing to do to a young married couple, so full of hope."

"So full of hormones. It helps them keep things in perspective."

"Party pooper."

"What's that?"

"You heard. Should have put that on your monument! Born a party pooper—Died a party pooper—Forever a party pooper."

Grandpa opened his mouth to begin another round but other people appeared and crowded around, stealing the attention. One young man dapperly dressed in smart 1930's argyle, called out excitedly, "Eddie!"

"Uncle Louie!"

Uncle Louie and Eddie shook hands and hugged.

"I was there, too," Uncle Louie said, "when you were born. I was looking after your grandma because your grandpa was not here yet."

Grandma curled her nose and upper lip, exactly the way Aunt Lois always did, and then sneered at Uncle Louie. "You two are just alike. You are both awful."

Brian turned to Eddie "There really are no secrets here, Eddie, but close your eyes anyway. There is someone who wants to surprise you."

Eddie closed his eyes.

"Okay. You can open them now," Brian said immediately.

Eddie opened them to find both he and Brian were no longer in the reception room. They now stood beside a great waterfall on a patch of velvet grass. A grizzly bear glanced at them as it wandered past. Eddie could hardly believe what else he saw.

"LARRY!"

Standing right beside the water's edge, a six-foot-long iguana faced him with its mouth open wide. Eddie and Larry ran to each other. Eddie gave Larry a big hug and Larry licked Eddie's face all over.

"Let me look at you," Eddie said and then stood back. Larry carried all the adornments of a mature iguana—rough plaited skin, huge black spines down his back and bright blue bands encircling his tail. "You look great! Harry will never believe this when I tell him."

Brian patted Larry's head. "It is great to have him here with us." He then put his hand on Eddie's shoulder and looked directly at him. "There is something that Larry wants you to know. He wants you to tell Melissa that he has no hard feelings toward her for stomping him to death in the shower. All that birthday cake you gave him made him thirsty and he heard the water running. Melissa just kind of took it wrong when he climbed right into the shower with her."

"I'm glad he's not mad at her. I really didn't think she meant to kill him. She's mean sometimes, but she's not a murderer."

"She is not."

"But it was really something—one minute I was feeding Larry cake, and the next he was gone." Eddie admired the spectacular cliffs and waterfall above. "What do you do for fun around here?"

"Whatever we want to do," Grandpa answered from out of

nowhere. All the relatives were again gathered around them. Eddie was caught off guard by their sudden popping in.

"Pick on me is what you do," Grandma said without missing a beat. She gave Grandpa a swift kick in the ankle.

"That's how I show my affection, woman."

"That is because you still do not know what affection is. Because you flunked 'Relationships 101.' And another thing, you never were any good at golf. You just drag that old thing around so people will think you were some kind of hot stuff."

"Now, there you go..."

Eddie turned to Brian with concern. "Do they always fight like this?"

Brian took Eddie aside while Grandpa and Grandma went at it further. "Do not worry about them. They love to spar. It is their most favorite thing to do."

"Don't they love each other any more?"

"They love each other very much."

Brian saw the real concern in Eddie's worried face. "You can put your mind at ease. Truth be told, they are just practicing."

"They practice bickering with each other?"

"They call it wrangling. Eddie, I need to tell you about Grandma and Grandpa."

"What?"

"They are famous—really famous."

"You're kidding?"

"Everybody here loves them."

"Everybody watches them fight?"

"You are quick! They put on quite a show. Right now it looks like Grandpa is winning, but that is only because Grandma saves all her best quips and quibbles for the Vesperian."

"What's that?"

"Grandma and Grandpa are famous stage performers. The Vesperian is a huge outdoor arena where they put on the show every evening. It is hilarious. They set up a boxing ring and they actually use referees and scorekeepers, and have rounds. It gets wild! And it always looks like Grandpa is going to win but old Grandma —"

"She's not old any more!"

"Young Grandma, she pulls out a whopper and knocks him flat every time. The people just roar! You are too new here to know Ed."

"Ed who?"

"His last name used to be Sullivan."

"I think I've heard of him."

"He is the one who organizes the show. He sleuths around looking for people with hidden talents who have never before performed. He walked by Grandma and Grandpa's house one day when they were out in the garden. They were just kidding around making fun of all the stupid things they and everybody else used to do back before they passed over. Ed could not see them because they were behind the hedge, but he heard them. He knew right then that they were going to be big. The rest is history."

"That's incredible."

"They are in such demand now, they have to practice every minute, practically nonstop, just to be ready for the next show. They have almost no time to themselves."

"Why do they do it then?"

"Because they are making other people feel good. And that is what it is all about."

"Can we go see them?"

"Their performance is not until this evening. If you want to go see a show, then I should tell you about my favorite thing to do around here."

"What's that?"

"Watching movies."

"You watch movies here?"

"All the time. Have you ever heard the saying 'All the world is a stage?'"

"Maybe."

"Shakespeare knew what he was talking about when he said it. It is true. All the world is a sound stage, where they make movies. Come here. I'll show you."

Once again Brian and Eddie were instantaneously transported to a new location.

"Whoa!" Eddie found himself walking up a great marble stairway. "This popping in and out thing is awesome. What do you call it?"

"There is no special word for it. It is just the way we get around. We travel at the speed of thought to where ever we want."

"WOW! I gotta figure out how to do it." Eddie looked up above him to the top of the stairs. "DOUBLE WOW!! What is this place?"

"Universal Video."

Towering above them, a monumental marble edifice more grand than those found in ancient Greece bore intricate and elaborate detailing beyond imagination. Eddie looked up at the massive portico over the entrance above them, carved with life-like scenes of people and animals. "This place is too awesome!"

They entered a great cavernous antechamber and Eddie stopped. The sheer grandeur and magnificence of this artful building evoked a sense of reverence and awe, and Eddie felt it. The walls glowed with an otherworldy translucency that disallowed any dark, shadowy corners or niches. The unfathomable intricasy of the gleaming marble parquet flooring alone appeared as if it took centuries to install.

"Should I take my shoe off?"

"Oh, no. Shoes are fine. There is no dust here so there is no such thing as dusty footprints."

"I have to think about that one. No dust. No sweeping. Does that mean no chores?"

"It depends on what you mean by chores."

Eddie heard their footsteps echo clearly and crisply off the walls. Then he was shocked to feel the gentle reverberations of the echoes pass back by them. He could not resist the urge to call out. "Hellooooooooooooooooooooooo." He paused to listen and feel the echo again. "I have never heard an echo like that! Like it goes on forever."

"We have perfect acoustics here. There is not a whisper anywhere that cannot be heard everywhere."

"That's intense. That's another one I'll have to think about." He did give a moment to thought as he continued to take in the spirit and scope of this incredible structure. "I feel like there should be statues of famous people in here, to help fill up all the empty space."

"We could not possibly do that," Brian said.

"Why not?"

"Here everyone is equal. We cannot lift up any one person by building a statue of them. We lift up everyone by building monuments to principles. I know that this is kind of heavy, but that is what this building is. You will understand this more a little later."

Seemingly endless halls radiated out from this great foyer like spokes on a wheel. Brian and Eddie finally reached the far side and entered one of the elegant hallways that really did appear to stretch on to infinity. They passed countless lighted open doorways every few feet on either side. Eddie saw that inside each door, a long room was lined floor to ceiling with shelves filled with small binder-like cartridges.

"Inside these rooms is the greatest collection of videos ever assembled anywhere in the universe. That is why it is called Universal Video."

"Incredible!" Eddie shook his head in awe. "This hallway goes on forever. And it's all movies."

"All the hallways are full of movies."

"What's the rental fee here?"

"In terms of money, movies are free."

"You're kidding! Free?"

"That does not mean there is no cost involved. Movies here are not like the ones back home. I need to warn you—movies here are completely uncensored. They can be quite offensive because you get to see it all."

"REALLY? I've never seen an uncensored movie before."

"It is a new experience. All the movies here are filmed live action and nothing is left to the imagination or on the editing room floor. What would you like to see? Name anybody past, present or future. Napoleon? Moses? Joan of Arc?"

Eddie paused to think.

Brian became anxious. "Who will it be?"

"Gosh, I don't know."

"There must be somebody whose life you would like to see or know about."

"How about Cindy Crystal."

"Good choice. One Cindy Crystal coming right up."

Brian and Eddie were instantly alone in a great and glorious motion picture theater, at the back of the center aisle. Once again Eddie was amazed at the exquisite beauty of the buildings. "I've never seen a theater like this one."

"They built them like this way back when. They were called Movie Palaces."

"Can we sit in the balcony?"

"Whereever you would like to sit is fine."

"Except the balcony is not the best view, huh?"

"Any seat in this theater is the best view because the screen adjusts."

"No way!"

"Yes way. All the way to the balcony."

They were removed to the balcony above. No sooner did they take their seats in the middle of the front row than a tuxedo-clad waiter showed up just beside them in the aisle. He balanced a large dome-lidded golden platter on one arm.

"Good day gentlemen. Would you care to order?"

"We haven't seen a menu yet," Eddie said. He looked at Brian and giggled.

"I think you should allow me to order for you, Eddie. The menu here is really extensive. What kind of juice would you like?"

"Don't they sell soda?"

"They only serve drinks that are good for you."

"B-o-r-i-n-g."

"You will change your mind once you taste the drinks here. You will not want soda ever again." Brian turned to the waiter. "Could we please have two Nectars number 117, and two large popcorns."

"Very good."

"Can I have extra butter?" Eddie said.

Brian turned. "The popcorn here does not need butter. Trust me."

The waiter smiled and lifted the lid from the platter with a sweeping arm movement to reveal two stemmed crystal glasses and two small footed golden buckets. "Two hot popcorns and two kiwi-coconut-cloudberry coolers." He handed the platter to Brian. "If you require anything else, I shall be right along. Thank you."

"Thank you."

With that the waiter simply went away.

Eddie's brow was heavy with thought. "How did the waiter know what we were going to order?"

"He did not know."

"How did he know what to bring on that platter?"

"He did not know what to bring either."

"How did our order get under that lid?"

"We ordered to be under there."

"So it was —" Eddie looked at the goblets and into the buckets as Brian placed the tray on a special platter rest device right between their seats. He noticed specifically the very small size of the popcorn buckets. "I thought you ordered large popcorns."

"I did."

"Maybe the waiter didn't hear you."

"These are large."

"These are the littlest large I've ever seen."

"It will be all you can eat."

"These puny little things? Now how long have you been dead?"

"Very funny."

Eddie picked up one of the golden buckets. "This is empty. They're both empty."

"They just look empty."

"Invisible popcorn?"

"False bottom. The corn pops up and presents itself when you are ready to eat it. That way it is always at its peak of freshness."

"And the butter?"

"If you want hot buttered popcorn, it will be hot buttered popcorn. Try it."

With a look of half disbelief, Eddie put his hand into the empty bucket and pulled out a fist full of popcorn. "This is the coolest thing I've ever seen!" He just stared at the popcorn in his hand.

"Eat it while it is still warm."

Eddie shoved the popcorn in his mouth and quickly reached into the bucket for more.

"You can have a different flavor every bite if you want—Caramel corn, cheese corn, chocolate corn. The popcorn knows what you are thinking and it will be whatever flavor you want it to be."

Eddie picked up one of the empty goblets and held it to his mouth and drank. And drank. And drank.

"Hey, slow down there partner."

Eddie pulled the glass from his mouth. "It's so good I couldn't stop. I know I shouldn't drink too much because I don't want to have to run to the bathroom in the middle of the movie."

"There is none of that here."

"They don't let you go during the movie? What do you do if you really got to go?"

"We do not need to go."

"What do you mean we don't need to go?"

"We never have the need to go to the bathroom. We do not even have bathrooms."

"Where does all the juice go?"

"All the good stuff is absorbed by your body."

"What about the not good stuff?"

"It is all good stuff."

"We should have come here years ago," Eddie said. "I never have liked bathrooms."

"Everything has its time. And I think it is time for a movie. Are you ready to watch the film?"

"Do we have to wait for other people to come?"

"We have the theater reserved. Just you and me."

"Really?"

"Really."

"Then I'm ready when you are."

"Put your feet up on the railing there and make yourself comfortable."

"Are you sure?"

"Go ahead."

"You're not just saying that to get me in trouble?"

"I would not do anything to cause you trouble."

"You used to. The last time you told me to put my feet up on the railing was at the civic auditorium, and I got in trouble."

"I have grown since then."

"Like two feet."

"And my two feet are going right up here." Brian plopped his feet up on the gleaming gold railing along the edge of the balcony right in front of them. "They actually do encourage you to put your feet up here. Anything to make you comfortable."

"Roll 'em," Brian called out and the giant diamond chandelier suspended from the ceiling above them began to dim. A music conductor way below them down in the orchestra pit, dressed in a black tuxedo, raised his arm and waved. Brian waved back and the conductor gave a down beat with his baton. A live full orchestra began a lush sweeping overture as the golden velvet curtain rose.

The screen lit up to a rosy pink. Brian turned to Eddie with a grin bursting out of his face. "Watch this!"

The entire screen rotated upward and forward to a position right in front of them.

"Whoa! Just when you think you've seen it all."

"A CINDY CRYSTAL FILM" scrolled across center screen in swirling cursive calligraphy encircled by white rose buds that bloomed while they watched. The soft light of a candle flame was the next image to fill the screen as it burned in front of a mirror. The actual flame and the reflected image gently flickered together and appeared as one.

The surroundings and background slowly came into focus revealing a thick pink candle held in the palms of Cindy Crystal's clasped hands.

"That's Cindy!" Eddie said.

"Yes."

"What's she doing?"

"She's making a Halloween wish. Just watch."

She gazed intently into the mirror and whispered a secret spell.

"Looking glass and candle's fire
Let thy magic intertwine.
Grant the wish that I desire —
This Halloween make Eddie mine.
So mote it be."

"What does she mean 'make Eddie mine?'"

"She just really wants to be your friend. She does not have friends. Most all the kids at school pick on her."

Cindy leaned forward, closed her eyes and gently placed her lips upon the mirror to seal her spell with a kiss.

"Is she really a witch?"

"Witch is only an earth term. It means nothing to us here. Cindy is simply trying to draw all the energy she can to help her in her quest for friends."

The film cut away to the Crystal Ball Salon where Cindy's mother, half in and half out of witch makeup was wishing her daughter luck. Cindy was dressed as Cinderella for the ball, hair done up beautifully with a glittering tiara tucked in front. Her evening gown shimmered with pearls and rhinestones. Topping it all off were her elbow length pale pink evening gloves with a pink diamond and white gold ring on her left hand.

"You look gorgeous, Sweetie. Like a princess."

Cindy beamed at her mother's compliment.

"I'm sorry that I can't take you myself, but going in a hired limousine is much more special anyway."

"Where's she going in a limo?" Eddie said.

"Shhhh. Just watch."

The Magic Hour

Mrs. Crystal hugged Cindy. "The driver all ready picked it up so you're good to go girl."

"Thanks for everything, Mom."

"You are welcome. Good luck, Sweetheart. I'll be waiting for you to find out everything."

Sandy kissed Cindy good-bye and then watched as her daughter literally danced out the front door of the salon to a waiting stretch limo. A kindly gray-haired driver in uniform, opened her door and they drove away.

Cindy fidgeted nervously as they passed through town.

The driver looked in his rear view mirror at Cindy in the back. "Must be some special man to receive this kind of attention."

"Oh, he is. Today's his birthday."

"Born on Halloween is he?"

"Oh, yes. That makes him all the more special."

"Any man would be honored to receive a gift like this from a princess like you."

Cindy glowed from his compliment. "You have the address don't you?"

"I do, thank you. And I know right where it is. I've actually been to the house before. Nice people."

They arrived at the house and the limo slowed.

"This is it, Miss."

The front view of the McCourt home as seen from across the street filled the screen.

"That's our house!" Eddie said. "That's what it looks like from over at the Buchanans."

"Shhhh. Just watch."

The driver turned the car around and pulled right up to the edge of the McCourt driveway, but parked obscured from the house by the large hedge across the front of the property. He opened Cindy's door and together they walked around to the front passenger door, which opened to reveal a magnificent tiered pink wedding-like cake resting on the seat.

"WOW!" Eddie was beside himself at the cake's magnificence. "That's a triple-layer cherry fudge cake with cream cheese and coconut filling!" A perplexed look struck his face. "Hey! Wait a minute. How'd I know that?"

Brian just smiled.

The driver carefully lifted the cake out of the car and carried it to the bottom of the drive.

"I can get it from here." Cindy reached her arms out to hold the huge cake.

"Are you sure? At least let me balance it on your arms for you."

"I got it." She fell forward from the weight, but caught her self. "I can do it."

"Good luck, Honey. I'll just be waiting here behind the hedge."

"Thank you."

Cindy clumsily walked up the driveway taking every care not to fall and sang a happy birthday melody in her sweetest voice. Her face radiated as she neared the house, her beaming smile literally stretched ear to ear. At the porch steps she looked up and stopped. And gasped! She saw the killed teddy bears dangling by their necks above above her.

Close shots of the individual dead bears flashed back and forth across the screen interspersed with close ups of Eddie's hand as it stabbed the Bearide of Frankenbear over and over right in the chest. Cindy screamed violently.

She saw the Bearide of Frankenbear stabbed through the heart and fell helplessly forward, head-long over into the cake. A deep red frosting rose atop the cake crushed into her chest and smeared a crimson stain right across and over her heart.

"STOP! STOP IT!" Eddie screamed, but the film played on.

Cindy and the cake landed on the cement steps and cake splattered up and down the porch, onto the driveway and even out onto the front lawn. She lay dead in the middle of the ruined cake.

"STOP IT! TURN IT OFF! CUT!"

With the word "CUT," the screen instantly went dark.

"Why did you show me that?"

"You asked to see Cindy Crystal's life. That is what she experienced today."

"I didn't know it was gonna be that!"

"Of course not. I did warn you though, that you would see it all. I told you that films here are uncensored. That is what you did to Cindy today."

"I did that to her?"

"You did. When you made the decision to execute the bears, you gave no thought whatsoever to how it might affect the person who gave you those bears."

"I didn't."

"Every single thing we do affects other people whether we think about it or not. All the great discoveries throughout history and the great and noble accomplishments of men are all recorded here in this library, but the most important lessons that history has to teach are simply the stories of how we treated others. You not only saw and heard what Cindy experienced today, you also felt what she experienced."

"It was awful."

"Yes, it was awful. You understand that now, because you now know the emotional cost of your actions to Cindy's life."

"I didn't understand that."

"The value in making mistakes is that we can learn from them and then become better people."

"Are all the movies like this?"

"It depends. If you mean are they all awful—they also record all the good things we do for people and how nice we are. Those can be very moving."

"How do they put that in a movie?"

"They use a special film stock that not only captures the sights and sounds of history, but it also captures the emotions. That is why the movies here pack such a punch."

"I don't feel good. I feel like I killed Cindy."

"In a way you did. You stabbed her spirit right in the heart."

"It was Tad's idea."

"It might have been Tad's idea initially, but the little voice inside of you said not to do it and you made the decision to do it anyway."

"I'm really sorry."

"I am not the one to whom you need to apologize. Her name is Cindy. And you should do it at your very first opportunity. The only way for her to be able to heal properly, is with your sincere apology, and that is the only way for you to really learn and grow from this as well. Will you apologize to her?"

"I will. I promise."

"Everyone has the little voice of conscience inside of them. It is a gift. And it will always tell you the right thing. If we do not listen to it or if we ignore it, it can be taken away."

Eddie pondered a moment. "Who is the little voice?"

"Everybody has loved ones who have died who care very much

about them. Even if they have never met them. Because these loved ones can see the big picture of our lives, they try to help us and warn us so that we do not make mistakes."

"You mean guardian angels?"

"You thought they only had guardian angels in the movies. They are real."

"Are you mine?"

"I am still new here. I have lots to learn before I can take on that kind of responsibility. Your guardian angel has been with you since the day you were born."

"Somebody's been following me around ever since I was born?"

"It is the same with everybody. People get help all the time that they do not even know about."

"Is he suppose to protect me?"

"That is one of the things he does."

"Where was he when the Erlking came and got me?"

"When you arrived here and climbed out of the carriage, did you look at the driver's face?"

"Just for a second. I was afraid to."

"Did he look familiar to you?"

"Maybe a little."

"He should have looked familiar because you have met him before. He is your guardian angel."

Eddie was taken aback. "The Erlking is my guardian angel?"

"No. No. No."

"Who is my guardian angel?"

"Uncle Louie."

"Uncle Louie? And he's the Erlking?"

"No! No! Please give me a minute to explain."

"Okay."

"Uncle Louie was right there in the woods with you. He did not leave you even for a minute."

"Why did he let the Erlking take me?"

"He did not take you. In your mind you believed that the Erlking was after you. You had already created that scenario so securely in your head, that there was nothing Uncle Louie could do but play along."

"So Uncle Louie's the one who really took me, but because I believed it was the Erlking, that's what I saw?"

"That is right."

"That wasn't very nice. Let me believe I was being taken away by the Erlking."

"After you fell and hit your head, you still had a long way to come. It was the logical thing to do. It was the only thing to do."

"It was still a crumby thing to do."

"That is the power of imagination, Eddie. Most people have no idea how powerful it really is. And why it is so important to always use it for positive purposes. By the time you reached this plane, though, the darkness and deception had to disperse and that is when you saw the coach and driver for what they really are."

"I was wondering what the deal was—why everything changed all of the sudden the way it did. So who is the Erlking?"

"The Erlking is a folk character created long ago to explain away childhood deaths that otherwise had no explanation."

"So he's not real?"

"The Erlking is very real. Because someone created him. That is the danger of human imagination run amuck. That is the danger of not controlling your thoughts. When we imagine something, we actually set energies and events into motion that can and will eventually bring our thoughts to fulfillment. Your imagination literally brought you here, Eddie."

"So when the Erlking knocked me down on the trail, was that my imagination, too?"

"No, no. You really were knocked down. But that was not the Erlking, that was a young man named Earl King – who likes to pretend that he is The Erlking."

"So what's his problem? Why's he so mean?"

"He had a very difficult day and was carrying a burden of anger."

"He didn't have to lay it on me, I didn't do anything to him. He's the one who knocked ME down."

"He really had had a difficult day. Sometimes, and especially at Halloween, he becomes a little haughty."

"What does that mean?"

"He acts too big for his britches."

"Oh. Cindy said he acts like he owns the place."

"Some of the time he does act that way, so today it was all arranged for him to encounter some diffficulties in order to bring him down to size."

"What happened?"

"He stepped out of bed this morning onto a golf ball."

"Ow."

"He twisted his ankle and really bruised his hip when he hit the floor. The funniest part about it is that he does not play golf."

"So how'd the golf ball get there?"

"I cannot say—trade secret. Anyway, then he pulled his Halloween costume out of the closet and found gaping moth holes all over in it. On his way to go buy a new costume, he was pulled over and ticketed for not having any license plates. It was then that he realized his custom plates – ERLKING – had been stolen. While he shopped, a big delivery truck rolled down the hill and smashed into his parked car and totalled it. He fought the rest of the day with the insurance company and finally was given a temporary replacement vehicle and then on the way here tonight his tire had a blow out."

"Rough day."

"So when the hem of his cape caught and ripped on your costume, he almost lost it. He really was not mad at you. He was just mad because things kept going wrong. Anyway, Earl King is not The Erlking even though he likes to pretend that he is. And there is no reason to be afraid of him. Later, you and he will have the chance to clear things up between you. So do not hold any grudges against him, okay?"

Eddie nodded.

"Just pretend that you are in his movie and before the movie is over everything will be wrapped up in a pretty bow."

"Okay. So can just anybody come here and watch these movies?"

"Anyone who lives in this realm. But not everyone lives here on this level. Some people when they pass over go to very different places than here."

"Bad places?"

"The right places for them based on how they lived their lives."

"Have you ever been to those places?"

"I have. I went with Grandpa once when he went to do some research."

"Was it scary?"

"I was more worried than scared, because the people there are so lonely and they do not understand how to let go of the negative thoughts that are holding them back."

"How did Uncle Louie die?"

"You should ask him yourself. He is right beside you."

"He is?" Eddie turned to look.

Uncle Louie appeared. "I am always right beside you."

"Uncle Louie, I know you were only four years old when you died, but are you able to talk about it?"

"Oh, sure. I do not have any qualms."

"What happened with you and Grandpa when you died?"

"We were playing along the top of the canal that was near our house, seeing who could make the biggest splash by pushing the biggest rock into the water. I made the biggest splash when I went in with the biggest rock and the whole side of the canal. Your Grandpa froze he was so scared. He was terrified as he watched me be swept away by the swift current. There really was nothing he could do. He was only seven himself, and the water would have carried him away as well. I have never blamed him for not jumping in to try to save me," Uncle Louie continued. "We would have both been killed. He had a difficult time with it his entire life, though. He felt guilty for not saving me, and he felt guilty because he knew that we were not supposed to play near the canal. We both knew that. Truth be told, your great great grandmother was right there beside your Grandpa—she had already passed on. She was on strict orders to hold him back because it was not yet his time."

"Now I understand why Grandpa joked about tombstones all the time. He was still hurting. Kind of like me."

"That is very insightful Eddie. You are very intelligent. You are a good boy. I have lots of fun taking care of you."

Grandpa McCourt appeared right beside them. "You are wise beyond your years, Eddie. I could not speak of that to anyone my whole life. It was just too painful."

"Talking about it helps the pain to go away," Eddie said.

"I understand that now, but I did not then."

"You joked about the tombstones because that was the only way you could deal with it."

"That is right. What your Uncle Louie did not tell you is that it was me who pushed that big rock in. I was jabbing a big stick behind it trying to dig all the dirt out when, KAPUSH! Not only the rock, but the whole canal embankment caved in taking Louie with it."

"I was feeling guilty that Brian died just like you were, Grandpa, 'cuz Louie died. I told him that we had to listen to the CD."

Brian turned to Eddie. "It was not your fault at all, Eddie. And the Erlking did not kill me. I just fell. Grandpa was there and saw the whole thing. It was not anyone's fault. It just happened. So, please, do not think that you are responsible for my death."

Eddie listened and accepted. "How come nobody believes that we don't really die when we die?"

"Because they are afraid to believe. Death is kind of like getting your report card in school. If you know that you did your best, you are not afraid. If you played around, you want to hide your report card and not even look at it. You want to pretend that it does not even exist. It is the same with life. Some people pretend that death is the end, that there is nothing after it. That way they do not have to worry about the mistakes they made."

Eddie sat thoughtfully for a moment.

"Does God live here?"

"Not far from here."

"He's a nice man, isn't he."

"Very."

"I can feel it."

"That feeling is love. Perfect love. Everyone here feels it for every living thing. There is no hate. Do you hate anyone?"

"Well, I used to hate Elliott Carney. Almost everybody does."

"How do you think that makes Elliott feel that everybody hates him? That everybody teases him all the time?"

"I DON'T WANNA SEE ANY MORE MOVIES!"

"When you are ready. I wish you had some idea, Eddie, how good you made Elliott feel when you stopped in at his house. He really does not have friends."

"I really didn't go to see him at first."

"I know. You only went there to use the telephone so you could get a ride home. But you were polite about it and Elliott thought you came to see him. Inspite of the initial reason for the visit, you were able to learn a little about Elliott and his world."

"He's a neat kid. I was really impressed once I got to know him."

"He is an impressive person and he will go far in life. It is the same with anyone. When we begin to understand them, our hearts can begin to embrace them."

"Even bullies like Tad?"

"Even bullies like Tad. As difficult as he is to like, if you really knew all the problems that he has in his life—the neglect, the abuse, his fears—it would be a little easier to like him even inspite of his bad habits."

"I know his dad's in prison."

"Not any more."

"Did he get out?"

"You remember when Tad went home with his mother from school?"

"I do."

"Tad's father was killed in a prison uprising. That's when Tad found out, that morning at school."

"Tad said he couldn't talk about it."

"He was hurting too much and he was afraid."

"Afraid of what?"

"Afraid of what all the kids would do if they found out his dad was in prison. That's why Tad acts like a bully. Not because he is strong, but because he is afraid and hurting inside. Do you know what is the opposite of love?"

"Hate?"

"It is fear. Hate is a weakness caused by fear. That is why bullies like Tad act the way they do. Because they are afraid and they are hiding their fear and weakness behind an attitude of hate. Love is the only real strength. It is the strongest force in the universe."

"I've heard that before."

"It is true."

"So what happened with Tad's father?"

"He was actually trying to calm the other inmates when he was caught in the fray. He was due to be released on parole next spring. He was learning from his mistakes and trying to make things right. Now, Eddie. You cannot talk to anyone about any of this except Tad. Not Mom. Not Dad. But do talk to Tad. Let him know you care and so do the other kids. Let him know they want to be his friend, but he must be nice."

"Have you seen his dad?"

"I have not. Tad's grandmother came to see me, though. She passed over some time ago. She has seen him. She says he is doing fine and has a really good attitude."

"That's good."

"But they are both worried sick about Tad. That is why she came to see me. She knows what good friends we have been with Tad. She told me how proud she was of you, Eddie, when you told him off after he tripped Cindy."

"He needed it."

"You are right. What he did was cruel and dangerous. But his grandmother begged me to ask you not to write him off as a friend. He needs you. He needs a friend who will stand up to him when he listens to the wrong voices and behaves badly. Tad was caught with the stolen CD's from Mr. Warburton's office."

"That was him?"

"He would have been expelled immediately because he was caught before, stealing money out of teachers' purses, but the principal was worried about him. Because of all the things on his record, Tad was to have gone to a Youth Services Retention Facility with one more strike. But with his dad dying, Mr. Warburton felt that he should stay with his family, so he did not report it."

"That was really nice of him," Eddie said.

"He cares about Tad. He knows that Tad has great potential with all his energy and enthusiam. He simply needs to learn responsiblity so he can use it constructively."

"How did they catch Tad? Cindy said she didn't say anything to anybody."

"A teacher on recess duty overheard Cindy accuse Tad."

"You have to watch what you say, huh?"

"Yes, indeed. Eddie, I want you to have Dad take Tad with you next time you go fishing or camping or anywhere. Take him in my place. Tad needs positive experiences."

"We can do that."

"There is an old saying that it takes a village to raise a boy. Tad needs help from many directions. I know you will help."

"I will."

"It will take patience. Working with angry youth is not easy, but it is important. We have a responsibility to love and accept everyone. I know that we can count on you, Eddie."

Eddie sat quietly to think on everything. "Does it ever rain here?"

"Only if we want it to. But even then, we do not get wet."

CHAPTER SIXTEEN

"EDDIE" echoed through the night woods as Sabbateurs stretched shoulder-to-shoulder in every direction and called his name. Their torches and flashlights cast an unearthly glow in the forest.

Lois and her new found friend, the Executioner, walked along with the searching crowds. They looked under bushes and inside of dead trees, literally combing the woods as they passed.

"We'll find him," Lois said. "We cannot help but find him with everybody looking. EDDIE! Oh, EDDIE!"

"Don't be so sure. We may not find him."

"Oh, stop! Of course we will."

"Think about it. A little kid with all these monsters coming after him. That could scare anybody to death, let alone a little kid. He may not want to be found."

"Oh, go look behind that log." She completely ignored his negative comment.

"Aye, wench. What ever you say."

Lois followed the Executioner to a large fallen tree. "You know, I do not even know your name yet."

"Call me Bert."

"I cannot say that I have ever been called a wench before. This is a first for me."

"And you're quite a wench at that!"

Lois cooed in the afterglow of his compliment. "It is rather exciting when you say that."

"You've come a long way tonight, Lois."

"How so?"

"When I first saw you, it was as plain as the mudpack on your face that you were one unhappy camper. The rule is nobody leaves here without having a good time. That's why I grabbed you. After a couple dances you loosened right up. Became a person again."

Lois was wide-eyed and all ears.

"The whole world is so uptight about one thing or another that it's lost its humanity. That's why we all come here tonight—to celebrate our humanness and share fellowship."

"But you don't even know what I really look like," Lois said.

"Doesn't matter. Humanity comes from the inside. That's where all the worth and beauty of a soul lies. For that matter, you don't know what I look like either under this hood."

"You're right. About it all. I do just have to ask, though. Why the executioner?"

"Used to be my nickname in a former life, back before I rejoined the human race instead of the rat race. It reminds me how far I've come and that I'm not going back."

"It is very decent of everyone to stop the party and search this way."

"Of course we would. You know I wasn't trying to be negative back there when I said we wouldn't find him. I want to find the little tyke as much as anyone."

"The lost boy, he's my brother's son."

"Is he now? Your nephew. I was only trying to see things from his perspective. With all these monsters coming after him, calling out his name—I was just thinking, that could send a little boy into hiding so he won't be found."

"You have a very valid point. Just look at this sight. The woods full of monsters carrying torches. It is frightful. I am so impressed that you would even think to understand his perspective."

"The first rule of accomplishing anything is try to understand the other's point of view."

"Now I really know we will find him, with all these good, intelligent people like you helping out."

"It pleases me to see you just relax and have a good time."

Lois was quite smitten with this man whose face she had never seen. His executioner's hood completely obscured it. "It's refreshing that everyone here has been so welcoming and friendly. I have truly had a good time."

"That's what it's all about. Getting along and enjoying each other's company."

"But especially you, Bert. I've never known such a nice brawny fellow as yourself."

"I think you're a swell person, too."

They looked at each other and shared a moment.

Meanwhile, back at Witches' Point up in the control tower, Sandy continued to spearhead and monitor the search effort.

She had immediately radioed the front entrance to check if Eddie had passed there, but he had not. She then masterfully organized and sent out the hundreds of party goers to hunt for Eddie in an orderly and coordinated manner. She next took the time to discuss some important things about Eddie with his parents. Cindy was also present, right beside her mother.

"Please, let me first say how sorry I am for the loss of your son, Brian," Sandy said. "I didn't know him, but when I heard that he had passed on I could only think of his poor parents going through every parent's worse nightmare, to bury a child."

The McCourts' demeanor softened as Sandy spoke.

"Also please know that I truly believe in my heart that your sweet little Eddie will be just fine, but I must tell you a few things. Tonight, he is on a quest that I don't think anyone could keep his determined heart from pursuing. Eddie says that Brian specifically told him to look for him tonight. With that, he was committed to reaching his brother."

"Why wouldn't Eddie talk to us?" his mother said.

Doctor McCourt nodded. "Yes. Why wouldn't he tell us that?"

"Maybe at the time you weren't open to hearing it. I know he said you didn't believe him that Brian was was still alive and communicating with him."

Mrs. McCourt put her hand to her face. "I can't believe we shut him out. We just thought he was refusing to accept that Brian died."

"Which is common in children," Sandy said.

"We turned our son away. I feel terrible."

"For whatever reason, he wasn't comfortable with your belief in what he believed, or in what he had already told you. So he would not open up to you."

"Eddie kept insisting that Brian wasn't dead," Doctor McCourt said. "At first we humored him. We figured it simply was denial. But then he started telling us things that Brian supposedly told him. And we still didn't believe him."

"Then he started telling us weird things, even unnerving things. Like the Giants were going to win. And about relatives we'd never heard of and when they died. We didn't know what to think. But just last night, for the first time, we finally started to really understand and believe him."

Sandy sat forward on the sofa. "At any rate, I've been around a lot of mediums and even more fakes. This young boy possesses something extraordinary."

"You really think so?" his parents both said.

"I know so. Genuine psychic abilities like Eddie possesses are divine spiritual gifts no less precious than any other God-given talent. It needs to be nurtured and cultivated so he does not turn away from it as he grows older. Gifts like his are given with the sole purpose of being able to bless people's lives."

Both Mrs. and Doctor McCourt could hardly believe that this woman whom they had never even met, knew their own child better than they did. They also were both touched by her understanding and her compassionate way.

"This is all well and good," Doctor McCourt said, "but why would Brian even know, let alone think to come here?"

"Before you pass complete judgement on us here, please let me explain a few more things. Anciently it was believed that on this night, Halloween—the most hallowed night of the year, the spirits of all those who passed on during the years came back one last time in search of their loved ones. The townsfolk would gather around great bonfires to light the way for the spirits and to show them where to come. Later tonight, we have what we call The Bonfires. A solemn time of meditation, if you will, with the fires. Some people use it to sober up, but most find it a reverent time to be close to their deceased loved ones. Some people have had extraordinary experiences over the years."

"It sounds quite unlike what we saw earlier," Mrs. McCourt said.

"Oh, it is. It is a quiet time, when everyone can be alone with their thoughts and feelings for those they have lost."

"We had no idea."

"Most people don't. Witches' Sabbath is not exactly what it appears to be on the surface. Our play is a little raucous, but that's all the further it goes. I'm sure you have your own opinions of the Witches' Sabbath the way every one does. But as for all the people who just quit partying and are now out searching for a little lost boy, they are good people who on this night can simply let go and have a little fun."

Cindy demurely sat forward on the sofa. "Mrs. McCourt? I'm really sorry for what I did at the cake walk tonight. It wasn't very nice of me. I was so angry and upset at Eddie for killing all the teddy bears, I didn't know what else to do to get back at him. I really am sorry."

"Thank you, Cindy, for your apology. But please know I'm sorry, too. Those adorable teddy bears, Eddie has enjoyed receiving them so much. I was so stressed out with finishing the cakes and getting ready for forty-five house guests —"

"Forty-five?" Sandy and Cindy both said in shock.

"Oh, yes. In fact, all forty-five of them are here. Anyway, I wasn't even aware of what Eddie had done. He owes you an apology and we will see that he does so."

Doctor McCourt nodded his head in agreement. "Not to change the subject, but are all these people really witches?"

Sandy grinned. "You mean do they have green skin and hairy warts? No. Do they practice withcraft? Some do, but even that is not necessarily what you might think. We can talk more later, but I think we should get back to the matter of finding your little boy."

"Please. What exactly did Brian say to Eddie about tonight?"

"He told him to look for him when time stands still."

Mrs. McCourt looked at her husband then turned to Sandy. "Pat and I were just talking about that before we came."

"Did Eddie tell you he was coming here tonight?" Sandy said.

Doctor McCourt shook his head. "As far as we thought, he was sleeping out over at a friend's home."

"How did you know to come here?"

"We had a phone call from someone who was concerned because they saw Cindy and Eddie walking through the cemetery a while ago."

"You see!" Sandy said. "Right there, you are being watched over. The odds of someone who knows you well enough to call you because they saw Eddie. I know we will find him. But I also know, looking at the time, we only have thirty minutes to do so."

The McCourts were astounded at Sandy and her perceptive abilities. Doctor McCourt looked at his watch.

"That's right. It's 1:30."

"So for thirty more minutes it's technically still one o'clock," Mrs. McCourt said. She turned to look at her husband the same moment he turned to look at her. "We need to tell him," they both said at the same time.

"We always intended to when the time was right," she next said.

"This is the right time."

The Magic Hour

"I agree. We just have to find him first."

Sandy stood up. "There is reason for concern."

"Mom?" Cindy tried to interrupt, but Sandy ignored her and kept talking.

"There is no way for us to know in what capacity they will meet. Whether Brian will come here, or whether Eddie will go there."

"Mom?" Cindy said again.

"Not while I'm talking. Now if Eddie does or has gone to visit Brian there on the other side, heaven only knows what trauma he may have suffered to sever the chord that binds us here. No one is ever released casually from this sphere."

"Oh, Dear God." Mrs. McCourt shut her eyes in prayer. "Please don't let anything happen to our Eddie."

"MOM! I know how to find Eddie!" Cindy said when the conversation lulled a moment.

"Cindy! Why didn't you say so?"

"I've been trying to for ten minutes."

"Oh, I'm sorry."

"I just have to call him on his walkie-talkie."

"Oh. Thank God!" Mrs. McCourt cried. "CALL HIM! CALL HIM!"

Cindy quickly pulled the walkie-talkie from her satchel. "EDDIE! COME IN, EDDIE! THIS IS CINDY. WHERE ARE YOU?"

There was no reply.

"LET ME CALL HIM!" Eddie's father took the walkie-talkie from Cindy. "EDDIE! CAN YOU HERE ME? THIS IS DAD!"

Still there was no reply.

"He could be out of range or his battery could be dead," Doctor McCourt said trying to be optimistic.

"Or he could have dropped it or something so it's not with him," Sandy said.

Cindy took a deep breath. "Or something could have happened to him so he can't answer."

His mother looked sick. "Ooooh! Don't say that, please."

Sandy put her arm around her. "Everything's going to be all right. We're going to find him."

Doctor McCourt put his hand on Cindy's shoulder. "We need to retrace his steps. Can you show us which way he left?"

"Sure. Come on!"

They all raced out the tower door and down the little road past the string of fires.

"He entered the path right there." Cindy pointed to where she and Eddie said good-bye.

Doctor McCourt started down the path. "We need to follow along here and continue to call him. Come on."

"There's a search button, too," Cindy said.

"Good idea! I'll press it."

He pushed the button but they heard only silence.

They hurried down into the woods and stopped every few hundred feet to call again on the walkie-talkie.

"Press the search button," Mrs. McCourt said.

They all stopped to listen but again heard only silence.

As they moved deeper into the forest, they worked their way closer to the other searching crowds. They pressed the search button and listened but only heard voices of others calling Eddie's name.

Sandy screamed with all her might! "EVERYBODY SHU-U-U-T U-U-U-UP!" Her voice was so loud it not only rattled the night air, it shook the trees. They all stopped and listened intently while Doctor McCourt pushed the search button yet again. This time their efforts were rewarded. Off in the distance—a faint electronic squeal.

"THAT'S HIM!" Eddie's mother screamed with excitement. "PRESS IT AGAIN! KEEP PRESSING IT!"

Again the same distant squeal was heard from off in the forest. Doctor McCourt repeatedly pressed the button as they all methodically worked their way through the dark woods toward the sound.

"OVER THERE!" Cindy took off through the trees.

"THE RAVINE!" Sandy said. "Come on!"

They fought through thick undergrowth and the beeping became louder.

Because she was shorter, Cindy made her way more quickly through a dense thicket. "THERE HE IS! THERE HE IS!" She approached a large rock on top of which sat Eddie's green high-top sneaker. She quickly examined the shoe and saw the sprigs of dry grass stuck all over in it. "I hate stickers."

Doctor McCourt came frantically running up. "WHERE IS HE?"

"His shoe!" Cindy handed him the sneaker.

Sandy and Mrs. McCourt finally caught up.

"Oh, Dear God. Please help us!" Mrs. McCourt cried out in desperation when she saw the shoe. Sandy put her arm around her and squeezed. "We'll find him. We'll find him."

Doctor McCourt picked up the other walkie-talkie off the ground beside the big rock. "We know he was here." His voice, too, shook with emotion. "Let's fan out and keep searching. We have to look under every bush and behind every tree. Let's split into pairs since we have two flashlights. We can cover more ground. Sandy, if you and Cindy will go that way, we'll go over here. And stay together as you search."

They broke off and went their different directions.

Sandy fought her way through a thicket of scrubby undergrowth and realized she could no longer see Cindy. "CINDY! WHERE ARE YOU?"

"I'm right over here, Mom, through the trees."

Sandy breathed a sigh of relief then focused back on Eddie. The more time passed, the more she began to doubt herself and her feelings of hope. "Eddie, oh, Eddie. Where can you be?"

A loud scream pierced the sky, followed by complete silence. Sandy and Cindy both froze.

"HE'S OVER HERE," a deep male voice called out breaking the tension. "BRING THE DOCTOR!"

Sandy and Cindy were close to the voice and rushed through the trees toward it. They both turned white as they approached a host of Sabbateurs silently clustered around in a circle. No one spoke. Sandy frantically pushed her way through the crowd.

"Let me through! Let me through!" She shrieked when she saw Eddie lying on the ground face down, He was still in the same position as when he first fell. A horned monster pushed his way through the bodies.

"LET ME THROUGH! I'M A DOCTOR!"

Sandy looked up at the sky. "Oh, please dear God, let him live." She knelt down beside Eddie then the doctor gently turned him over. Dried blood covered his face. Cindy saw Eddie and turned away in hysterics. Sandy panicked and screamed. "GET AN AMBULANCE!"

CHAPTER SEVENTEEN

"Where are we going?" Eddie asked while he and Brian walked down a coral pink cobblestone promenade that gently wound down a lush embankment.

"Some place fun."

"Just tell me."

"It's called Camel-Lot."

"No way!"

"Yes way!"

"LET'S GO! I'm there!"

Eddie noticed exotic pink stone towers and strangely twisting turrets rising to astonishing heights above the trees just ahead.

"Is that it?"

"It is."

"It looks better than I even imagined."

They arrived at the front of a splendiferous pink stone castle that at once looked ancient and new. Both stopped to take in the sight. Pink and white lotus blossoms as tall as trees rose from the water garden that encircled the bottom of the castle. Blooming vines scaled the walls to dizzying heights.

"I can't believe I'm actually here at Camelot," Eddie said.

"This is not where King Arthur lives."

"But I thought you said —"

"This is Camel-Lot."

"Camel-Lot. What's that?"

"Where people go to ride camels."

"Nah!"

"Yes. Come on inside."

They crossed a bridge and entered the castle proper to find more breathtaking water gardens full of fountains, reflecting pools and great statues of all different kinds of animals.

Eddie's eyes roamed in attempt to take it all in. "I've never seen so many animal statues before."

"That is because this is a Creature Co-op."

"What does that mean?"

"It is one of the places where a whole wide range of animals come to give public service."

"The animals give public service?"

"Everyone and everything contributes here and does their part. Most of the time the animals enjoy being with themselves, but they realize that they have responsibilities to others just the way we do. So, here the animals donate their time as guides to give people the opportunity to experience nature in a way that they may never have before."

"This is wild."

"More than you know. Depending on which animal guide you pick—rhinoceros, elephant, ostrich, polar bear or whichever—the scenarios are all diferent."

They came upon an exquisite, much larger than life sculpture of a snow leopard. From a distance, the statue appeared to be made of bronze or some fine metal but as they drew near, it became crystalline transparent, with a brilliant light source radiating out from within the statue itself. The effect was dazzling and hypnotic. Eddie stared unable to move he was so entranced by the display.

"That light means the Snow Leopard Safari is open right now," Brian said.

"Can we go?"

"I have already made arrangements for Dromedary Dream."

"What's that?"

"A camel ed-venture into the deep desert."

Eddie did not appear particularly pleased. "Why'd you pick that one?"

"Out of respect for the camels. They are the ones who started this whole thing."

"You're kidding?"

"No. It began with just a handful of camels volunteering, but it became so popular that it has grown into quite an attraction. There are so many different ed-ventures now, it would practically take a lifetime to experience them all. Everyone wanted to keep the original name because it is so cute."

"That's pretty cool, really."

"You are going to enjoy it very much."

"So all these different animal statues represent different animal adventures?"

"That is right. Only here we call them ed-ventures because they are learning-based experiences."

Brian and Eddie continued to walk along a grand colonnade with repetitive sweeping arches. Toward the inside of the castle grounds, directly across from each archway was another animal sculpture. But on the opposing side, back under the colonnade, the matching arches led into the actual ed-ventures.

"This orangutan statue," Brian said, "represents the guide for the Orangutan Odyssey, which is right through the arch there. And the next one is Panda Passage."

"All the guides aren't riding animals?"

"Not at all. The orangutans hold your hand. There is a lot of vine riding involved, too, in this one."

"Isn't that dangerous?"

"Not here. You only fall if you want to."

"I like that approach."

"We just need to change our clothes and we are ready to go."

"I didn't bring any other clothes."

"Not a problem. They have clothes here. Just step behind that screen there."

"That glass wall? That's a changing screen? You can see right through it."

"Yes. It is a changing screen. You step behind it and you change. Try it."

"With a smirky grin on his face, Eddie followed Brian behind the clear plate wall. POOF! They were ready to go. Bare chested and bare foot, they donned matching psychedelic green and orange aloha surfer trunks with coordinating foreign legion caps, complete with back flaps. Identical black mirror sunglasses completed their picture of cool.

"I'm sold! I love it here," Eddie said.

"But you have hardly even seen anything, really."

"I've seen enough to know I like it here. Speaking of seeing things. Look at you! You're all hairy."

"That is what happens when you grow up."

"I can't believe how much hair you have on your legs."

"I take after mom's side of the family."

"And your armpits, too. You have more hair than dad does."

"You will have just as much hair when you get a little older."

"You think so?"

"I know so. We are twins. Remember?"
"Oh, yeah. Cool."
"Shall we go meet the camels?"
"Ready when you are. But, are we gonna need sun screen if we're going into the desert?'
"Not here."
"What about mosquito repellent? Are we going anywhere near water?"
"There are no mosquitos at this level, but there are places that have them. You do not want to go there. I promise."
"Well, let's not. But let's go."

Opposite a great statue of a noble-looking camel, the boys stepped through an archway into a vast painted desert setting. Two sleek, white, one-humped camels stood waiting just ahead of them, bedecked with ornate purple and gold trappings fit for the magi.

"Eddie, this is Ester. She will be your camel guide. And that is Sultana, my guide. They both say they are pleased to meet you."

"How do you know what the camels are thinking?"

"After you have been here a while, you begin to understand on a different level than just talking. It is pure communication—mind to mind."

"You hear with your mind instead of your ears!"

"That is exactly it."

"Cindy's mom explained it to me."

"She was right. So seasoned guests, people who have lived here a while, can speak directly with the guides. They can actually talk to the animals while they are on the ed-venture. It really adds to the experience."

"Well, Ester and Sultana, I'm glad to meet you two, too."

Ester and Sultana knelt down so the boys could climb up into the saddles. Brian climbed up first. "Riding a camel is a little different than riding a horse. They wobble back and forth because of the way they move their legs. It might feel funny at first."

The camels stood back up and Eddie swayed to the side almost falling off, but he caught himself just in time.

"Don't worry. You will not fall unless you want to."

Ester, Eddie's camel, rolled her lips back in a big teethy smile.

"Ester says you won't fall unless she wants you to."

"Very funny, Ester," Eddie said.

"Camels have traditionally gotten a bad rap as stubborn creatures, but they really are delightful when you get to know them."

The sheer vastness of the scenic desert vista before them defied description. Rolling coral pink sand dunes stretched as far as they could see.

Eddie was unnerved a little by the sight. "We're going to ride across all that?"

"We will be there before you know it."

"Be where?"

"The first stop on our itinerary."

"Where's that?"

"It is a surprise."

"You're full of it, aren't you. Surprises I mean."

They looked at each other and smiled. The camels took off with the boys bouncing up and down and laughing as they went. Up one dune and down the next, each sand hill seemed to grow larger than the last. The dunes become dotted, then covered with millions of gorgeous white sand poppies with deep purple centers.

"We're getting close to the oasis," Brian said. "It should be just over the next dune or so."

"It looks like it should be hot here, but it's not."

"This only looks like a desert. It is what the animals we are going to see are used to, so that is where they are comfortable. Does that make any sense?"

"I think so."

Over two more dunes the desert opened onto a sweeping verdant landscape dotted with turquoise pools. They entered a smooth grassy area on the outskirts of the oasis and passed an adorable family of desert hares playing with a pair of bat-eared foxes. The animals really appeared to enjoy each other's company and were not disturbed in the least by either the camels' or the boys' presence.

"Hey! Look at all those zebras." Eddie said, excitedly pointing to a large herd grazing ahead of them in tall grass.

"Look closely at their stripes, Eddie."

He noticed the animals only had soft brown stripes on their heads and necks. The rest of their bodies were completely white. "What's the matter with them? What happened to all their stripes?"

"Nothing is the matter with them. They actually are not zebras. They are quaggas."

"Quaggas?"

"They are a relative to the zebra that was driven to extinction back on earth some time ago. This is the only place you will ever see them."

"They're beautiful animals."

"They are very friendly, too. Reach down and scratch one behind the ears as we pass through them."

The quaggas looked up when the camels entered the herd's space. Eddie reached down as one particularly large quagga nudged his head against Ester's side. He vigorously scratched right behind its ears. The quagga rolled its lips way back and brayed with an outrageous grin. The boys laughed at both the funny sound and the comical expression. The quagga shook its head and stepped back. Then more quaggas crowded forward so their ears could also be rubbed. Quite the riotous chorus resulted as Brian and Eddie attempted to scratch them all.

Still more quaggas gathered around and they, too, all rolled their lips back and brayed with clamorous volume. At first their brassy voicings seemed random and unruly but their cacophony of dissonant sounds quickly modulated into an energetic quagga chorale with interweaving polyphonic melodies and intricate harmonies. The oasis came alive while the quaggas sang their equine hearts out. Their quavering voices seemed to be a sort of reveille, awakening or calling all creatures within hearing range. A pride of lions came bounding out of a nearby grove of trees and met up with a pack of spotted hyenas emerging from the tall grass.

The lions immediately joined in the music-making. They crooned a repetitious deep growl that created a pulsing rhythm underneath the quaggas voices.

The hyenas broke into a delirious descant solo, their soprano-like voices dancing high above all the others.

Baboons howling, jackals yelping, horned bills squawking, and antelope bleating all added further levels of musical color and complexity. This apparently well-rehearsed anamalian oratorio came to a dynamic close with a screeching pair of Bateleur snake eagles somersaulting down from high above over and over until they landed right on top of Ester's and Sultana's heads.

The boys were completely enthralled by the whole performance. They clapped and clapped while Eddie gazed goggle-eyed at the powerful red-faced, black and white bird sitting right in front of him.

"You can touch him. He will not hurt you."

Eddie stroked the silky feathers on the birds neck, still with a look of disbelief on his face. "This whole thing is the coolest whatever-ya-call-it I've ever seen."

"I just wish you could understand what they all were saying."

"What were they saying?"

"There's too much to translate right now, but it was a sort of welcome."

The quaggas pulled away and the lions rubbed up against the side of the camels just the way dometic cats do.

"They want you to come down and rub their bellies, and then they will give you a bath."

"Like lick me all over? A cat tongue that big?"

The camels knelt down and the boys dismounted. The lions immediately rolled over onto their backs. No sooner did they start to rub bellies, one with each hand, than three purring cheetahs pressed up against the boys' backs, competing for attention.

"Oh, look! A honey badger," Brian said. A squat little creature with a white back and black legs waddled through the lions. Just before reaching Eddie, it tucked itself into a ball and rolled right up to his leg and flopped belly up. It, too, wanted a tummy rub.

Eddie laughed. The little creature was so cute. "I think this is the funnest thing I've ever done. There's only one problem with it."

"What is that?"

"I can't ever tell anybody about it. They'll just think I was talking about some ride at Disneyland."

"I would not worry about it too much."

A herd of oryx waited patiently for their turn to receive attention. Their graceful white bodies with extremely long slim black horns and black facial markings were especially eye-catching. As Eddie admired them, something over near the edge of the closest pool drew his gaze. He saw many large brilliant pink blobs lying on the grass.

"What on earth are those?"

Brian smiled. "That is the first time I have heard that phrase used here."

"So what are they? They look like giant pink cream puffs."

"Those are pink hippos."

"Yeah right. What are they really?"

"They really are pink hippopotami."

"Pink hippopotamuses? I've heard of pink elephants but that was in a cartoon."

"We have those, too."

"Get real! A color coordinated animal adventure?"

Both camels turned their heads and looked right at Eddie, as if in disbelief.

Eddie looked around him at the pond and its environs. "Pink waterlilies. Pink flamingos. Pink hippos. Pink sand. I'm beginning to think there is way too much pink in the world."

"The pink hippos are very real. Walk over to them if you do not believe me. They are gentle."

"That's okay. I do believe you."

"Pink hippos are not exclusively found here. Occasionally you can find one back in the earth sphere. There they call them albinos. Normally hippos have dark pigmentation in their skin that protects them from the sun. Because the sun is never harsh here, hippos do not need dark skin pigmentation. They look bright pink because of all the superficial blood vessels near the surface of the skin."

"How do you know so much about all these animals?"

"I read the tour manual ahead of time."

"But how do you remember everything?"

"Have you ever heard of total recall?"

"Oh, yeah. It's a Schwartzenegger movie."

"The words 'total recall' mean you remember everything you hear or read. It is one of the perks of living here. All these animals are only the beginning. When we have more time, there are many more to see. We need to move along now."

The boys remounted the camels and climbed out of the oasis valley. Once again desert dunes stretched before them as they jostled up and down on their camel guides.

"Do they ever have sand storms here, like in 'Lawrence of Arabia?'" Eddie said with a gleam in his eye.

"Do you want one?"

Before Eddie could answer, both camels again turned their heads and looked straight at him. With a wry little grin, Eddie excitedly nodded his head up and down.

"Okay, then. See that big dune way over there on the horizon?" Brian pointed to an enormous distant sand dune. "We will see you there!"

WHISSSSSSSSSSSSSH! The sky blackened instantly with a blinding sheet of sand that whipped past and did not end. Eddie could not even see his hand in front of his face let alone Brian or the distant horizon where he was supposed to be going. He was almost blown right off as he struggled to stay atop Ester, who managed somehow to stay upright against the combative wind.

Eddie started to laugh. And laugh. He continued to laugh with the whipping sand beating against him. He laughed so hard that again he almost fell off just from laughing.

On and on he and his camel guide braved the storm until at long last, and still laughing, he reached the distant dune where the storm abated as suddenly as it began.

Eddie saw Brian waiting for him. "That was the funnest thing I've ever done!"

"I am glad you so much enjoyed it. Did you notice how the sand kind of tickled?"

"Yeah! It tickled alot. That's why I was laughing so hard."

"I was too. We have really great sand here!"

"I can't believe we have been riding for hours and I'm not even saddle sore."

"I know it seems like hours. The camel knows better than to do that to you."

"Is that how it works?"

"At least here."

They rode over the crest of another dune and saw that it rolled down to a shimmering crystal sea. They stopped along the pristine shoreline and looked out. The water was so clear, with no visual distortion, that not only were the colorful stones on the sea bottom visible, but the brilliant fish swimming past were seeable as well.

"If you take your glasses off you can see better," Brian said.

"No way. There'll be too much glare."

"There is no glare."

Eddie removed his sunglasses and looked at the sea. Though glistening in the bright sun shine, the reflected light off the water appeared soft and perfectly polarized to the eye. No harsh glare was to be seen anywhere.

"So why'd we wear these?"

"Because we wanted to look cool."

"Right, man." Eddie put his sunglasses back on.

"How about a swim? The camels will wait for us. They want us to experience everything we can while we are here."

They both jumped down and tossed off their hats and glasses and ran toward a gentle surf. Brian reached the water first and ran right out on top of it. Eddie, come on. You can walk on this water."

Eddie stopped at the water's edge and looked out at Brian.

"This water will support you in whatever you want to do. Step right up on it. It is no big deal."

Hesitantly, Eddie put his foot onto the shallows. "Hey! It works. It's hard. But it's soft." Gaining confidence, he walked right out to Brian.

"Now you can say that you have walked on water."

"This is heavy."

"If you say heavy —"

"Aaaah!" Eddie started to drop down into the sea.

"You will sink. It is okay. Just go with it. To really experience this water, you have to sink down into it."

Eddie raised his eyebrows questioningly.

"It is impossible to drown here, so just relax and think s-i-n-k."

Trusting in what Brian not only said, but in what he saw him doing, Eddie laid back in the water and began to listlessly float downward. The gentle caress of the water, like thousands of tiny fingers softly massaging, created a tingling yet soothing sensation that put him totally at ease and lulled him off into a sleeplike dreamy state. Even with his eyes closed, he could with perfect clarity, see the bedazzling display of color all around him. Most of the colors he had never even seen before. The light that passed not only through the water, but that radiated out in expanding bursts of color from each minute water molecule, created a kaleidoscopic experience beyond words. The colors burst like great fireworks all around him to the accompaniment of delicate tinkling chimes.

Eddie felt something lifting him from under both his feet. He opened his eyes.

"OOOH MY GOSH! BRIAN! LOOK AT ME!" Eddie rose above the water's surface and surfed along. Brian also, like Eddie, rode the back of two dolphins swimming just below the surface of the sea.

"This is way better than boogie boarding!" Eddie said.

The dolphins carried the boys side by side far out into the sea then brought them right back up to the shoreline where they jumped off and walked up onto the beach.

Eddie started to shake off. "We forgot to bring towels."

"Do you need a towel?"

"Rad! No drip water." Eddie looked down at his dry swim trunks and legs. He even lifted his feet to look at the bottoms. "The sand doesn't stick to you. But it sure feels good under my feet."

"Lie down and see how good it really feels."

Eddie laid down. "Wow! It feels like that bed we put the quarter in at that hotel in Las Vegas."

"It feels better than that! Each little particle of sand is at the perfect temperature working with all the others to massage you and make you feel good."

"How come it does that?"

"Just like the water and everything else, it knows the first rule of happiness is to make others happy."

"How does sand know how to do that?"

"Because it has intelligence, just like the water and the flowers. All matter has it."

"I just can't get over the fact that everything is so perfect here. Why would anyone want to live anywhere else?"

Eddie noticed many glowing white sails had appeared out on the water. Against the topaz color of the sea they created a stunning visual sight. He watched all the boats head toward a jewel-like emerald green island nestled on the horizon. "What's out there?"

"A very special place," Brian said with reverence in his voice. "We can go there together sometime, but it is more than just a day trip. How about some pink lemonade?"

"Sure."

"Great. I know just the place."

The two rode on through lush pine forests and across a mountainside beneath massive snow-capped granite peaks and came upon a small lake. They stopped beside a sweeping pink marble verandah between two giant urns that billowed over with sprays of luminous orchid blossoms. They dismounted from their camels and Brian reached to an overhanging tree branch and plucked two pink lemons.

"What are those?" Eddie said.

"Pink lemons."

"Not more pink!"

They both sat at a small table already set with two crystal glasses.

"Pink is a perfectly beautiful color," Brian said. "Watch this." He held a lemon over one of the glasses and gently squeezed. WHOOSH! The glass filled right to the rim with bright pink pulpy juice. "*Voila!* Pink lemonade."

Eddie made a sour face.

"Try it." Brian held up his glass. "Lemons here are sweet." He then handed the other lemon to Eddie who gave it a good looking over.

"Looks like a real lemon except it's pink."

"It is a real lemon. Now hold it right over the glass and squeeze gently. It will do the work for you. It wants you to drink it."

Eddie barely positioned the lemon over the other glass— WHOOSH! Much to his delight, the glass filled just like Brian's did. They touched their glasses together.

"Cheers," and they drank their juice.

"Wow! This stuff is great, too," Eddie said. "Tastes like raspberry lemonade only better. We should grow some of these back home."

"I am not sure the pink lemon trees can tolerate the climate there."

"Hey, where'd it go?" Eddie realized the lemon he just squeezed had completely disappeared. "The lemon, where'd it go?"

"Back to the tree."

"What do you mean?"

"It withered away."

"But where'd it go? It's gone."

"It went back to the tree. It was no longer needed so it returned to its element—back to the tree."

"This is going to take me a while to get used to all of this. Everything popping in and out. But I have a question. If we are twins, then why am I not grown up like you are?"

"Because you still have the same consciousness that you had on earth. In this world, you can be as old as you want to be."

"So I can have a beard if I want to?"

"If you really want it."

"That's kind of neat. I have another question, too."

"Okay."

"What is with all the pink anyway? This patio is pink. The flowers are pink. The lemons. Even the sand dunes. How come there is so much of it?"

"Sometime I will fully explain it to you. It is too involved for right now. And this will probably sound a little hoakie to say, but you remember we talked about how everyone here has perfect love for every other living thing?"

"Yeah."

"And how everything here, because it has intelligence, also feels that perfect love for every other thing?"

"I'm with you."

"Pink is the color of universal love and has deep symbolic—"

"Wait a minute. You just lost me."

"I was afraid of that."

"This is way too heavy. The rocks and the water love me? That's why they're pink?"

"That is a small part of it. That is why everyone and everything here is so giving. Because they feel nothing but love. When you love someone, you want them to be happy."

"I can understand that. I respect it, too. But it still doesn't mean I have to wear pink shirts does it?

"Heavens no."

"That's a relief."

Eddie looked around and admired the lush forest that swept down to the water's edge.

"So, is this place heaven?"

"Some people call it that. It actually has several different names."

"I thought heaven had palm trees, like California."

"Heaven has any kind of trees you want."

Eddie noticed across the lake a golden meadow ablaze with yellow flowers. To one side sat three cottages painted the same bright yellow as all the blooms around them.

"Does somebody live over there?" he said.

"You'll never guess who."

"Tell me."

"It is someone you studied about in school just this week."

"Who? I can't think of anybody."

"He painted 'Sunflowers' and 'Starry Night.'"

"Not Vincent van Gogh?"

"The same."

"He lives here? I mean over there?"

"He lives in the middle house."

"Who lives in the other houses next to him?"

"Vincent and Theo, his brothers."

"Wait a minute. Vincent lives in the middle you said."

"Yes. And before you get any further confused. Vincent's younger brother with whom he was always so close is Theo. And Vincent had an older brother also named Vincent who was stillborn."

"Does that mean born dead?"

"It does. Vincent and Vincent and Theo are inseperable now. They are like the Three Musketeers off on all kinds of creative adventures together. It would be great for you to meet them, but they are away on a concert tour."

"They do concerts?"

"A tour to attend concerts."

"Oh." Eddie paused a moment. "Didn't Vincent commit —?"

"I know what you are thinking. There were some issues in the way he passed. He had some serious mental problems at the time. But aside from that, he has worked through everything."

"That's good. I'm glad. I was feeling sad for him."

"No need now. I wish you could meet his wife. She is so adorable."

"He wasn't married."

"Not back then. Her name is Reiko. Sometime I will take you over there."

"You promise?"

"I promise."

"Someday we'll have houses side by side just like them."

"You can bet on it."

Brian looked up suddenly. "Oh, good. Andy is here." A tall young man of twenty with full wavy dark hair appeared on the verandah just beside him. The design on his summery shirt had a distinct look of the 1960's. He stepped right up to Eddie and extended his hand.

"Hi. I'm Andy."

"Hi. I'm Eddie."

"It is really nice to finally meet you." They shook hands vigorously. "Brian has been telling me all about you, Eddie. It seems that you have been having some kind of girl trouble lately, huh?"

"Yeah. I guess."

"Sometimes it is kind of hard to know what to do in those circumstances."

"I know," Eddie said.

"That is kind of why I came to see you, because I have been having some girl trouble too."

Eddie perked up. Andy pulled up a chair out of nowhere and sat right in front of him. "Some time ago I was engaged to your school teacher, Miss Pleasant."

Eddie's jaw dropped. "You were gonna marry that old thing? She's really a nice lady but she's way too old for you."

Andy chuckled out loud. "She was not always old, Eddie. This was a long time ago when we were both young. Margaret and I were very much in love. We planned on spending our lives together. But then I was killed in the Vietnam War, and that was the end of our plans."

Eddie knew neither how to respond nor how to deal with this information. He swallowed hard then blinked even harder.

Andy stood up just as a handsome young Asian man appeared right between him and Brian. The pleasant smiles with which he and Andy greeted and embraced evidenced a long friendship. "Eddie, I would like you to meet Tran."

He and Eddie cordially shook hands.

"Tran is the man who killed me."

Eddie looked at Tran with his eyes opened wide.

"He was killed, too, the very next day. We are good friends now. Eddie, I need your help in order to solve a problem that I have."

"What can I do?"

"First, I want you to please just look down at your feet."

Eddie was puzzled by Andy's simple request but obliged. He bowed his head and looked down at his feet. He saw an old, floral needlepoint rug beneath them. He looked back up and jumped with alarm. He and Andy were no longer on the lakeside verandah. They were now in Miss Pleasant's house, in her bedroom. She sat right beside them in front of her bureau, and struggled to remove her Raggedy Ann makeup from the carnival. Her wig was off, leaving her real hair smashed flat to her head. In her old tattered bath robe, she was not a pretty sight.

Eddie was afraid to either speak or move.

"She cannot see or hear us," Andy said to set Eddie at ease. "I asked you to look at your feet so you would not get dizzy when we traveled."

Eddie looked around and saw that the room was filled with all sorts and sizes of Raggedy Ann and Andy dolls. The bureau top was covered with old photos of Andy and Miss Pleasant.

She wiped makeup from her left cheek and unexpectedly cringed in pain. Right below her left eye her skin was black and purple. She had a huge unusually-shaped black eye.

"Miss Pleasant has a shiner!"

"In the shape of Cindy's flashlight."

Miss Pleasant continued to wipe away her makeup and forty years of pain and sorrow gradually became visible on her face. She suddenly looked years and years older than she had ever looked before. Eddie could not believe how old she looked.

"Miss Pleasant, as you call her, is the crazy lady who takes Cracker Jacks to the cemetery."

"She is?"

"And I am the one to whom she takes them."

"That's your tombstone?"

"I am Andrew Valentine."

"Oh, gosh! I'm really sorry we ate 'em."

"Not to worry. I am glad you did. At least someone was able to enjoy them. I certainly cannot eat them. But Miss Pleasant, inspite of what she does, is not really crazy. She just has so much pain, that she cannot think clearly. If she could, she would know that our love is still alive. Because love never dies. Only bodies do."

Even though Miss Pleasant could not hear or even sense Andy's presence, her movements and expressions somehow seemed choreographed to his every comment, as she, too, recounted in her mind a life never lived. She picked up a faded photo of the two of them dressed in Raggedy Ann and Raggedy Andy costumes, pictured as they sat together on a bale of hay.

"You see that picture that she is holding? The last time Margaret and I were together was at a barn dance on Halloween night almost forty years ago. That is when that photo was taken. I knew the army was going to ship me out the next day, so I planned a big surprise for her. I rigged the dance contest so we would win and the prize they gave us was a box of Cracker Jacks. We sat out on a bale of hay and ate them in the moonlight. When we got down to the toy surprise, she found the diamond engagement ring that I had hidden inside."

While Andy spoke Miss Pleasant opened a well-worn jewelry box and removed an old Victorian era diamond ring. Her mouth quivered with pain when she tried it on and found it still fit her finger.

"That ring belonged to my grandmother. She gave it to me especially to give to Margaret. The very next day after I gave it to her, I was shipped half a world away."

Andy paused with emotion. He, too, was overcome.

"Margaret has never forgiven me for dying. She is still angry because of the life she never had. She wanted to have a family. I wanted a family. We both did. But as it turned out, she has been alone all these years. She has lived her whole adult life feeling bitterness toward me and toward Tran, whom she has never even met." Andy turned toward Eddie so choked up he could barely speak. "Eddie. You must tell Maggie that you saw me. You must tell her that I have forgiven the man who killed me and so must she. I have tried and tried to reach her in her dreams, but she is harboring so much anger and bitterness, I cannot even begin to get through. Tell her please to forgive. It is so important." Andy took Eddie's hands in his and looked straight into his eyes. "Will you please promise me that you will tell her?"

Eddie, deeply moved by Andy's plea, heartily nodded.

"There is a letter from me over here..."

Eddie and Andy were instantly standing in the entrance hall right beside the front door.

"Stuck behind the tin liner of this mail slot." Andy lifted the flap to an old-fashioned mail slot in the wall. "It's where no one would ever find it and only a little arm like yours could ever reach it. I wrote this letter to Margaret and mailed it three days before I died. It has been hidden there nearly forty years. I want you to give it to her and tell her to read it out loud."

Eddie was speechless from these further revelations.

"I wish that I had the time to explain everything in detail, but tell her that she must read it out loud." Andy's speech became faster and faster. Eddie could barely keep up he spoke with such urgency. "You will need money for a bouquet of roses. Very specifically, I need you to give her eleven red ones and one white one. Maggie will know exactly what it means. Take them with you when you go to get the letter so that she receives them all at the same time. Now, between the third and fourth steps of your front porch, a nineteen-eleven silver dollar is lodged down in a crack. It is worth more than enough to pay for the roses. Keep the change and spend it on yourself."

Andy stepped over to the fireplace and slowly ran his hands down the mantel, then turned around. "And tell Maggie that as she reads the letter, I will be standing right here, in front of the fireplace..." Emotion cracked Andy's voice as Miss Pleasant entered the front room from the other side. She looked straight at the spot where Andy stood, though she could not see him. Andy looked straight back at her. "With all the love in my heart burning bright." Andy put both hands to his face to wipe his streaming eyes. "I am sure you have lots of questions Eddie, I'm sorry, but I have to get you back this instant!"

FWOOM!

Eddie was again seated on the lakeside verandah with Brian. He sat quietly, almost dumbfounded, and pondered. Brian knew not to speak because he knew Eddie's thoughts and feelings as he contemplated the things that Andy shared with and asked of him. The two of them enjoyed a comfortable silence together.

Finally, Brian spoke first. He knew it was time. "It is a lot to take in."

Eddie did not respond immediately, but after a few more moments, he did. "I have a question."

"Okay."

"Where was your guardian angel when you fell out of the treehouse?"

"This might be difficult for you to understand, but it was my turn to move on."

"What does that mean?"

"It means that you are suppose to go on and live your life without me there."

"But I don't want to."

"You will be a much stronger person because of this experience, because of my passing. You will be able to help more people because of the better understanding that you now have of what is really important in life."

"I've given it a lot of thought, and I've decided to stay here with you. I like it here."

"But it is not your time, Eddie. Your life on earth is a gift. A gift of time. A gift of time to experience things that you can only experience there. Because it is a gift, your life is not yours to decide when it is over."

"But I don't want to go back."

Brian sat forward in his chair with a focused intensity. He took

Eddie's hands in his own and held them tightly. "Do you ever want to see Mom and Dad and Melissa again?"

"Yes. I want to see them."

No sooner were the words uttered from his mouth than Eddie started to feel dizzy.

"I love you, Eddie. Tell Mom and Dad and Melissa —"

Before Brian could finish his sentence, Eddie was pulled backwards by some extreme force.

"I love them tooooooooooooo."

CHAPTER EIGHTEEN

The church bell in the old cathedral in downtown Middleway chimed one o'clock—Bong!—the second time tonight. The sound of the bell resonated over the town and out onto East Mountain, where crowds of Sabbateurs stood over Doctor McCourt while he determinedly performed cardio pulmonary resuscitation on Eddie. He lost one son. He was committed that he would not lose this one.

Eddie moved slightly and coughed.

"EDDIE? CAN YOU HEAR ME?" his father said.

Eddie groaned then came to. His father's concerned face was the first thing he saw, completely surrounded by smiling monsters.

"EDDIE!" Doctor McCourt was overcome with emotion. He scooped his son up in his arms and hugged him with all his might. They both cried a flood of tears into each others arms.

"D—Dad. I can't breathe!"

His father released his grip and gave Eddie a kiss on the forehead next to a big bump right at his hairline. "Thank you! Oh, thank you God! For sending back our little boy."

Teary-eyed Sandy stepped forward through all the monster faces. "We've been praying that you'd come back to us, Eddie."

The crowd opened and Mrs. McCourt pressed through. She dropped to her knees and also hugged Eddie so tightly he could hardly breathe. "Oh, Eddie!" She wept openly. He cried openly. Doctor McCourt wiped his still teary eyes, so grateful to have not lost another son.

"We need to get Eddie to the hospital," he said.

"I'm okay, Dad. I just fell in the forest and hit my head on that big tree."

"I can see that. You've got quite the goose egg. I want to run some X-rays."

"Really, Dad! I know you're the doctor, but I'm all right. I'm not going to die. Brian even told me so."

"You saw him?"

"We've been together for a long time."

Both of his parents paused at Eddie's words that he had been with his brother.

His father swallowed to clear the lump in his throat. "I believe you son. How'd Brian look?"

"He looked great. He was all grown up with a beard and everything."

"Really?"

"Oh, yeah. He's even taller than you are."

"That's great."

"Oh, Dad. I never told you, but when you were working on Brian in the hospital, he was floating all over the place right up above you."

"Is that so?"

Everyone kept talking to Eddie, but he did not hear them. His mind spun around with everything that had occurred. He looked all around to further gather his bearings. The sight of all the monsters with their torches helped him realize that he really was re-earthbound.

The lady vampire with the really long hair walked up. She now had warm caring eyes. "We've all been praying for you, Eddie."

"Thank you."

Cindy stepped forward. "The whole Witches' Sabbath shut down, and everyone came to look for you in the woods because we were all worried about you."

"That was really nice of everybody."

The McCourts expressed their thanks to everyone for helping. A low fog horn rumbled through the woods to signal the Resumption of the Witches' Sabbath. Loud rock music followed and the Sabbateurs all started back.

"Shall we head back, too?" Eddie's mother said, looking wearied but at least not worried.

Doctor McCourt looked to Sandy. "I guess the only way out of here is back to the castle and the bus?"

"That's it."

"I'll carry Eddie, then."

"I can walk, Dad."

"Are you sure you're okay, Eddie?" his mother said. "Your eyes look far away."

"I'm fine. Really. I'm just thinkin' about everything."

"All right then, Sweetheart."

"Oh, Eddie," Cindy said handing him his sneaker. "I cleaned out all the stickers for you."

"Gee, thanks. I really hate stickers."

"Me too."

Everyone made their way to the trail and began the return walk up the mountain. Eddie was lost in thought while the others all chatted. The McCourts told Sandy how impressed they were with the way she organized the search effort, and how amazed they were when the entire party shut down to help.

"They're all good people here," Sandy said. "Some of them look a bit brutish, even without their costumes, but there isn't one of them who wouldn't give you the shirt off his back if you needed it."

"We are impressed," Doctor McCourt said.

"Did you notice the time when Eddie was revived?"

"I wasn't thinking about the time."

"He came to right as the clock struck one, for the second time. I don't know for certain, but I imagine he left on his journey at the stroke of one as well."

Doctor and Mrs. McCourt looked at each other. "It's time to tell him," they both said at the same time.

He nodded. "We always intended to when the time was right."

"This is the right time. Tonight."

Doctor McCourt looked at Sandy. "Earlier I asked if everyone who comes here practices witchcraft?"

"Not at all. But even those of us who do—it isn't necessarily what you may be thinking. We don't practice the dark craft. We follow an ancient, peaceful, earth religion. With a name like McCourt, these things are part of your heritage whether you know it or not."

"You think so?"

"You've most likely got Celtic blood in you. I know the witch thing bothers some people. We might have a different way, but deep down we're no different than you folks."

"That's a nice way of putting it," Mrs. McCourt said.

"And as far as the Witches' Sabbath, the stigma helps keep our numbers in check so we're not overrun."

"Who pays for all this?"

"We have some overhead, but virtually everything is donated or contributed. And if you think the Pub at the carnival has haute

Halloween cuisine, stick around to see the culinary creations for the Feast of Samhain."

Doctor McCourt's ears pricked up. "Samhain?"

"It's the ancient name for Halloween. It means end of summer or harvest festival, depending on which book you look in. But that is what tonight is, a harvest festival coupled with a New Years celebration."

"How so?"

"October 31st was the last night of the Celtic calendar. And that's where all the merry making comes in."

"Not so different really, then, from other celebrations."

"Not at all. And the proceeds from tonight —"

"Proceeds?"

"Yes, indeed. People pay well to get in. Not here at the gate but through contributions in advance. We do not handle any money here. But all the proceeds go straight to Children's Charities."

"We had no clue."

"Most people don't. No one does it for notoriety. No one's name goes on a bronze plaque. It's done quietly with no T.V. reporters. But no one gets in without contributing, and the totals might astound you. You also might be surprised by who is behind some of the makeup."

"We were already impressed with you, but the more we get to know the more impressed we are becoming."

"Well, thank you. I'm flattered and humbled by your comment." They reached the bottom of the castle grounds. "I really wish you would consider staying for the rest of the evening."

"It's a little roudy for the kids."

"In addition to the food, the quiet time is said by many to be the most spiritual experience they've ever had."

Doctor McCourt grinned. "We can't leave anyway."

"Why not?" his wife said.

"Lois."

"Oh. You're right. Not until all forty-four of her girls are all rounded up."

Sandy placed a hand on each of their shoulders. "It's settled then. You're not leaving until you have at least broken bread with us. I hope you all have good appetites."

Cindy was beside herself to hear the McCourts had decided to stay.

"If we are going to stay," Doctor McCourt said, "we really should do it as a family. It's not fair for us all to party all night and leave Melissa home alone wondering where we are. I'll call a cab to pick her up."

"Very good idea."

He stepped away to find a quiet spot then called a taxi company on his cell phone, that had been tucked in his pocket.

"There are no taxis available to take someone to the Witches' Sabbath," the dispatcher said.

"Oh, come on. You must have something. I'll throw in a fifty dollar tip."

"There is one—"

"I'll take it!" he said before hearing the particulars.

"It's a stretch limo with a minimum dispatch fee of $150. With your tip, it brings the total to $213.20 with tax."

"TWO HUNDRED THIRTEEN DOLLARS?"

"And twenty cents."

"All right!" Doctor McCourt took a deep breath. "The address is 353 Pineview."

"Oh. I know that address," the dispatcher said. "I've already been to that house once today."

"You have?"

"The little Cinderella girl."

"Oh. no."

"Oh, yes. Such a painful experience. I'm not sure I'm up to going back there for any price. In fact, I'm gonna have to pass."

"Just make it an even $250!"

"Give me your card number and I'll be there in five."

Doctor McCourt hung up fuming. He took a minute to catch his breath before he called his daughter.

"Melissa?"

"Oh. Hi, Dad."

"We found Eddie and he's fine."

"That's great. So you'll be coming home now?"

"We want you to come join us here at the Witches Sabbath."

"Dad? Are you all right?"

"I'm fine."

"Did you just hear yourself? You said you want me to come join you at the Witches' Sabbath."

The limousine will be there in five minutes. And I've already given the driver instructions on how to get here."

"Limo? Is this for real?"

"I've never been more serious, Sweetie. It's costing me $250 just to get you here."

"Dad?"

"Yes?"

"If I stay home, can I have the two hundred and fifty dollars?"

"Tell the driver to hurry. We'll be waiting for you."

"All right. I'll see you at the Witches' Sabbath."

Doctor McCourt hung up and realized the celebration was again at full bore—music blasting, people dancing everywhere. Over in the crowds he saw Lois dancing with a werewolf in a wheelchair. He energetically bounced up and down in wheel chair wheelies. Lois had a Miss America smile plastered on her face. Her own brother could hardly recognize her she looked so different. Even through the gobs of nightcream still stuck to her face, she appeared to be a new person with her normally curled-up-in-disgust lip stretched smooth and flat with a smile. She continually rubbed her finger tip back and forth across her upper lip as she danced.

Lois had even sought out her own four girls and instructed them to release their upper lips, because it was unladylike, uncouth, and just plain uncomfortable.

Doctor MCourt walked back to where Sandy was still speaking with Mrs. McCourt.

"A brief overview so you know what to expect. The party runs until 3:00 and then the Feast of Samhain and The Bonfires begin. Both are done in complete silence. This will probably be a new experience for you."

"Dinner with no verbal communication?" Mrs. McCourt said. "I can recall quite a few actually, where everyone sat in silence."

"If you're like us, we try to forget those dinners." Sandy chuckled.

"We do, too."

"The idea of the silent time, came from the past when utter silence was mandated in order that even the faintest whispering from the other side could be detected by anyone and everyone. Even a hint of a whisper on the breeze."

"Sounds quite compelling, sitting all together in silence with the fires burning."

"It is. Even at the feast, or when people come back and ask for more juice or a second helping or whatever by holding up an empty glass with a smile, you learn more about how to get along with people when words are not an issue. Because without words we all have a common heart."

"How true."

"Now, at the feast, all the food is accompanied by detailed descriptions with ingredients listed. Not all our celebrants are meat eaters. There are many exquisite vegan and vegetarian dishes as well."

"Bring it on!" Doctor McCourt said.

"And one more thing. Before you eat, we pass out little packets of paper and pencils. Everyone writes down their New Year's resolutions, and lists all their bad habits that they are going to sacrifice, or offer to the fires to help make the world a better place for the coming twelve months."

Mrs. McCourt was overwhelmed by all that Sandy had shared. "I have quite the new understanding now, of this event. I can see all kinds of reasons for people to come."

"Different people come for different reasons. Many because of the Bonfires. Many more because of the fun and fellowship. Everybody dances with everybody. The uglier you are, the more people love you and the more everybody wants to dance with you. Where else can you go and experience that?" Sandy became a little choked up. "You see those two round little witches over there?" Sandy pointed into the crowds.

The McCourts nodded.

"Those two old sisters live the year round for the comraderie they feel here tonight. They don't really have hairy warts all over them, but no one ever wants to dance with them anywhere else like they do here. They have the time of their lives just getting ready. They spend almost a week putting on their makeup."

The McCourts were speechless at these further revelations. Mrs. McCourt shook her head in disbelief. "I can only imagine how that would make them feel."

"Where else could those two possibly be the belles of the ball? You see that man in the toga they're dancing with, the really hairy one? Tonight he doesn't have to hide who he is. He's shiny bald on top but he's all hair from the neck down. He always wears long sleeve shirts, never wears shorts or even sandals. In junior high people started calling him gorilla feet, and they still do."

"That's nothing to be ashamed of, but how wonderful that he doesn't have to feel ashamed here."

"Almost everyone here has a story. Let me call those two old girls over for you to meet them. They are delightful."

Sandy walked over to the twin witches and the man in the toga. After a word, they all accompanied her back through the crowds.

The very hairy man with a shiny bald head, wore a long black toga slung over his left shoulder with Roman sandals strapped up his legs. Black rings around his eyes and vampire teeth gave him a menacing appearance. He and the ladies approached and his gaze met with Doctor McCourt's. They both smiled.

"John?"

"Pat? Welcome, welcome. And Elizabeth, nice to see you here."

"Thank you."

"You all know each other?" Sandy said.

"Sure we do. John's chief administrator at the hospital."

"Great. No need to introduce you then to my favorite furball." Sandy squeezed John and gave him a kiss on the cheek. He smiled. The others did not know whether to chuckle or not.

"I've never seen you out of a suit and tie," Doctor McCourt said.

"Tonight I can celebrate the monster within." The others chuckled.

"We can all be proud of who we really are here," one of the witches said, "without people pointing at us and calling us some kind of a freak."

Sandy looked to the McCourts. "Let me introduce you both to Ludwiga and Lucinda." The two matching witches both half curtsied and half bowed at the same time, each bending their inner leg as they stood side-by-side and extended their outer arms to create a perfect butterfly bow.

"Charmed. We're sure."

Mrs. McCourt tilted her head and smiled. "We're the ones who are charmed, by your coquettishly bewitching way."

"Here at Witches' Sabbath we use only first names," Lucinda said. "And you two are?"

"Pat and Liz."

"Thank you. We'll remember those. This must be your first year."

"We didn't exactly know what to wear. Next year we'll know better."

Doctor McCourt looked at his wife in disbelief.

"No matter," Ludwiga said. "Everyone's welcome regardless of how they are dressed because this is a celebration of what's on the inside, not the outside."

The blasting music suddenly took a turn. A strange, macabre song with a syncopated rhythm started to play, deafeningly. Both Ludwiga and Lucinda shrieked.

"OH! Come with us. This is our most favorite—The Transylvanian Tango." They grabbed the McCourts, and with John in tow as well, dragged them into the dancing crowds.

The McCourts immediately saw other people they knew. They saw Lois dancing with a slimey green sea monster who was actually deputy mayor. He twirled her around and she went back and forth between him and her executioner.

"Isn't that Beth Iverson's daughter over there?" Mrs. McCourt said.

"It is. She's the one who lost her arm at the zoo when she was little. Look how much fun she is having."

The McCourts saw things with totally new eyes—things that had simply slipped past their fields of vision before.

Sandy realized that both Cindy and Eddie had not been around for quite some time. She looked and found them sitting on the edge of the draw bridge. Cindy noticed her mother approaching.

"Mom! You won't believe the things Eddie has been telling me. Eddie went to a movie palace and saw a whole Cindy Crystal Film. He watched and felt how it hurt me when I saw the bears and fell into the cake. You were right, Mom." She started to cry.

"Oh, Sweetie."

"Cindy. I didn't want to make you cry," Eddie said.

Sandy put her arm around Eddie. "It's okay. It's a happy cry." Sandy gave her daughter a hug. "May I sit down with you two for a minute?"

"Sure."

"Eddie, it sounds like you had quite an experience on the other side."

"I did."

"That's very kind of you to share some of it with Cindy."

"I wanted to."

"Did you happen to notice what time it was when you came back and your father revived you?"

"Hut uh. I wasn't thinking about the time."

"It was exactly one o'clock—the second one."

"Really? When I fell and hit my head, the first thing I heard was the one o'clock bell."

"So you were gone exactly one hour. One magic hour. You probably learned more in that sixty minutes than many people learn in a lifetime."

"I learned alot. It's hard to believe it was only an hour. It seemed so long. Brian and I did lots of stuff."

"They don't have time there the way we do. It's timeless. Past, present and future are all one. And I know that's difficult to understand from our perspective. Tonight, during the one o'clock hour when we are also timeless, is the only time during the year when our two worlds are in sync."

The three of them sat quietly a moment, then Sandy spoke again. "Why don't you two come and dance?"

"I want to hear more of Eddie's stories," Cindy said.

Sandy smiled. "That's fine, Sweetie. Well, if you two will excuse me..." Sandy wanted to hear more, too. She was so touched by what little she had heard of his experience, she wondered if he would be willing to share some of it with everyone there. She walked off to find his parents, who were fine with the idea as long as Eddie wanted to. They simply asked that he not speak until Melissa arrived, which would be anytime. Sandy then went back and asked Eddie. Though he was nervous, he was anxious to tell about his experience. He felt it was important to tell about it.

The stretch limousine drove right up in front of the castle with Melissa standing up out of the sunroof, swaying to the music. Lois and everyone else saw Melissa's grand entrance and rushed over before the limo stopped. With her Aunt Lois and a mob of monsters swarming the limo, Melissa became afraid and dropped back down inside.

"MELISSA?" Lois said.

"MELISSA? MELISSA?" everybody said.

Melissa at last opened her door. The Driver would not even get out.

Lois threw her arms around her niece before she even stepped out and hugged her tight. "Oh. Melissa. I'm so glad you could join us."

Melissa looked around to see if this was some kind of a joke while the limo squealed away in a cloud of dust.

Lois took Melissa's hands in hers. "We are all having such a wonderful time, we would not want you to miss out on it. And I want to apologize —"

"No, no. Let me apologize."

"No! Let me apologize."

"No! I won't."

"Then let me thank you, for your courage and honesty in those helpful things you said to me earlier."

Melissa's jaw almost hit her knees as it fell open.

"I had no idea that people thought of me as a witch."

Melissa was flabbergasted. She simply could not speak.

"Come along now. We've got some partying to do. Everyone – THIS IS MELISSA."

Before Melissa could even turn her head Ludwiga and Lucinda had her by the arms on either side and they were off dancing in the crowds.

The party continued on with riotous good fun, but eventually the music slowed, becoming mellow and soulful. The celebrants all took seats again as they had in the beginning.

Sandy rounded up all the McCourts and her own daughter and took them to the front row of the arena where she introduced them to some friends. They all squeezed in together to make more room. Sandy then stepped onto the stage between two blazing fires and spoke into a microphone.

"We want to thank everyone for coming again this year and supporting us. And thank you for your generous contributions to the children. As you all know, Feast of Samhain begins shortly. But first I want to beg all your pardons for a slight breach in tradition. Before we proceed we have a rare opportunity tonight to hear about an extraordinary experience by one of our youngest celebrants. Sandy looked down at Eddie. While we all squeezed an extra hour of partying in because of the time change, our young friend Eddie was out experiencing the real magic that this night has to offer. Thank you all for your willingness to help look for him earlier. Eddie lost his identical twin brother Brian recently, and ever since he's been on a quest to prove that somehow, somewhere his brother is still alive. I've asked him to share with us a glimpse of what he experienced. Let's have a warm witches' welcome for Eddie."

Eddie stepped up onto the stage and Sandy gave him a big hug. He stood before the microphone and looked out at all the monsters filling the amphitheater. This time he did not see scary people. He saw good people in great Halloween costumes. He wiped a tear from his eye and began to speak.

"I'm sorry I was so much trouble to everybody, that you all had to quit partying and come look for me. I really appreciate it. Thank you. My brother, Brian died on Friday night three weeks ago. He fell out of the treehouse. I was asleep and I had this awful dream that I was falling and falling. Just before I hit the ground I woke up screaming. That's when I looked over and saw that Brian was gone. He wasn't in his sleeeping bag and the hatch door was open. I crawled over and looked out but it was all dark so I couldn't see. I tried to use my flashlight but the battery burned out, so I climbed down anyway. When I got to the bottom of the tree I stepped on something. It was him."

Eddie started to cry and could not talk for a minute. "I tried to wake him up but he wouldn't. I started screaming for help and I ran into the house to get my mom and dad. My dad's a doctor—I knew he could help. We all went running back out with flashlights and my dad did CPR on him while my mom called the ambulance. They tried all night at the hospital but nobody could bring him back. I didn't want him to be dead."

The entire arena melted with emotion. Monster makeup ran down almost every cheek. Eddie's parents could barely stand to relive their son's death, and especially not through their little boy's eyes and heart.

"Anyway," he said after he wiped his eyes with his sleeve, "I kept dreaming about being with Brian. We played together up in the mountains at Rainbow Lake. But the dreams felt real. They didn't feel like dreams. And we talked about stuff—real stuff—and I knew he wasn't really dead, or we couldn't talk about stuff. Then I heard about the bonfires up here, and the spirits of the people that died are suppose to come here. So I came here 'cuz I didn't know where else to go. But I didn't feel good after I got here. And I didn't think Brian would come here so I left. When I was walking down the path, I got scared and I ran off into the woods. That's when I fell and hit my head on a big log. Then the Erlking came and took me away in his black hearse. I knew I was gonna die 'cuz I couldn't breathe. But all of the sudden, it was like this explosion and I wasn't in the forest anymore. I was in a beautiful place with flowers and meadows. And my brother was there. Except I didn't know it was him at first because he wasn't ten years old anymore. Because he was all grown up with a beard and everything. At first I didn't believe it was him. But it was him. He even had the two little moles under his left eye. That was the only difference between us."

Eddie stopped a moment when he noticed how heavily his entire family was weeping. "Brian and me, we talked a long time and we saw Grandma and Grandpa and lots of other relatives I've never met before. Everybody was there. Even Brian's iguana Larry was there, too." Eddie looked at Melissa and smiled. "My Grandma and Grandpa weren't old anymore. They were younger than my parents. Then Brian and me, we did lots of things together. We went and saw a movie, only it wasn't like the movies here. I learned lots of things from it. I learned lots of things when I was with Brian over there. I learned the most important thing is caring for other people's feelings. There's somebody I want to apologize to again. I did something that really hurt her feelings. I'm really sorry Cindy that I killed the bears."

Cindy clutched her mother's arm while Eddie continued.

"It was kind of a joke, and I didn't realize how it would hurt you when I did it. Please accept my apology and be my friend. I met with my guardian angel, Uncle Louie. He's my grandpa's brother who died when he was only four years old. I asked him how he died. He said he and my grandpa were playing along a canal pushing big rocks in to make splashes. Grandpa pushed in the biggest rock, but Louie made the biggest splash when the whole side of the canal caved in with Grandpa's rock.

The whole audience looked like the sobbing lion in "The Wizard of Oz."

"I learned that everybody has guardian angels who watch over them and help them to know what to do. But sometimes it is time for people to move on and we have to accept that even if it's hard. Brian and me, we did all kinds of neat fun stuff together. We went lots of awesome places but the most important thing is I learned we all have a responsibility to treat people with kindness and respect. When people act mean or rude it's because they're hurting inside. We can like anybody if we understand them and we can understand them if we take the time to get to know them. That's what I learned."

No one clapped. The entire arena was silent. Eddie looked to Sandy. Red-eyed and weeping, she stood and walked back to the stage.

"No one is clapping Eddie, because we are all so deeply touched. No one wants to disturb the special spirit that you have shared. Thank you very much."

Eddie sat with his family while Sandy struggled to talk through her emotions.

"I feel like we could say our benediction right now and call it a night. Just a few things I need to go over with everyone before our time of silence begins. I apologize if it sounds like a checklist. It is. If there is anyone who has not received a paper packet, please raise your hand so we can pass you one."

Lois and all her girls, among a few others, raised their hands.

"For anyone unacquainted, the paper inside is to write down all your bad habits and character traits that you will then offer to the fires as sacrifice in your personal quest to progress and become a better person this coming year. You also can write out emergency messages if needed, but anyone who breaks the quiet with even a whisper, will be directed to leave immediately. When your offerings are complete, feel free to proceed to the banquet tables in an orderly fashion. Remember this is not a race. Take your time. There is plenty of food. Restrooms are in both directions. Anyone may leave at any time. But it also must be done in silence. It is a pleasant evening tonight, but there are plenty of blankets and cushions for everyone. So feel free to pick them up from the stacks on either side of the arena. The next few hours are not an endurance test to see who can stay awake. Feel free to sleep to free your mind to roam with the spirits of your departed loves ones. And finally, when the first rays of morning light streak above the mountains behind us, we know the spirits have again returned to the realm of the dead. We will then extinguish the fires for another year and the benediction will be pronounced within the privacy of each person's own heart. Again, thank you all for your love and support. Now, Earl will pronounce the invocation and blessing for the Feast of Samhain and The Bonfires."

The very person with whom Eddie had an encounter earlier this evening on the trail to the Witches' Sabbath, the being of complete blackness, walked onto the stage. With the glow of fires on both sides of him, he appeared shadowy and not of the world.

"Before I begin, I first want to thank Eddie for sharing. Those are important lessons to learn. How great to learn them so young. For most of us it takes a life time to learn them, I know because I have yet to learn them. I also want to extend my sincere apologies to Eddie. I feel rather unworthy to be up here following him. I fear that I may have contributed to his feeling of fright earlier this evening when he was the unfortunate recipient of some of my misdirected rage." He looked right at Eddie. "The anger you saw in my eyes really was not towards you. I had some problems earlier and hadn't had time to cool off. I am very sorry that I knocked you down and that I frightened you."

As he spoke, Eddie noticed that some of his teeth showed white where the tooth black had worn off. Eddie was pleased with the apology. It helped to wrap the evening's experiences up in a bow. "Please accept my apologies." Eddie smiled and nodded at Earl, who smiled back.

"With that said, and with Eddie's forgiveness, I would like to proceed." He looked to the sky. "The wheel of time has turned and once again brought us to this crossroads which marks both the end and the beginning of the year. On this Hallowed Eve when the loving spirits of the dead walk among us, we give thanks for all the bounties bestowed upon us these past twelve months. We ask for humble hearts filled with gratitude to carry us through the coming year. And we ask for caring hearts given in service and understanding. May the food before us provide us with sustenance and the strength of the earth to carry us in our divine task of living worthy lives. Some are new to the power of silence. Within the quiet, we may all find the comfort that we seek, and the reaffirmation of love for which we yearn. May we honestly and sincerely offer our faults to purify ourselves that we may come to a unity of love. And as it is willed—so mote it be."

Earl stepped from the stage, leaving only the crackling ring of fires. The hundreds of formerly riotous party goers, who now sat quietly throughout the amphitheater, began to hum a strange and haunting melody in unison. Their intoning voices softly filled the arena with a tuneful sense of unity. Lois and the girls, scattered about the crowd, could not believe their ears.

The tune that everyone was humming was the very melody they were humming earlier in the night, and that they had regularly sung for years. The girls joined in in four-part harmony and the amphitheater took on an aural glow in addition to the bonfires' glow.

Everyone was thrilled. Faces lit up as the ethereal effect of the girls' sweet young voices floated like a vapor rising above the rest.

Bong! The distant bell tower began to chime. Bong! It was three o'clock in the morning. Bong!

The humming finally concluded after many repeats, and the arena sat in complete silence. A gentle breeze blew through and rustled all the adjacent trees.

Some Sabbateurs now began to quietly open their envelopes and write out their resolutions for good. A trickle of monsters and witches made its way down to the stage and carefully tossed paper offerings into the fires. They then walked off toward the far side of the castle where the banquet was served, beside even more bonfires.

More Sabbateurs, including Lois, stepped down to the front. With a big smile, she stood before the great blaze with both hands full of folded papers. She threw her resolutions into the flames and watched as they caught fire and floated into the air as glowing embers.

The McCourts all wrote out their own committments to be better people during the next twelve months. Mrs. McCourt resolved to be less judgemental of others; to be more accepting and not cast opinions. She also commited to more fully give of her real self in service and not just for the Halloween Carnival, but throughout the year where ever help was needed.

Doctor McCourt promised to not bet anymore—to keep his promise to his wife, no matter how difficult. He also vowed to be there more for his family and for others around him who may need his help, regardless of their needs. And he promised to be more aware so that he could help.

Melissa pledged to not be so snotty to her only brother and to be considerate of others. She also promised to not say rude things even if people deserved it. Lastly, she wrote that she would more willingly help her mother around the house.

Eddie simply penciled on one of the little pages "I will be a friend to everyone," implying all that the word friend entails.

They tossed their folded resolutions into the flames and made their way to the banquet area with all the others.

The line to the serving tables was long, but all waited patiently and silently, with much smiling and nodding. They neared the tables and were bowled over with what they beheld—a feast fit for royalty. Spread before them was the most beautiful and lavish display of food any of them had ever seen. Each serving dish was artfully presented and garnished. Jack-o'-lanterns and colorful autumn leaves decoratively filled every inch of space between the actual serving trays.

Though many were traditional Halloween dishes, most were completely new to the McCourts—soul cakes, boxty, barm brack and crowdie to name just a few.

Mrs. McCourt could not make up her mind which of the tureens of soup she should try first. She finally narrowed the field to Autumn Bisque and Harvest Stew, while her husband heaped on the cornbread and deep dish venison pot pie.

A clearly printed card beside each item explained the dish and listed the ingredients so no one felt intimidated.

Eddie reached for the serving utensil to the colcannon—mashed potatoes with parsnips and onions, but his arm was not long enough. Immediately, five monster hands appeared to assist.

Everyone loaded their plates and with a large cup of Witches' Brew cider, then all returned to their seats in the arena to eat.

The whole family silently ate their meals and their thoughts all turned to Brian. They stared into the fires right in front of them. Melissa almost thought she saw his face in the crackling blaze.

Lois, already finished with her meal, showed up with her huge smile still plastered across her face. Her constant smiling had caused much of her mud pack to crack and fall off, so she looked rather ghastly in the glow of the fires. Mrs. McCourt scooted over to allow her room to sit down next to her. Lois smiled at her and she genuinely smiled back.

They all finished their meals and Doctor McCourt took away the trays and returned loaded down with blankets and cushions. Everyone snuggled and settled in.

Lois took her sister-in-law's hand and squeezed it. She then patted it with her other hand. Lois and Elizabeth sat together in comfortable, undemanding silence.

Doctor McCourt's mind traveled back to his childhood when he and Lois were little. A tidal wave of memories flooded his mind. He recalled his grandparents and everyone at a big family picnic. He remembered he was stung in the foot by a bee when he was playing in the grass without his shoes. That was the last time he ever saw his great-grandfather.

Mrs. McCourt took a trip down memory lane, as well. She thought about how fun it was to have a baby in the house when Melissa was born, and then came the twins. She recalled her shock at learning how much noise two mischievous toddlers could make. Her thoughts lingered then on Brian.

Even Melissa pondered on her two little brothers and how much she really did love them both.

Eddie curled up in a blanket and laid his head down on his father's lap. He promptly slumbered off and began to dream. He returned to the lakeside verandah where he and Brian drank fresh-squeezed pink lemonade. Brian was seated at the same little cafe table.

Brian had a sparkle in his eye. "Shall we go?"

"Are they home?"

"They are not only home, they are waiting for us."

"Let's fly!"

Eddie and Brian were instantly transported across the lake to the three yellow cottages. Except now, they were French blue."

Eddie's face looked puzzled. "These were yellow like one second ago!"

"They are still yellow. Step to your left about ten paces."

Eddie followed Brian's suggestion and to his surprise, they were still yellow, at least from where he was now standing. "What's the deal?" Eddie stepped back to his right. POOF! The houses changed back to blue.

"I'll let Reiko explain."

Over a low fieldstone wall laced with rambling pale blue sweet peas, a vibrant and breathtaking flower garden enraptured them both. Their eyes could barely take in the masses of flowers all in various shades and tints of blue. From the palest, almost white daisies to the deepest dark blue dahlias, the garden was electric in color but cool and soothing in effect. They walked along the wall and stepped through a charming country gate that billowed over with racemes of incandescent blue wisteria blossoms.

"Welcome," a sweet lady's voice said.

Before them stood a petite woman in an elegantly simple dress. She wore a stylishly floppy sunhat trimmed with fresh blue cornflowers. Her poise and demeanor bespoke a real lady.

Brian looked to her as though her knew her well. "Reiko. This is my brother, Eddie."

"It is very nice to meet you, Eddie."

"Nice to meet you, too." He could not help but notice her warm dark brown eyes and her caring smile. With natural blush in her smooth cheeks and with her shimmering black hair falling gently over her bare shoulders, she was a vision of loveliness. Eddie thought she was the most beautiful person he had ever seen. Reiko slightly bowed her head and blushed in embarassment.

"Thank you, Eddie. That is very kind."

Eddie blushed. "Oh. That's right. You don't have to talk here for people to hear you."

"I am very flattered. But there is an even more beautiful lady right over there on that bench who bears a striking resemblance to the two of you. You should go say hello."

The boys looked across the garden to where a lady gracefully sat on a carved stone bench. She also wore a hat that partially obscured her face. She stood and walked toward them. Brian smiled knowingly.

"Mom."

"Brian."

Mrs. McCourt gently placed her palms against Brian's cheeks and cradled his face the way only a mother would do. They both sweetly looked into each other's eyes until they could stand it no longer. Rapt with emotion, they embraced.

Eddie and Reiko were deeply touched with the unfolding scene. Neither spoke so as not to disturb.

For the longest time mother and son held each other tight. When they finally released, Mrs. McCourt turned to Eddie. "You come here, too, so I can give you a hug." Eddie and his mother embraced.

"Mom? How did you get here?" Eddie said.

"Nothing can keep two spirits apart that are bonded by love," Reiko said in reply.

"But how did you even know where to find us?"

Reiko stepped forward. "The love literally pulls you together, regardless of where you are. There is no need to look. You simply go to that other person, whereever they are."

"I just know I couldn't stay away," Mrs. McCourt said. She then turned again to Brian with tearing eyes. "I had to come see you."

"I am so glad you did!"

She took her son's hand in her own. "There is so much to say and yet nothing to say. I just had to be with you." They hugged again.

"Reiko," Brian said, "Eddie was asking about why your house became blue so suddenly. Would you mind explaining just a little for us all?"

Reiko smiled. "You are too young, Eddie, to know about husband and wife disagreements but that basically is what it is all about. You see, Vincent's favorite color is yellow so I wanted the house and garden to reflect that. But he said no. The house and garden should be blue because that is my favorite color. We are both stubborn because our intentions are based on love, and a desire to please the other. So, we reached a compromise. We split the difference."

"What do you mean?"

"If you approach the house from one side it is blue, as well as all the flowers. If you approach the house from the other it is yellow."

"I don't really get it."

"The color of the house," Brian began to explain further, "depends on from which direction you first look at it. When we were across the lake we were looking at it from the right side, so it was yellow."

"Oh! So the left side direction is blue."

"That is right. I know it sounds silly but we both love each other so much neither is willing to give in."

"That's really neat. So if I walk over there," Eddie crossed the front walk. "WOW! It's yellow. And all the flowers, too."

"Even the songbirds in residence. Over there they are yellow warblers and over here they are mountain bluebirds."

"I think it's enchanting," Mrs. McCourt said.

"It seems like everything Vincent and I do together is disjointed and split down the middle. We also agreed on a cultural exchange program. He would teach me European cultures and I would teach him Asian cultures. Out front here is our Cottage Garden, but the dewey path around the side there leads to the Tea Garden and the Meditation Garden."

"We should all be so cross-culturally enriched."

"Ah! The boys are back," Reiko said.

"Hello! Hello! Hello!" Three gentlemen dressed in Japanese kimonos stepped out of the house into the garden. Wooden geta on their feet clacked on the stepping stones as they walked.

Reiko pointed to their feet. "That is how I knew they were on their way. I could hear their shoes."

One of the men kissed Reiko.

"Gentlemen, you know Brian."

They all shook hands warmly.

"This is his mother, Elizabeth, and his brother, Eddie."

Vincent stepped forward. "It is a pleasure to meet a woman as beautiful as yourself."

"Enchante, Madame," his brother Vincent said. He gently lifted her hand and kissed it.

She blushed. "Moi aussi, Monsieur."

Theo took her hand from Vincent. "Very pleased to meet you."

"The pleasure is all mine."

Vincent turned to Eddie. "It is also a pleasure to make your acquaintance, young sir."

"We studied all about you in school this week."

"That is very kind of your teacher to include me in your curriculum." Vincent pulled down on his ear lobe. "You see. I have my ear back."

"That's great!"

"It is the first thing about which everyone asks."

"Do you still paint?"

"Yes, indeed."

Reiko placed her hand on her husband's shoulder. "Eddie and his mother are just visiting."

"Well then. Enough about me. We need to go somewhere and celebrate the visit. We should take you to Empyreal Park. Enrico is singing. His arias are simply seraphic."

"Enrico Caruso?" Mrs. McCourt said.

"The same."

"Oh, my!" She put her hand to her chest. "It sounds so exciting."

"And then we could stop by the Heliac Theater," Vincent's brother Vincent said, "where John is performing all his latest along with some of his old favorites." He broke into song—"All you need is love!"

"Oh, dear! When can we go?" she said.

Theo stepped forward. And we must do a gallery stroll! The works here span the milenniums. And you can see all of Vincent's best."

B-R-R-R-R-I-N-G. A phone rang.

"A phone?" Eddie looked around at everyone's puzzled faces. "They don't even have phones here."

B-R-R-R-R-I-N-G. It rang again. Doctor McCourt walked around the corner of the house.

"Dad? What are you doing here?"

"I came to see Brian."

The Magic Hour

B-R-R-R-R-R-I-N-G. The phone rang a third time. Eddie, his mother and his father were all instantly back at the Witches' Sabbath. The phone rang yet again in Doctor McCourt's pocket, the fourth time. He was completely surrounded by the hooded ones, the men in black robes with the skull faces. He reached into his pocket and turned it off. The men pointed to the far side of the arena and then gestured for him to stand. He rose and looked to his flabbergasted wife. She stood, too. And then Eddie and Melissa. They all started to walk when the same sweet humming that began the silence once again softly filled the air. This time as before, Lois' girls' joined in. Again their voices wafted above the others. Surrounded by the forbidding black robes, the McCourt family was not only escorted from the arena, but all the way to the parking lot beside the bus.

Lois, who was still sitting back on the front row, assessed the situation and rose to her feet. With her head held high, she confidently stood before the fires and looked to the crowd above. Without gestures or motions, the Brownies stood where ever they were. They all saw Lois and knew through silent, nonverbal communication, that it was time to go. One by one they made their way forward and formed a line in front of the fires. Lois and all forty four girls calmly walked from the arena humming softly as they went. When they arrived at the bus, the girls calmly boarded.

Sandy came running up, all out of breath. "Don't go yet!" she half whispered. "I am so sorry that happened to you. I didn't even think to say anything about a cell phone."

"I'm sorry to have disturbed everyone," Doctor McCourt said. "I forgot it was even in my pocket. Anyway, it was kind of fun being escorted by the bouncers from hell."

"The singing almost made it fell special," Mrs. McCourt said.

"That's why we do it. To soften the blow."

"It worked."

"It's good for us to get all these kids home to bed," Doctor McCourt said. "All's well that ends well."

Mrs. McCourt hugged Sandy. "And thanks to you, this night ended very well. Thank you for everything. I cannot say it sincerely enough."

Sandy took Mrs. McCourt's arm in hers. "Come by the salon some time. I would love to do your hair and to get to know you better. I think we have more in common than we know."

"I'd like that. I will come by. Sandy. I don't think you've met my sister-in-law Lois."

"Nice to meet you," Lois said.

"It's a pleasure to meet you. You come by the salon, too."

"Thank you."

Sandy handed them both a little package wrapped in Halloween tissue paper.

"What's this?"

"Just a token for being here tonight. Everybody leaves with something."

They all hugged again and swapped fond thanks and good-byes. Sandy apologized for Cindy not saying good-bye. She didn't want to wake her, because of the lovely dream she had had about her grandmother last year.

Eddie suddenly bolted from the bus and ran right up to Sandy. He threw his arms around her and hugged her as tight as he could. They shared a wonderful, nonverbal moment and then just as quickly, he dashed back into the the bus.

Inside the bus, the girls on the front row on both sides jumped up to clear seats for the McCourts. Melissa and Eddie sat behind the driver's seat and their parents just across the aisle.

Doctor McCourt asked Lois if she would drop him off at the hospital on the way home. That was the source of the ill-fated phone call.

"I'd be delighted to," she said. "And I even know where it is."

The drive home was virtually silent. The girls who were not deep in sleep were too droopey-eyed to even make a peep. Doctor McCourt also dozed while Mrs. McCourt unwrapped the small package Sandy gave her. Inside she found a little framed work of calligraphy.

"We all have a common heart
when words depart."

She pondered on the profound truth of this little saying and then thought back on how much she had learned tonight and over the past days, before she, too, nodded off.

Lois looked in the mirror as she drove, and saw Eddie sitting up right behind her, wide awake. He could also see her face in the mirror.

"Eddie, We're all glad that you're still here with us."

"Thank you, Aunt Lois. Me, too."

"I was so impressed with your talk. Not only with what you said, but how well you did it. Standing up there in front of all those people all by yourself. I would have been terrified."

"Thank you. I really wasn't scared. People become afraid when they don't understand something. I understood that all those people quit their big party to come look for me in the woods. I understood that they all cared about me so I wasn't afraid."

"You're wise beyond your years young man. I'm so very proud to be related to you. I know I can learn much more from you, too."

"Thank you."

"Was it really wonderful over there?"

"I never wanted to leave it. But Brian told me it was important for me to come back and help everybody."

"I know you've helped me."

"I'm glad."

"I think someone whispered to me during the bonfires," she said.

"They probably did."

"At first I thought it was just the wind."

"What did they say?"

"It was a woman's voice. She told me she loves me and that I was on the right track, now."

"Did you recognize the voice?"

"I think it was your grandmother."

"She's your mom."

"That's right."

"Uncle Louie is the one who whispers things to me, to not do bad stuff and to be nice. I think he helps me remember my test questions at school, too."

"Do you think my mother is my guardian angel?"

"I don't know. But I know she watches over you. They all watch over us all."

Lois started to weep.

"Are you all right, Aunt Lois?"

"Thank you, Eddie. I've never been better."

The bus arrived in town and Lois drove straight to the hospital's main entrance. "Patrick. We're at the hospital."

Doctor and Mrs. McCourt both woke up. They kissed each other and exchanged good-byes.

"Thank you, Lois," he said stepping to the door."

"Oh, Patrick. I'm so grateful you took us to the Witches' Sabbath. We had such a marvelous time."

"We're very pleased that you all enjoyed yourselves so much. I've got to run, but stay in touch."

"Oh, I will."

He gave her a hug. "Drive safely."

"Good-bye, Uncle Patrick," Lois' daughters called out.

Doctor McCourt turned around with a huge grin. "Good-bye, girls."

"Good-bye, Dad," Eddie and Melissa said.

"Good-bye, you two. Good-bye everybody!" He stepped out the door.

The bus drove on to the McCourt house. They pulled into the drive and Lois asked the girls to collect their things and then come right back out to the bus. "We're going to drive straight on home." Lois relished the idea of driving all those hours in silence with the girls sleeping.

While the girls assembled their things, Mrs. McCourt and Lois exchanged very cordial words.

"I feel like tonight, during the bonfires," Lois said, "we communicated more than we ever have, and we didn't speak a single word. How can that be?"

"It's quite something. Did you open your little present from Sandy?"

"Not yet."

"I don't want to spoil it for you so I won't say much, but it really explains it all."

"And the people tonight. There isn't a more loving group of souls. I wasn't abused or taken advantage of. I don't know if everyone felt sorry for me or what. I looked so awful, but everybody wanted to dance with me. I mean everybody."

"That's wonderful Lois."

"It was so exciting Everyone there wanted me to have a good time. And I did—the time of my life. And I owe it all to you and your family."

"Thank you, Lois. It was a rewarding experience for us all."

"And those things I said earlier about never wanting to see you all again. I want you to know I am very sorry. I acted imprudently and with an uncaring heart. From here on out I'm going to be the kind of sister-in-law you would want me to be."

The Magic Hour

"Thank you, Lois. I feel the same way. We all grew from our experiences this Halloween."

They hugged and shared a moment.

Lois kissed Elizabeth on the cheek. "Thank you for putting up with me."

Lois was simply reborn a cheerful person instead of the sourpuss she had been her entire life. "And where are those cute kids?" She followed Mrs. McCourt into the house.

"Eddie. Aunt Lois is leaving!" his mother said.

He ran into the front hall and gave Lois a big hug. She kissed him and rubbed his hair. "You keep up the good work, okay? Someone has to keep us all in line, you know."

"I will," he said. "And thanks for coming."

"My pleasure, thank you. Good-bye Melissa." They hugged and both started to cry. Lois wiped her cheek. "Thank you again, Melissa. I owe you a great deal."

They all walked Lois out to the bus. She and her four daughters, who up to this point had been indistinguishable from the other Brownie girls, except for their formerly curled noses, surrounded Mrs. McCourt.

"Thank you, Aunt Elizabeth." The girls all together hugged and kissed her and then moved on to hug Melissa and then Eddie, who was a little stiff in the process.

Each Brownie girl, all forty of them, then went through the same good-bye procedure to Mrs. McCourt, Melissa and lastly Eddie. He politely and respectfully returned the hugs but not the pats.

CHAPTER NINETEEN

At last, quiet reigned again in the McCourt household. With Lois and the girls gone, everyone made ready for sleep. Eddie climbed into bed and noticed Melissa lingering just outside his open bedroom door.

"Larry forgives you," he said. "He knows you didn't mean to kill him."

"I didn't really. I'm sorry that I did. I didn't mean for him to die, poor thing. I'm glad you didn't die."

"Me too."

"If you did, then Mom would only have me to pick on."

"I know you don't really mean that. Because otherwise, I would have to pick up this pillow —" Eddie grabbed a pillow and whopped Melissa. "And hit you really hard."

Melissa grabbed the pillow and swung it back at Eddie.

"MELISSA!" Mrs. McCourt walked into the room. "He probably has a concussion!"

Melissa gave Eddie a quick hug and walked out.

Eddie's mother sat down on the bed beside him.

"Mom, I know why Grandpa gave tombstones to everybody for presents."

"You do?"

"Yeah. Grandpa and I talked about it. He didn't do it because he was mean or anything. Because he had so much pain about how Louie died. He felt guilty. The only way he could deal with it was to laugh about it."

"That's really something Eddie, that you can understand that."

"You know. I think it would be really fun to give people tombstones as gifts. And it's something they can really use."

"Oh, no! You're going to be just like your grandfather."

"That won't be bad."

"No. It won't. But I have to tell you just how proud we were of you tonight."

"Thanks. I really learned alot tonight."

"We all learned alot tonight, thanks to you. We all came closer together as a family, too."

"Even Aunt Lois."

"I know. She and I had a very nice talk."

Mrs. McCourt reached down beside the bed and then held up two paper mache masks, the ones that Brian and Eddie made in school. They looked like identical death masks of two young faces. She held one out to Eddie. "This one is Brian's, isn't it?"

"How'd you know?"

She smiled. "I didn't think you were ready to see them before. But the little voice just told me you were."

"Mom. You wouldn't even believe how beautiful it was there. And they had all your favorite flowers. That purple one that's your favorite—what's it called?"

"Heliotrope."

"You should have seen it. It glowed like a neon sign. And it smelled like heaven just like you said."

"It sounds like it was a wonderful place."

"It was. I told Brian I wanted to stay there with him."

"Oh, Sweetie. I am so glad you didn't. If we'd have lost you, it would have killed the whole family."

"Then we'd all be together on the other side. Just like in my dream."

"You had a dream about that?"

"During The Bonfires. You were there. Do you remember?"

"I know I dozed off."

"You were there, Mom, with me and Brian."

"I feel like maybe I did dream about Brian, but I really can't remember anything."

"You hugged him and kissed him over and over. You wouldn't let go of his hand the whole time."

"I wish I could remember."

"If you can't remember, then you don't know where we were then either, do you?"

"I don't, Sweetie."

"We were at Vincent van Gogh's house."

"Not really."

"Yes, really. His garden was unbelievable. And his wife, she was a knockout."

"Eddie. You're not just making this up?"

"Honest, Mom."

"All I can say is that even though I don't remember anything, I do have this satisfying and peaceful feeling that Brian is near."

"He is. He always will be."

"That's very comforting to know. Eddie. There is something that I need to tell you. Your father wanted to be here with me to tell you together, but you know he had to go to the hospital."

"To help people."

"That's right."

"So what is it?"

"It's about your birthday."

"What about it?"

"You remember when I asked you what you wanted for your birthday?"

"I do."

"Do you remember what your answer was?"

"I said I just wanted to be with Brian. I didn't want any stuff."

"That was a very beautiful and sincere wish. Your father and I have been meaning to tell you this for sometime, but have been waiting for the right opportunity. Tonight is the right time."

"What?"

"You know how Brian was born on Halloween?"

"Yeah. Just like me."

"Do you know what time it was when he was born?"

"Hut uh. I never heard."

"He was born at 11:57 P.M. That is three minutes before midnight on Halloween."

"What time was I born?"

"You know how Brian was just a little older than you?"

"Yeah, so what time was I born?"

"You were born an hour and three minutes later."

"That's one o'clock."

"Exactly one o'clock. But it isn't Halloween anymore."

"How come?"

"Because after midnight, it becomes November 1st."

Eddie's face tightened. "So I wasn't born on Halloween?"

"You weren't. But think about what just happened tonight. You wanted to be with Brian on your birthday."

"At one o'clock! Tonight one o'clock was like an hour long!"

"That's right."

"That's the coolest thing! So I was really with Brian on my birthday, exactly?"

"Exactly. The Magic Hour belongs to you Eddie. We didn't tell you when you were little because actually one AM is still Halloweeen night and it would not have seemed fair for only one of you to have had your birthday on a holiday."

"This is great, Mom! The Magic Hour—one o'clock AM November 1st. That's my birthday. Thanks for telling me."

"You are welcome. Thank you for being so understanding."

"I really got my birthday wish, huh?"

"You certainly did. I'm sure it was because you deserved it. You are a good boy and we appreciate it. And you know that we love you?"

"I do. I love you, too. And Brian said for me to tell you he loves you."

Mrs. McCourt leaned over to kiss Eddie.

"Hoo-hoot, hoo-hoooo."

"Ah. Mr. Bones is back," she said. "I haven't heard him in the garden for weeks."

"Not since the night Brian died."

"Hoo-hoot, hoo-hoooo."

"He must be right out my window." Eddie sat up and looked out. The night bird with the brilliant golden eyes sat on a branch just feet from the window.

"Hoo-hoot, hoo-hoooo."

"Mom, what do you think it means that he's back?"

"To me it's reassuring. It tells me everything is back to normal and as it should be."

"I think so, too."

"Let him sing you to sleep, now. We'll talk more in the morning." She leaned over and kissed him again. "Good night. Sleep well."

"Good night, Mom."

The church bells rang out in the morning over a seemingly deserted town Even church services were all moved to the afternoon to accommodate everyone sleeping in on this the morning after.

The midday bells chimed as the first real sign of life emerged in the McCourt household. Inspite of getting to bed after it was already light, Doctor McCourt stirred before anyone else. He made a cup of tea and went out on to the verandah to enjoy the air. Quite some time passed as he thought about all that had transpired lately in his life and in the lives of his family. He pondered on last night and what extraordinary things took place that resulted in bringing his family closer together. He heard Eddie's bare feet walk toward the front door.

"Hey, Dad."

"Good morning, Punkin. Did you get some sleep?"

"I did. How about you?"

"I had a good sleep."

Eddie rubbed his eyes. "Aren't you gonna watch the game? It's probably more than half over already. It's an early one."

"Not today."

"How come?"

"It's not quite as exciting when you already know how it's going to end."

"I didn't think about that. Did you bet?"

"I promised your mother I wouldn't bet anymore."

"That's too bad. You should have waited just a little longer and then made the promise. You could've made a lot of money."

"That's okay. Keeping promises is more important. Come on out and sit by me."

Eddie squeezed into the oversized chair beside his father.

"This is one of those stay in your pajama kind of days' don't you think?"

"I do," Eddie said.

"I can't tell you how proud we were of you last night. Everyone there was so impressed and touched by you and what you said."

"Thanks, Dad. It was all true."

"I know it was."

"We're really glad, too, that you didn't stay there on the other side."

"You should've seen Brian, Dad. He was all grown up, with a beard and really hairy legs and armpits. He's more hairy than you are."

"Oh, is he?"

"Yup. We went swimming and you could see his hair everywhere."

"Takes after your mother's family then."

"That's what he said. He also said I was gonna be hairy like him, too, 'cuz we're twins."

"That makes sense."

"You know what's the coolest? They have no-drip water. You don't even get wet."

"Sounds neat. Last night you said Grandpa wasn't old anymore."
"Nope. Not even as old as you."
"So I suppose he had more hair than I have, too."
"He wasn't bald anymore. He had normal hair."
"Sounds like everyone has more hair than me."
"Sorry, Dad."
"It's okay."
"But you know that hair is not really what's important."
"I know." His father rubbed his palm across the big bare spot on top of his head.
"Oh, Dad. Will you help me with something?"
"Sure."
"I need to get those teddy bears down."
"I'll go right now and get the ladder."
His father retrieved the ladder and climbed up to untie the ropes.
"Dad, if you can just hand them to me, I'll undo the nooses."
"How'd you get these up here in the first place?"
"Tad shimmied up and slung the ropes over the beam."
"What ever happened to Tad? Weren't you going to sleep over at his house last night?"
Eddie did not answer. His hesitancy spoke volumes to his father.
"Are you two still friends?"
Eddie's face showed that he had to think before he could answer. "Yes. I think I'm probably the only friend he's got."
"Does he have a difficult time making friends?"
"He has a hard life and it shows."
"I know his father's not around, and I think his mother works about three jobs."
" I know he needs people in his life. With Brian gone now, can we take him fishing and stuff with us in Brian's place?"
"Sure we can."
"There's an old saying, a village raises a boy. That's what Tad needs."
"That's right. My father used to say that. Where'd you hear it?"
"From Brian."
"He's obviously hanging around his grandfather. That's great! We'll do everything we can to help Tad. Deal?"
"Deal. Thanks, Dad. You know, that was naughty of you to sneak in your cell phone last night."

"I didn't sneak it in. I just forgot I even had it. And besides, it's only naughty if you know you're not supposed to do it."

"You probably don't remember anything about your dreams last night."

"Not really."

"That's okay then." Eddie wanted to tell his father how he disrupted his dream last night but did not want him to feel bad, so he said nothing. "Thanks for helping me with these bears."

"Anytime, son."

Eddie placed the four monsters on a porch chair and walked into the house with the single monsterette, the Bearide of Frankenbear. "Good morning, Mom." They passed in the front hall.

"Good morning, Eddie. She walked into the kitchen and turned on the television to the football game.

Back outside, Doctor McCourt hung the ladder back up in the top of the carport. He glanced at the car knowing he had four flat tires to fix. All four of the tires were miraculously full of air. "HONEY! Come here. Quick! HONEY. COME HERE, PLEASE!"

Mrs. McCourt walked on to the porch. "What's wrong?"

"Nothing's wrong. It's what's right. LOOK! The tires."

"Thanks for pumping them up, Dear."

"I didn't do it. I thought you must have."

"I only do cakes. Must have been the Good Halloween Fairy or the Great Pumpkin. All I know is they were fine when I went out earlier."

"You went out?"

"Early."

"After I got home?"

"While you were asleep."

From inside the house, the deafening sounds of a sportscaster calling a football game blasted out through the screen door into the neighborhood. The volume was so deafeningly loud both Doctor and Mrs. McCourt covered their ears. The voice of the broadcaster went crazy with excitement. "UNBELIEVABLE! THE GIANT'S SCORE! Five. Four. Three. Two. One. And the Giants WIN! This is one of the biggest upsets of the year ladies and gentlemen. With only six seconds left the Giants complete a forty-seven yard field goal —" The noise shut off.

"DID YOU HEAR IT?" Eddie yelled from inside the house.

"THANK YOU! YES WE DID!"

Mrs. McCourt turned to her husband and looked him straight in the eyes. "Did you bet?"

"I was going to, but then I remembered my promise to you."

She affectionately kissed him. "I really appreciate you following through on your promise like that. I know how difficult it probably was for you."

"I wanted you to see that I am a man of my word."

"Now, I don't want you to feel too bad about the money you could have made, okay? Just don't even think about it."

"I won't."

A sly grin streaked across her face.

"You didn't. Did you?" he said.

"I did."

"Oh, honey! How much did you place?"

"A lot."

"How much is alot?"

"I just figured that these were exceptional and extraordinary circumstances and that I had an obligation to do it."

"You're not going to tell me are you?"

"At first I wasn't sure about what Eddie said, but after a few days as things developed —"

"At least tell me what the odds were."

She kissed her husband again.

He jokingly scowled. "You are cruel!"

"Would you rather I had not told you?"

"No. I'm glad you did. Now we have some common ground."

"No we don't. You're not a betting man."

"How could you?"

"I didn't make any promises not to bet. I didn't need to."

"At least tell me what you're going to do with all the money."

"That I will do. Every penny is going to Children's Charities. We're going to stretch it as far as we can. After last night, I realized that we have a broader obligation to help than I had thought. I also realized that Brian didn't give us a tip so we could just go indulge ourselves in extravagance. That was a gift designed to be shared."

"When did you place the bet?"

"Early this morning when everyone else was still asleep."

"You sly little thing. I'm really proud of you."

"I'm proud of you, too. But there's more."

"You have to at least tell me how you even knew where to place your bet."

"Sandy and I placed our bets together."

"The Crystal woman?"

"Sandy Crystal, yes. All the money is going to help the children. She and I are going to be very busy working out all the details."

"I'm even more proud of you."

"Last night I didn't know if I was going to make it through the night when we thought we had lost Eddie. But I learned so much from Sandy. She knew our own son better than we did. I am so grateful that she had faith and confidence in what he was saying right from the beginning. We owe her alot. She brought us back together as a family. Even Lois, my gosh. She was a real person when she left. She was actually someone you could have a normal conversation with."

"They say adversity makes you stronger if you allow it to. Hopefully we are all stronger and better people now."

"Where is everybody?" Melissa stepped onto the porch. "Where did those come from?"

"What's that dear?" Mrs. McCourt said.

"Those roses."

"I didn't know there were any roses."

Melissa pulled a card from a spectacular bouquet of long-stemmed red roses nestled between two of the bent-willow arm chairs. "Oh. They're for Eddie. She must still be sending him things." She handed the card to her mother. "Here, Mom. You can open it."

"It's for Eddie."

"You're not going to open it?"

"No. We'll let Eddie open it. EDDIE. There's a present here for you on the porch."

"WHAT?" He dashed out the door with the Frankenbride teddy in his hand. Her wounded chest was sewn back together with crude stitches of black yarn. She looked even cuter now and more like a Frankenstein.

"The bouquet by the chair."

"Flowers? Who's sending me flowers?"

"I don't know. Here's the card."

He ripped open the little envelope.

the magic hour

Dear Eddie,

Last night when we kissed I felt something between us, and it wasn't germs. But I realize now that we care for each other as friends and friends are very important. I just want you to know that I still respect you. Even more now. Thank you for the apology. It was more than I could ask for. Thank you for being my friend.

Forever your friend,
Cindy Crystal

Eddie looked at the bouquet. In the midday light now streaming onto the covered porch, a single white rose bud glowed vibrantly against the red of all the other buds. He counted the roses right out loud. "One - two - three - four - five - six – seven - eight - nine - ten - eleven red and one white. ANDY! MISS PLEASANT! I won't need to use the silver dollar."

"What silver dollar?" his father said.

"Who's Andy?" said his mother.

Eddie looked down at the porch steps. Right between the third and fourth step was the largest piece of shattered pumpkin from last night. He dropped to his knees and pushed it aside. After he scraped pumpkin slop and soil from the crack between the steps with his fingers, the tarnished edge of a silver dollar became barely visible. "It's really there! I can give it to Cindy."

His father stood and peered down over his shoulder. "What's really there?"

Eddie jumped up with the dollar in hand, and frantically ran around his father toward the roses.

His mother stood up. "Eddie! What's wrong?"

"No time to talk!" He grabbed the roses with both hands and ran back past his parents and down the porch steps.

"WHERE ARE YOU GOING?"

"I GOTTA GO HELP ANDY!"

"WHO'S ANDY?"

"I'LL TELL YOU ABOUT IT WHEN I GET BACK!"

Eddie zipped down the driveway on his bicycle with the vase of roses balanced in one arm. Still in his pajamas, he rode through the quiet streets of town as fast as his legs could peddle, all the while struggling to hold on to the big bouquet.

He rode right up to Miss Pleasant's porch and jumped off. His bike crashed in the bushes as he raced up the steps. Carefully placing the roses down right in front of the door, he dragged a milk box from the far side of the porch over under the mail slot and jumped up on it. Peeking in the mail slot, he saw only darkness. He reached his arm down inside to feel around and made scratching sounds with his fingernails as he tried to find the lost letter.

Inside the house Miss Pleasant drank her middle-of-the-day morning coffee. She heard the odd scratching noises. "Who's out there?"

Eddie was too focused to even hear her. Miss Pleasant called out again and yanked open the front door. Still in her tattered robe, she looked terrible with her black eye and lack of sleep. She was jolted by the sight of the bouquet of roses on her porch right in front of her. She stared at the flowers and did not see Eddie. She mentally counted the roses and her hand went up to her mouth in disbelief. She turned away and finally noticed Eddie up on her milk box with his arm lost into her mail slot.

"Eddie! What on earth are you doing?"

"I'm trying to fix something."

"What can possibly be wrong with my mail slot?"

"Nothing's wrong with your mail slot. It's something else, and I'm trying to fix it."

At last he touched the envelope with his finger tips and shrieked with joy. He jumped down from the milk box with the letter in hand and landed practically on top of the roses. He tried to balance himself, but fell backwards across the porch. Miss Pleasant gasped and pushed open the screen door in an effort to help but banged the roses and Eddie as well. He and the roses flew right off the porch into the bushes.

"Eddie! Are you alright?" She hurried down the steps and helped pull him up. She saw the letter still clutched tightly in his hand, an envelope yellowed with time, and immediately recognized the all too familiar penmanship and the old stamp. The blood flushed from her face, but her pallor quickly turned to red-faced anger. "Eddie McCourt! Were you trying to take my mail?"

"No! Miss Pleasant. I was trying to get it to you! It's been stuck in your mail slot for almost forty years!" Eddie handed her the letter. She was dumbfounded and could not respond. Her eyes welled and her heart swelled with emotion.

Eddie noticed black smear marks down either side of her nose, where her makeup had run down with her tears. With her hair still smashed flat and her black eye, her appearance was quite frightful. She did not look like the gentle Miss Pleasant that Eddie had always known, however, he understood that she was in much pain.

"Miss Pleasant. I need to talk to you."

"I should think you do."

Miss Pleasant tucked the envelope into her robe pocket and the two of them picked up the scattered roses together. Eddie watched the tender way she cradled each flower stem in her arms.

"Do you want me to go buy you another vase?" Eddie said.

"No, thank you, Eddie. I have vases in the house."

They stepped inside the house. She asked Eddie to sit down while she went into the kitchen to place the roses in water. Eddie looked around at the room and tried to remember everything that Andy instructed him to do the night before.

Miss Pleasant carried the roses back into the room all beautifully arranged in an old fashioned cut glass vase. Eddie keenly watched her as she walked toward him and set the bouquet down right in the middle of the table on a lace doily.

"They're even prettier in that vase," he said.

"Thank you, Eddie." She sat down next to him and placed the unopened letter on the table. "Now, Eddie. Will you please tell me who these roses are for and how you knew that the letter was there."

"The roses are for you."

"Thank you, Eddie. That is very kind of you."

"They're not from me. I'm just delivering them."

"Then who are they from?"

"Andy."

"Andy who?"

"Andy Valentine. The man you were gonna marry."

Anger again flashed across Miss Pleasant's face. "How dare you play a joke like this on me!"

"Miss Pleasant, please understand, this isn't a joke! This is real!"

"How could you possibly know about Andy and me? Who told you?"

Eddie swallowed hard.

"He did. Miss Pleasant, I know this is gonna be hard for you to believe, but Andy told me. He told me himself. Last night I fell in the woods and hit my head. That's when I met him and he told me all about you. Last night when you were sitting in your bedroom in front of your mirror taking your makeup off, we were standing right there."

She clutched the front of her robe and pulled it tightly closed.

"He told me all about the Cracker Jacks and how you got engaged and everything."

"How can this be?"

"Andy told me to tell you that he's forgave the man who killed him and that you should too."

Miss Pleasant was further dumbfounded at Eddie's words. She moaned in pain.

"The man who killed him's name is Tran. He got killed the day after Andy did. Tran is really a nice guy. He and Andy are buddies now. Andy said you have bitterness in your heart 'cuz Andy died on you. He wants you to get rid of it."

Eddie's words pierced Miss Pleasant to her very core. How could this child possibly know about her secret sacred love. She stood up from the table shaking uncontrollably. She tried to walk but had to hold onto the table for support. She turned from the table but stopped and turned back. She picked up the vase of roses and teetered with it over to the fireplace. With her back to Eddie, she held the vase close to her chest. He saw her face in the mirror on the wall above the fireplace. She placed the vase up on the mantel and gently pulled the white rose from the bouquet. Holding it to her nose, she softly recited to herself a little verse from long ago. "Eleven red say I love you—A single white means forever true. Eddie," she said, "how did you know to bring eleven red roses and one white one?"

"Andy told me to. He said you'd know what it meant."

"And the letter?"

"He told me the letter was in the box. Andy wrote it three days before he died."

Miss Pleasant turned around with tears streaming down her cheeks. "It's been there all these years. Right under my nose." She started back to the table but fell. Eddie jumped from his chair and caught her. He held her elbow and helped her return to the table. She flopped down in her chair and stared at the old envelope.

"Andy said for you to read the letter out loud."

Miss Pleasant looked right at Eddie. This was all way too much for her. She broke her gaze and looked down at the letter, the proof of what Eddie said. She tenderly picked it up and held it to her heart, as if it was the most precious thing that she had ever held. "Out loud?"

"He said you had to."

She reached for a silver letter opener in the center of the table but the old glue on the envelope was so dried out the seal was lost. Her hands trembled as she opened the letter, then her entire body began to shake.

"I don't know if I can go through with this."

Eddie gently placed his hand on her wrist. She put the letter back down on the table, pulled a wadded handkerchief from her bath robe pocket and wiped her eyes.

> *"My Dearest Maggie,*
>
> *How are you my darling? How can I possibly express all the love that I feel for you, except to say that being apart from you all this time has only made my heart grow even fonder, and yearn even more intently to kiss your sweet face. The very thought of being with you again is my sole source of strength to carry forward.*
>
> *Even though we are a world apart, it is as though I see your every move and feel your every thought. I love you, Maggie. With all my heart I love you. I am counting the days until I can again hold you tight within my embrace, and express in person my unfailing love. Press on in faith and courage. The battle will soon be over and then we will never be separated again. Love and roses.*
>
> *Eternally your Valentine,*
>
> *Andy.*

Miss Pleasant was simply overcome. Sobbing uncontrollably, she tried to stand up but collapsed right back into her chair.

"Miss Pleasant! Are you all right?"

She was not able to reply. Not able to sit still, she tried to stand again. This time, with Eddie's help, she managed to rise to her feet. "HELP ME TO THE MANTEL! I don't know why but I have to get to the fireplace!"

Eddie helped her walk to the fireplace right in front of the roses.

"Miss Pleasant? Are you all right?"

She half nodded. "Yes, Dear. I'm fine."

"How come you wanted to come back over here to the fireplace?"

"I don't know. For some reason I just feel this is where I should be right now." She put her hand to her forehead as if checking for fever. "I suddenly feel warm. Very warm indeed."

"Andy said that when you read the letter he would be standing right here in front of the fireplace with his love burning bright."

"Oooooh. Andy? Are you here? Can you hear me?"

Both Eddie and Miss Pleasant stood in complete silence, as if they awaited a reply.

"Andy. I love you, I forgive you. Can you forgive me?"

Again her pleas were met with silence.

"Andyyyyyyyyyy."

A blinding burst of sunlight flooded in the windows. BONGGG! It filled the entire front room with the soft golden light of autumn. BONGGG! The church bell in the near-by old cathedral once again began to chime. BONGGG! The very foundation of the house appeared to quake with its resonant tones. BONGGG! The sound of the bell reverberated through the house and out over the entire neighborhood. BONGGG! In the midday light, the once magical Halloween images throughout town now appeared drab and lifeless. BONGGG! The twinkling Halloween window displays had somehow all lost their appeal. BONGGG! The allure and the mystique of the darkness of just the night before was completely dispelled. BONGGG! Planters of flowers were visible everywhere, where before they were obscured by darkness. BONGGG! Their delicate beauty seemed to welcome this new day with a feeling of hope and joy. BONGGG! The Celtic cross atop the cathedral stood as a great gun sight against the bright sky. BONGGG! The echo of the bell continued to rise and to spread. BONGGG! The valley, the mountains, the forests beyond, all echoed with the call to grace.

About the Author

James S. Crowley was born in Idaho Falls, Idaho and graduated from the University of Utah in Salt Lake City. A skilled artist and classically trained singer, he has devoted his life to the art of storytelling. Whether writing screenplays for the motion picture industry, designing and building prize-willing floats, or performing on stage, James is always sharing a story. Many years in the creation, *The Magic Hour* marks his debut in writing novels.

Also an avid collector and importer of Asian antiquities, he wrote the critically acclaimed *Wabi Sabi Style*—a lifestyles book on Japanese aesthetics in Western application.

He and his wife currently reside in Utah.